BLOOD SISTERS

ALSO BY VANESSA LILLIE

For the Best
Little Voices

BLOOD SISTERS

~~~~~

Vanessa Lillie

BERKLEY
New York

BERKLEY
An imprint of Penguin Random House LLC
penguinrandomhouse.com

Copyright © 2023 by Vanessa Lillie
Penguin Random House supports copyright. Copyright fuels creativity, encourages diverse voices,
promotes free speech, and creates a vibrant culture. Thank you for buying an authorized edition of
this book and for complying with copyright laws by not reproducing, scanning, or distributing
any part of it in any form without permission. You are supporting writers and allowing
Penguin Random House to continue to publish books for every reader.

BERKLEY and the BERKLEY & B colophon are registered trademarks of
Penguin Random House LLC.

Library of Congress Cataloging-in-Publication Data

Names: Lillie, Vanessa, author.
Title: Blood sisters / Vanessa Lillie.
Description: New York: Berkley, [2023]
Identifiers: LCCN 2022057957 (print) | LCCN 2022057958 (ebook) |
ISBN 9780593550113 (hardcover) | ISBN 9780593550120 (ebook)
Subjects: LCGFT: Novels. | Detective and mystery fiction.
Classification: LCC PS3612.I424 B56 2023 (print) |
LCC PS3612.I424 (ebook) | DDC 813/.6—dc23/eng/20221208
LC record available at https://lccn.loc.gov/2022057957
LC ebook record available at https://lccn.loc.gov/2022057958

Printed in the United States of America
2nd Printing

Book design by George Towne
Interior Art: watercolor background © white snow / Shutterstock Images

FOR THE BELOVED WOMEN WHO WALKED BEFORE ME

Tame Doe
Nanyehi (Nancy Ward)
Ka-Ti Walker
Sah-li Walker (Brewer)
Mary Jane Walker (Harlow)
Areta Knight (Walker)
Bessie Knight (Gilbert)
Carla Lillie (Knight)

What happens to the land happens to the women.

—Native wisdom

AGILVGI (SISTER)

A devil kicks in the front door, but he's holding a pistol instead of a pitchfork. The three of us girls, watching TV in a tangle of relaxed limbs on the floor, grab one another and scream.

"Tsgilis!" I call out the name of Cherokee evil spirits from stories around campfires meant to scare us, as a real one fills the narrow doorway. His white plastic mask and horns glow with all that dark night behind him. He stomps his nasty boots into the small trailer with a *thud-thud, thud-thud.*

A second devil follows on the metal stairs. The trailer creaks like a roller coaster to hell. Syd clings to my arm as tight as when we play Indian rope burn with the boys at school.

"Sister, are they raven mockers?" Syd hisses, referring to the soul-stealing Cherokee witches older cousins told us about.

"Them are dollar-store masks." My voice shakes though I try to sound tough. "Ain't no witch wearing that."

The two white Tsgilis are not long and lean, but thick like tree stumps. I wonder if the real devil wears a shiny vest or prom tuxedo. No way he looks like these two in their sweat-stained shirts tight across their beer bellies.

Terror triggers a baptism over my body. A flood of helplessness spreads from my chest and washes down to my curled toes. It's a feeling of smallness only those who live nowhere with nothing understand.

The moment stretches and their horned plastic masks catch the light in the wobbling ceiling fan. Pale blue eyes focus on us. I swear the frozen grins on the masks curl.

"You girls stay put," yells the first devil. He stabs a fat finger at where we're trembling in the center of the living room. The other devil beside him barely lifts his mask to spit chew on the ratty carpet.

My heart thumps in my ears, but I try not to let on. I'm pretty sure these kinda men are like wild dogs, surviving on meanness and the smell of fear.

"Where's your daddy?" the second devil hisses at me like he hasn't already scared us bad enough.

Our gazes whip around at one another like tetherballs. Syd's always insisted we're old enough to be alone, even out in the middle of nowhere. *I can handle it. I'd never let anything hurt you.*

The truth is, out here, out nowhere, no one can be saved.

The only sound in the trailer is cheesy laughs from *Full House* on the TV. We stay quiet except for muffled sobs. Usually at least one of us can comfort the others when something goes wrong. Not tonight. Maybe not ever again.

We scoot closer together until our arms are around each other. Skin to skin, warm and familiar. We bow our heads like we're asking for forgiveness at the pastor's altar call.

There is a click and the devil aims his pistol right at the center of where we're clinging to one another. "You girls don't got no voice now? Yapping usually, ain't ya?"

I glare at that devil and see his eyes flash blue. I realize he's stared at me before. Watched me, even, from high up in the trees along the fence line. This devil is a hunter, just like Tsgilis.

"Now, listen here," the first devil calls. "Tell us where your daddy keeps his money from that skunk weed he's been selling."

Only canned laughter from the TV breaks the silence.

"We can make you talk," the other devil barks. "Or we can make you beg." He aims his gun and fires right at the screen. I've heard shots ring out plenty, but in this small room, the sound is a piercing explosion like a firework gone wrong.

We shiver and sob but don't say shit.

The devil with the gun lunges at us. "Have it your way." He jams the pistol inches from my face. "Start with the pretty one. That'll teach her daddy." Then he points the gun at Syd. "Put this one that looks like a boy in a closet. I'll tie that one up."

We scream for each other, arms outstretched, as we're ripped apart.

"Luna!"

"Syd!"

"Emma Lou!"

Syd tries to kick the devil who's grabbed her under the arms. She stops fighting quicker than I'd ever expect. She's supposed to protect us. To save us when we step wrong. But then I see why she lost her fight. The devil is dragging Syd to the tiny storage closet by the kitchen. She knows what I know: there's a loaded shotgun in there.

I'm flipped hard onto my stomach, and my face is shoved into the carpet by a nasty boot.

I pull away, but the hard toe connects with my jaw. Fresh pain blooms as I squeeze my eyes shut and try to slow my breathing. To stop shivering. To not give these wild dogs what they want.

Play possum, that's what we do in the middle of nowhere to survive.

Play dead until Sister saves us from the devils.

I go completely still except for a prayer on my lips, whispering to a god who's never answered out here, out nowhere, *Let Agilvgi send the Tsgilis back to hell.*

1

EXETER, RHODE ISLAND
Fifteen Years Later
TUESDAY, MAY 6, 2008

I brush wet dirt from the skull's damaged eye socket and wonder if my sister is dead.

The thought is an old habit. Normally, I barely notice; the fear is like a clear film that floats past my eye to be blinked away and forgotten.

Footsteps crunch to draw me away from worries about my only sister, Emma Lou, in rural Oklahoma. My focus returns to this hilltop near the Sandy Brook hiking loop in Rhode Island. Where I stand is not an area for hikers. I am on Narragansett Native land, which means I need to hurry to preserve the scene from whoever is headed this way.

I drop the toothbrush caked in mud and hustle to my backpack. I open the bag as I hear the snap of someone moving past the yellow caution tape I used to lock down the site yesterday evening.

Grabbing a soft cotton sheet from my bag, I fling it into the air to cover the entire skeleton I excavated from the earth this morning. An air pocket floats beneath the sheet as if the bones are trying to rise and leave the shallow grave.

I narrow my eyes to see who's coming over the hill. I half wave, relieved, at the sight of a familiar too-thin face with neat brown hair. He's in his usual loose jeans and starched yellow polo with a tribal seal stitched on the pocket.

"You pretty far along, Syd?" asks Ellis Reed, the Narragansett Tribal Historic Preservation Officer I work with the most. "Coroner won't like it."

"They're short-staffed and sending an intern." I don't hide my annoyance as I toss him a can of bug spray. "Starting before dawn means some college kid won't screw up our chances of an ID on the remains." I pause and decide to stick to this half-truth. Sharing that I'm in a hurry and meeting my wife in a couple of hours for an appointment will only lead to more questions.

"Kutaputush." Ellis says thanks in Narragansett, then coats himself with a thick layer of spray. These damp woods will have mosquitoes already out for blood. He tosses the can onto the ground and then crosses his arms as he stares down at what brought us here. "Appreciate the sheet."

Not that I need to explain as much to Ellis, but it should be common practice to cover remains. To treat the dead with respect and not as a spectacle. Especially bones like these, uncovered by accident, because they were never meant to be found.

"Can I take a look?" he asks.

"I didn't wait. I'm almost done," I warn as I retie my short black hair at the nape of my neck.

The Bureau of Indian Affairs, or BIA, says I shouldn't have excavated until Ellis, as the tribal representative, and the coroner showed. But my new boss works from the BIA headquarters, one thousand miles away, and from what I've heard about her, she wouldn't let an intern screw up her dig site either. Not that I asked.

I lift the sheet straight into the air and ball the fabric into my arms with a sniff of the fancy detergent my wife likes. She was softly snoring this morning when I gave up on sleep and came back here with my headlamp and excavation equipment. After two days of finding nothing of significance in my geological survey of the area, I was shocked to strike bone. With the last rays of sunlight at my back, I made the call to Ellis.

He blows out a long breath. "I'm glad you found her."

I nod once and follow his gaze to where I've brushed away the layers of earth around the delicate bones still wearing a dirty white dress. The arms and legs are fanned out like she was making a snow angel.

I'm lucky to work with Ellis because he treats me with respect, something the BIA hasn't traditionally given to tribal leaders like him. He could see me as just the BIA, the oldest bureau in the government. Created by the Department of War to exterminate Native people, culture, and ways of life across this "new" country "discovered" by men like Columbus and colonized by Pilgrims and founding fathers, despite the tens of thousands of years of Native life that preceded them.

The modern charge of the BIA is different, of course, but the bad blood rightfully remains. The culture at the BIA is changing, so there are more of us who see our job in a new way, especially since it's personal to me. I've never shared this with Ellis, but I'm Native, too. Cherokee from Oklahoma out here on Narragansett land in Rhode Island. But I look white, and I refuse to be the white woman who brings up her Cherokee heritage when it's convenient, selectively dropping it into a conversation with people who live Native life every day.

As part of a new generation in the agency—and Native myself—I do my best to make inroads with tribes and show that I'm here to help, not harm. But there's three hundred years of terrible history that tells another story.

I also greatly respect Ellis as a tribal leader who must live in two worlds. The need to preserve the past but also continue building the tribe's future through what's allowed by the government. He must find some version of balance between what the tribe needs to continue existing—language, land base, culture, medicine—and what the government will agree to give.

My role as an archeologist is simpler. I see myself as a midwife to the past for the future. To support the tribes by advocating for what they need to continue traditions that honor their thousands of years of history as they carry this knowledge into the future.

"Syd? Did you hear me?"

"Sorry."

He clears his throat. "Small cranium size."

I focus back on the bones between us. "Even without the dress, the narrow ridges of the eyebrows suggest female to me."

He crouches near the feet. "What's the stratigraphy?"

I almost grin at his question, which shows his knowledge extends well beyond what's needed for his job title. It's something I immediately respected in him when we first met after I took this job five years ago. I like to think he appreciates it in me, too. Neither of us is a fan of the status quo, especially not when it comes to justice.

"The same layer of earth," I say. "Two feet four inches deep, except the skull and feet were three inches higher on each side."

"Shallow grave dug fast," he says with a sigh. "What do you make of the skull fracture?"

A memory of Emma Lou in a screaming fight with her ex-boyfriend floats past, but I return focus. I want to step beyond the status quo of my job, too. To not let my sister and all her problems distract me from justice.

I drop to my knees and return to the position I was in right before he arrived, toothbrush and all. I take away a few more layers of mud on the right eye socket, where the fracture begins. "There's a section of avulsed bone on the right cheek." I pause as Ellis squats next to me, and I point out where the face was cut, starting at the left eye socket. "The trauma extends from the inferior orbital border under the eye socket to the left canine tooth root."

He tightens his lips like a flinch. "Stabbed in the face."

"There's only blood splatter along the left shoulder." I motion to the small spot I'd noticed when inspecting the dress. "Her assailant—let's take a wild guess and assume *he*—could have grabbed her from behind and stabbed her as he held her. I didn't see any more trauma, though, so this was the only injury by the knife. But that wouldn't necessarily kill her."

"You can tell all that?"

"Best guess," I say, because that's all I can do with the constraints of time, money, and going gray before seeing any lab results. Plus, I'm not a forensic archeologist, a specialist in excavating crime scenes. I studied it in school, extensively, but kept returning to the land and culture over labs and bones—to honor indigenous history and support projects that make the future possible.

Ellis rubs under his eyes, as if he wishes there was more available than guesses. "Keep going, please," he says with a weariness I understand. This is not an average day.

I fumble with the flashlight in my pocket but manage to click it on. The sun is only starting to rise, and we need more light to properly examine the neck bones. "This break indicates a laryngeal fracture. The attacker probably stood on her neck until she suffocated or bled to death."

Ellis blows out a long breath. "How old, do you think?"

"Late teens, early twenties."

"Just the right age to disappear." He scrapes his knuckles under his clean-shaven chin. "What about the dress?"

"Machine stiches. No tag on any seams or initials sewn inside."

"We're not that lucky."

"Well, I wouldn't say that." I reach over to a brown paper bag holding our only clue. I use my pencil to lift out a pink plastic quartz Swatch watch. "Looks like something from the eighties."

"Yeah," he says with the lightness of memory in his voice. "My sister and her friends had Swatches like that when they were teenagers. Probably 'eighty-five."

Trends in teenage culture are fascinating, no matter the decade, but I stay on topic. "Approximate year of death would help. We can see if there are any missing women in the national database."

"There were plenty of women that went missing back then," he says. "Maybe ran off, maybe not. Few reported, though."

There's no need for me to say what comes next in his reasoning. Even if someone did report it to the police, it's unlikely anything would be done, let alone actually filing a report or contacting the FBI, which has jurisdiction over reservation land.

I ease the watch back into the paper bag and set it aside. I doubt there's a print, and if there is we won't know for a year. Maybe more. Not for old bones on Native land.

As the BIA's regional archeologist, I may not have legal jurisdiction to actually investigate—that's usually a tribal officer's job—but these bones were found by me on land that I'm responsible for. That's an obligation extending beyond man's laws into the laws of nature, which I've always respected. I can at least help by doing as much legwork as possible to bring a name to the remains and answers to the family.

"I'll get started with a missing person report first thing," I say, though I don't hide the tone of my voice that suggests it's a waste of time. The FBI manages Native land, but missing Native women and girls don't typically garner their precious attention and resources. "She deserves us trying, at least."

I stare at the blood splatter on the white dress and worry again about Emma Lou. I remember her the last time I was home. No one had warned me she was using again. I found her strung out in our family's living room, under a picture our mom bought at a Quapaw tribe powwow called *Madonna of the Plains*. A Native woman in a buckskin dress gazing bravely into the distance as she holds tight her baby in a cradleboard.

I've often thought I carry my worry for Sister the same way, strapped to my back, but all burden, no blessing.

The worry grew heavier with Emma Lou's parade of boyfriends with short tempers who were well trained in tearful apologies. But that was nothing to the drugs. My mom had her dismissive attitude and Baptist prayer circle, and my dad had his avoidance. It always fell to me to actually find Emma Lou and bring her home, full of more drugs than sense. Then she'd do it again. And again. The worry grew too large, and if I had kept going back home to Picher, it would have broken us both.

The wind unfolds in a gust that rattles the silent acres of trees around us. Chills spread along my arms, and I wish I didn't hear my grandmother's words, but I do: *This wind is a messenger. There will be news from Unetlanvhi.*

I'm in no mood to search for signs of the Great Spirit. I'm fighting the idea of Emma Lou's death taking root. As if my grandmother's god is saying this time the worry of failing to save my sister will not painlessly float past my eye.

"The intern is here," Ellis says as a van bumps along the narrow path.

The wheels spin deep tracks in the spring mud and crush the plants and few wildflowers edging the trail. I already don't like this intern, and I haven't even met him yet.

I dig the toe of my boot into the mud and try to release the worry for Emma Lou. I swore I was done when I said goodbye to Sister three years ago in a hospital bed. I haven't returned to Oklahoma since. Instead I am here seeking justice and peace for what's been hidden in the earth.

"Let's go," I say, relieved at the kick of anger instead of helpless fear. "That intern sure as hell isn't going to screw up my scene."

2

The coroner's van jerks to a sudden stop as if striking an invisible tree. The driver's-side door flies open, and a tall kid dressed head to toe in blue scrubs, a medical apron, and a surgical cap nearly falls to the ground. He takes only a few steps before he starts flailing his arms and yelling. "You already started?!"

In that second, I am justified in my choice to dig alone, even if it's breaking regulations set long ago. I glance at Ellis, then back to the kid. "I'm the one digging. We start when I say."

"I wanted to do it," he says with a whine in his voice. "You were supposed to wait!"

"Wait for the coroner." I cross my arms. "You're an intern."

"I represent the coroner, thank you very much." He leans forward and jams his balled fists onto his hips. There's something maternal in the pose. I almost smile, guessing his mother probably uses the same one.

"Let's try this again. I'm Ellis Reed from the Narragansett

tribal office," he says kindly, and steps toward the kid with a wave. "This is Syd Walker, archeologist from BIA. There's plenty to do."

"This dig is for my senior thesis." The kid's eyes go wide and honestly look gleeful when he glances at the skeleton. "I have to know everything."

"These remains were a human being," Ellis says firmly. "Not a science project."

The kid stands up taller, but his fists go back to his hips. "I have experience with Indian remains."

That's unlikely, since I'd know about it, given any remains on tribal land in this region of the country get called in to me and Ellis. "What experience?"

"My university has Indian hair and skeletons. We've studied them in class."

"At least use the term 'indigenous,' kid, since you're not Native yourself," I snap.

The kid smirks as if I'm the dumbest person in the world. My guess is an older sibling passed that down.

Ellis makes eye contact and shakes his head to keep me from continuing the lecture. Many colleges are disrespectful to Native graves and artifacts, going so far as to get a law passed to keep what they stole. Hiding behind the robes of judges to justify human remains and sacred objects being stolen and abandoned to shelves. Many universities paint a tidy and offensively inaccurate history of all indigenous people: discovery by colonists, removal from land, forced dispersal onto reservations and so-called Indian Territory, and now merely history to be studied.

As if we aren't still here. As if by being here, we are evidence of their crimes.

I take a deep breath to calm down because I know I can't blame all that on the kid. "Fine. You can look at my notes," I murmur.

"Nice!" He does a fist pump and shuffles over to my write-in-rain notepad and sketches. With an extra-loud sigh, he drops onto the ground and starts to read.

I return to the remains with my toothbrush and camera to take more photos now that we're getting some sunlight. Ellis still needs his flashlight as he inspects the broken neck bones. He starts to make his own sketch, which will be shared with tribal leaders.

"Wait a second." The kid looks up from the notes in a huff. "*You* found this skeleton?"

I finish taking photos around the skull before answering. "Yeah."

"I thought it was an Indian ceremony. Or *indigenous* ceremony." He flips a few pages, then tosses my notebook onto the ground. "Like a burial thing."

"Why would a coroner be involved in a Native burial ceremony?" Ellis asks, kinder than he should.

"Well . . . I don't know," the kid stammers. "I need, like . . . facts and stuff for my thesis. So, what happened?"

I don't answer and instead do one more brush of the left eye socket.

"I'm Jeremiah, by the way." He plops down next to me in a gangly heap. "Is that a toothbrush?"

"Mmm-hmm," I say. "Simple tools are best."

He snorts toward Ellis, who doesn't respond. "How'd you find it?"

I stare at the kid—Jeremiah—who looks genuinely curious and maybe a little nervous. I should be kind. I was an intern, too, once, for the BIA, though not willfully ignorant like this unega, as my dad would utter about ignorant white people under his breath.

"At the BIA, I perform resource surveys," I begin. "In this case, there are internet cables being run through three miles of

Narragansett land. Before that work can begin, we make sure there aren't any artifacts or unknown grave sites that need to be reburied and protected."

"You're an archeologist," he says, as if I don't know. "Aren't you supposed to be digging up stuff for museums or whatever?"

"No."

"Really?" He glances at Ellis. "That sound right to you?"

"Would you want your grandmother's bones displayed at your college?" Ellis asks. "How about her favorite pots or plates for students to joke about or study how crude they were? Would you like your classmates to say things like, 'That's decent for a poor white lady in the 1950s who didn't know better'?"

"My grandma wasn't poor," Jeremiah says.

Ellis grins. "Then I bet she really wouldn't have liked to be treated that way."

We sit in blessed silence for a few minutes, and I think of a buckskin shirt I saw in the Smithsonian Museum. It belonged to an Oglala Lakota man whose body was seized at his death and kept in cold storage for 130 years. He was allowed to be taken home by his family only after the Native American Graves Protection and Repatriation Act was passed in 1990.

"What do you do during one of your land surveys?" Jeremiah asks me.

I am trying to stop what's happened since Columbus stepped foot in this hemisphere. To honor the history and culture of those who lived here for at least ten thousand years before that cataclysmic moment. But that's not what he's asking, so I keep it to myself.

"Every few feet, I scoop and sift the dirt to make sure there isn't anything underneath that needs to be preserved. In this case, I found an arm bone. Then saw a machine-stitched cotton sleeve, which told me the remains were post-contact."

"Contact with what?"

"White people," I say. "The bones are preserved too well to be prior to the Revolutionary War."

"Like prehistoric?"

"There were thousands of years of Native history here before a single ship arrived," I say. "You should call it precontact. Do you need a pen?"

"I'll remember." He blinks toward Ellis. "So when does the burial ritual start? Can I take pictures or does that steal souls or whatever?"

Ellis slowly grinds his jaw, and I'm glad to see his patience wane. "We'll need DNA testing first. To be sure she's Narragansett. Then we'll have a ceremony."

Jeremiah scratches at his surgical cap. "But this month, right?"

"No," I say. "Try a year, if we're lucky. Based on the trauma inflicted on the cranium, this is a cold-case murder victim. Labs are backlogged years."

His eyes go wide. "Murder, huh? My adviser would probably think that's wicked cool."

I wonder if I can blame the "wicked cool" *Saw* movie franchise for this kind of dumbass wanting to be a medical examiner.

Jeremiah grins at the turn of events, and for a moment I consider helping him so he'll leave. I could walk him through the Munsell color chart for identifying soil types. I could explain how we measure stratigraphy and each layer of earth. I could show him ranges of soil acidity and what that means for remains. I could even walk him through my photos and share the process the skeleton will go through in the lab.

Naw.

"I think we're ready to move her," I say to Jeremiah. "Did you bring the cadaver bag?"

"The skull has almost detached," Ellis says. "Probably due to the larynx injury. Do you have foil to wrap it?"

"Whoa, wait just a minute." Jeremiah holds up his hands. "I need more information for my paper." He clears his throat. "Please?"

I shake my head because sometimes I'm a real sucker. "The left maxilla had sharp-force trauma." He's watching me, so I continue. "Likely perimortem. Do you know what that means?"

"Oh, um, like the injury caused her death?" He leans over the skull.

"She may have been running away and got caught from behind. Grabbed around the waist with one arm and attacked from this angle with the knife directly into the left side of her face." I pause to act out how the killer could have been positioned. "She was pulling away when the knife went in. There's little blood splatter because she was turning from him."

"Man, he went for the face." Jeremiah stares for a few seconds. "So that's what killed her?"

I shrug and brush a stray black hair into my stubby ponytail. "I'm not a forensic archeologist. There are no fancy labs or cutting-edge technology for quick answers."

"So what's the point?"

My gaze narrows at his arrogant freckled face. "Justice."

"Catching the bad guys who did it," he says with a confident nod.

"That's only one part," I say. "Returning sacred pottery to the right tribal leaders is justice. Finding a mass grave site after a battle so a proper burial can be given is justice. Uncovering the remains of a woman who was held down on the ground with a boot on her throat to bleed out after getting stabbed in the face is justice."

He flinches and points toward my tools. "Can I use the tooth-brush? If I'm careful?"

Ellis only shrugs, so I hand the kid a worn one that shouldn't do any damage.

I go to find another lens for my camera to take more photos of the skull, since we have extra time. The photos will be used at every level and every stage, from forensic investigation to family identification. As I'm searching my backpack, I hear my flip phone vibrating. I hurry to answer when I see the caller ID.

"Hey, boss. I was going to call you on my way back to the of-fice. The dig is going well. We—"

"I'm not calling for an update, Syd." She inhales deeply, and I picture my new boss, Jo Mankiller, from the one time I met her. She's looking out toward downtown Nashville in a glass-walled office on the top floor of the Bureau of Indian Affairs regional headquarters.

Jo is young for a regional director, and after being ignored by my last boss on his way to retiring to the panhandle of Florida, I'm still trying to figure her out. "I just landed at the Providence airport, Syd. You need to pack a bag and meet me for a briefing. I've got you assigned to a regional detail."

"What?" I take a few steps away for privacy and stumble for a moment. "Why?"

"A skull was found in Oklahoma. On BIA-managed land."

I keep myself from saying *So?* Remains are found on Native land all the time. Me being from the state shouldn't matter. I know she's new to the job, but surely she's aware of that much. "Is the region so hard up for an archeologist that—"

"The skull was found in Picher."

"Oh." I brace myself against a tree. "That's where I'm from."

"I know, Syd."

Of course she did. I'd told her in her office a few months ago during our first and only meeting about the night with the devils. The murder of Luna and her parents.

Tell me something true about yourself, Syd.

Before I'd been able to stop myself, I told my new boss about that night—even though it'd taken me two years before I'd had the courage to tell my wife, Mal.

My best friend, Luna Myers, and her parents were murdered by two men in devil masks . . .

I'd meant what I said at the end of my rambling to her: I believe in the importance of justice above all else, from murdered girls to family heirlooms meant to remain buried in sacred places.

"Where did you find the skull?" I ask firmly as the wind rustles pine needles overhead like a warning.

"I'm sorry, Syd, I know this is . . . personal for you."

"Where?"

Jo gently clears her throat, and her voice is strong and calm. "On the Myers land."

Luna Myers. Her family land going back to the Quapaw tribe allotment. Right across four acres of cornfield from my family's Cherokee homestead.

The Myers land. Where Emma Lou and I almost died. Where I didn't save Luna.

"Syd? I'll see you at the airport?"

None of it matters. I haven't stepped foot in Northeast Oklahoma in three years, and I intend to keep it that way. "We'll talk in an hour."

3

After we load the Narragansett woman's remains into the coroner's van, I mention meeting my boss to Ellis, to explain why I can't stick around for a debrief.

"She wants me to go on a regional detail." I cross my arms tight across my long-sleeved BIA polo. "To Northeast Oklahoma, where I'm from. I'll get out of it."

"Might not be that easy. Your boss had to pull some strings to get you assigned a detail outside your region," Ellis says kindly, but there's a warning in there.

I grit my molars for a moment because he's not wrong. With current politics in the BIA, it's damn near impossible to drop in from an outside region.

"Shit," I murmur, and clear my throat when it tightens.

"Not excited to see your family?" Ellis guesses correctly with a half grin.

"About as excited as they are to see me."

"It's never easy with blood." Ellis watches Jeremiah drive

down the narrow path, slowly this time. "Did your boss transfer from another BIA region?"

"Jo is from the Office of Justice Services."

"OJS?" Ellis whistles. "BIA police force? Huh. Don't hear about those kinds of transfers much."

"She was a special agent. Whatever that means."

"Means you don't want her knocking on your door."

As far as I knew, OJS was all about drugs. Drug trafficking, particularly, and they had to work well with the FBI since the US government is still landlord on most Native land. That dynamic worked fine because all the FBI cared about was drugs, too.

But now that she'd left OJS and was a new BIA regional director, Jo was very focused on bones. On women who were missing. There's no way she could have done that over at OJS unless there was a mountain of drugs buried with the woman's remains.

"Nice that she seems to give a shit," I say, meaning it. "But there's no reason for me to go."

Ellis checks his watch. "I'll swing by my sister's place after lunch. Start asking around about girls who went missing when she was in high school. I'll call you in a day or so. Good luck with the new boss."

"I'll need it," I say lamely, but I'm determined to get out of this assignment. Someone in the Oklahoma region should be involved instead of me.

If that logic doesn't work, then I can be honest with Jo and explain I need to be here for Mal after her doctor visit today. She didn't cry after the disappointing appointment two months ago, but she was still pretty down.

She's been trying to get pregnant for almost two years. Or, I guess, *we've* been trying to get pregnant. Becoming a mother by thirty wasn't on my radar until Mal, who'd be almost thirty-two if the baby were born this year.

In the beginning, I went to every appointment. Partly to support her, and partly because of my fear that her wish would come true. We'd be parents.

Guilt knocks around in my gut as I irrationally wonder if I'd somehow wished away her happiness with my fear.

I say goodbye to Ellis and hurry to the start of the hiking loop, where I parked my truck. I cough a few times and continue to walk. Normally, the dark quiet of the woods is calming, but today the effect is the opposite.

Tension is everywhere in my body: pressing in my chest, churning in my gut, grinding my molars together, and balling my toes in my boots.

Part of it is worrying about Mal and her disappointment while I hide my relief. Part is about this other skull's appearance in my day. Best guess, she's like the Narragansett woman: hidden in the earth with the intention she'd never be found.

My truck is ahead, and in the passenger seat I see a flash of dirty-blond hair, a halo of frizz, and a blurry face from a memory fifteen years old.

Not again.

My vision narrows as my chest seizes, and I can't catch my breath.

I drop to my knees and listen. It takes a moment to hear something, anything, over the blood rushing in my ears and heart knocking in my chest. I search for the Cherokee words my grandma Ama taught me.

The short and sweet chirp of a totsuhwa, or cardinal, finally grounds me. I open my eyes and see a magnolia tree. I listen again, hearing in the branches a tsisquoga. I can almost make out the robin's orange color in the tree.

This is my calming tool that Grandma Ama suggested when I told her about my panicking symptoms. She said to search for sacred things.

Listen for birds singing songs of our ancestors.

Seek out the trees of the Cherokee.

The cedar, pine, spruce, laurel, and holly are green throughout the darkest days of winter.

It took practice, but I learned to move my focus beyond my body, to the earth around me, until I could release myself from panic's tight grasp.

The twisting in my chest starts to unfurl as I listen to the screech of the tlaiga, or blue jay. I rise from the mud, relief steadying my heartbeat, and take a few steps and a few more. As I approach the truck, my breathing is normal. No flash of brownish blond keeps my pace steady.

That was a trick of the eye. I open the truck door.

I'm not seeing dead girls again.

4

As I pull into our long driveway, Boone Lake shimmers at the edge of the sloping lawn. The peace I usually feel seeing the view is interrupted by Mal's red Acura still in the driveway.

I grab the sheet I used at the grave site, dusted in dirt, but leave my equipment and tools in the passenger seat. Hurrying up the deck stairs, I pause at the side door of our house, which is slightly open.

"Mal?" I call as I step inside, and my gaze darts around to the open area connecting our kitchen, living room, and dining room, all empty. "Mal? Are you home?"

I hurry around the sofa and cross the dining room to the hallway that leads to the bedrooms. I make it to the last doorway, gasping as if I've run the ten miles from the dig site to home.

My wife sits at the edge of our bed with her back to me. Mal faces the large windows toward the lake and is unusually still. Light reflects off our wedding photo, from the courthouse steps in Massachusetts, the only state that's legalized gay marriage.

I drop the sheet and move closer. Her chest rises and falls in a sleeveless red silk dress. Her optometrist coat is still hanging in dry-cleaner plastic. She holds her flip phone in her hands like a bird nest.

"Mal?"

Her light brown eyes blink at me. "Did I call you?" She glances down at the phone with a frown. "Wait, I didn't. Why are you home? Is everything okay?"

I let out a long breath that she's fine, if distracted.

She shifts on our bed and tucks a knee so she's facing me. As on most days, I'm struck by her beauty. Every color comes alive on her skin, a rich burnt umber that perfectly highlights her freckled nose and cheeks.

"Are you okay, babe?" Mal asks again, still cradling the phone.

I answer her with my own question. "Who called?"

She smiles as if hiding a secret. "The doctor."

I take a step forward into the bedroom. "Oh."

"Dr. Grigsby had a patient go into labor, so she had to cancel our appointment."

"Oh."

"She called herself because she had news. *Good* news. We have good news." Mal rises slowly and drops the phone on our bed. "We're pregnant, Syd. It's early, but everything looks great."

She steps closer and intertwines our fingers. I know mine are clammy. I know I've lost color in my face. I know I'm not good enough to be anyone's mother.

"Syd, isn't this what we wanted?" She smiles softly as if waiting for me to join her in long-awaited joy.

I can only nod, on autopilot. "I love seeing you happy."

Her head dips to the side and several dark braids fall forward. "I know what you're doing."

I try to stay calm but feel as if I've been caught. "I'm not doing anything."

She crosses her arms. "You've tried to keep the idea of this baby at a distance. Like how you tried to keep me at a distance when we got serious."

"That was college," I say, hating how defensive I sound. "I've grown up."

Mal smiles at me like she sees right through my posturing. Which she does. She always confronts and clears up what's hanging in the air between us. "I love you, so I helped you through those issues. Looking back, it helped me with clinicals, actually. The kids I work with who don't want vision therapy are a lot like dealing with a twentysomething scared of commitment."

"Hilarious."

"I'm not joking about this, though, babe." Mal raises her eyebrows. "You're disappearing."

I will not see dead girls. "No, I'm not. I'm right here. I want what you want."

"That's the problem exactly." She stares deeper into my gaze, never flinching, always honest. "You're saying what you think you should. Not what's in your heart."

"That's not what's happening," I argue, more with myself.

"Well, I know I am happy. Time to celebrate." She grins, and I feel her joy is beyond me, outside of me, somewhere new that doesn't require me at all. "I'm going to call the girls and then go see my mom to tell her in person. Want to come?"

"They're going to flip." I kiss her deeply as if trying to tether us back together. Then I remember I have news, too, now an excuse for not joining her. "I've got to go to the airport. My boss is waiting."

"At the Providence airport?" She heads over to the bed and picks up her phone. "Isn't she in Nashville normally?"

"Jo wants to talk about a case in person." I shrug as if that'll soften the surprise of what I'm about to say. "Jo thinks I need to go on a regional assignment. There was a skeleton found in Northeast Oklahoma."

Her mouth makes a perfect O. "And she wants you to go there and . . ."

"I'm going to tell her no. We have too much going on. I can't leave you. Not now."

"I didn't ask you to do that." Mal strides across the room and tears the dry-cleaner plastic off her doctor's coat. "Do you know where the remains were found? Is it another missing woman no one cares about?"

"They found the skull on land near my parents' house. The farm across the field—"

"Where your friend and her parents were murdered?"

Thump-thump.

Everything is dark and muffled. The coats and jackets around me smell of mothballs and my eyes sting, already wet from terrified tears.

I am fifteen again. I am back in that trailer. I must save the girls.

Luna.

Emma Lou.

Perhaps it was Grandma Ama's Unetlanvhi. The Great Spirit led the devil to put me in this particular closet. The loaded rifle is a familiar weight.

I told the girls we'd always be safe. A promise I had no business making. I said I'd protect them both. Another promise I'd break.

"Where did you go?" Mal whispers, taking my hands again.

I can't admit the past is returning. That I'm doing more than dreaming of gunpowder and hearing that single shot.

I return to Mal. To this moment that should be the beginning of a true happiness. I have to stay here.

"After what happened with Emma Lou, I swore I wasn't going back to Oklahoma until we were ready. I am far from ready. Still, I have to pack a bag, just in case."

She nods once as if I'm lying to myself, which maybe I am. Still I leave her to call her girlfriends, and I pack quickly while half listening to her exciting news being repeated.

"I'm heading out." I step back into the bedroom with my bag. "I'll call you when I land."

"Okay," she says softly, more to herself. "Okay." Mal rolls her shoulders back with a deep inhale. Her reset, she calls it when she's hit a wall. "This might be good timing, Syd."

"Really?" I don't hide the hurt in my voice. "Sounds like you want me to leave."

"Are you picking a fight?"

I lift her hand and put it to my lips rather than apologize. "I'll call you after. I love you."

"Put the sheet in the washer," she says as I leave our bedroom. I don't need to turn around to know she's smiling.

I drop the dirty sheet into the machine and try not to think of the woman's skull that rested beneath it. Or of the skull waiting in Oklahoma for me.

Or that somehow I'll have to live with disappointing them all.

I'm angry as I head toward my truck, probably the most at myself. I'm not paying attention as I drop into the driver's seat and slam the door.

But maybe that's why she's come back now, when I wasn't looking.

Her voice is unchanged after fifteen years. She's not screaming my name this time. Instead, she's calm and cool. She blows a bubble, and I flinch at the pop, shocked I can hear the sound.

I close my eyes tight, thinking darkness can somehow stop what has been a long time coming. If I can't see that fuzzy halo of dirty-blond hair, perhaps she's not there.

Thump-thump.

"Oh, Syd. Just because you left me to die back then doesn't mean you get to ignore me now."

5

~~~~~

Of course, I'd seen Ghost Luna before. Hell, I saw her earlier today. The messy halo of hair. But it'd been a while. Years, in fact, during dark times, difficult times. Before Mal and before Rhode Island.

"Aren't you tired of so many girls going missing?" Ghost Luna smacks her gum and there's the scent of Bubblicious Watermelon. "You can actually do something."

My hand is trembling as I crank up the radio to drown out her voice, or rather, my memory of her voice. Trauma lives in the body. That night with the devils has manifested itself in my life in more ways than I care to acknowledge. I don't know why it's here now, but I never do until it's gone.

The radio commercial cuts to blast the 1993 hit "Cherub Rock" by the Smashing Pumpkins. Our favorite song that year. Our last night together, we'd had the song on repeat while I made popcorn. We'd screamed, *Let me out!* Then the devils darkened the door.

I slam the dial to shut it off.

After gripping the wheel for a moment, I put the truck into drive. I can't be seeing dead girls. I certainly can't be hearing them either.

The silent treatment works, and it's quiet on the twenty-minute drive to Rhode Island's T.F. Green Airport. I pull into the short-term parking lot closest to the airport.

"You'll have to repark or pay an assload when you're back," Ghost Luna says.

I almost laugh as I wheel into the spot. Is this figment of my imagination trying to save me money? I don't look at her, but she's there. She pops another bubble, and I nearly fall out of the truck trying to get away.

"Don't forget your bag," she calls.

I slam the door instead of answering. I don't need my bag because I'm not going to Oklahoma.

Once I'm through a set of sliding glass doors, I pass a huge wooden sailboat by the tourist welcome counter. I head down the escalator to the recently renovated baggage claim area, where, oddly enough, there is a bar. I don't turn around, but I feel her or it or whatever you call your mind on the verge of snapping.

Jo Mankiller sits at a high-top table in front of a margarita the size of her head. She waves as I approach, and I give her a polite nod before sitting down. Her black hair is cut into a stylish bob. Turquoise beaded earrings dangle above her white collared shirt, and I think of the slang "tradish." As if Jo is dressing the part of a traditional Native American leader.

"You can tell this state was run by Italian Catholics," she says with a grin. "They even have a bar where you pick up your luggage."

"No blue laws either. They sell beer and wine cold." That doesn't happen in some places, including Oklahoma. "As if that'll stop people from cracking them open in the car."

"Nothing like a roadie." She raises the giant glass but doesn't take a sip. In fact, it looks completely full. There's a stack of folders in front of her. She's been working, but she's putting on a "cool boss" show.

My chair is uncomfortable, and I shift, trying not to look around and see ghosts. I keep my focus squarely on Jo. "You settling into the job okay?"

"There wasn't much to settle into. Your old boss seemed more concerned with bass fishing."

"Worked for me. Something to be said for doing your job however you want."

"So I'm told." Jo smiles coolly.

"Don't the folks in OJS get to do whatever they want?" I lean forward. "Or is that why you transferred to BIA?"

The cool gaze remains. "There were many reasons why I left, but let's shift gears. How did it go with Ellis and the remains you found?"

"Female, likely young. Stabbed in the face by some piece of shit, I'm sure. She was wearing a Swatch, one of those plastic watches from the eighties—"

"I'm familiar."

"Ellis is going to ask around. Not hopeless, but not ideal."

"The relationship you've developed with the Narragansett tribe is impressive."

That may be true, but the praise bothers me. "I give them common courtesy. Something everyone in BIA should do."

"But they don't."

I cross my arms. "Things are changing."

"Not fast enough for me." She stabs the large twisty straw into her drink. "You want anything, or can we get into it?"

I'm eager to hear her pitch. In my five years of working for the BIA, I'd been assigned two other details, an unmarked grave in rural Massachusetts and an extra set of hands for a big resource survey in Connecticut. Neither had a criminal investigation component, and technically, what Jo was asking was far outside my job description. I wave my hand for her to continue. I'm ready with my arguments. I'm not getting on that plane.

"I've been studying the cases of missing people in different BIA regions. A lot of girls—women—have disappeared where you're from."

I nod, because of course they had. It was a sad fact of rural life. Of a disinterested police force. Of ignorant assumptions about missing Native girls—drugs, prostitution, runaways—that kept anyone from looking. Not to mention issues of tribal versus nontribal land. Questions of which police should be involved. Who has jurisdiction and over which people?

Jo places one hand over the other, her large turquoise and silver rings catching the light. "I got the call about the skull because the regional director of the Northeast Oklahoma office owes me a favor."

I hold my breath for a moment because I realize she did pull strings to get me assigned to this detail. "It's not a good time for me. For my wife and me."

Jo sits back, and I realize it's the same motion she made in her office that led me to spill my guts about the night with the devils. It's a simple gesture, not closed off, but not exactly welcoming. It's as if she's saying, *Prove it.*

Jo had mentioned she was close with her father, who just recently passed away. I wonder if he'd taught her that gesture, maybe after she tried sneaking back into the house, or didn't tell him about a new dent in the bumper.

It works on me again, and I can't stop myself. "Mal, my wife, just found out she's—we're—pregnant."

"Congratulations."

"She's been wanting this for a while. I need to be there for her."

"She asked you to stay?"

"Oh. No."

"You still have something like nine months before the baby will arrive, I believe."

"Oh. Yes. But . . . my family." I stop there as if those two words are a complete sentence or well-articulated thought. Still, if you know, you know.

Jo nods as if she does. "Family is complicated."

"I haven't been back in a while. Last time, my sister OD'd. We found her, Mal and me."

"That's awful. I'm sorry."

"She has a daughter. My niece. Gracie. I didn't think she'd stay on drugs after she . . . became a mother. Kind of breaks my heart."

"The dad is—"

"In prison, thank God," I say, thinking of the last time I saw Cody. That led to the last time I saw my family. I'd brought Mal to meet my parents when they rather surprisingly offered to host a wedding reception for us back in Oklahoma.

I'd been relieved at their offer. It was as if my parents were saying they forgave me for never bringing Mal home. As if my parents understood I didn't know how to reconcile the broken version of me that left Picher with this new version—a college graduate in love with a wonderful woman and ready to take a good government job and buy a house in a state they'd never been to. Those versions of me are incompatible and wouldn't know each other. Maybe most ridiculous, I worried this new version might disappear by going back.

The night before the reception, I should have been hanging twinkle lights in the yard or wrapping plastic utensils in napkins tied with ribbons for guests to grab at the end of the cake line. Instead, Mal and I were searching for Emma Lou.

I don't know if I'll ever forgive Sister for the day I saved her life instead of celebrating my relationship with Mal, which saved mine.

Not the way I'd dreamed of introducing her to my roots. *Welcome to the family, Mal.* Running around to meth houses and abandoned buildings where Sister used to hang out and score.

Cody had her in some random trailer a friend of a friend told us about. We found him first, zoned out, but then suddenly, he snapped awake. He launched himself from the floor as I ran to Emma Lou to find her almost dead, her shirt lifted up over her unhealed C-section scar. Her breathing was shallow, and she wasn't responsive.

Cody screamed at us that Emma Lou was fine. He got in my face and said to leave her alone. Threatened to get his gun. He was high, and I'm sure there was a weapon somewhere, but I'd thankfully already called the ambulance. He admitted to the paramedics that she'd done meth and snorted some opioids. They gave her Narcan right there before rushing her to the ER.

Then Cody had the nerve to show up at the hospital to see her. Crying about how he loved her. That he really would marry her this time. That he'd be a good dad to Gracie. Emma Lou didn't hesitate to take him back.

That's when I knew. That's when I told her. *I can't stand by you if you choose him. He'll kill you, one way or another.*

"It's family," Jo murmurs. "Never easy." She scoots the margarita to the side. For a moment, I think she's going to take my hand. Instead, she pulls something from a folder and slides it across the table. "You recognize this, Syd?"

I pick up the square plastic ID badge. It's familiar before I even know why. I stare at a photo of me from when I was an intern for the BIA during my junior year of college. "Where did you get this?"

The me in that photo was only six years removed from the night with the devils. She still woke up smelling smoke and crying for Luna. She was desperate to leave Oklahoma behind. She was struggling to accept herself as Two Spirit because she felt empty, as if she didn't even have one. She'd meet Mal that fall and realize what it meant to find your person. That it's worth healing yourself so you can be better for someone else.

From behind me, I hear a voice. "Help her."

I don't turn around but continue to stare at my younger self. "Where did you find my old badge?"

Jo takes it from my line of sight and returns it to the folder. "Your badge was placed inside the mouth of the skeleton."

I flinch at the words, the implication. "What?"

"Either someone really wants your help or they're warning you to stay away. I vote the former, though there's good reason for the latter. The regional director didn't report the badge yet. He agrees you should be involved."

"It feels like I already am."

"It could be dangerous, Syd. But I'm asking you to go, not telling you."

"The timing couldn't be worse."

Jo slides two photos from the same folder as the badge. I don't have to look at them to know the images will stay with me for the rest of my life.

I pull the photograph closer, and it's a skull on a metal lab tray. There's a light layer of dirt, similar to the skull this morning, indicating it was also hidden beneath the earth. There are notations of size and shape. Female. Young. Like a terrible song on repeat.

The next photo is from the scene. The skull rests in a tree, wedged where the two main branches split. A deep V that seemed almost grown to hold it perfectly in place. My old badge, my young face, dangles between white teeth.

"She didn't die with it in her mouth, if that's what you're wondering."

"Jesus," I murmur at Jo, because the thought hadn't occurred to me. Now that she'd said it, how could I think of anything else?

"You were born and raised there. Your family still lives there. That's your lineage, Syd. The places we're from live within our DNA."

"I haven't been back in years. I'd planned to keep it that way." There's a pause, and I feel the weight of something unsaid. "What else?"

"The Northeast Oklahoma regional director is letting you take this detail because I asked. I approached the region's supervisor first, and she's not happy about it. She didn't want your help. Didn't want help of any kind, in fact."

That's strange. Every region is understaffed. Budgets are stretched. Not to mention, Jo outranks the supervisor. I didn't even realize "no" was an option.

"I was shocked she refused help," Jo continues, "especially since she's requested our support for similar cases in the past."

"Really?"

"They don't even have an archeologist on staff right now.

There's not an agency in the country who'd refuse help. Her dad was the former regional director—"

"Sue Dove, yeah, I know her." Know her favorite ice cream. Know who she had a crush on in high school. Know the smell of her first car and her slushie order from the Sonic in Miami. Know I haven't seen her since high school graduation. I'd peaced out of her life—cruelly, I'm sure she believes, and I wouldn't argue. I doubt she'd work with me unless her boss's boss told her to. "What'd she say?"

"That she was already handling it," Jo says with surprise in her voice.

"What about local police?" I ask, though I already know the answer.

"Keeping them in the loop, whatever that means. She had quick answers for everything, which I never trust." Jo clears her throat. "I don't advise you to either, no matter the history."

The Sue I remember didn't lie, especially about things that mattered. But maybe we've both changed. "This seems outside my job scope and definitely outside of your jurisdiction."

"Look, Superintendent Dove has been on my radar. She's investigated several missing and murdered Native women cases and went above and beyond. She seems smart, maybe even the type to keep climbing. But this isn't adding up."

"You sound frustrated."

"We should have been Superintendent Dove's first call. Instead, she's dodging us."

"There are lots of reasons she wouldn't want my help," I say, not willing to get into them.

"This a small-town, know-everyone's-business kind of thing?"

"More like 'I doubt she wants to see my face' kind of thing."

Jo nods as if she understands, though there's no way she could.

I'd left Sue and our friendship behind when I went to college. I can't really explain why. I'd left my sister and my family behind, too.

"How long are you going to hide?" asks a voice from behind me.

Jo stares at me. "Syd, how long are you going to hide?"

I draw back in my seat, the power of the echo—the question—coming from outside me and from within.

There was a skull in my hands this morning. Now another skull with my name literally in its mouth. It felt like the remains, from these unknown women, were reaching out for my help. As if the earth itself was tired of waiting.

I cannot hide if I'm going to uncover the truth.

"Okay," I say simply, and I wonder if I ever really had a choice.

"Here's the one time I'm saying this to you." Jo pauses and papers shuffle before the snap of a briefcase. "You will work well with others. You will use the resources of this agency to figure out what they're hiding. You will absolutely not let small-town bullshit get within a mile of this investigation."

"I hear you."

"You better do more than that. Call me when you get to the Myers place."

"One condition."

She frowns. "Continue."

"Don't take me off the Narragansett site. It's likely a cold-case murder, and I want to support Ellis and the tribe so they can get answers and bury her."

"You've developed a good relationship there," Jo says in a matter-of-fact way. "We're getting a lot of pushback on redrawing water rights out West. It'd be helpful if BIA wasn't seen as the interfering assholes for once."

"Dare to dream," I say. "So I can work the case with Ellis while I'm gone?"

"As long as it doesn't pull your focus too much."

"I'll go get my bag," I say. "And I need to repark my truck in long-term."

"Told your ass," Ghost Luna murmurs.

Jo rises and there's not a trace of satisfaction on her face. Perhaps she's mirroring my own anxiety. Perhaps she has her own.

She hands me the folder but doesn't let go as I tighten my grip. "This is about more than the skull and the badge. You need to figure out what they're hiding."

6

~~~~

After a full flight from Providence to Atlanta, the back of the next plane is blissfully empty on the leg to Tulsa. In a quiet row, I turn on the overhead light and take out the file from Jo. The photos slide onto the open tray, and I'm staring at my young face dangling from the teeth of a skull.

"Damn, in the mouth? That's messed up."

I smell bubble gum and glance over only long enough to see Ghost Luna in the aisle seat.

"The mouth is an interesting choice," she continues. "As if he's trying to keep her quiet."

"He who?" I ask, breaking my rule and turning toward her.

Her face is clearer than even my memory allows. The round dark eyes are familiar, but there's something not there. She shrugs and pops a bubble. "It's always a he."

I am mad at myself for indulging my trauma. As if I need to let it dominate one more aspect of my life.

Staring out the small window at the clouds, I wonder if Mal

is out celebrating with her friends over brunch at CAV this afternoon. Or if her mom is making her favorite pork chop dinner on Sunday.

I called Mal in the truck after I moved to the long-term parking garage. The conversation had been short but loaded with uncertainty.

"What did you mean when you said the timing was good for me to go?" I'd asked.

"That you should take some time," she'd said. "This is an opportunity."

"For what?"

"To be sure this baby, this family, is really what you want."

I'd almost lied then. Almost told my wife I'd always wanted a baby, a family. That whatever she wanted, I wanted it, too. Instead, I told the truth: "I love you."

"Never been on a plane," Ghost Luna says as she stretches. "They got a pisser?"

I snap my gaze over to her. "What?"

"Joking, Syd. Jesus." She crosses her stretched arms and closes her eyes.

I swallow the *I'm sorry. Forgive me.* I am terrified of what this figment of my imagination would say.

How could I ever forgive you? It should have been you.

Tears sting my eyes, so I return to the folder as I blink them away. I start with the photos, flipping through the small stack. There are more images of the skull in the lab. There's only one photo of the skull with the badge, my badge, in its mouth. It's a different shape than the rest, which makes me think it was printed separately and kept out of the official file. If that's true, the regional director really is sticking his neck out to keep this quiet.

But why?

I stare at the badge in the photo, and I'm sure of one thing: somebody wants me back in Picher. They are calling me to the Myers property, where three people were murdered because I couldn't save them.

This person knows me. Knows where I work. Knows what I do. Knows only what's under the earth could bring me home.

Ghost Luna leaves me alone as I get my luggage from the baggage claim—no bar—and stare at the wall murals celebrating Oklahoma. There are sports teams and a painting of a grinning Will Rogers. The second-largest image, taking up almost as much as the college football mural, commemorates the Oklahoma Land Run of 1889.

I frown at the white people smiling as they drive covered wagons with happy children in the back. There are a few people painted stabbing white flags into "unassigned land." Left out of the mural is that this land wasn't unclaimed, but actually "Indian Territory," after tribes were forced from their homelands to Oklahoma. But history repeated itself when this land was taken by the government because it was profitable and coveted by white people who didn't like paying leases to Native landowners to use it.

I'm thinking about the false narratives we've been told as I head toward the rental car place. There's no line and the bored guy running it lets me pick out any car I want. Of course I choose the Jeep Cherokee in a glossy red.

The sun has almost set as I float along the pristinely paved turnpike. That's what Okies call every highway. Mal laughs when

I slip up and use the term in Rhode Island. Though I'd never call any of our highways pristine.

Ghost Luna leaves me alone as I pass the Hard Rock Casino and there's no panic attack as I zoom by the huge QuikTrip gas station that signals I'm outside the Tulsa city limits. I remain calm and focused on the hour-plus drive directly northeast. As if my body is telling me this is where I'm meant to be.

I hum along to the local country station playing old gospel, Barbara Mandrell singing "Power in the Blood."

> *Would you be free from the burden of sin?*
> *There's power in the blood, power in the blood.*
> *Would you o'er evil a victory win?*
> *There's wonderful power in the blood.*

The last time I was on this road Mal was beside me. She'd been awed by an Oklahoma sunset. All that flat land spanning toward a glowing pink-and-lavender sky that wraps the senses like a familiar blanket. Ahead is a pecan grove that looks like it's on fire.

My grandma Ama told me once that "pecan" is a Native word. I headed to the tribal library and found it was indeed from the Algonquin tribe's word "pakani," which means "a nut too hard to crack by hand."

I would sit with my grandma, her red apron full of pecans, as she split the hard brown shells with her silver nutcracker. She said the pecan trees were a comfort to Native tribes removed from their homelands in the South and forced to Oklahoma, which is a Choctaw word for "brave people." She said lots of people have heard of the Trail of Tears, but not many know what it means.

She talked about how gun-drawn soldiers on horses led imprisoned Native people along a one-thousand-mile journey away from their homes to Oklahoma.

"Our family saw the familiar pecan tree rising up in welcome," my grandmother said as she handed me a cracked shell. "The pecan was something in this new land from the home they'd been forced to leave."

The memory leaves an emptiness in my chest. I miss my grandma and pass the grove in a blur.

Now I focus back on the glow of the Phillips 66 sign announcing gas is almost three dollars a gallon. I could have chosen something more economical, but with the BIA picking up the tab, it was hard to resist.

I slow the Jeep down as I approach a giant glowing bridge of glass and steel across the turnpike. It was once called the Glass House restaurant; McDonald's bought it in the sixties, making it the largest in the world at the time. At night, it looks like a spaceship hovering over the highway, until you see the glowing yellow arches.

There's no motel in Picher, and it's honestly a relief to be heading toward nearby Miami, pronounced *Mi-am-MUH*. It's the largest town in Ottawa County, and to quote my cousin Rayna, that's a lot like being the best Goofy at Disneyland. *Who gives a shit?*

Miami does have a Super Walmart, across from the old Walmart, which was turned into a church. I imagine what we convert old Walmarts into will be a popular topic when future generations study this era in American civilization.

The Microtel Inn & Suites is the nicest hotel in Miami, and again Rayna's Goofy-at-Disney analogy applies. Still, it's nice to step into an air-conditioned lobby as I roll in my suitcase, which has more digging tools than clothes and shoes.

There's no one at the desk. My finger hovers over the tiny call bell, but that feels a little rude. A TV somewhere in the back blares news about Clinton's win against Obama in the Pennsylvania primary.

"Hello?" I call in as kind a voice as possible.

The TV goes silent and an older man in a rumpled polyester uniform ambles to the desk. He frowns as if it's a mystery why someone might show up at a hotel at night with a suitcase.

"I didn't have time to make a reservation," I explain. "Just need one room for one night. Government rate."

He grunts and takes my ID. He types slowly and with force as if tapping out this inconvenience. I stroll over to the small waiting area with corporate furniture but don't sit. I need to text Mal.

I delete the first three:

I wish you were here. I wish I wasn't.

Miss you. Please don't leave me.

Made it! Funny story, I'm seeing Luna again! LOL 👻

I decide to just text I thought of her on the drive and will call her in the morning.

No response.

After several sighs and murmured swears, the printer begins to whir. I return to the desk already on edge when the music in the lobby suddenly blasts "Cherub Rock."

I gasp at the opening lines and cover my ears like a child.

"New speaker system," he yells, shaking his head.

I snatch the keyholder and bill from his hand and nearly run out the door.

"Wait, you wanted a double, right?" he calls. "You planning to have company?"

I don't answer his question but instead hurry toward the shadowy but familiar figure waiting for me on the other side of the sliding doors.

I'm not sure if ghosts sleep, but I do know that she sure as hell isn't sleeping next to me.

MISSING

PICHER, OKLAHOMA
TUESDAY, MAY 6, 2008

He's going to kill me this time, I know it.

I open my eyes to see where he's left me to die.

The room is dark and bare.

I lie on the nasty floor as a chemical smell burns my nose.

"Help," I rasp, my voice unrecognizable.

My skin is tight and clammy and feels like I'm being eaten by fire ants.

He really gave me some bad shit this time.

I blink at the tiniest bit of sunlight peeking through a crack in the plywood board nailed over a window.

I scratch my face and feel the most recent cuts around my wrists. I hate how I've been marked by this man.

I hate everything between us except the one thing I love most.

My darling baby girl. *How will you survive without me?*

I curl into the darkness and refuse to think of the terror leading up to this room, this time.

I shake as another wave of withdrawal begins in full force.
How many times must I beat death?
Must I escape one devil for another?
I hear his truck pull up and I scream.
Let me out.
Let me out.

7

~~~~~

My dreams are filled with dead girls, their skulls shining white despite the thick mud. When I wake, I am certain only I can find them.

"They are waiting for you," says a voice muffled by the rattle of the motel room's air-conditioning.

Pressing my palms into my eyes, I try to both wake up and get a grip. My grandma Ama told me that I'd see Luna's spirit because we're still connected. That the terrible night had made the veil between worlds thin.

I ache to talk to my grandma Ama, who saw the real me in a way I've only experienced with Mal.

"We have the same eyes, Nigohilvi. We see the world in a way meant to share. Do not close yourself to this gift."

I dangle my legs off the bed and blink at a sliver of dawn peeking through where the curtains don't connect in the only window.

I wonder if I should call Mal now or after my dig at the Myers place. It might still be morning when I finish, but I doubt it. I study my jitters. Ask myself what I think a phone call could accomplish that a text could not.

Call me when you can. I love you.

It's a little bit chickenshit, not calling her. But I'm about to step foot in the last place on earth I'd ever want to be. So I'll cut myself some slack this morning. At least until I've had coffee.

Anxious to begin, I'm showered, repacked, and out the door in twenty minutes. The hotel is near the main road to Picher, a nine-mile drive from Miami. I grab a to-go coffee from the empty lobby after I drop off my key, and I drive.

My mind stays on Mal, especially since the last time I was on this road she was sitting beside me.

Mal didn't believe me when I described my hometown as a ghost town. We first met far away from Picher, on the other side of the state. I was a bartender at this honky-tonk, close to where we both went to college at Northeastern State University in Tahlequah, Oklahoma. I was a senior, and she was about to graduate from optometry school in vision therapy for kids.

She sipped her beer and listened as I told her how at first, Picher was in a region called Indian Territory, the very northeast corner of Oklahoma, where tribes were forced to migrate after their homes and businesses were taken.

"I've heard of the Trail of Tears," Mal said.

"Cherokee aren't the only tribe who walked that trail," I said. "And injustice didn't stop after they arrived."

I shared that my family is Cherokee and my parents live on my dad's family's allotment lands outside Picher.

"Allotment?"

"My family had homes and land and businesses in Tennessee, but that land was stolen once President Andrew Jackson"—I paused to make a spit noise toward the floor as I always do at his name—"ignored the Supreme Court ruling against his Indian Removal Act. All the treaties and protections tribes had made since white people arrived were ripped up. My family had been there for thousands of years and we were removed, as they called it, to Oklahoma."

Mal took my hand for a second. "My ancestors were removed, too. By ship. From homes and businesses they'd had for thousands of years. Removal doesn't even begin to describe what's been done."

I didn't know Mal's family history yet, though she'd tell me later that week on our first date. How her mother was a professor at Brown University, a place founded and supported by men who'd made their fortunes enslaving her very ancestors.

I slid her a fresh beer. "What's the saying, 'We are our ancestors' wildest dreams'?"

She smiled as if I'd done something right. "Tell me more about Picher and the Quapaw tribe."

I explained that much of the land owned by members of the Quapaw tribe became valuable once minerals were found there. In the early 1900s, everyone was making money, even the Quapaw who owned the land where the town of Picher sprang up. Not that their success was allowed for long. BIA, my very employer, leased or even sold the Quapaw land to mining companies against the wishes of the tribe. The BIA kept the money, generation after generation, over the course of a century.

This new mining district was a point of pride for the state. A place of new opportunity for the thousands of mostly white people who moved to our tiny corner of the state in the 1920s. A true boomtown that produced the lead for most of the bullets in both world wars.

Over thirty years, the miners and huge machines pulled out twenty billion dollars' worth of rocks and minerals from the earth. Leftovers were then chipped and sorted into tiny pieces called chat.

"They called us 'chat rats' growing up," I said to Mal. "White or Native, we were all rats."

At its peak, the chat piles in Picher looked like a gray mountain range looming on the prairie. It brought money and black lung, as they called silicosis, which killed both my great-grandfathers.

But all things end—or, in Picher's case, go completely bust. By the mid-1950s, almost all the mines were stripped of anything worth selling and abandoned. The jobs gone. Only cavernous mines below and mountains of leftover chat above. Quickly ticking time bombs for everyone left behind.

For as long as I can remember, backyards and streets were caving in from collapsing abandoned mineshafts and caverns below. The streams run a metallic orange, though my dad says when he swam in them as a boy they were clear. Or at least that's how he remembers it.

The groundwater is full of lead. The chat poisons our land and toxins are kicked up into the air we breathe. We were left with a town that looks like the surface of the moon and is just as inhabitable.

As Mal finished her second on-the-house Budweiser, I told her how hardly anything grows in Picher. The fields are full of huge mounds of rocks, ripped from the earth to be chipped small and piled high. Even when a tree somehow survives, it grows from polluted soil and drinks polluted water that poisons the ground.

"Do you glow at night?" she asked with a little devious grin that I've never stopped loving.

"One more of these and we'll find out," I said.

As if I'd conjured the town from my memory, I turn onto the highway that leads straight through Picher. The chat piles are smaller than they once were but still rise ahead of me.

I could tell I'm in Oklahoma with my eyes shut. There's a quiet to flat land. To some it's peaceful, but to me it's always felt empty.

There's a buzz living near a city like Providence in Rhode Island. I liked the energy the first time Mal and I visited her family, and that's one of the reasons why Mal and I chose it as our new home—plus the BIA needed someone with my specialty in that region.

I've never said it out loud, but I imagine even when our bones are dust, we leave behind energy. Most people only think of America and this land going back hundreds of years, starting with the Pilgrims. But the energy of the Native people goes back ten thousand years that we know of, probably more. All those steps and breath and laughter and tears. It cannot all disappear.

I think of that energy when I'm digging into the earth. I think of that energy when I'm watching Mal inhale and exhale. When I find a bone or a piece of a flint arrowhead. More than anything, I want justice when that energy is stolen.

The Myers land is about a mile from our family's property, and my Jeep bumps along the now abandoned acreage. If I turned around, I could see the roof of our family home and barn. Instead, my gaze stays forward, over to a split oak tree on the fence line almost exactly halfway between my family's house and the old Myers property. "There's our tree," Ghost Luna says from the back seat and then disappears. The three of us girls would climb that oak to get over the fence, or even just hang out in the thick branches.

Sometimes we'd leave notes or little presents for one another deep inside where the tree had rotted. The memory makes me happy for a moment and then depressed. What stupid things did I write to Luna when I should have said so much more?

Living east of Picher means we're literally on the state line. You can see Kansas from the roofs and trees. For some reason I thought of Kansas as prairie and Oklahoma as land. Maybe because land sounds like a commodity where the value had been decided, parsed, and distributed to the tribes crowded into this corner of the state.

Prairie seemed freer. Like years ago, before the white men and before fences. No land allotments to be taken and given and taken again.

Wasn't that the ironic thing about the slur "Indian giver"? As if we had any say in the give-and-take. More accurately, anything worth giving would be taken away and only returned when it was worth nothing. Actually, nothing would be better, because what was left was killing us.

At the entrance to the long, washed-out driveway, there's a telephone pole with a BIA sign warning US PROPERTY NO TRESPASSING. The four words are more commonly posted than stop signs in Picher. There's something sparkling under it, and I throw the Jeep into park.

My boots crunch on the brownish-orange dirt road as I head over to the old light pole and find one of those metal plant hooks nailed into the rotting wood. Dangling from it is a handmade mobile, like would hang over a crib.

I run my fingers along the different shapes, all phases of the moon, connected by long strands of silver and blue beads. Chimes tinkle at my touch. There are four small dream catchers tied onto the sides, gently wrapped in brown leather ribbon with hawk feathers dangling down, twisting among the moons. That makes me smile because even though they're more hippie than Cherokee, I've always loved dream catchers, especially with all my nightmares.

On the ground are sage and cedar bundles. A tall dollar-store candle with the Virgin Mary lifting her eyes to the heavens is burnt all the way down. I squat to inspect a faded package that has clearly been rained on and dried out several times. The narrow rectangle shape is familiar.

"You know what that is."

I don't turn around at Ghost Luna's voice, the tone of it a warning, like a snake rattling under a rock.

I narrow my eyes to read the faded letters: BUBBLICIOUS WATERMELON.

"Emma Lou," I whisper to the small memorial I know my sister created for Luna. Sister started beading several years ago with our great-aunt Mercy, who was eager to pass down any traditions. For a moment I consider finding a lighter and burning some of the cedar. Watching the smoke rise among the moons.

I hurry back to the Jeep and put it in drive. I'm not here to remember my past. I'm here to make sure someone else's isn't forgotten, no matter how many years they were hidden.

At the end of the driveway, not even the old barn remains, razed along with the trailer after the fire. I can hear my breath in the quiet truck as I try to see the present and ignore the past.

As I stare at the fences, I think of my grandma Ama, who complained about them from barbed wire to cattle. They came with the white men, their government, and their money, she'd explained. They also came with a new view of land—a thing to

be owned, sold, mined, and stolen at any cost, from broken treaties to human lives.

As I get out of my government-paid-for rental, I know I'm
upholding this view by working for the BIA. An agency created
to manage the system the government created to control and, in
many cases, eliminate Native peoples' relationship with the land.
Grandma Ama wanted to be sure we understood, no law or fence
or thousand-mile trail could create a break in this bond.

*Land is our culture. Land is our birthright. Land heals us and
feeds us and connects us with our ancestors. When the land leaves Native hands, the balance is broken until returned.*

But I am trying to help, I want to argue, *even if it's within the
system. That counts, doesn't it?*

There is no balance on the Myers land, or perhaps this is what
the Creator left after so much death. I begin to walk through the
yard, which is now overrun with small trees, waist-high weeds,
and even a patch of poison ivy I manage to avoid. I struggle
against fifteen years of the land taking back its dominion.

The past is everywhere. I hear the laughter of three girls on
the tire swing. I feel the bark cutting into my skin as I fish out a
note hidden in a tree.

With the good memories come the bad. The devils through
the door. Spray of glass from the shot-out TV. To see Luna,
maybe already dead, lying on the threadbare carpet with a devil
in her face. The shotgun blast.

Only one bullet. Only one bullet.

Escaping with Emma Lou and hiding until there was a terrible explosion, killing who wasn't already dead.

I barely remember the funerals. My only memory is a few
notes of my grandma Ama singing "Amazing Grace" in Chero-

kee over three caskets. Mom pressed a red rose from that day in our family Cherokee Bible.

My boots crunch along the gentle slope of the yard, and I keep going until I approach one of our other favorite trees for hiding messages. It's cordoned off in bright yellow DO NOT CROSS tape that no one bothered to take down after the area was cleared by local authorities. This is where the skull was found.

I set down my sorter and tools before finding the folder in my bag. I hold up the photo that's smaller than all the others. The only one from the scene with my badge in the skull's mouth. The image aligns perfectly, and I realize my guess was wrong that this tree was the only place the skull could have been wedged.

There are a half dozen other trees nearby that would work. One even has a large rotted-out area on the bottom that could have held the skull perfectly.

"Something special about this tree."

"Yeah," I respond before I realize I'm not actually talking to anyone.

Annoyed, I focus on the file and brief notes. Someone anonymously called the skull in to the BIA office. The scene was inspected, photographs taken, but nothing else of consequence found. Cadaver dogs were brought in and found nothing. Metal detectors also found nothing.

No one could see this spot from the road. Likely the person who put it there was the same person who called it in.

I walk a circle around the yellow tape. I'll start close to the tree to see if anything was dropped in the soil when the skull was *placed*, is what the note had said.

"Displayed, is more like it," says Ghost Luna.

I don't let myself look around at the acres that need to be

searched and feel overwhelmed. I focus on this area in this moment. First things first, a few feet at a time.

My shovel goes into the grass and deeper to dirt. My body relaxes at this familiar movement. A calmness brought by the search for answers. Of possibly being near the truth.

I dump the soil and shake. The dirt falls through the holes. Only an earthworm wiggles and squirms in the bottom. I drop him back into the upturned dirt and move two more feet to the next quadrant. I dig again.

Hours pass quickly with absolutely nothing to show for it. I stop for a drink of water and wipe the sweat from my face.

"This isn't working," Ghost Luna says. "You're not looking, not really."

"I'm doing my job." I stare out at the upturned earth. A job at an organization that's failed a lot of people who went missing.

"What was someone trying to do?" she asks, now closer, just behind me.

"Get my attention."

"They could have put that skull anywhere." She pauses and smacks her gum. "But they didn't pick anywhere."

My gaze goes to the tree. I grab my gloves and jog over. Running my hands over the bark, I feel knots and creases. I get closer and see scrapes from a pocketknife or rocks. Near the V is a giant heart with our initials in order of age: S + EL + L.

There are other trees, fence posts, and even a big rock where the skull could have been placed. But it wasn't. Instead, someone put it right in the spot where we'd hide notes and little presents as girls.

Surely it's coincidence, my fear argues. There are only two people alive who know what that tree meant among us girls. I know I didn't do it, and if it was Emma Lou, well, why?

My fingers remember this tree as I reach deep inside hoping there's not some rabid animal waiting. I bump the bottom and skitter my fingers around leaves and sticks. My finger brushes something else. I gently pull it out.

A small, rolled-up piece of paper rests in my palm like a caterpillar. But there's something inside. I can feel a weight heavier than paper. I unspool a receipt from the Otter Stop gas station. My face falls at the only item bought, Bubblicious Watermelon.

"What the hell did you do, Sister?" I whisper.

"There's something in it."

My hands tremble as I reach the object at the center. A ring slides out. It's not a smooth band but has twisted gold braid circling something in the center.

Ghost Luna whistles. "You know what that is?"

It's familiar, of course. This figment of my imagination knows what it is, then on some level I do, too. Still, I whisper, "What?"

"It's a panda coin ring. Like the rich bitches wore back in the day."

I angle the face of the ring toward me. The coin at the center has a panda bear chewing a long stick of bamboo.

"There's something on the back."

I tip the ring so the panda on the coin is facing down. Using my small flashlight, I peer closer to see an image of a Chinese palace with stacked square roofs.

"What's the date, Syd?"

"Nineteen ninety-one." I look at Ghost Luna. "Two years before the devils." I check the date on the receipt, which is from the day the skull was found.

"There's something scribbled . . ." I murmur and hold the paper under the light. Two words at the bottom, right where the ring was folded into the paper: **FIND ME**.

"Told ya."

There's a noise at the entrance to the property, where someone has parked.

I hurry over to find an evidence bag before heading toward the road. I've only made it a few yards when I see that it's my dad's faded lime-green pickup. My phone buzzes in my pocket. My mother is calling.

"Something's not right, Syd."

"Dad!" I yell, but he's already back in the truck and pulling away as I run to try to catch him. "Dad!"

I'm there in time for a cloud of dust to roll over me, and as it clears I picture my dad, his hands firm on the wheel at ten and two. His salt-and-pepper hair tied in a thin ponytail that my mom has threatened to cut off since their first date. He's tall and lean where my mom is short and curvy, like a five-foot-in-heels tornado.

The dust clears, and I realize he was standing at the memorial Emma Lou created for Luna. There's something new at the telephone pole. Dad nailed a piece of paper right under the NO TRESPASSING sign. As I run toward it, the word at the top stops me cold: MISSING.

Taking up most of the poster is the smiling face of Emma Lou. Sister is missing. The words on the receipt echo, **FIND ME**.

8

~~~~~

"You've never seen that picture of Emma Lou."

The statement from Ghost Luna breaks through my panic. I tear my gaze from my sister's face printed on a MISSING poster in stark black and white. The photo is cropped close and a little blurred, but Sister is clear-eyed and smiling. Her hair is longer than I remember and there's a confidence I've never seen before.

I read the words on the poster like a list of ingredients in my worst fears come true: "Emma Lou Walker, 28, 5'6", 130 pounds. Missing 7 days. Last seen in blue flower-print dress. Hair in braids. Car also missing. Silver Grand Am 2008. Contact Noah Walker with any information. Anonymous welcome."

"She got new wheels," Ghost Luna murmurs.

"With what money?" I say, as if that matters, surprised to feel anger amid my fear. "She's been gone a week before. When she was using."

"She's clean, though. Or that's what she said the last time you called. Why are you assuming the worst?"

"Sometimes the worst is also the most likely."

I start back toward the tree where I found the skull. My steps are loud in the quiet of the late afternoon. My stomach grumbles, but I stay focused on a familiar checklist:

Call dirtbag friends.

Check trailers out east.

Call hospitals.

Knock on a few doors of other dirtbag friends.

Find an old dealer or two at pool hall.

Drag her high ass home.

My hands are shaking as I throw my tools into the Jeep. I place the evidence bag carefully on the back-seat floorboard. I need to talk to Jo before I hand this over to Sue and the BIA regional office. All that has to wait.

"Agilvgi, where are you?" Ghost Luna says in a singsong voice from the back of the Jeep.

I let out a long breath. My grip on the steering wheel is turning my knuckles white. I twist the key and the engine roars. As I drive, there's dread, like I've been caught. Instead of a teenager sneaking back into the house, I am an adult trying to pass unseen. As if I thought I could come here like an outsider and save myself from the pain home always brings.

I've gone maybe a quarter of a mile before I pull over in a ditch halfway down the road with our family's fields, full of sweet corn already three feet tall. For a moment, I remember days of eating corn with Emma Lou and Luna fresh from the field with butter dripping down our fingers as we clung to the little holders shaped like corncobs.

My throat tightens with a familiar pain. Not saving my sister. Again.

I pick up my cell phone and dial Mal. I wipe a few tears as it rings.

"Hey, babe," she says, sounding happy.

"Hi," I say, trying to sound calm and normal.

"What's wrong?"

Tears fall down my face. I hate myself for crying over something I didn't do a damn thing to stop. "Emma Lou is missing again."

"Oh my God," Mal says. "That's awful. Do you think it's drugs?"

"Of course it's drugs," I snap, then take a couple of shaky breaths. "I'm sorry."

"What did your parents say?" she asks gently.

"I haven't seen them yet."

"Where are you staying?"

"At a hotel. I'm here on business! I'm sorry." I clear my throat to get my tone under control. "I'm here on business. I didn't really plan to see my family—"

"Syd, are you serious? You were going to be across a damn cornfield from your family and you weren't going to see them? After three years?"

Ghost Luna appears with her arms crossed in the passenger seat. "Mmm-hmm."

I squeeze my eyes closed. "I am a complete failure, Mal. You don't want to have this baby with me."

Her tone is calm. "I didn't say that."

"But how could you? I can't protect anything I love."

"Love isn't about protection. In fact, it's what makes us vulnerable to pain. That's why it's so scary."

"Well, I'm fucking terrified of being a parent. I'm sorry, but it's true."

"Listen, you've had some bad news. Let's talk more later, after you've spoken to your parents. Okay? I love you."

"I love you, too," I whisper, and hang up.

"I can't believe she married you," Ghost Luna says from the passenger seat.

My shoulders fall. "Don't you think I say that to myself every time I see her?"

"That can't be healthy."

I throw the phone at her and it lands with a *thump* in the empty seat.

Taking a deep breath, I scrub my face with my hands. I'm not going to help anyone like this. I need to calm down and get focused. After I drain my water bottle, I toss it into the back with my luggage. I brought everything with me since I wasn't sure where I'd stay tonight.

I turn down the long dirt road to my family home, all on the same twenty-acre government allotment given to our family after the Trail of Tears.

Though we are Cherokee, most of the land around us and in Picher was part of the Quapaw tribe's forced resettlement. Not that you'd know it. White people had long ago taken the land— often through legal channels and with the BIA managing it all— once they knew valuable minerals were underneath.

The Jeep rattles over the cattle guard as I creep along the unpaved driveway. I catch a profile on the southern edge of the family cemetery near the first headstones. My heart thumps, *Emma Lou*, but it's not. It's Ghost Luna walking in the section with the oldest graves, each thin but carefully preserved by our family, generation after generation, as others filled in the ground around them.

I cannot think about gravestones right now or I'll go crazy.

Crazier. I get out of the Jeep, slamming the door as my phone buzzes.

"Mom," I answer as I head toward the front porch of our single-story farmhouse.

"Syd, I'm glad I caught you. I have some news."

"Sister is missing."

Mom gasps. "Did Aunt Mercy call you?"

"No, I saw the poster."

"Oh, your father's got a bee in his bonnet. Been putting those papers up all over— Wait. What did you say?"

I stay silent, not meaning to be so dramatic, but I'm on the porch. I know Mom is calling me from the landline near the kitchen window. I step in front of it. "Hi, Mom."

She screams and drops the phone. Her footsteps pound over to the screen door. "I thought you were a ghost!"

"Sorry," I say. "I'm real."

"Come here, then." She opens her arms like it's a reflex of motherhood. "What are you doing here?"

"BIA work." I give her a quick hug. "What's going on with Emma Lou?"

"She's missing," Mom says flatly.

"Yeah, I read that on the freaking—"

"Mam-maw?" a tiny voice calls from inside.

"I'm out here, Gracie girl."

I take a breath to stifle my petulant tone. Parents know how to push buttons because they install them.

Mom looks thin in a floral top and nice skirt. Her hair in a bun is gray at the roots. There are more wrinkles on her forehead and around her eyes than I remember. She looks weary.

The screen door swings open, and my niece in a pirate costume runs onto the porch. Her little pigtails are strawberry blond and she has a heart-shaped face and dark brown eyes like Emma Lou's. "You talking to Mommy?" Her excited bare feet freeze in place as she sees me. "Oh."

I swallow as my throat burns with tears. They're raising a grandchild. Not full-time, not until recently, but it's day in and day out with them both living here. I blink the tears away quickly, but there's no denying it's been a tough three years for them all. Not that I've been here to see it or help.

"I'm your aunt Syd." I give a little wave as Gracie wraps her small body around my mom's leg. "Me and your aunt Mal mail you books and toys every month?"

"I like the books. Can you send candy?"

"What kind of candy?"

"Pirate candy." She crosses her arms. "Like red licor-ishes."

"You got it." I glance at Mom, whose gaze flutters like a hummingbird around her granddaughter. "Dad around?"

"He just left," Mom says. "He needed to get ready for the meeting tonight at the Miami Civic Center. How's Mal?"

"Good," I say, not wanting to change topics. "What meeting?"

"The Picher buyout meeting. We're leaving in a half hour, after dinner. I pray no one throws a punch this time."

I laugh, but she doesn't. "Seriously?"

"Gracie, go finish your meat loaf, please." Mom pauses as Gracie hesitantly goes back inside. "This committee has been a nightmare for your father. For all of us. Telling people their houses are worth a quarter of what they expect."

While it's called the Picher buyout, what matters more is that the town is part of the Tar Creek Superfund Site, an environmental disaster area that not only makes selling a house impossible, but also poisons those who breathe the air, drink the water, and live on any part of the polluted land. Now the state is trying to buy out every house in those dangerous forty miles.

"Are you considering taking the buyout now?" I ask.

"I'd be fine with it, but I'm not the one deciding."

It had been an argument between my parents since there was talk of house buyouts. Dad never pretended his "hard no" was about money. He wouldn't discuss leaving behind land our family had to walk across half the country to get after our ancestral homes were stolen. He sounded more and more like my grandma Ama.

"The civic center is next to the police station, so maybe the drunk and rowdy ones won't come." Mom wipes a hand on her apron. "You eat?"

"No," I say, and lower my voice. "But what's going on with Sister?"

Her jaw tightens. "We're praying. Your dad is hanging his posters. There's a search tomorrow night."

"A search? I can look right now."

She frowns at me. "Where?"

"The usual spots. Druggie and dealer friends."

"She doesn't hang around with them anymore. She's clean."

"Mom." I cross my arms. "She's done this before."

"Don't I know it, Syd. But she's changed. She's been on the straight and narrow. She's a great mom."

"So you don't think this is drugs?" My throat tightens at how much worse this alternative theory would be for Sister. "Then what? She's run off? Been . . . kidnapped?"

"She goes on long walks sometimes. Maybe she needed a break . . . I don't know. We all deal with things different." Mom swipes away a tear and any emotion with it. Her voice and gaze return to stern detachment. "The Good Lord hears our prayers. But he also helps those who help themselves." She turns on her heel toward the door. "Now, come get your meat loaf. You look like you're about to blow away."

The door slams in my face, and I take a step forward but stop. The fields seem quieter. The gravestones larger somehow, as if taunting me. Like they know the earth holds new secrets about my sister along with the other skulls.

FIND ME.

I consider telling my mom about the message, though I don't know what exactly I found. I need to run it by Jo first. See who she thinks we can trust within the local BIA to look into it.

The screen door flies open and Mom is there with a plate but glaring into the distance. "Syd Alma Walker. Did you rent a car?"

"I'm here for work." I take the meat loaf that's shoved my way. "The BIA is paying."

"We woulda picked you up."

"I got in late."

"Last night? Oh, for heaven's sake. You aren't staying in a hotel?"

"I have my bag. I'll stay here." This would be my mom's real worry. "I want to help with Sister."

"You said you wanted to stay *away* from all that."

"Well, I'm here."

"You sure are," Mom says. "Don't eat your plate on the porch like a raccoon."

I follow her inside and feel all the nerves of being back in my childhood home. Everything is the same. I stand in the small kitchen that leads to the living room. The Salvation Army store mismatched chairs and a sagging green couch. The brown living room carpet that abruptly stops for dull white linoleum into the kitchen. At the small dining room table, Gracie is mushing her little cut-up pieces of meat loaf.

"I'm done, Mam-maw. Ice cream?"

"You can eat it on the porch. I'm tired of cleaning today."

Gracie runs over to where I'm standing by the refrigerator. "Ice cream, please."

Still balancing the plate, I heave open the bottom freezer drawer with a familiar heft. How many times did we get into the ice cream here as girls? "Ooooh, sundae cups?"

"Yes! And spoon, please. I don't like little one in it."

"You're very good at giving directions." I open the cup and grab a small spoon. "Do you need help taking it outside?"

She grabs them from me before she runs out the door. "No. Bye!"

Mom drops a CorningWare dish of limp green beans on the table. "Frozen from last season, but not too bad. Cooked them with bacon."

"Thanks," I say, and ease into the chair with my plate. "How worried are you about Sister?"

"I don't know." Mom slams on the sink faucet and begins to violently wash the dishes.

My dinner is eaten in silence as I try to focus on why I'm here. I inhale the delicious meat loaf slathered in a brown sugar ketchup. The green beans are better than all right, or maybe I'm just starving. Once the kitchen is quiet, I take my plate over to the sink. "I can dry."

I don't wait for the inevitable "No," but instead pluck the fork she's holding right out of her hand. Swiping it with a clean towel, I drop it into the drawer and pick up a bowl from beside the sink. "I'd like to go to the buyout meeting."

Mom scrapes my plate into the garbage under the sink. "Oh,

Syd, you don't want to do that. People are not at their best right now. Even your father lost his temper."

That really surprises me. "I can handle it."

"You don't want to see our town like this." She washes the plate and then hands it to me. "I wish you'd listen."

"You know better than to expect that from me."

"From anyone these days," Mom says with a deep sigh.

A quiet settles between us as we finish the dishes. I wonder how to better understand what's happened to Sister. I try to not make it about me, but I'm hurt that no one called me until today.

Then I remind myself I'm here for work. The skull and the badge.

"One thing, Mom. Did you clean out my room recently?" With the question blurted out, there's a gnawing tension in my chest. I'm more nervous than I want to admit about my badge being in the skull's mouth. "Did the church have a sale or anything?"

"I donated a couple boxes to the Salvation Army a while back. Take a shower and relax. Skip the meeting. We won't be more than a couple hours." She grabs her purse and keys. "Gracie girl, we need to get."

I listen to them chatter on the porch. Cup and spoon disposed of and seat belts buckled. The outside and inside go silent, and I let out a long breath.

There are no footsteps, but I can feel Ghost Luna's presence. "Sister's not with me."

That almost breaks me. Not that she'd know. Not that she's real. Still, I let out a shaky breath of relief and stand. "I'm going to that meeting."

"I was going to haunt you until you did. Booooo!"

I shake my head and almost laugh. There was never any question. A gathering of people from Picher is too good an opportunity to pass up. Someone there knows something about Sister and maybe even the skull. After avoiding everyone in my hometown for three years, the only way back is a baptism by fire.

9

~~~~~

I park my Jeep under one of a dozen lampposts in the lot full of trucks and old sedans. Police vehicles are quiet in front of the station next door to the Miami Civic Center, where a couple of officers are waving people inside. I scan the crowd, searching for Emma Lou.

"She's not there."

I ignore Ghost Luna, which is a lot easier if she's not calling me out.

"Weird being back here."

She's also right about that. The civic center is all roof, almost no windows, which I guess is mid-century modern architecture. It reminds me of what people in the 1950s thought the future would look like. The building is the shape of a barrel cut down the middle and dropped on its flat side, the roofline so close to the ground it looks like you could step right onto the dark shingles from the sidewalk.

There have been fifty years of proms and weddings, sports

wins and losses, community meetings and arts and crafts fairs. My grandma Ama said the Klan held rallies there, too.

My heart begins to thump, and it's all I can hear in my Jeep, which is quiet now. I pushed my anxiety deep down during the drive, but now that I'm actually here, I can feel the pressure build again.

"Isn't that Aunt Missy?"

"Yeah," I say in an exhale of relief. My dad's cousin Missy, whom I've always considered more of an auntie, is smoking a cigarette straight ahead. She's talking to an old man who's familiar in that potbellied scarecrow way of old men around town that I grew up with.

"Some things never change," Ghost Luna says.

I'm honestly relieved to see Aunt Missy is exactly the same as always: brown hair crimped and teased into a spectacular poof. She's wearing a ripped shirt that shows lots of cleavage with her tight jeans. That normalcy pulls me out of my panic and out of the Jeep.

I click the automatic locks and beeline toward Aunt Missy.

Her ornery grin spreads when she sees me. "Hey there, girlie!" She waves and throws down her cigarette, stubbing it out with the spike of her heel. "I just saw your momma and dad rushing inside like a bat outta hell. Too busy to tell me you were in town, I guess."

My breathing relaxes as I head toward her open arms. She squeezes me like a baby against her chest. "Any news on your sister?"

I shake my head and sink into her warm embrace. The overly sweet perfume and skin always running hot. "I just found out."

"I've been asking around, but nothing." Aunt Missy squeezes tighter. "It's the damnedest thing. Poof. Thin air."

"I really thought she'd stay clean," I murmur. "For Gracie at least."

"Addiction is a tricky bitch. Hey, you know Rayna will flip when she sees you."

I pull from the embrace with an excited gasp at news of her daughter, my crazy cousin, who is one of my favorite people in the world. "I didn't know she was out." Rayna ran into an undercover cop when she was trying to help a bad boyfriend sell some pills to pay off his dealer.

"Good behavior." Aunt Missy beams. "Go see her at Buffalo Run Casino after this shitshow."

"Mom said these meetings get a little rowdy." I nod toward the entrance. "You take the buyout for your house?"

She glances at the old man, still smoking. "We're among the holdouts. The wood on my house is worth twice what they're offering. Same here for Mr. Huckle."

Ah, that's where I knew him from. He owns the pool hall in town, though I'm not sure if it's still open. A lot can change in three years. "Good to see you."

He bobs his head in a faded Okie Burger hat and keeps smoking.

"What about the land you all own?" I ask. Aunt Missy and Rayna have houses on Quapaw land that belonged to the family on Missy's mother's side. And there's more land, I think.

"They're just offering on the houses. The land ain't even a part of the discussion," she says. "Besides, the land is BIA managed. Hardly seen a cent going back three generations at least."

"I'll look into it for you." I feel shame, not for the first time, that my employer has a history of doing more harm than good for the people we're supposed to serve.

She snorts and gives me a "Bless your heart" look. "I don't

even know where to tell you to look. Picher, Miami, Welch. My momma's dad said we got land all over Ottawa County."

"You should get paid for the land, finally, and be compensated for the pollution and remediation."

"How about an ass like JLo while we're dreaming," she says with a snort.

"I'm not joking, Aunt Missy. It's not right."

"I need enough buyout money to afford a house somewhere that won't poison every pet I got."

"Oh no," I say, thinking of their cute beagle. "Bernie?"

"Had a tumor the size of a grapefruit growing out his neck." She sniffs and wipes under her thick mascara. "Weighs on me."

"We better get in there," mutters Mr. Huckle as he throws his cigarette over the rail.

I put my arm around Aunt Missy, for my own comfort as much as hers, and follow them inside. Stepping into the large rectangular entryway, I inhale the familiar tennis-ball-like smell of the gymnasium, which is lit up like there's a game tonight.

"They got the posters here," Mr. Huckle says, and points inside.

At first I think he means posters of Emma Lou, but I don't see her face anywhere as we walk inside.

Aunt Missy pulls my arm. "You gotta see my house."

In the big gym entry area where normally they buy and sell tickets, there are a dozen posters on easels with maps of Picher showing houses, property lines, and shading based on the likelihood of a sinkhole.

Aunt Missy stands near a poster in the middle, and I examine it as she begins to explain. "Both Rayna's place and mine could sink a foot if the West Netta mine collapses. Most of the houses on our block, too."

The Netta mine was full of lead so rich, the pillars required to keep the mine from collapsing have been whittled away or stolen completely. "That's really scary," I say.

"Dipshits are always out at Netta, though. Who knows what they're doing."

"The who?" I laugh.

"Young shitasses working for the Dawesons. You see someone with a yellow bandana, they're one of 'em. And stay away."

Daweson. A name I want to avoid at all costs. It leads to my own sinkhole.

I squeeze her arm. "Maybe you should take the money."

"I couldn't buy a trailer off Highway 69 for what they're offering. Then I'd have to live there." She laughs, a smoker's cough with a little lounge singer to it. "Look here, Syd. This is the map that started all this mess." She points at a map that shows where lead levels are elevated, which is pretty much everywhere in Picher.

"The first buyout of Picher houses was two years ago, because of this map. Kids having lead levels eleven times what they should be."

"How many took the buyout?" I ask.

"About fifty families with small kids, and I get that," says Aunt Missy. "They say lead poisoning can make you crazy, especially if it starts when you're little. You should have heard the scientist. Talking about more likely jail time, bipolar, drug abuse, cancers, diabetes, you name it." She sighs and stares closely at her house on the map. "If I'd had the money, I would have left when Rayna was a baby."

"Don't get down on yourself, Missy." Mr. Huckle takes out a pack of tobacco chew and crams a wad in his lip. "We need to keep our community together. They're trying to throw a little money at us and wipe their hands clean like they didn't create this mess."

Mr. Huckle spits on the floor near where the Miami mascot, a "wardog," which is basically a bulldog, has been painted with a spiky collar. Two women walking inside gasp and hurry past him.

"Is moving so bad?" I ask. "You'd be closer to the Super Walmart."

"I don't like Miami." He swats his hand as if we're being attacked by flies. Then he glares at the trophy case glowing on the main wall. "Too stuck-up and impersonal."

"So no matter what, you won't take the money?" I ask.

"I'll get carried out feetfirst." He spits again. "Even if my damn toes are black from lead poisoning."

"More like orange from Tar Creek," Aunt Missy says, and adjusts her big purse. "Let's get in there. I don't want to miss the yelling."

"Hey!" shouts a man's voice from the water fountain. "You Noah's girl? The one that works for the Indians?"

"What the hell do you want?" Missy says. "She ain't got nothing to do with all this, Mr. McClain."

The man marches over to us in his pressed shirt and worn khakis. "Listen here, you tell your daddy we know he's in on this scam. Wouldn't be surprised if it's got something to do with tribes. Always taking, ain't ya."

It's difficult to know where to start with this old fucker. I turn to Aunt Missy with a grin to let her know I'm happy to engage.

"I got this, Syd." She pats my arm. "Mr. McClain, you always were mean, but I didn't know you were so racist. Let me sum this up. Ain't no Native in this corner of the state that's here by choice. Our families got forced here. Then anything that could help us get out of here was taken away. Money, language, culture, decent education."

He lets out a long whiskey breath. "I ain't getting into all that history shit, Missy. Noah ain't taking the buyout because he knows he'll get a lot more money at the end." He jams a finger in my face. "Listen here, your daddy is screwing us good, honest folks of Picher to line his own Indian pockets. We ain't going to stand for it. First your sister goes missing, then who knows."

"Get the hell back inside," Aunt Missy says, "before I tell the cops to look in your shithole house for evidence."

He lets out a wheezy laugh. "Like they'd listen to one of you."

In the man's eyes, I see a whiskey-fueled rage. I realize I haven't seen this kind of anger in a while. The burning gaze hungry for a place to send decades of wrongs, resentments, and likely true injustices. Maybe that's the saddest part. If he wasn't so ignorant, he'd see that the people he hates and villainizes have more in common with him than the better-off white people where he thinks he belongs.

I let Aunt Missy take my arm, and we leave him cursing us.

"Ignore that dickweed." Aunt Missy leads us into the gymnasium, where I watched basketball tournaments and went to the circus.

I can feel the angry energy even without all the scowls and glares. I don't know what Mr. McClain wanted or why he's mad, but he's not the only one. There are at least 150 people sitting or standing on the wooden bleachers and the room is vibrating with anger.

"Bigger crowd than a revival," I say.

"Wouldn't know. Preachers don't come to Picher no more." Aunt Missy nods toward the front row. "Your mom is there with all the wives of the buyout committee."

At the center of the gymnasium is a table with six men and a microphone in the middle. There's also a lectern. My dad is talking to the man in the center, who's in a suit and has a sign that reads, CHAIRMAN RHETT CAINE, ESQ.

Dad's shoulders are tightly drawn, as if the conversation is serious, which makes sense, given what Missy and my mother have told me about the buyout process. I know my dad feels an obligation to Picher, and maybe the land itself. But I would never have guessed that loyalty was stronger than his need to stay in the background. I don't think I've ever seen him in front of a group of people in my life.

"You can sit with me if you want. I keep it cool in the back." Aunt Missy elbows me, and I follow along. I spot my mom with her arms crossed in conversation with one of the wives.

We make our way up the retractable wooden bleachers. Aunt Missy stops to talk to a couple, and I continue to follow Mr. Huckle. He eases onto a bench at the top, and then Aunt Missy drops between us. I'm relieved to be sitting and hopefully somewhat anonymous. A few people glance our way as we get settled.

"Do you see any of Emma Lou's friends?" I ask, wondering what exactly I hope to find at this meeting. "People I should talk to who might know something?"

Aunt Missy flips some hair off her shoulder and too-sweet perfume follows. "Of course she's friends with people here. The whole damn town is worried."

I nod, feeling stupid and grateful Aunt Missy dropped it there. The truth is, I don't really recognize that many people. I start to bounce my leg and wonder if coming here was a mistake. An overstep, both for my family and for my job.

"Hey." Aunt Missy puts a hand on my bouncing knee. "One thing at a time, okay? Don't listen to the gossip."

"What gossip?" I ask.

"Drugs. Stealing money and hightailing it out of town."

"Well, I believe the first one," I say, feeling ashamed.

"I think she needed a break. Trust me, we'll find her. Oh, there's your dad getting our attention. He looks dead on his feet."

Dad does look exhausted, and I wave along with Aunt Missy. He grins at us and looks extra Cherokee next to the panel of white men, though any of them could be Native, too. In Oklahoma, where they crammed thirty-nine tribes along with white people, we are a mix. Maybe "whitewash" is the more accurate word.

Dad glances at my mom and points at where I'm sitting in the bleachers. Mom stops her conversation and stands up. She shakes her head at me, and then when she looks to Aunt Missy, any warmth disappears.

"June sure has a stick up her ass tonight," Aunt Missy says, giving Mom an extra-big wave.

Mom has always hated Aunt Missy and never thought much of Rayna either. Mom and Aunt Missy have opposite approaches to life in a place that's either poor or real poor. Mom always had a pristine house, stitched and pressed clothes, and a judgmental stare. That's her armor.

Aunt Missy rolled with life. Six dogs in the yard, dirty kid in hand-me-downs that should have been thrown away, and wild friends over at all hours. Aunt Missy would let me sneak sips of wine cooler that would go spraying out of my mouth after she told a dirty joke. Aunt Missy and Rayna had a real friendship, which I'd never have believed is possible for mothers and daughters if I hadn't seen it with them.

Mom sits down as the gymnasium gets quiet. A man I don't recognize rises from the table and identifies himself as head of the Miami Chamber of Commerce. He starts his remarks, which are mostly a plea for patience as they look for funding and kindness as they try to find the best path forward. There are as many groans as eye rolls, it seems.

"They mostly got Miami people on this committee," says Missy. "Nobody trusts it."

"What about my dad?" I watch him and his hunched shoulders. Since I last saw him, he looks weary, but also unsettled, like one of the nervous lions in cages pacing before the circus starts.

"No one expects him to do much, honestly. Not with all the players involved."

"When can we talk money?" someone shouts. "These buyout estimates are a joke!"

"We're saving questions for the end," says the committee chair.

"You gave the Redders twice what we got offered. We have one more bathroom!" shouts someone else. "Something stinks to high heaven!"

The crowd applauds. "Are the Redders going to stand up for themselves?" I ask Aunt Missy.

"Girlie, you know they ain't here. They got paid. This is for people pissed off enough to drive to Miami to give the committee a piece of their mind."

She appears to be exactly right. Person after person has their say, shouting at the committee, often to a round of applause.

My dad hardly speaks. He hands files over to the chairman, who flips through them to address each complaint. The man who got in my face earlier stands at the mic to complain about his buyout offer.

"Now, Mr. McClain," Chairman Caine says as he flips through a few pages. "The assessment says your house is 1,256 square feet. We did our calculation, and the price—"

"We did updates to the kitchen last year," he yells. "You can't measure us against some of these others."

People begin to shout at Mr. McClain, who points his hand at one family in particular. "You ain't so much as painted in a decade. There's no comparison, square foot or not."

"Lipstick on a pig don't change the price at the fair," yells the man Mr. McClain seems to be angry with.

An older woman stands up beside that man. "We got three hundred feet on you. That should up our price."

More yelling, more literal finger-pointing.

"That's enough discussion for now," the chairman shouts. "Someone from the state is here to talk about where we're going to find the funds to continue the buyout."

"They're short thirty million." Missy smirks. "We'll be lucky to see a cent."

The speaker from the governor's office asks for cooperation. He cites that seven hundred people in Picher are qualified for a buyout, and they've had fewer than three hundred acceptances.

"Then pay us what we're owed!" shouts Mr. McClain, which gets the crowd going again.

I glance down at my mother, who's ramrod straight. I understand what she meant when she said that this wasn't Picher at its best. While I know I'm negative about where I'm from, the truth is that there is a lot of good. That's part of why it's so hard for people to let go.

We'd watch out for one another's kids. We'd help out when someone was short on their polluted water bill or needed time on their rent. Even after Luna and her parents were murdered, when there were terrible rumors saying they'd gotten themselves killed or even that Sister and I had something to do with it, people would stop by our house to check on us. Maybe rubbernecking our pain, but they'd still come with a casserole and a prayer.

Missy lets out a long sigh. "It's everyone for themselves now. No one talks about relocating the town or keeping the community together. It's all money. Probably what they wanted all along. Better to keep us fighting and distracted."

I frown at her. "For what?"

She shrugs. "A lot of contracts coming out of this work. Possibilities of selling chat again, which would mean big money. Anytime money is involved, there's good people and bad people first in line. Who can tell which is which?"

"Dad is helping," I insist. "He cares about the land."

"Sure. But you only got Cherokee blood. Lots of history of Cherokee trying to be friends with whites. Signing treaties and giving over rights, like white people would honor a damn thing. Guess how that worked out for everyone?"

There's bitterness in her voice, as there's a right to be. Her great-grandmother on her mom's Quapaw side had all her land taken away or "put in trust" by the BIA to manage. Land that was so valuable, they'd called her the richest woman in the world at the time. Except the BIA never handed over the money. Not that it's the fault of Cherokees. But when there's pain, there's blame. Sometimes it's easier to lash out at the person sitting next to you instead of those actually responsible.

There's an announcement that the meeting is taking a break. Missy stands and waves toward the entrance. "There's that cute niece of yours. You seen her yet?"

"I did earlier." I already have a smile as I turn and catch sight of Gracie in a man's arms. "Who's got her?"

Missy waves again as the man turns. "Don't you recognize Emma Lou's baby daddy? Cody got out of jail right before Rayna."

I lunge forward and Missy tries to grab my arm, but I shake her off. That piece of shit forced drugs on Emma Lou and, knowing him, could be tied to her disappearance or even worse.

Jail is the only place he belongs.

That's why I finally sent him there.

He's out now and everything clicks into place.

My questions about Sister are answered.

Cody got Sister hooked on drugs again and now she's missing.

I know he knows where.

But for right now, I'd sooner break his arms than see them hold my niece for one more second.

10

"Y ou mad at Dada?"

Gracie clings to the neck of her father. Cody Daweson is a multigenerational piece of shit with sad eyes that cried my sister back to him again and again. And apparently, again.

"No, I'm not mad." I smile and try to ignore Cody, who's staring at me like I might clock him.

Gracie shifts in Cody's arms to look around the noisy gymnasium as everyone takes a break before the next section of the meeting. "Is Momma with you now?"

I flinch at her small voice full of pain. "She's not, sweetie."

Cody's face goes red, and the deep color spreads to the tattoo on his neck of a heart with two swords through the center. "We'll find Momma," he says. "She's busy buying you presents."

Gracie giggles and rubs her face into his tattoo. "Lovies?"

"Sure." Cody looks embarrassed. He yells over my shoulder toward the bleachers, "Hey, June, I gotta get going."

Mom is talking to the same woman as earlier. She holds up a

finger, which gives me a few more seconds. "When was the last time you saw Sister?" I step toward him as he eases back. "The truth."

He sticks out his jaw as if I'm getting on his nerves. "Momma will be back soon," he says to Gracie, and looks at me as if he's using his daughter as a shield.

I smile at Gracie and say sweetly, "That's not an answer, Cody."

He slides around me and darts over to the bleachers. He jams Gracie at my mom. "Your daughter hasn't changed at all. I'm not putting up with her shit."

"Get going, then. I'll take Gracie." Mom slices me a cold glance as she slides her onto her hip. "Kiss your dada bye, honey."

Gracie does and he barely acknowledges her. He struts to the exit like he's flexing in the jail yard. I start to go after him, but my arm is held back. "Hold on there, girlie."

"I have some questions for him." I pull away from Aunt Missy, but she's still hanging on tight.

"I understand, but he wasn't going to talk to you. Not now. Do you really want to do this in front of Gracie?" She waits for me to relax my arm. "Go see Rayna. She'll take you to Cody. You don't want to be with him alone."

"What's that mean?"

"That there's bad blood, but I'm not telling you anything you don't know." Aunt Missy shifts as my mom starts toward us. "I need a cigarette. You should get out of here."

I give Aunt Missy a quick goodbye and head over to my mom.

"Gracie, you want Aunt Syd to hold you?"

She immediately shakes her head no. "Snack, Mam-maw."

"I got Goldfish crackers in my purse," Mom says to me. I grab her purse from the bench and unzip it as I return.

I reach her as I'm peering inside for the crackers. There are a dozen small white prescription bags with large labels stapled to the top. "What are those for, Mom?"

She grabs the purse from me and digs deeper. "Here are your fishies."

Gracie snatches them out of Mom's hand. "Paw-paw want some?"

"Go see." She puts Gracie down, and she runs over to the table where Dad is talking to the Chairman Caine guy again. "Why you looking at me like that?"

I swallow thickly. "Are you sick? What's with all the prescriptions?"

"I'm delivering them to people here," Mom says, as if I've just asked the dumbest question in the world. "Look, you need to be nice to Cody. He's really stepped up since he got out. He and Sister are happy."

"She's happy, huh? Right this very second?"

Mom flinches as if realizing what she's said. "I doubt she is at the moment, Lord knows. But we'll get her back on track soon and—"

"June!" A woman swoops between us in a swoosh of good highlights and a red leather jacket to hug Mom. "I've got great news."

"Hello?" I say, annoyed. "We're in the middle of—"

The woman faces me, and I flush as if embarrassed, but I don't know why. I try to place her, but she's back to facing Mom. "We got permission from the local police for the search tomorrow night. Tyler will take care of all the logistics. Have to give him tasks so he stays out of trouble, right?"

"Who's Tyler?" I ask, knowing about the search but not that other people are organizing it.

Mom blinks at me as if I'm being rude. "Deandre and her husband, Tyler, have organized the search party for Emma Lou." Mom grins but there's no smile in her eyes. "We're so grateful to you both."

I blink at the name just as Deandre squeezes Mom's shoulders. "They're about to call me up, and I'll make the announcement. We'll find her." She turns to me with the same pitying look. "Glad you're here, Syd."

"Deandre," I say softly, the name so familiar, but I can't place it. Then I see her pale blue eyes and remember as she arrives at the podium with a wave. "Wait, that's Dea? Dea D?"

Mom snickers. "She's not a Daweson anymore. She's Deandre Monterey. Married the mayor's son. Didn't you have a crush on her?"

"No," I say, shooting her a look. "We were friends . . . before."

"Friends" is maybe an overstatement. I followed her around all through Picher elementary and middle school. I did everything she asked, laughed at every joke, and gave her "ups" to save her spot in every recess line. I worshipped Dea D, and she knew it. I finally got invited to a slumber party at her house for her fifteenth birthday. It'd been a great night: four-wheeler rides, spying on her older cousins, and eating wild blackberries off the bush until our stomachs ached.

But a few months later, her uncles wore devil masks and murdered my best friend and her parents. A night leading to five deaths. Luna and her parents. The only silver lining was the devils, twin brothers Pete and Skeet Daweson, burned up in that trailer.

The whole Daweson family stuck to themselves after that. Deandre moved from town to the family compound out in the tiny area of Devil's Promenade on the Oklahoma-Missouri border, about nine miles southeast of Picher.

I hadn't thought about Deandre in a while. I try not to think about anyone in that family, including her cousin Cody.

I grind my teeth so tight my jaw aches. As Deandre adjusts the mic, the room falls silent. It's annoying that she's even prettier now than she was in high school. Her hair is still a golden brown, but there are lots of blond highlights. She's got on a great lipstick and her skin glows, maybe Botox. Her red jacket is tight, and she did not have those boobs in high school. Of that, I am certain.

I take a seat next to Mom and rub my palms along my scrubby brown work pants. I hate how old insecurities, when back at the source, so easily return to roost.

"Hello, everyone," Deandre says as the gymnasium quiets. "I have two quick announcements before the meeting starts. First, there's pop and pizza after tonight's meeting, and it's sponsored by Wings Recovery." She pauses as the crowd murmurs some appreciation. Her expression turns serious. "Now then, as you all may have heard, Emma Lou Walker is missing. My husband, Tyler, and I are organizing a search, with help from June and Noah, of course. Please join us tomorrow at five p.m. at the Picher fire station."

"You let a *Daweson* organize a search party for Emma Lou?" I snap at Mom.

"Gracie's father is a Daweson and there's no way around it. Plus, she's the only one who offered," Mom says through a gritted smile toward Deandre, who's crossing the gym in high-heeled boots. She waves goodbye our way, and I reflexively wave back. At Deandre's smirk, I realize the wave was for Mom, not me.

My face is on fire, and I am fifteen all over again.

"You okay, Syd?"

I glance up at my dad holding Gracie. "A little shocked," I say. "At the kind of people we rely on for help these days."

Dad's forehead creases as he puts Gracie in Mom's lap. "You didn't tell her yet?"

"Tell me what?" I send Mom a look.

"Give me a hug, kid," Dad says, and I do, but I don't drop the scowl.

"What's she supposed to tell me?" I ask him.

Dad raises his hands and steps away as he always does when he senses conflict. "I gotta get back there." He taps Gracie's nose and hurries over to the main area, where someone on the committee is setting up a presentation screen.

"Mom, please." I lean close to her. "What is going on?"

"Deandre is the physician's assistant for Dr. Canter," Mom says quietly, her gaze darting around.

I almost laugh. "Dr. Candy is still in business?" Even in high school he was known as the doctor who'd get you whatever you wanted. The whole cheerleading squad was on his "candy" that kept them skinny and peppy. I'm sure it was basically legal speed. "What does that have to do with Emma Lou?"

"Sister delivers prescriptions for Wings, his clinic. I'm part-time in the office to make ends meet on the farm." Mom pats her purse. "I'm filling in deliveries until Emma Lou is back. Deandre's Dr. Canter's partner in the business. She's . . . our boss."

My jaw falls open. I keep from saying, *My sister the drug addict is delivering drugs?* Instead, I watch Gracie chew her snack and try to tamp down my anger or at least breathe through the guilt that all of this is news to me.

Mom is watching me like she can see this open wound. "Don't look at me like that. You weren't here. You don't know."

I stand up, needing to get some air. I try to bite back the anger.

"Where are you going?"

I get close to her ear. "You and Sister can't help yourself when it comes to that godforsaken family. No wonder you wouldn't tell me who you were working for. You should be ashamed."

Mom stands and takes my arm. "Carol, can you watch Gracie a minute?" she says to the woman she'd been talking to, who's a little farther down the bench. Carol nods and scoots closer to my niece. "Let's go."

Mom nearly drags me outside and marches us around the civic center until we're in the shadows.

I yank my arm away from her like a petulant teenager. "What the hell, Mom?"

"Don't use that language around me."

I roll my eyes. Mom is very selective about who can say what around her.

"What's on your mind about that family?" Mom glances around. "But say it just to me. Now. And never in public."

My toes are tight in my boots and my left foot starts to cramp. I tap it on the grass as I string questions together. "Dea runs Dr. Candy's place? Wings or whatever it's called? Doing what?"

"They prescribe OxyContin, mostly, for pain management. Some people don't have cars or can't make it to Miami, so Sister delivers."

I shake my head, because of course that family would suddenly be interested in making money on drugs legally. "How'd she get involved in the first place? And you?"

"Cody," Mom says quietly. "He knew Deandre needed help and your sister needed a job. Raising a kid takes money."

"And you?" I ask. "You had the stomach to cash a check from the Dawesons, too?"

"More than I could stomach losing our home." Mom stares out toward the parking lot for a moment. "Or the Walker land."

"Mom," I whisper. "You didn't say anything . . ."

"Not much to say, Syd. The school cut your dad's hours back. Funding isn't there for a full-time Native student counselor. Wings is good money. And it helps people. There's a lot of pain around here."

There was a huge uptick in doctors prescribing opioids in Rhode Island, too. It seemed pain was suddenly everywhere and solvable with a pill.

"ODs dropped ten percent." Mom sounds like a radio spot for Dr. Candy. "Besides, we deliver other types of prescriptions."

"I've never even seen you take a Tylenol, Mom." I pause and try to hear my breath. To ground myself, as Mal says, and not react from a place of fear or anger. "Dea's uncles killed Luna and her parents. They tried to kill us. You and Sister are . . . taking money from that scum-of-the-earth family."

Mom crosses her arms and her floral blouse waves in the warm breeze. "It's been fifteen years and those uncles are long dead. Cody loves Gracie more than life. It's easy to judge when you're not here. One thing happens, then another. This is where things stand now."

The truth hurts and I push back. "Fine, I'm out of here. I'm going to see Rayna." I know my mom will hate that. I'm annoyed with myself, too, that I'm back to being the teenager.

"Syd Alma Walker, if you stay at a hotel tonight, so help me."

"I'll stay at the house, but I'll probably be late."

She grunts as if that's barely acceptable.

I stomp off toward the Jeep and my hands are shaking as I pull the keys from my pocket. I watch Mom go safely inside the civic center and then take long breaths, leaning against the door in the lamppost light.

I have never felt so far away from my family.

A whole new chapter began for Emma Lou, and they didn't share it with me. I know I chose to stay away, but I do call sometimes. Once a month, usually, hopefully. No one had said anything.

"Did you ask?" Ghost Luna's voice whispers from the darkness.

We usually talk about my job and what's new with Mal. I chat with Gracie and hear what letters she's drawing. The letter "T" was last month. She'd mailed me a turkey drawing using her handprint and painted the fingertips like feathers. I got out my turkey call and made gobble noises that caused her and Emma Lou to bust a gut. The last few calls, Mom told me what she was planting in her vegetable garden this spring. Dad told me about working on a new outreach program for the high school kids he counsels. They had plenty of opportunity to tell me, so it must be something else. Something Mom and Sister didn't want me to know.

I can run through phone calls and ways that I've tried to stay connected all I want, but that doesn't change the truth. "They're hiding something from you," Ghost Luna says at my ear, whispering the truth I don't want to admit.

They hid their lives from me.

11

〰〰〰

I pull up to the Buffalo Run Casino full of guilt for all that went unsaid, especially by me, and that includes with my cousin Rayna. I didn't once reach out while she was in prison.

The parking lot is big enough for a fleet of cars and the trucks that hauled them. The Peoria Tribe built this casino only three years ago. It's going so well for the almost three-thousand-member tribe that owns it that they're breaking ground on a new hotel next door. In front of me, I take in the casino's wooden beams and head toward the large awning leading to several sets of glass doors.

"You think Rayna's pissed at you?"

I shoot Ghost Luna a look, pausing my steps.

"Got gum on your shoes?" barks a man's voice behind me. "I'll be late for keno."

I step aside, annoyed he didn't go around. "Sorry."

His saggy face wrinkles even more as he gazes up from a Rascal scooter. His eyes are the exact light blue that indicates he's a Daweson, kin to that den of devils. All with those pale eyes and stupid nicknames. "Don't screw with a man's livelihood."

Even if I don't know his name, he's certainly one of them. That aura of nastiness permeates on a cellular level. "I'm not stopping you, old man," I murmur under the whir of the scooter's tiny engine working hard.

He zooms past and raises his middle finger on the hand not steering.

I release a long, shaky breath and follow him inside to a giant windowless room. Ghost Luna is gone, and I'm grateful for that small mercy.

The sensory overload is immediate: row after row of slot machines flash and ding; table games are crowded as people wait for seats to open; the big bar in the middle is three people deep clamoring for drinks. I glance toward a restaurant in the back, the facade a replica of the local Coleman Theatre, built with mining money. Buffalo Run is not large by Vegas standards, but as one of six casinos crowded into this part of the state, it's part of what keeps Oklahoma at the top of the list of most casinos per capita.

Before I look for my cousin, I make myself follow this Daweson. Isn't this what I feared most? Seeing these terrible people living and breathing where Luna and her parents aren't.

The Daweson waves at the security guard and motors past the table games. Before he heads toward the KENO sign in the back, he scooters to a group of people at one of the few tables in the roped-off bar area. Most look half his age, but they have the Daweson dark hair and, I bet, those eyes. There are nods toward him, but most stick to their drinks, scroll through their Black-

Berries, or text on their flip phones. I hate the sight of this group, and find time has barely dulled the edges of this knife-sharp pain.

A woman who is older than the rest returns to the table. Her white hair is long and braided down her back. Turquoise glistens in her ears. It takes me a moment, but I recognize Deandre's mom, Manda. Even before the night with the Daweson brothers, the real devils Pete and Skeet, Dad never liked me going to the compound.

Manda rises from the head of the table and saunters over to the old man on the scooter. She jams a wad of cash at him with hardly an acknowledgment and returns to her seat.

Before she sits, she looks across the casino and finds me staring. Her eyes narrow in recognition. I see the pale blue eyes, even from this distance. Her mouth presses into an angry thin line. I don't look away.

I welcome her anger. I am proud I shot her brother, Skeet, to save my sister. That my bullet might have been what killed him. The report was inconclusive, since a stray bullet hit the propane tank, causing a massive explosion after Sister and I escaped.

"They burned up?" I'd asked Sue's dad as he read details of the report. "Did they suffer?"

"Not enough," he'd said. "We'll leave the rest to the devil."

When I found out that both Skeet and Pete died that night, that's when I first understood real justice. The kind that has nothing to do with laws on paper written by white men who called us savages in those founding documents. Instead, it is the righteous order of the world.

Only Emma Lou and I escaped that night. Those devils might be dead, but Luna and her parents were murdered.

When I'd seen the fire with my own eyes, I'd been terrified

for Luna. I hadn't known she was already dead inside along with her parents, who'd shown up sometime after I got Emma Lou out of there. That the flames only killed devils.

"Well, fry my prairie oysters," says a familiar voice behind me.

I turn to see Rayna in all her casino waitress glory: black padded bustier, too-short schoolgirl skirt, and name tag that says RAY. Her hair is the same long, kinky curls, but with a few dyed purple pieces underneath. She's skinny as always, with her acne-scarred cheeks and perceptive gaze that rarely misses anything—except an undercover officer a couple of times.

"Hey, cuz." I give her a shy hug and am relieved to turn away from the Dawesons. "Sorry to just show up."

She snorts. "You family, girl. You can always show up. Unless you want money. I cannot help you there."

I smile, relieved she seems the same older cousin with attitude. I try to hide my pity that so little has changed for her. "You doing okay?"

"Obviously." She gestures up and down at her outfit and then all around at the casino. "How's your fancy-ass life with your hot doc wifey?"

An old happiness returns that Rayna still cares enough to tease me. After the devils, she was the only one who didn't treat me like I was shattered glass. When I left the house more, she'd let me tag along. Trying to keep up with her smart-ass attitude made me feel normal again, or as close as I'd ever get to it. She pushed until I pushed back. She forced me to live until I could do it on my own.

"Life is fine." Something tight in my chest loosens, and I can't hold back saying, "Mal is pregnant."

"Way to lock that shit down, girl!" She shoves my shoulder. "Why do you have that deer-in-the-headlights look?"

I notice another female server, who is in black shorts and a Buffalo Run tank top. "Is that the actual uniform?"

"Changing the subject, cuz?"

"Yes. Why do you look like a stripper?"

"'Cause I wore this when I was stripping." Rayna flips her hair. "Lost a little weight in prison and fits like a glove."

"Not up top." I point at the padding that's visible. "Still stuffing your bra."

"You know what?" She grabs the back of my head and shoves my face into the padding. "Guys would still pay twenty for a ride on this motorboat, baby."

I pull away and laugh loud, as more uncertainty eases. "How was jail this time?"

"Pretty good. No complaints." Rayna pulls on one of her necklaces, running the pendant up and down. "Skin cleared up. Lost ten pounds." She leans close. "Had fantastic sex. You scissor sisters know how to do it."

I laugh. "Well, we own the equipment."

"That's for damn sure. Had me popped and locked." She does a funny little wiggle and we both laugh.

"I assume you're back with an ex?"

She itches at her hair before smoothing her skirt. She's always been restless, like a goldfish swimming around and around, no matter how dirty the bowl. "Me and Bo Don are hanging out."

"Isn't he dead?"

"That's Donny Jo. Drowned while noodle fishing." She wiggles her fingers, since that's all the bait noodlers use when they jam their fists into holes on the lake or river floor. "Dumb but hung. RIP."

"So, you're back with Bo Don," I say to get her to focus. "Is it serious?"

"As a heart attack."

I remember him being a lazy piece of shit. "You can do better."

"I'm out of the can. He's out of the can. Chat rat fairy tale. Cinder-fucking-ella."

"Or shitty parole judge."

"How about a little support, cuz?" She loops her arm through mine. "Missed you."

"Ray!" shouts a man behind the bar in a white collared shirt and limp bow tie. "Drop these drinks."

"I don't want to get you in trouble," I say, pulling away. "I can sit in your section until your shift is over."

"One sec." She leads me toward the man at the end of the bar, where there are about a dozen sweating drinks waiting. "I'm outta here, Melvin," she yells toward the guy who I assume is her manager.

"Like hell, Ray." He throws a rag down and stomps over in khakis pulled way too high. "Your skinny ass ain't going nowhere. You got drinks to drop."

She toggles her head back and forth. "I hear you. I do. But I don't give a single solitary shit."

His long pale face lights up to a bright red. "Excuse me?"

She winks at me. "Know how I got this job?"

I keep my smile from her angry manager and smirk back at her. "Winning personality?"

"That's right, and . . ." She clenches her fist and opens her mouth to make a blow-job motion. "Won Melvy over and over and over."

I grimace and watch the red disappear, and he's pale now.

"R-R-Ray . . . now, see here . . ." he stammers.

"I'm pretty sure I was the first woman to ever touch his dick." She squishes his cheeks. "You'd have married me right then and there, Melvy."

He lets out an exasperated breath that causes his thin lips to vibrate.

"Though . . ." She plucks a shot off the tray and throws it back. "His mom's basement is pretty nice."

"You're such a piece of work," Melvin says as he steps back, nervously glancing at the couple closest to us at the bar, who are clearly enjoying the show. "You miss your shift tomorrow, you're fired."

"Spanks a lot." Rayna puts both her hands on the back of his head. I recognize the move, though he seems clueless as his eyes go wide. He squeals as she jams his face into her bustier padding.

The couple laugh, and he's bright red again.

"Want anything?" she asks me as she motions at the tray of drinks, but I shake my head no. "We're outtie five thousand, Melvy!" Rayna lets out a loud hyena laugh that always draws every eye, and she knows it.

"Is he going to fire you?" I stare at her red-faced manager.

She grabs her purse from under the bar and we're arm in arm again. As we head toward the exit, she leans closer. "Naw, he won't do shit. Harassing my ass all the damn time. I might lawyer up. Retire with all that har-ass money."

I feel relieved this little show hasn't done much damage. "Can you help me find Cody Daweson?"

"Now, that sounds like trouble."

"I have some questions for him about Emma Lou."

Rayna waves bye to a couple of people as we approach a back

exit. "I do have on the right outfit. And who knows, maybe some extra cash."

I realize I have no idea where we're going. "What do you mean?"

She lightly bumps me with her hip and then hauls open the door. "If any of the dancers are no-shows, Cody can just throw me on the pole."

12

Remember this old biddy?" Rayna points toward the white Dodge Neon she's had since high school. "We've both been ridden a lot of miles, but we're still kicking."

"I have a rental," I offer, but I'm already reaching for the handle.

"Naw," she says. "We'll get it on the flip back to Picher."

Rayna drops into the Neon and leans over to unlock the passenger door. There's the same creak from more than a decade ago as I ease into the seat.

"You want to grab a drink before?" She digs around in her giant purse. "You look like you need one."

"I don't drink anymore," I explain. "Not good for my anxiety."

"Neither is life sober." She reaches over and smacks my knees, so I scoot them. Digging past a stack of white napkins in the glove compartment, she pulls out a mini bottle of Jameson and cracks the cap.

I tap a small dream catcher around her rearview mirror. "NDN represent?" I tease.

"Emma Lou made it for me. She's not the only one with bad dreams." She takes a small sip and lets out a breath. "Sister was the last person in this car with me. Day she disappeared."

I slowly buckle my seat belt, imagining Emma Lou doing the same thing. "Could you tell she was using again?"

"I don't look close." Rayna takes another drink before turning on the car. "She was more scattered than usual, I guess. Worried about Cody. She was . . . jittery, so maybe coming down. Who knows, life is hard around here, cuz."

The back of my head drops against the seat. "You're staying clean? From drugs, anyway."

"Weekly drug tests or I'll get fired." She starts feeling under my seat. "Actually, Emma Lou had drug tests at Wings. She took it seriously. If someone was smoking weed around her, she'd leave."

"You can fake those tests," I say without thinking, reflexively. "Did you ask around about her using?"

"Sure." She pulls a CD case out from under my seat. "Didn't get anywhere."

The loud motor is the only sound for a few seconds. Rayna flips through the pages of CDs. "The meth business has changed since you left. Used to be locally made." She shakes her head as if reflecting on a farmers' market stand with fantastic tomatoes. "Word is, meth is starting to come from Mexico. Made in labs the size of football fields."

"McMeth?" I offer.

"Guess so." She smacks on the dome light and holds up the case. "I never can find the one I want."

I picture Manda at the head of the table in the casino. They dealt in plain view in Picher neighborhoods. White-boy posers with sagging pants and backward hats would nod at Emma Lou, as if drugs made our families friends. Cops never seemed to get involved, maybe too lazy, maybe paid off or just smart enough to not go against a family like the Dawesons. "Are the Dawesons still involved with drugs?"

Rayna pulls out a CD, squints, and puts it back. "If you're dealing meth in Northeast Oklahoma, they are."

I grind my teeth, anxious to get going. Even if Cody doesn't have Emma Lou drugged out at his place, he likely knows where she would lie low. The worry I want to ignore is that if he's waited this long to do anything about it, he might not want Sister found.

"Gotcha." Rayna waves the CD in my face. "The one I want is always hiding behind another. Hope you like Oklahoma Red Dirt country. This one's about how them Oklahoma boys roll their joints too long."

She slips the disc into the ancient player. The kind the face pops off for security. The song is a live version, and as the lead singer starts playing to the excited crowd, Rayna peels out of the parking lot.

Feeling hot and anxious, I roll down my window. I close my eyes and listen as the breeze blows over my face. The smell of dew-wet fields and blacktop roads takes me away for a moment. "Are we really going to a strip club?" I ask, unsure if Rayna was joking about getting on the pole when we left.

"The Body Shop is basically a bar with boobs," Rayna says as we cross the Spring River heading out east of Miami.

"It's named after the lotion store in the mall?"

She snorts. "Actually, I heard Deandre only got the license because the city thought she was opening a repair shop."

"Deandre opened a strip club?" I snicker, thinking of her boss-babe act earlier in the night.

"Well, Cody manages it. Keeping it in the family. Hey, didn't you have a crush on *her* in high school?"

"No," I lie, and swat at her shoulder. "I guess I should be relieved Emma Lou isn't working there, too."

"Okay, judgy," Rayna says, sounding a little hurt. "Don't knock it till you rock it."

"Sorry," I say, meaning it. "You are amazing, on and off the pole."

She makes a crude gesture with her tongue and two fingers as we pass a trailer park near a run-down motel off Highway 69. "Bunch of Picher people moved in there. Mom keeps whining it's the only place she can afford with the buyout money."

I remember Aunt Missy mentioning that at the civic center earlier. "Is it that bad?"

"You'll see babies in diapers running around with dealers and meth heads. A real Shangri-la."

I catch a glimpse of several trailer homes lined up, but nothing looks particularly different from other trailer parks, which I've never been snobby about. I had plenty of friends and family in homes with wheels and without. We continue over a hill and past a pro-life billboard. Rayna takes a left and pulls into a gravel parking lot. There's a bright marquee sign that says, MIDGET MONDAY IS BACK!

"She's a regular from Texas." Rayna nods toward the sign as she pulls into the small lot behind the club, which is more grass than gravel. "Real pro, but every tip that night goes her way, so girls working get bitchy."

I'm relieved it's not Monday. I never liked strip clubs, even if it was my cool cousin dragging me there. Desire has never worked like that for me. Not with sad eyes and C-section scars that meant the kids were at home while Momma worked. I've heard there are places where women make good money and get treated fairly by their employers and protected from men who want more than their actual job entails. But around here, it never looked that way.

Rayna parks between two big trucks. "If Manager Melvin shows up, you gotta give me a sign so I can sneak out the back."

I think she's joking, but I'm not sure as we get out. There's a bass beat rattling from inside a rectangular building with white metal siding.

We head toward the front, and my anger returns as I think about seeing Cody and getting stonewalled again. The possibility that somewhere in his dumbass head is information about my sister has both my fists clenched tight and itching to do something.

As we approach the door, which is propped open, Rayna holds us back. "You look like you're about to punch someone."

I put a hand to my face and realize I'm flushed. "I really want to find Sister."

"We will," she says. "But there's big-time security here. Like, do not mess with them. The police never get involved, if you know what I mean."

"I'll stay cool." I inhale and exhale to prove it.

Rayna puts her hands on her skinny hips. "Syd Alma Walker, you better not get our asses beat."

I motion for her to lead the way, and a very muscular door guy with a yellow bandana around his neck waves Rayna through.

"It's topless girls, bottomless beer night," he says gruffly in my ear, and then pats me down.

Rayna is watching me closely, but I keep calm and follow her inside.

The Body Shop is a giant rectangular room with a long bar right inside and a round stage with a pole in the middle. There are men everywhere—in the rows of chairs, at tables, and in a long line at the bar. I notice the door guy isn't the only one with one of those yellow bandanas around his neck. There's at least a half dozen others.

The music is vibrating in my ears as my boot crunches on a Solo cup, one of several scattered around like the floor is a frat-party lawn. A banner behind the packed bar reads, YOUR HOMETOWN BAR WITH BOOBS.

Right on cue, the opening notes of "Touch My Body" by Mariah Carey start bumping. A too-skinny woman, twenty years old, tops, begins to circle the pole in a pink lace thong. I turn away, wishing for that empowered look instead of vacant and high.

"Let's find Cody," I say, and scan the crowd.

"He'll be in the back." Rayna waves at the woman on the stage, who gives her a listless tip of the head before swinging her leg around the pole and folding herself over.

She leads us toward a door marked WOMEN'S RESTROOM, and inside is a big room with faded purple paint. There are two dingy mirrors with Hollywood vanity ball lights. Four topless women look up with skeptical frowns.

"My dimpled ass," says a woman applying a thick layer of makeup over a bruise on her arm. "What do you want, Rayna?"

"To see the boss," I answer for her. "He around?"

The woman smacks her gum. "Cody ain't holding, if that's what you're after."

"He's not? No wonder you're so cranky," Rayna says. "Coke

and a smile, right? Skittles and a smile, maybe? I don't know what the kids are calling it."

A door swings open and Cody freezes where he stands. "What are you doing here?"

"Well, that's a greeting for family," Rayna says brightly. "Hello, how are you?"

"He looks twitchy," I say, and Rayna elbows me.

"This is a private place of business," Cody says loud, but likely he can go louder depending on how I react. "I won't be harassed."

I cross my arms. "Call the police. Tell them *you're* being harassed by women at the Body Shop."

A couple of the ladies snicker from their folding chairs as they continue to get ready.

"What do you want?" he says to me.

"I need a few minutes," I answer. "Alone."

Rayna puts her fingers lightly on my arm. "Let me go with you."

I shake my head and pull away. "Five minutes, Cody. In your office."

Cody glances at Rayna, who shrugs as if I'm being unreasonable to the druggie boyfriend who I'm betting knows exactly where I can find my sister. "Stay on the other side of the desk," he says.

Rayna sends me a warning glance, and I nod that she has nothing to worry about. A lie, but I can't wait one more second to talk to this asshole.

I close the door behind us and glance at the paneled walls and nude calendar from two years ago, where it's always Ms. July.

He drops into a creaking chair behind the too-big faux-wood desk separating us. He nods toward the calendar. "Before my time. She danced here."

"Congratulations." I cross my arms tight, but it doesn't ease the crackling live-wire feeling under my skin. "What can you tell me about Emma Lou?"

"She's missing," he says. "Gracie is a mess."

"I can't believe Emma Lou lets you see her."

"See my own damn daughter? We're back together."

"So you say." I try to slow my breath, but I can't. "You've tried to kill her before. I don't put it past you now."

He jabs his tongue into his cheek. "I don't give two shits what you think."

I step closer to his desk, even though I know I shouldn't. My fear for Emma Lou is a fuel for my anger with Cody that goes back all the way to the night with the devils. "I will find Sister and get her into treatment."

Cody leans back in his chair with a big smirk on his face. "She don't need rehab."

"Says the guy who hasn't been sober since fifteen."

He blinks at me as if he's surprised I noticed. "I saw some fucked up shit that year."

I almost laugh. "Yeah, me too. I was actually inside the trailer that night."

"Fuck you, Syd. That was my uncles, not me, okay?"

This is an old fight between us. That night with the devils, Cody was supposed to come by Luna's trailer. He and Emma Lou were already seeing each other. He'd gone to pick up Sue in Miami after the football game was over so she could hang out, too. But they never showed. Or that's what they told the police.

My guess is he did know something was going to happen. That's why he never showed until it was over. "I remember headlights."

He sucks at his top teeth. "You saw Luna's parents coming home."

"It was your truck I saw." I swallow, certain, though with no real evidence other than a feeling.

"You're here to fight with me about something that happened fifteen years ago? That I had no idea was happening and wasn't there for?" He glances at the big digital clock on the wall. "Three minutes left."

I press my palms into the top of his filthy desk. "Where is Emma Lou?"

His brown eyes go cold, as if he is steeling himself for the lie. "I don't have any idea, okay?"

"Not okay at all, Cody. The fact that you are okay tells me all I need to know."

He jams his fingers into his shaggy brown hair. "You don't know how I'm doing. What I'm going through. You ain't even around."

"I know she almost died because of you. That you tried to keep me from taking her to the hospital."

He swears under his breath. "I was fucked up back then. I'm not that person no more."

I laugh loudly and his mouth curls into a cruel twitch. My jagged nails are sharp in the palms of my hands as I see the devil masks. I think of blue eyes, even though he didn't inherit them. I believe he was there that night. He knew his uncles were, too. He left us all to die. Even if Emma Lou never believed it. And he's been slowly killing my sister ever since.

"Hey!" he shouts, and I'm over the desk, swinging right at his face. He bobs, but my other hand connects.

He slams back against the wall and yells, "Security!"

In seconds the door busts open, and it's not the door-man, but two tall, skinny guys with yellow bandanas hiding their faces.

I go completely still as every instinct says *Run*. I barely move before the first one grabs me by the shoulders and hauls me out of the office. He shoves me toward the exit door and Rayna runs across the room and jumps onto his back.

"Leave my goddamn cousin alone, you dipshit!" she screams.

He bucks her off, and she lands with a thud on her side. But then she's back up and we're both being shoved toward the door.

The push outside is so hard we land in the gravel. My palms and knees are on fire from the rocks, but I manage to scramble up and help Rayna do the same. We start to run toward the field on the other side of the parked cars, but there are three more guys with those yellow bandanas covering their faces.

"Shit, shit, shit," Rayna says, pulling us backward.

The one closest to us pulls out a pistol. "Facedown on the ground, bitches."

I search around for Cody, but he's nowhere. "We'll get out of here. It's a family matter."

"You ain't his family," the one with the gun says. "Now, face-down."

There's fear in Rayna's eyes as we drop to the ground. "Not even here a full day and you're already pissing off the dipshits."

"Don't call us that, bitch." A *whoosh* and *thud* as a boot connects with Rayna, who then curls toward me with a moan. "I told your ass."

I lift my head to scream at him, but Rayna yanks me down. "Shut your mouth."

I go back on my stomach and one of them zip-ties our hands.

"Hurry and get the truck," he says once we're both bound. "Let's take these bitches for a ride."

13

~~~~~~

Facedown in the bed of a pickup, I tug on the zip tie around my wrists. It tears my skin like a ring of fire.

"We are plucked and fucked now," Rayna murmurs from under her curly hair, which has fallen over her face in my direction. "Wish I'd had one last cigarette."

I start to argue that we'll be okay, but my quivering chin won't allow the lie. "I'm really sorry," I whisper.

Tiny rocks in this filthy truck bed dig into my cheek. I shift to relieve the pain, but there are just more on the other side. We listen to male voices discuss where to take us. Chat piles out west. Trailer in the outlaw lands. Shooting range. I try to discern how many men are there. As if facts will do anything when we're facedown and nearly hog-tied.

Boots thump and the truck bounces as someone jumps into the back. A flashlight shines right in my eyes. He gets close and his hot breath reeks of whiskey and Corn Nuts. "We can definitely handle these two," he says with a high-pitched laugh. No doubt they're all revved up from the tit club like raging testosterone transforms the world into their urinal.

I pull harder against the plastic ties and feel warm, wet blood on my wrists. I think of white dresses and women's bodies—so many of them Native—tossed in shallow graves, arms out like snow angels in the dirt or zip-tied behind their backs, fates all the same.

"Breathe slower, cuz," Rayna whispers, and I realize I'm almost hyperventilating.

The terror in my throat is not for my life, but for Rayna and Emma Lou. For the skull with my badge. For Mal and the baby I would have learned to love and somehow protected. I've failed them all.

"Hey!" shouts a guy's voice. "Stop just a goddamn minute."

I realize it's Cody. I shift to see, but the light is still directly on my face. "We're all good here, man," says the whiskey guy standing over me.

"Look, that's my girl's sister, okay? And her cousin. I can handle it."

"No, man, you couldn't. It's a damn good thing we were here when you screamed 'SECURITY!' like a little bitch." The other guys start laughing, but he continues. "It's playtime, right, girls?" He shoves a boot into my side.

"Cody, please!" I yell, desperate now, realizing he's our only chance.

One of the guys says, "Cody, please," and others repeat it like some terrible, mocking echo.

"Cody can't help you girls, no." He steps over me toward the truck cab and taps the roof. "Let's get out of here."

"Syd, I'm sorry," Cody yells.

The truck engine roars, and the tailgate slams shut with a *whoop*. "See you at the chat piles, boys."

As the truck peels out, I roll into Rayna as she's slammed into the side. We cough as dirt from the spinning wheels swirls and covers us like fumes.

I don't even think we've left the parking lot when the truck slams on its brakes. "Who is that?" yells the one standing over us. "Oh shit."

There is total silence until a door flies open and shuts loudly. At the stomp of shoes, not boots, I twist my neck to listen harder.

"Kaleb Winifred Dove," yells a woman's voice. "You dumbass. Cut them loose or I'll call Mom."

That name, Kaleb Dove. I knew this guy when he was pissing the bed. He's Sue Dove's little brother.

"This ain't your business," he says, now sounding more scared than tough.

"Do I need to draw my weapon?" she yells, still at a distance. Then the crunch of what sounds like heels in the dirt road. Someone is on the side of the truck. "You cannot tie up people." She sounds as if she's scolding a child. "I don't care who your boss is, Kaleb."

"Sue?" I call out into the darkness, shocked that the BIA region's superintendent would be here of all places. "It's me, Syd Walker."

The steps stop for a moment, then rush over. "Jesus, I'm so sorry." She goes around to the back of the truck and climbs inside.

Her shoes appear beside my face—they are heels. Tall heels. She crouches down, and I lift my head slightly to the side. I blink at her glittery skirt catching in the moonlight and think of how male birds evolved to have colorful feathers to attract a mate. She pulls me up and steadies me by my shoulders. "Keep breathing until there's one of me."

I search for the sounds of birds, but it's quiet. I inhale, wanting to smell a pine or spruce, the evergreen trees of the Cherokee.

Breathing helps, and finally Sue's narrow face is in focus. She looks a bit older, but there's that light in her gaze that goes beyond pretty and blond. A calm nature that was rare among teenagers and that I desperately needed. I don't remember her wearing so much makeup. Or any, for that matter. The sparkle skirt catches my eye again, especially with a gun holster around it. Her top has a heart cutout pulled tight across her cleavage.

"I'm okay," I say. "Help her, please."

She lets go of my shoulders and watches me for a few seconds. She turns with her hand on her holstered gun and stares down. "Shit, Rayna, is that you? One second, girl." Sue lifts Rayna up and eases her back onto the side of the truck.

"Don't you look the Real Housewives of Ottawa County. We interrupt your date?" Rayna says with a cough and then clears her throat. "White-trash Mr. Wonderful?"

"Nothing wonderful about him." Sue holds her by the shoulders, too. "I haven't seen you since you got out."

"Too good for dirtbags and slot sluts at Buffalo Run?" Rayna says in her sweet, sarcastic way—versus straight-up bitch.

"I've seen my fair share of dirtbags." She takes a knife out of her holster and quickly cuts the ties.

The second Rayna is free, she jumps up and kicks Kaleb right between the legs. He drops like a sack of potatoes with a big grunt. "Little bit of your own medicine," Rayna says as she stands over him, then kicks him in the ribs.

A couple of dipshits yell at her, but that ends when Sue puts her hand on her gun. "You move, you get shot. Next time, I'll just do it."

"You were pulling pretty hard, Syd." Sue helps me stand and examines my wrists. "That doesn't look good."

Blood is dripping steady enough to see it on the ground. "I'll be fine."

Sue snatches the bandana off her brother and wraps it around one wrist. "Hey, Keater, let me have yours."

"Screw you, Deputy Barbie," says the one closest to the truck.

She reaches up to grab him by the ear and twists. "You want me to ask again?"

He cries out and hands his bandana to her in a huff before she lets him go.

She wraps it around my other wrist. "You pressing charges?"

"We didn't do nothing wrong," Kaleb says as he slowly sits up and scoots farther from Rayna. "You know we're security for the Dawesons. This is their property."

Sue glances at me as if he has a point, which he does. "You're a moron, Kaleb. You got a right to patrol, but I got a right to be sure it's legal. You tie people up without cause again, and I'll get the sheriff involved."

He points at me. "She attacked Cody."

Sue turns toward the back of the building. "You pressing charges?" she yells.

"Not right this second," calls Cody.

"Then we're done here."

We finally get out of the truck, and the dipshits start to scatter until they're packed into two big trucks. Once the engines roar, they start with the threats and curse us before they peel out. Dirt spews in their wake.

My breathing speeds up again and it's all I can hear until Cody comes up to me. He squeezes my shoulder. Hard.

"You okay?"

"What do you care?" I pull away. "You're a piece of shit like everyone in your family."

"I didn't ask them to do that," Cody spits out.

"I've seen firsthand these dipshits are everywhere, and having guys like this around my niece or Emma Lou is dangerous," I say, not hiding the threat. I am scared, but the trembling in my body is from anger. "How did you ever get back in my family? After everything you've done."

Sue puts a hand on my shoulder. "Listen, Syd—"

"Don't you defend him." When I face her, the past shimmers between us. Because it's possible not only was Cody there that last night at Luna's, but Sue could have been, too. I get in Cody's face. "I will find my sister. I don't care how many shitholes I have to bust through. She's getting clean and she's getting you out of her life."

"God, you've always been such a bitch," Cody murmurs as his chin quivers. "Take this and get out of here."

He shoves a piece of paper in my hand, and I flip it open and see Emma Lou's name and medical information. A heart shape in pink highlighter is drawn around one word in the blood results section. "POSITIVE."

"Emma Lou is two months along." Cody's voice cracks. "We didn't tell anybody yet, but we're excited. Gracie's going to be a big sister."

I can't stop staring at the word. "Oh my God, Cody."

"She's clean. She was going to stay clean." He angrily swipes a tear. "Emma Lou was always saying how smart you are, but you're worse than dumb because you act like you got it all figured out. That's dangerous."

I stare at the heart-shaped scribble. "I'm trying to help."

"Help?" He pauses to spit onto the ground. "Well, you can start by backing off me, or you will never see any of us again."

AGILVGI

I dream I am one of his girls.
    We are stacked in a pile, smooth legs and glossy lips and mascara-streaked cheeks.

I needed to be the only one.

I was for so long.

Someone grabs my shoulders.

I wake up screaming.

The room is a dull black, like I'm under a blanket, and I suck air to survive.

My head hits the floor as he drags me.

I know his rough hands.

I know his voice when he whispers, "They're looking for you. Need a better place to hide."

He throws me over his shoulder as if I'm nothing.

I'm in fresh air for the first time in days, weeks, I don't know.

A bright light ahead. Is it the Spook Light?

I see the prison I'm leaving.

An old trailer in the outlaw lands. I smell gasoline.

My vision blurs and my stomach cramps sharp, worse than before.

I begin to sob as he sets the trailer on fire as if I was never there.

14

THURSDAY, MAY 8, 2008

My wrists throbbing wakes me, and I open my eyes to tiny plastic stars no longer glowing now that the sun is up. I remember Mom on a ladder and the smells of fresh paint and the hot glue gun as we covered my bedroom's popcorn ceiling with the small stars. It was less a solar system and more a softly glowing blanket above me.

It'd take another five years before I could lie in complete darkness without the smell of mothballs returning to trigger a panic attack.

My body feels heavy in my childhood bed. A creaky metal daybed that had been donated when my family moved in with my grandma Ama after the devils. The Dawesons owned the house my parents rented in town. A place Mom wanted to live. Dad made us move immediately, not caring that he lost the deposit. The decision had nothing to do with money, though I know Dad would never pay a cent to that family after what happened. Or that's what I thought, but now it seems we're more than willing to let them pay us.

I'd been relieved to be busy after losing Luna. I was tired of crying. I packed my room and most of the house since Mom and Dad were busy with Emma Lou. I heard them arguing the last night we were in that rental. *We got too close, June, too comfortable. We gotta go back to my family's land. To keep together what's left of us.*

But it's so close to what happened, Noah.

So we remember and don't let it happen again.

Maybe their plan worked for a while, but I never felt together with my family. We were like broken pieces trying to be forced into a puzzle. I sit up and the bed squeaks. We certainly aren't together now that Emma Lou is missing.

I exhale and wonder how long I can keep Sister's pregnancy from my parents. I have proven to myself, day after day, I can keep secrets. But this secret is no more mine to share than mine to keep.

Glancing out the window, I stare in the direction of where the skull was found. Where my badge was lodged between the teeth like a taunt. I feel pulled in half, to do my job or to find my sister.

"It's weird being back here," says Ghost Luna from the corner. She's clearer here at my parents' home, as if being close to her body in the graveyard makes her spirit stronger.

My ears register the murmur of cartoons from a TV. For a moment, I see a young Emma Lou on her belly. Her skinny legs like windshield wipers in her Strawberry Shortcake nightgown. She yells for me to hurry because *She-Ra* is almost on. Mom brings us honey toast. Those mornings, we were happy. Before the devils. Before we lost Luna. Before we lost what we were or what we could be.

"June has gotten messy the past few years." Ghost Luna points at a messy stack of boxes and containers I noticed last night when I got home. My room has changed. Mom's sewing stuff is in here instead of the hallway closet. The small boxes of thread and fabric are piled on my old desk haphazardly, which isn't like my mom. Her sewing machine is in the chair with a thick layer of dust on the faded blue cover. My room is a dumping ground. The Mom I know was particular about keeping our rooms as they were. Perhaps with Gracie joining, things changed.

I don't like how much this bothers me, especially as a woman with a wife and a child on the way. Feeling silly, I pull my phone out of the charger.

"You better call your wife."

I don't throw the phone, but I think about it. Of course I want to ignore the phone and Mal so I don't have to face any questions about last night. Especially given how dangerous it got—or could have if Sue hadn't intervened. The scared girl who used to sleep here would have given in to my fears, but I know better. I am better, because of Mal.

She answers on the first ring, her voice scratchy.

"Sorry I didn't call last night." I swallow some emotion. "Things took a turn when I went looking for Emma Lou. How are you?"

"I'm great." Mal takes a long, sleepy inhale and there are familiar creaks from our bed. "What happened?"

"Cody is out of prison."

"What? After what he did to your sister?"

I feel terrible that I dragged Mal into that part of my life. That she had to go to that trailer and see my sister half-dead. Hear Cody yelling at me and trying to convince us to leave them alone, or said another way, just let Emma Lou die. "I guess he got out early."

"I'm sorry." She clears her throat. "Where did you see him?"

I tell her more about the buyouts. How people will be leaving Picher for the first time in their lives. A place the mines brought their families two or three generations ago, a place they never left. But it's not only those with houses getting screwed over. Like Aunt Missy, there are people, Native people, mostly Quapaw, who won't see a cent from this buyout, even though it's their land. As if the only people, mostly white people, who should be compensated are those who built houses on land that wasn't theirs in the first place.

"So people like your aunt Missy had family who walked the Trail of Tears. Then had that land taken away, or at least the rights on it, when those minerals were found on it. Then companies came in and destroyed that land. Leaving literal poison behind. Now she's trying to make enough to start again, and she's not getting close?"

"It's as awful as that," I say. "She doesn't seem mad exactly. Almost as if she expected to get kicked again."

"Your dad is on the committee?"

"Yeah, I think he's doing his best, but he's pretty much set up for failure. No one is going to be happy."

"What happens after all the people in Picher are gone?"

"No one knows. Some people say we should just flood it and turn it into marshland. Return everything to the earth."

The bed creaks and I hear her get up and start across the room. I know she's putting on her lavender robe and then I hear her soft footsteps toward the kitchen for coffee. "So you went looking for your sister after?"

"My cousin Rayna and I ran into some trouble last night. Vigilante guys threw us in the back of their truck—"

"What?"

"Yeah, we're fine. Local BIA got involved. It was pretty scary."

"Who were they? Community police or something?" Mal says, her voice tense with emotion.

"Sort of. I was trying to talk to Cody."

"You think he has something to do with Emma Lou . . . missing?"

"If it's drugs, then yeah. That whole damn Daweson family is up to their necks, legal and illegal."

"Legal?" Mal clears her throat. "That's new."

"A lot is new," I say, not elaborating that Emma Lou and my mother are part of that next generation of drug dealing.

"Be careful, Syd," she says. "You can't just go in swinging. You haven't been there in three years."

My face flushes, but I don't offer that I did literally go in swinging. As good as it felt, I shouldn't have hit Cody. "I'm from here. I know this place. It was bad luck."

There's a long pause, and I know she's considering if this fight is worth it. We've had plenty of conversations like this before. It drives her crazy when I "go rogue" when there are people who can help. "Anyway," I say, hoping we can skip ahead. "I keep seeing Dawesons. Not just Cody, but this friend I used to have, Deandre, and her mom. They're everywhere."

"Deandre?" She laughs a little. "Is that Dea D? The one you had a crush on?"

I roll my eyes at the ceiling. "That was a long time ago."

"How's she looking?"

I let the smile at the edge of my mouth spread. Mal is trying to cheer me up, and I appreciate it. Honestly, I need it. "She looks pretty good, actually. Got highlights and wears stilettos now. The kind with the red on the bottom."

"What'd you say about her bottom?"

I laugh along with Mal. "I gotta go, babe. Found some evidence yesterday. Need to meet with Sue at the regional office."

"You cannot do this on your own, Syd." There's more rustling, as if she's trying to be emphatic. "This is dangerous. You start doing your loner thing and you could end up missing, too. Or dead. Who knows who planted that skull for you and why. You're living for more than yourself."

"I know it." I lightly touch where the zip ties cut my wrists. "Did you tell your friends? What did your mom say?"

"Everyone is really excited. My mom cried."

"That's great," I say, meaning it while wishing I could feel the same way. I hate missing out on her joy and excitement. To witness something she's wanted for so long finally happen.

"Will you call me later?" Mal asks, her voice clear, as if she's prepared for any answer.

"There's a search party for Emma Lou tonight," I say. "I'll try you after, okay?"

"Sure," she says. "Please be careful."

We hang up and guilt spins the room. After a few minutes of deep breaths, I return to the thin mattress and quilted bedspread. The truth is I'm always pinned within these four walls. No matter who I married or where I moved, it was always going to be tenuous. Because everything good is taken away.

I try to focus on why I'm here, and being back also reminds me of what's worked to find Emma Lou in the past. Where she'd sometimes go. Out east of town, to start. Then the outlaw lands, named after a few miles of what would probably be called the sticks, mostly abandoned, and near a town that's been dead for decades. The search party tonight will not include the outlaw lands. It's too dangerous there, which means it's exactly where I need to go.

Leaving my bedroom, I step into the short hallway, where cartoons blare. Rayna's light snores float out of Emma Lou's room. She'd been too scared to sleep alone in her house, and I was relieved she agreed to come with me.

I enter the living room with a smile on my face, but my niece isn't there. The bright morning sun streams through the window. There are no signs of life either, except a cup of coffee and a fresh stick of butter next to the *Miami News-Record*.

My bare feet leave the carpet for the linoleum. I stare out the window over the kitchen sink and see my parents with Gracie in the nearest field. She snuggles into my mom's shoulder. My sister not being with them is a sharp pain.

I slip on Mom's worn garden shoes and head toward them. Not all of Oklahoma is flat, but our land certainly falls to stereotype. There is nothing but greening fields stretching out to more fields.

I weave through a small grove of persimmon trees and come to a new garden planted closer to the house. I can't resist taking a look and grin when I see the mounds of soil with early shoots of corn, squash, and beans. This is a Three Sisters Garden, the trio of vegetables that's the heart of Native agriculture. I haven't seen one planted since my grandma was alive. She'd use the plant's Cherokee names, selu, tuya, and iya.

A wave of grief hits me as I remember Grandma in her apron telling us about the long relationship the Cherokee have had with these plants. I may have rolled my eyes, but I secretly loved how she shared stories and connections in everything around us.

I crouch down to run my fingers over the tall, thin corn stalks. Soon they'll provide a place for the bean plants to climb so they aren't overwhelmed by the sprawling squash vines. The beans will provide nitrogen to the soil and help stabilize the corn during high winds. The squash leaves provide cover for the soil to stay moist and keep out weeds.

The Three Sisters have a symbiotic relationship. To Grandma, they held truths that should be kept alive and even honored. *We do not survive without the land. We must nurture and not only take.*

I squat down to pull a couple of weeds from one corner. There is a whisper inside me about whose hands planted this garden, but I don't have the courage to confirm it was Emma Lou who has nurtured this land and carried on the tradition. I also know that without help, she won't see the harvest.

I walk along the fence line, toward my parents and niece. As I approach, my gaze follows theirs out to the fields stretching to the horizon. "You looking for Charlie?" I call.

Gracie peeks over Mom's shoulder, gives a quick nod, then hides her eyes again.

I hadn't noticed last night, but Dad looks thinner, though his shoulders are still wide and strong. "You can see his horns." He points toward the old homestead, a now crumbling house built by the family who walked the Trail of Tears from Monroe County, Tennessee, to Northeast Oklahoma.

I squint, and sure enough, there is the top of the hulking bison's fuzzy head near a split tree. I'm glad to have something silly to talk about first. Dad likes to avoid difficult conversations, not that I'm going to let him this time. "Has he been good?" I ask with a little smirk.

"Been three weeks," Dad says, bragging about how long it's been since Charlie escaped and ran through downtown Picher. Sort of like the NO ACCIDENTS FOR X DAYS sign at a construction site. Dad reaches over to tickle Gracie's bare foot that hangs off my mom's hip. "You want to ride the buffalo?"

She giggles but doesn't look up as the sun lights her hair. The dirty blond with gold streaks is the same color as Emma Lou's and Luna's when they were her age. Gracie's legs are already tanned even though it's early spring, and that's like us girls, too. Gracie could have been the fourth of the so-called triplets.

I can't rush trust, even with a three-year-old. Phone calls aren't a relationship. They're a stopgap at best.

"I saw you last night, remember? Me and your aunt Mal send you books."

She makes a little whining noise, and I frown at Dad. "She thought Rayna was her momma," he says quietly.

My heart hurts from a new pain. To see how my sister's disappearance impacts her child. I'd worried about my niece, of course, but that's not the same as the experience firsthand. How scary it must be for such a young child to only know she wants her momma, who's not there.

"She's fine, aren't you?" Mom says in her bullish way, which usually works as a Band-Aid rather than a cure. "We're looking for birds. Gracie, where's the next one?"

She keeps her head hidden, so I scan the trees until I see a flash of red. "I spy with my little eye a red cardinal."

Her little head shoots up. "Where you see it?"

"By the persimmon grove."

"The dancing trees," Dad says of the long, skinny trunks that gently curve like a wave ripples after a skipping stone. Gracie's eyes go wide in the direction of the grove. "Want your aunt Syd to take you over there?"

My heart speeds up, and I hold out my arms to take her. She starts to go but shrinks back. "Mam-maw go, too."

"Sure, sunshine." Mom turns on her heel and starts her steady stride across the dewy grass.

"Say good morning to the ancestors," my dad calls.

I laugh. "You do that now?" I ask Mom, trying to keep pace.

My grandma had always called good morning and good night to our family cemetery. I thought Mom hated it.

She shrugs. "What's important feels different with grandchildren."

I gaze at the cemetery as I follow along. The main path leads to the first grave, the wife of the first Walker on this Oklahoma land. Grandma Ama said everything had been taken away from us: our land, our language, even children were taken from families to "kill the Indian and save the child" in residential schools that ripped families apart.

I had heard the stories but still had trouble imagining what my grandmother described. What had been passed down to her from her grandparents' experience, not another story. She shared what she knew from the past to warn me of the future.

The small cemetery gate is closed. I glance up at WALKER spelled in iron. In another month, honeysuckle vines will grow to reach the letters until Dad cuts them back.

"Good morning, *annadestors*!" Gracie calls as Mom pauses near the entrance. She points at a sparrow sitting on one of the thin, older graves.

"She'd stay here all day if I let her," Mom says.

Emma Lou is the same. She loves our family cemetery in a way I never understood.

Growing up, I resented the constant reminder of aunts and uncles, grandparents, people I loved, dead and in the ground. Other graves were for people I had no connection to other than the blood that was no longer in their veins. Their names known only because they were carved on a thin gravestone. An uneasy peace with death comes early when you're raised by the family cemetery.

There are people I knew and loved buried there now. My grandma

Ama is there. My grandfather and his two sisters, with Aunt Mercy's grave ready and waiting for her body, which is more normal than not around here. Next is the sweet face of an angel on a grave from a cousin who drowned as a toddler. There's Luna and her parents. The only graves not of our lineage, but certainly of our hearts.

There's a flash of Ghost Luna out in the newer section, near her own grave. I hear my grandma Ama singing "Amazing Grace" in Cherokee. Remember my relief and horror at having the remains of my best friend resting so close to our house. Her still-young parents hadn't bought plots, of course. And there was no insurance money. So Dad had offered to bury them with our family, and it felt right, despite the unconscionable wrongness of their murders.

Ghost Luna stands over her own grave, and even though I know she's not real, it's an ache without end seeing someone mourn their short life lost.

Mom leads us away from the cemetery and points. "I heard the red bird chirp there."

Gracie's little hand cups her ear. I am grateful for the distraction my niece provides as I try to temper this homecoming nostalgia. I grin at her and realize having a child around makes me want to try harder to be upbeat and positive. As if there's an audience and you want to be your best self standing on the stage. I want to share this thought with Mal, but I worry it'll give her the wrong idea.

I'm not ready for that stage. I was never meant for that spotlight. Maybe any spotlight.

The sharp call of a cardinal breaks my thoughts, and Gracie, like a pro, doesn't say anything until the bird is silent.

"There!" She confidently pokes her finger toward the bird-feeders, where he lands on the ground, a red drop in green.

"Boo jay, Mam-maw," Gracie whispers, and points to the top of the red bud tree. "My Gracie loves boo jays."

"Your who?" I ask her.

"She has an imaginary friend that she calls Gracie," Mom says. "Totally normal."

I hold up my hands. "I didn't say it wasn't normal. Emma Lou had that little imaginary friend-goat she'd feed, remember?"

Mom ignores me, so we head toward the bird. He screeches his annoyance.

"Does he remind you of a dinosaur?" I ask Gracie. "That's where they come from."

She giggles. "That's a boo jay."

"But he comes from a T. rex. Grrrrrrr."

"You silly." Gracie shakes her head. "That not a dino."

I bop my finger on her nose. "Guess they don't teach evolution in pre-K."

"They don't even teach it in the high school," Mom says, not sounding particularly bothered by it.

I feel the divide between us. How she clings to her religion. A language I never spoke or wanted to understand. A way of life that hates how I love. "Look, another boo jay, Gracie." I point at an elm tree closer to the house.

"Let's sneak," she whispers.

Mom puts her down, barefoot, and I don't say anything, though I'm worried about stickers, the little brown burs that scratch at skin. Even through socks, they can draw blood.

"What are you up to today?" I ask as Gracie dances away.

"I have to work," she says sharply. "I'll be home early for the search party."

"Oh," I say. "I'll help, of course."

"Talk to your dad." She raises her hands. "I'm leaving this in the hands of the Lord. He'll bring her home safe."

I start to argue but stop myself. "I hope so, Mom."

I put my arm around her thin shoulders, and we watch Gracie try to sneak up on another red bird. Mom's face is pinched in pain. A hard look that I imagine has been used by generations of women who managed to survive on these plains.

Mom pulls away from me and nods toward Rayna's car. "Sister's room smells like whiskey now. Your cousin does it to herself. Like Missy."

"I'm sorry about Rayna being in Emma Lou's room." I chew on the inside of my cheek. "Last thing I'd want to do is upset Gracie."

She heads up the porch, and I follow. "Kids recover fast. Some kids. You always did."

I could sleep at night, if that's what she means. I didn't wake up screaming like Emma Lou. I didn't run out to the graves or fields to yell at the devil to take me instead.

"Why is all your sewing stuff in my room?" I ask.

Mom reaches for the screen door handle but pauses at my question. "Emma Lou needed the hallway closet for work. It's locked, if you're wondering. And no, I don't have the key. It's one of those number locks. Like a bike lock, I guess."

She stares at me as if there's more she's not saying. Or maybe she knows I'm holding back secrets, too. But how can I form those words?

I was tied up in the back of a pickup last night with a gun pointed at me.

I punched Cody.

Mal is pregnant.

Emma Lou is pregnant.

Lord knows what the drugs are doing to that poor baby.

My jaw remains tight, molars pressing into molars, keeping all these truths locked away.

I hear Mal: *You're doing your loner thing.*

I search for true words I can say but then see a cloud of chat blowing up from the road.

"Dada!" Gracie starts to run toward the dust.

"He's early," Mom says.

There is no wind today, and the dust swirls and lingers like a bad omen, a reminder even, of an old lesson. You can only hide secrets if you're the only one who knows.

15

~~~~~

Cody pulls up to the house in a 2008 Ford, so I guess the strip club business is good. He springs out of the door like the blade of a snapped-open jackknife. "I'm getting Gracie early," he calls as Mom approaches.

"Sure," she says, but it's in a placating tone as if she's only revealed her first card. "Let me get her breakfast. You want eggs?"

I walk up behind Mom, who's got one foot in the grass and the other in the dirt of the driveway by the truck's back tire. Then I see what's got Mom angling. Cody looks terrible. And that's coming from someone who already hates the sight of him.

He's glaring at me, and it makes the bruise I gave him under his right eye flush darker. His eyes are rimmed in red like he's been up all night putting God knows what into his body. There's a slight tremor in both his arms as he pulls on his ratty baseball cap.

"I don't want eggs, June. I want my daughter. She can eat at home."

"All right, then. I'll get her backpack."

Mom heads toward the house. Seeing her fold to Cody makes me want to do the opposite. Ghost Luna approaches the scene, almost like a warning, but I take a step closer to him. "You're not doing anything stupid."

"Like what?"

"Keeping Gracie from her family. Doing it when you're in no condition to take care of a child."

"What do you know about taking care of a child?" He sticks out his stubbly jaw. "She's safe with me."

I swallow thickly at the implication. "Is she not safe here?"

"I don't know." His voice is quiet. "I want her with me."

I glance at where Gracie is dancing around my dad. She's near her momma's garden. "I'm searching town and the outlaw lands," I say, trying not to sound like a gawking tourist. As if I have a right to look there as much as anyone. "If Sister is . . . pregnant, then I don't know how you aren't doing the same."

"We don't all get to do whatever the fuck we want. I have a business to run. I have responsibilities. I have to take care of my family—"

"Like you took care of Emma Lou?"

He spits on the ground. "You better be careful where you look, Syd."

"Look for what?" my dad asks, suddenly behind me.

Cody rolls his shoulders. "Your daughter is going to the outlaw lands to search for Emma Lou."

"Really?" he asks. "By yourself?"

"I'll be fine."

Cody snickers, the sound sticking in his throat. "People are out there because they don't want to be found. Trust me, you don't want them to find you either."

"Are you threatening me?" I take another step closer and his fists clench.

"I'll drive you, Syd." Dad puts a hand on my shoulder. "I'd like to look, too."

"Dad, you don't need to, really."

"Doing your loner thing," says Ghost Luna from behind me.

"Take him up on the offer," Cody says, and there's that threat again.

Dad's gaze has grown concerned, if not suspicious. "You don't need me, but I'd like to go. If Gracie isn't around, I get stir-crazy with your mom taking Emma Lou's shifts at Wings."

Dad is lying because he's like me, and we love to be alone. Live for it, in a lot of ways. But I see he's worried, and he's had enough of that lately. "Sure."

"Dada!" yells Gracie with a little backpack bouncing on her shoulders. Mom trails behind with a Barbie suitcase.

"What all did you bring, girl?" He scoops her into his wiry arms. "We got plenty of clothes at the house."

"I need princess dresses, Dada. For me and Gracie."

"She's got an imaginary friend," Cody says quickly. "Ain't nothing wrong with her."

"Don't think you're in a place to judge," says Ghost Luna from somewhere I don't care to find.

"I think it's cute," I say to my niece.

"We packed every princess dress in the house." Mom holds up her hands. "Had to have her way. Like her momma."

"Or her sister," Cody says to me. He doesn't wait for a response and instead loads Gracie into the car seat in his truck cab. He pulls out fast, the dust shooting up into the air.

Mom fires a look in Dad's direction, then marches toward the house. "I'm making scrambled eggs. If no one eats them, fine by me."

"We're heading out," I call. "But thanks."

Mom turns to send another look to both of us but doesn't say anything until the porch door slams.

"Cody is doing his best," Dad says.

"Is he?" I glare toward the dirt cloud over the road from Cody's truck. "He seems like the same old druggie dickhead."

Dad presses his lips together as if really considering what I'm saying. "He's trying."

I blink at him. "I wish he was still in jail."

"Well, you did your best there," Dad says with some edge to his tone.

Standing on these ancestral acres, I feel like an outsider. As if Cody living near here, no matter what he did or does, connects him more to my family. As if it's only proximity, not behavior, that counts. "Let me get my stuff, and we can go."

I hurry inside, not acknowledging my mother beating the eggs in a bowl like they owe her money. I grab my phone and wallet and peek in to see Rayna is still sleeping. I leave a little note on the Wings notepad on the nightstand—*Be back soon*—and hurry out the door.

The faded green truck is running with Dad behind the wheel. I slide into the passenger seat, already warm from the morning sun. There's duct tape over a hole in the middle where Emma Lou accidentally jammed her fishing pole. The radio only picks up the local gospel station and the tape deck eject button hasn't worked since I could drive.

Dad pats the steering wheel, and I shake my head affectionately that the old girl is still running.

"We should check the rentals east of town," I say about the area I'd usually go first.

"Those are boarded up," he says. "Dawesons owned most of them. They were first in line to be bought out."

"How much have they made so far?"

Dad makes a small humming noise. "Almost three hundred thousand."

"It's Quapaw land," I say, angry that they made money on something that wasn't theirs.

"The BIA let them lease it generations back, so they built on it. That's what they were paid for, whether it's their land or not."

"Lease, huh?" I say, remembering another terrible thing the BIA did to Native landowners. Taking the land and putting the rent in "trusts" that were never paid. "The BIA didn't actually collect the rent. Or if they did, they kept it."

"It's complicated." Dad's shoulders slacken as if he can't keep up this toe-the-line act. "I was glad those shacks were vacated. Vern's place has a sinkhole in the front yard. Emma Lou used to hang out there."

My mind flashes to finding Emma Lou wild and barefoot trying to build a garden for angels with the scrap metal in the front yard. You can always tell the meth houses by all the trash. She'd hit and kicked and screamed when I'd dragged her away. That might have been the time she bit me.

Dad goes slow down the dirt road until the landscape shifts from green fields to the lunar landscape of my hometown.

Huge hills of shimmering white gravel chat rise from flat emptiness. Some of the hills are hundreds of feet high. The beauty of chat is a dangerous illusion, like the promises made by the companies who leased the land for the rights to dig it up and eventually abandon it.

My grandma said there was once a chat pile so high you could see it miles away in Miami, like a mountain grew on the prairie.

An eighteen-wheeler blasts by us on Highway 69, which takes us to downtown Picher. Dad presses the gas, and we're speeding past landscape filled with not just chat, but rusted-out machines, concrete columns, scattered trash, and old junk cars.

We pass a large chat pile I remember from high school. Guys would build a bonfire to burn anything not bolted down, from tires to paint cans. As everyone got drunker, they'd slide down the piles of chat on cardboard boxes like it was the first snow.

I watched, afraid to seem like I cared. I remember Dea D would be there. Deandre, I guess. I hated how she'd draw my gaze. Always popular, since her mom was happy to supply booze and drugs. She'd sometimes look my way. I'd wonder if she was remembering when we were friends. Or if she was remembering her uncles made it so we never could be again.

But I was never able to focus on Deandre for long because I'd need to watch Emma Lou. She'd dance too close to the fire. Slide down the chat on a piece of cardboard despite not being able to see what she was headed for. Flirt with a dumbass guy to make Cody jealous, best case. Other times, she'd wander off in the dangerous dark, searching. For the rabbit in the moon. For the devil. For Luna. I was tired of asking by then because the answers never made sense.

Things weren't good with Sister, but drugs made all the delusions and incessant searching so much worse. "You think she was clean?" I ask finally.

Dad sighs and taps a finger on the steering wheel. "I do. She was doing good. Real good. She liked her job. Gracie was happy. Cody seems to have calmed down."

I cross my arms and keep my skepticism to myself. "So Sister is great and then *poof*?"

"Well . . ." Dad clicks a little from the side of his mouth. "She'd been talking about Luna again. Visiting the grave more. Leaving little trinkets on her tombstone with Gracie. Called it her angel garden."

"Yeah," I say, thinking of the meth head's house, though I had helped her build plenty of them when we were girls. "But where would she go?" My gaze snaps to my dad as I picture Emma Lou wandering the chat piles. Sleeping in our family cemetery when Aunt Mercy told her the veil was thin. "She was looking for Luna's ghost again? Why didn't you stop her?"

The question hangs in the silence as Dad slows down once we hit the city limits. My dad's face has turned pinkish, a sign of a temper he's never lost.

I stare up at the town's water tower with the faded red letters spelling PICHER and in smaller letters underneath GORILLAS SINCE 1918. Sometimes you'd see cartoons with gorillas smiling in mining hats, like the canary in the coal mine, I guess.

"Sister wanted to remember." Dad clears his throat. "You made your choice to stay away. We chose to stay together and deal with pain in our own ways. I know I haven't always done my best, but—"

"No, Dad, I'm sorry," I say, knowing I was too callous. Living far away has allowed me to compartmentalize and, in some ways, move on. My parents and Emma Lou see Luna's family, who still live in Picher. Dad's the school's Native counselor, so he advises Luna's cousins. Helps explain to the parents what's needed for the local junior or state college or vocational school. My parents had two children survive, while Luna and her parents are dead.

Emma Lou and I are survivors, the only survivors, and every

day I try to remember our lives are a gift. Even if it was given through blood. "Of course remembering Luna matters." I pick at the small scar on the tip of my pointer finger and miss Emma Lou as much as Luna.

"Most people don't think about it," he says. "It's been fifteen years this month and everyone has moved on. Emma Lou wanted to have a remembrance ceremony on the Myers land. But the BIA wasn't going to allow that. She put a little mobile up."

"I had no idea the BIA owned the Myers land until this assignment," I say, not wanting to linger on how much I want that ceremony to happen. Even if I have no right to be there.

"They manage it. Like all the other Native land that was once valuable. Not that many saw a cent."

I don't know how many times I've been asked if I was raised on a reservation. But that's not how things were done in Northeast Oklahoma. People were given plots of land, allotments, instead of all being forced into one area.

I think of Missy's land, both the Cherokee and Quapaw allotments. "Someone should sue."

Dad grins at me. "Yeah, right. Those courts ain't made for us."

We pass the pharmacy and post office. Pause at the only stoplight and continue past the volunteer fire station, where the search will begin tonight. Dad is heading for the outlaw lands, a place I didn't have to go often, thankfully, with Emma Lou usually being strung out in town.

More chat piles rise as we leave the town and Dad turns onto a dirt road.

I open the glove box and dig through McDonald's napkins and truck registration forms for Dad's small binoculars.

"I've looked every day since she went missing," Dad says. "Strange no one has found her car."

I focus the binoculars and scan the first trailer, easily a quarter mile off the main road. There are several rusted-out cars near it, but none of them are Emma Lou's Grand Am.

We pass another four trailers in the next several miles. This is not the kind of place where you could just knock and ask for a cup of sugar. I've yet to see a window not boarded up or covered in newspaper or aluminum foil.

"Meth is changing right now," Dad says as he turns down another long, empty dirt road. "State passed laws so dealers can't buy the over-the-counter stuff they need to cook. Not that it's stopped meth use. People have to find it from new places."

I drop the binoculars between us. "Like Deandre?"

"That's all legal." Dad shakes his head. "I mean meth is coming from Mexico now."

I glance at him. "That'll bring cartels, Dad."

He suddenly slams on his brakes, and I look ahead. There's a twist of smoke rising into the air. I grab the binoculars and focus on orange flames erupting from a trailer.

Thick black smoke curls into the air. I look closer and there's a truck outside. "Someone is there. We should go see if they need help."

Dad throws the truck in reverse. "That's the last thing they'll want."

"Dad, what if Sister is in there?"

He shakes his head. "Somebody is burning a meth trailer. It happens all the time out here, likely a retaliation thing. We do not want to get involved."

Dad drives fast down the road and he's turning back toward home. But seeing that fire has taken me back to that night.

"Can we go by Luna's place?" I ask, not realizing that's where I wanted to go until I hear myself say it. "I want to see Sister's memorial for her again."

Dad doesn't say anything, continues to drive. He parks by the mobile and turns off the truck. "Burning trailers bring back some bad memories, kid."

"Same for me," I say softly, staring at Emma Lou's face on the poster.

"I didn't see you and Emma Lou hiding in the field at first."

"We were out there awhile," I say. Dad and Mom had been at my grandma Ama's since we were at Luna's. Dad called the fire department as soon as he saw the flames. Then he'd run to find us.

"Worst moment of my life was looking across the fields from the kitchen window to see the Myers trailer on fire. Felt like . . . my soul was ripped out of my body knowing both my girls were inside."

"I don't remember Luna's parents coming back. I barely remember anything while we were out there hiding until you found us."

"I was about to run into the fire. You stood up from behind some bushes and had Sister in a bear hug."

"You would have died if you'd run into those flames."

"I was more than prepared for that." His gaze is so haunted as he shuts his eyes. "I was not leaving my girls to burn up and die alone. But I found you. I'll never forgive myself for not being able to save the Myers family."

I could say, *It's not your fault*, but I'd be a hypocrite since I live with the same regret, too.

When Dad found us, he put his hands on both our shoulders, and it was as if he had broken a trance: we snapped. I started screaming and Emma Lou was finally free to run toward the fire. Dad caught her and took us home. I don't remember anything else that night. Hushed whispers, maybe, Mom and Dad scared as they floated from my room and back to Emma Lou's. Dad took us to the BIA police the next day. Sue's dad, Ronny, took my statement.

You didn't die because you used that gun, little girl.

You should be proud.

There was only one bullet. One bullet.

If there'd been two, you'd have killed them both.

Don't let it eat you up.

Only one bullet, little girl, only one.

If somehow there had been two bullets, surely I could have stopped them both. No matter the bile rising in my throat. No matter the tremble in my fingers and tears in my eyes. If another life must be taken, I could do that for Luna.

The questions lingered longer than the rumors, but it always came back to drugs and money.

Why else would the Daweson brothers visit at night with guns?

Myers had his share of drug troubles, right?

Couldn't keep a job.

Selling weed.

Just like his old man.

Living off the government.

I had few answers in the aftermath. Superintendent Ronny Dove seemed to agree with the rumors. He pieced the night together in a press conference, announcing that the remains of all five bodies had been identified. Luna's father owed drug money to the two Dawesons. Something went wrong. Shots fired and an explosion that burned through the night. He mentioned two juveniles had escaped. He didn't release our names, but everyone knew.

There were rumors I'd shot the whole family and taken the money.

No other witnesses. Though I'd always questioned if Cody and Sue had been there and were too scared to get help.

Now Sister is gone again.

"If you think Sister is clean, why aren't you going crazy?" I ask him.

He lets out a long exhale. "Aunt Mercy says she's alive." He holds up his hands before I can lay into him. "I've always been a sucker for hope. This time feels different."

"Different how?"

Dad stares in the direction of their trailer. Tall grasses grow around concrete blocks that indicate something else was once there. "Sister didn't hide from the devil like when you were girls. This time, she was chasing him. Aunt Mercy says . . . maybe she found him."

My gaze connects with his before I say, "Maybe he's been here all along."

16

〜〜〜

I adjust my sunglasses in the noon sun outside the Bureau of Indian Affairs Eastern Oklahoma office. I'd talked to Jo briefly this morning and she confirmed what I guessed: I needed to give Sue the ring as potential evidence.

"Don't trust her, but act like you're playing along," Jo had said.

"A peace offering?"

"Or Trojan horse. Your call."

The BIA building is alone in a field about a mile down the road from Miami High School. Last I looked at the BIA organizational chart, there are twenty people working here.

In contrast, Rhode Island is in the Eastern US region of the BIA, which does not comprise half of one state like this office, but rather twenty-seven states. That's how many indigenous people were forced to this part of Oklahoma.

When I was little, I remember asking my grandma, *Isn't everyone a little Indian?* After all, Mom said we were "part Cherokee."

Rayna was Cherokee and Quapaw. Luna was Cherokee, too, going to the same free doctors and dentists that we did.

Grandma seemed angry at my question. *You* are *Cherokee. Counting blood is for white people.*

That became clear in college. When people learned I'm Cherokee, they often asked "how much," as if I needed to be validated or dismissed. If I felt defensive, I'd say, "I'm on the tribal rolls" or "My family walked the Trail of Tears." But if I wanted to leave the conversation, I'd say another truth, "A sixty-fourth," and try to ignore whatever comment came next. Usually, *Oh, so not like half or anything. Not* that *much.*

I never had the courage to ask how much blood *they* thought is enough for me to claim my heritage.

Not that I had an easy answer. Mixing of blood is a complicated topic among tribes, the Cherokee especially, who seemed to engage in it as early as anyone. It's even complicated within my family. My grandfather—a white farmer—died many years before I was born. Grandma Ama never spoke of him, and I always had the sense that she'd never have chosen him to marry. She had mentioned that her parents wanted her to marry a white man. That mixing of blood was a strategy they chose for survival.

So does that make me less Cherokee?

Staring out at the flat land, I see my grandma shelling black walnuts as her gaze turns hard. She looked across the fields where the family's original house was crumbling. These moments of warning often happened on the porch when she was cracking nuts or snapping peas as her mother and her mother's mother had done.

They're trying to erase us. Every story you tell. Every bead you sew and wear. Every heirloom you honor and pass down. Every Cherokee word you speak. We bring our ancestors closer so they can guide us back to the land.

As I head toward the tinted glass and simple boxy shape of the BIA building, I realize I became an archeologist out of anger. I might have rolled my eyes at my grandma's talk of a Great Spirit, but I hated the idea of our stories and history being stolen along with the land.

Even as my longing for connection grows, it's difficult when so much of our legacy is a story of injustice. As if barbed wires have been woven into our family blankets.

My boots crunch on the gravel pathway leading to locked double doors. I press the buzzer and a woman says hello.

"I'm here to see Sue," I say.

"Superintendent Dove?"

"Yeah, I'm on regional assignment. Syd Walker."

Instead of responding, the woman buzzes the door open, and I head inside. I knew Sue started working for the Bureau of Indian Affairs while she was in college, so a couple of years before me. Being in different parts of the country meant we never had a reason to work together or even talk about our shared employer. I hadn't realized she'd moved up to the top job in the region. She had to be the youngest superintendent of the twelve regional agencies, maybe by a decade.

The door closes hard behind me and there is a small waiting room with a map of Ottawa County on the wall. An older woman waves for me to keep walking. I stride past cubicles on both sides, envious of what it'd be like to be in an office like this instead of basically working out of my truck.

The hallway ends, and I turn right toward what look like the larger offices. Before I can confirm my hunch, Sue steps out from behind a door. There are two men behind her, and I recognize one of them from the buyout meeting.

"This is Syd Walker, Noah's daughter," Sue says casually to them, as if this was the plan all along.

The men ask me to tell my parents hi and then leave without saying who the hi is from.

Sue is in a tight skirt and crisp white shirt. She's balancing a laptop on a yellow legal pad, with a shiny pen behind her ear. "I thought you'd come by next week after you're settled," she says, and starts walking.

I follow quickly and she opens another door labeled SUPER-INTENDENT DOVE. "Did they use the same sign for your dad?" I ask.

She grins at me. "Good guess."

Sue was nostalgic growing up. She seemed to revere the past. It never bothered her to get teased for wearing her mom's dresses after she passed away. I'd go with her to the Salvation Army store, where she only bought used and vintage. I grin to myself as I realize she didn't even get a new job but took over her dad's.

As if the thought conjured him, I lock eyes with a painting of Ronny Dove on the wall. He's serious in his worn gray Stetson and turquoise-studded bolo tie in his flashy—for Miami—gray suit.

Sue's office has a big tinted window that overlooks an empty field. Telephone wires cross in the distance, and a red-tailed hawk circles a patch of land looking for lunch. I start to point it out but realize she must see them every day.

"How are your wrists?" she asks after the door is shut.

"Okay." I touch the left one, which still throbs even after fresh bandages and antiseptic. "Your brother grew up."

She shakes her head as if he's just pelted us with a water balloon. "It's a post-military phase. Not many jobs right now that pay cash and don't ask questions."

I chew on the inside of my cheek to keep things professional. "I wonder what would have happened if you didn't show up."

She pulls the pen from behind her ear and drops it onto her desk. "Stay away from them so you don't find out."

"Rayna says everyone calls them the dipshits."

"I've heard that," Sue says. "I'm sure you weren't thrilled to know your sister and mother were working for the Dawesons either."

I raise my eyebrows. "But that's on the up-and-up, right?"

"As far as I know," Sue says coolly. "Look, if you want to concentrate on your sister for a few days—"

"I can do more than one thing at a time. In fact, I brought some evidence."

I hand her two plastic bags, one with the ring and one with the receipt unrolled. Her eyebrows shoot up. "We had the metal detectors out."

"It wasn't in the ground," I say. "It was deep inside the tree where the skull was placed."

"We shouldn't have missed that." Sue's neck flushes red. "So it's a receipt for gum and a . . . what are those rings called?"

"Panda coin ring." I watch as she inspects it closer. "From 1991."

"Shit, does that say *Find me*?" Sue blows out a breath. "Where did you get this?"

I swallow to keep my patience. "Inside the tree where the skull was placed. It's rotted out. We used to hide messages in it as girls."

Sue nods, though she and I weren't close when we did that. She was more my teenage friend than a girlhood buddy. "So you think this is from Emma Lou? And the skull, too?"

I sigh, because honestly that just doesn't sound like Emma Lou.

"How would you know?" asks Ghost Luna, pulling my gaze to her in the corner of the room. "A lot can change in three years."

"What?" Sue asks.

"Sorry, just distracted." I turn back toward Sue. "It was maybe Emma Lou. The gum was Luna's favorite. Emma Lou might've made a little memorial for her."

Sue shakes her head. "They should have gotten your sister some real help."

I swallow my reply because it wouldn't help either of us. It's one thing for me to have criticisms of Emma Lou or how my family deals with her issues, but I'm not interested in two cents from someone outside the family.

Ghost Luna makes a ticking noise. "Don't you think that's how your family sees you?"

"What's with those old boxes?" I ask Sue, wanting an immediate change in topic.

She stands up from her desk and approaches a small stack. "This is what survived the flood. The buyout committee requested allotment maps for any land the BIA doesn't manage."

I remember hearing their old office in Miami was wiped out by the swollen Neosho River during a hundred-year-flood situation. "Was the flood before your dad retired?" I ask, and head over toward the boxes. "I doubt much was online."

"Hardly anything," Sue says, sounding frustrated.

"I'm surprised the buyout committee cares about the allotment land. The way I understand it, people are only getting paid for houses."

"These are highly complicated matters." Sue returns to her chair and gestures for me to follow back across the room. "Everyone is doing their best in difficult circumstances."

"You sound like a press release." I drop into the chair across from her desk and think of my aunt Missy and how she's being paid for only her house, not the land she rightly owns. "Shouldn't the BIA be advocating that the tribal members who own the land get paid the money? Instead of the white people who built houses on it and didn't pay rent?"

Sue flashes a diplomatic smile. "Our office is not getting involved in the buyout process."

"That's so convenient," I say, not sure why I'm itching to lay into her, considering she rescued me and Rayna last night. "The BIA got involved when there was lead found on Quapaw land. Or even when a Quapaw person was thriving as a landlord to a business. The BIA stepped right in and took the land away. Legally got the landowners ruled incompetent. Most never saw a dime."

"Sheesh," says Sue. "Feels like I'm at a tribal council meeting."

"Maybe you should listen."

"You and I always argued," she says with a smile. "Couple Tauruses."

"Whatever, you're a cusp," I say. "Two-faced Gemini."

"I still have the book of birthdays," she says, referring to the astrology book we loved as teenagers. "I should look up a few colleagues who are driving me crazy."

In that moment, I can almost see my best friend. There's the pull to share parts of my life with a person who once knew so many of my secrets. "Seems like BIA should do more. Finally help tribes."

"Bad blood spilled is a stain that never goes away," Sue says quietly. "I'm proud to be helping the tribes. Proud to advocate for people who have been silenced."

I nod and don't argue, because sometimes I tell myself the

same thing. She's still looking at me in that old way, like nothing I do surprises her.

This moment is familiar, reminding me of when I told her I felt different from other girls. That my grandma told me I was Two Spirit—a new term at the time in 1990—which, in a simple way, means I have both the masculine and feminine spirits within me. Being Two Spirit is an honor that goes back long before any labels or colonist beliefs. It's a sacred role that honors Native life outside of how non-indigenous view gender.

But sure, Two Spirit often means gay. And Sue didn't point a finger in my face and yell, *I knew it!* Or ask if I was in love with her. Or ask if it happened because of the devils. Or ask if that meant I'd lied to her when I said I liked a boy from our class (which I hadn't lied about). All scenarios I'd imagined a thousand times as an excuse to keep who I was hidden from everyone, even her. All she said was she was glad I told her.

I don't want to return to those days, because I have changed, and she certainly has, too. "Anything in those flood boxes related to the skull case?" I ask.

"Naw," Sue says quickly. "The case is only a folder at this point." She pulls a set of keys out of her pocket to unlock and open a drawer. She locks it again before dropping the file onto the desk. "No prints on the skull or anything. Damnedest thing."

I glance at my suitcase, where the case file contains the intern badge Sue doesn't know about yet. If she did, she could easily use the evidence and my connection to the case to get me thrown off it. "My boss said you didn't want me here."

Sue sighs as if that was something she wished I didn't know. "Look, I have this handled. More people, more problems. See last night."

"What can you tell me about the skull?"

Sue pushes the folder across her desk. "An anonymous tip. Called in to the front desk here. Answered, so no recording. Male, though."

Grabbing the file, I drop back into the chair and flip it open. There hadn't been any additional analysis on the skull. "How long until we know more?"

"Hoping a favor pays off and we get lab results soon. Wouldn't hold my breath."

"The local police don't seem interested. You're certain since it was Quapaw land that the skull is from someone Native?"

"That's my view."

"My boss, Jo, says you've been more receptive to missing and murdered Native women than most."

There's a flash of pride in her big brown eyes. I remember how her dad called her a Cherokee princess, even though that's something only white people claim. "I'm aware that Native girls go missing and there's not a lot of recourse for families."

"Except you didn't want help with this one?"

She smirks at me. "This is a cold case at best. I've got a lot more on my radar."

"Well, I'll do my best to stay out of your way."

We stare at each other for a moment as if we both recognize all we know of the other and all we don't. "Our former archeologist left all his stuff when he quit to go deal blackjack."

I nod my gratitude, though that's the least she should do for an agent assigned here.

She glances at her watch. "I gotta get going."

"Lunch date?" I ask as I stand.

"Hardly." She flushes a little as she grabs her purse over the back of her chair. "They're naming Eighth Street after my dad. I have a mic check for a speech I'm giving at a big ceremony tonight at the Coleman Theatre. Sorry to miss the search for your sister."

"We'll have plenty of help. I'm sure he'd be proud." I think of how little I saw Sue's dad, even though she and I were together all the time in high school. Ronny Dove was always working, and I only had one terrible occasion to see him do that firsthand.

Only one bullet.

"He'd have loved having a street named after him," she says, her eyes a little watery. "I'll try to rush the labs on these items you found. Let me know if you find anything else on the Myers land."

"I will," I lie.

She pauses before opening the door but doesn't look back at me. "Strange that you're back and your sister is gone. You're the only thing left from that terrible night. Almost feels like you're a clue."

I cross my arms, not sure what she's getting at, exactly.

"Maybe you need to dig there, too, Syd."

17

~~~~~

Growing up, people from Miami called people from Picher chat rats. We called them stuck-up. It wasn't much of a rivalry since we were in different sports divisions and Picher had about five percent of their population. I could see their point when comparing Picher's sparse few blocks of mostly boarded-up businesses surrounded by piles of chat to Miami's bustling downtown, which included the historic Coleman Theatre, built with Picher mine fortune money.

There are restaurants, fast food, and a big library with pretty statues outside. A tourism billboard has the town's pronunciation, *Mi-am-MUH*. Like the better-off cousin who gets a new bike for Christmas every year, and Picher is the cousin too proud to take the hand-me-down.

A sign says CHAPTERS, and I'm surprised to see a charming bookstore with little café tables outside where people are sipping from Starbucks cups. I turn toward the hospital and other medical buildings clustered in the few blocks past the Pizza Hut Express.

I arrive at Dr. Candy's medical building in the same location, but I'm pretty sure it used to be puke-yellow stucco. Now it's a warm cream with shingle siding. Pansies are edged around a copper birdbath. There's a bench if someone wanted to sit outside a doctor's office to enjoy fresh air and the cars zipping down A Street.

I park next to my dad's green truck in the small lot across the street. First I text Jo to let her know about the meeting with Sue. Then I text my mom that I'm swinging by and leave the Jeep quickly so she doesn't have time to answer with a no. I cross the one-way street toward the front entrance. There's a new sign, WINGS AD-DICTION RECOVERY, written over angel wings. The birdbath is empty except for cigarette butts.

Mom is outside waiting for me as I approach the glass door. She's wearing nice slacks and another brightly printed floral shirt. I didn't think she owned anything other than drab browns. "Is that from Stage?" I ask, referring to the only clothing store I could imagine my mom shopping at other than Walmart.

"Deandre sells clothes." Mom reaches into her purse and pulls out a gold lipstick tube. I stifle a gasp as she spreads a deep red color across her lips. She didn't even wear lip gloss at my wedding. "And makeup. She has a whole group of women selling for her."

"Like a pyramid scheme?"

"No." Mom pops her lips as she spreads the color. "But I went to a party at her house and bought some stuff. She wants me to join her . . . Sales Squad, she calls it. Bless her heart. Like I'm going to go onto Facebook and bother my friends with girl-power inspirational quotes to buy these flower tops."

I know she's trying to make light of it, but I'm unsettled. Not that she looks different—that would be too simple. More that she's changed, and she wants everyone to see it. Another reminder of how much I don't understand. "Is money that tight?" I ask.

She glances around. "I'm done getting into it with you. You aren't here, so it's not your business. Now, what do you need?"

I push down the snotty response and try for mature. "I have a few questions for Deandre. Short and sweet, I promise."

"Your sister needs this job. I need this job. Don't screw anything up." Mom doesn't wait for a response and instead opens the door for me to go inside.

We head straight into a waiting room with a dozen chairs, all empty, except for two women sitting across from each other. Both have bouncing legs and seem to be in a scratching contest. Not that I mean to be unsympathetic. Addiction is terrible. I'm skeptical of how much good these places do, handing out opioids for a hangnail. Feels like when they'd put real cocaine in Coca-Cola. Like something we'll look back on as a terrible, profit-led mistake.

Mom waves at the woman farthest from us. "Debbie, how you doing?" The woman turns with a scowl. "I know," Mom says softly. "We'll get you fixed up soon."

A slightly familiar-looking lady rises from behind a glass partition. There is a CASH ONLY sign on one side. On the other, a NO FIREARMS with Yosemite Sam circled and a line through him.

This only reminds me of why Emma Lou should never have been working here, even if the drugs are legal.

"Well, is that Syd?" the woman behind the glass says with warm eyes to match her grandmotherly face. Her grayish hair has streaks of purple that coordinate with her skirt and top. Deandre collection, if I had to guess. "I haven't seen you since your wedding reception. Oh—" Her face flushes. "I guess I didn't see you, actually. I saw your parents. And the wedding picture in the paper."

"It's good to see you now." I get close enough to read her name tag. "Trudy, how you been?"

"Can't complain." She snaps a folder shut. "Let me buzz you gals in."

Mom leads the way into the office, where Trudy is bringing over a bag. "Here you go, June. Be sure to go back by if they don't answer their door the first time."

"I call, too," Mom says, seeming defensive.

"This is different than checking people in, June." She smiles as if trying to make a joke. There's an undercurrent to her tone. As if Mom isn't quite doing Emma Lou's job right. "People with bills don't answer unknown numbers. Heck, I don't either."

"I'll go by twice and call." Mom puts a hand on my shoulder. "Syd wanted to say hi to Deandre. Is she back from lunch?"

"What a good girl to come help find Emma Lou." Trudy's demeanor shifts back to grandmother. "They'll find her. I'm sure it's a misunderstanding. Having fun with her girls or maybe took off with a new guy."

Mom provides a fake smile. "I bet you're right."

"I love your top," I say to her. "Is it the same as Mom's? From one of those parties?"

"Of course," Trudy says with a wink. "This is from Deandre's latest collection. You have to get there fast if you want one."

"She makes the clothes?" I say, surprised.

"She sells them." Trudy brushes a hand across the ruffle neckline. "Only at her parties. VIP." She wiggles her shoulders. "June, you better get going. There's twenty-five in there. Thursdays are busy-busy."

Mom hefts the bag over her narrow shoulder. "Short and sweet," she says to me with her hard look that could have endured the dust bowl.

"I'm not going to pitch a tent," I say with some whine in my voice. Mom smiles at Trudy and then leaves quickly. I'd imagine delivering that many prescriptions would take all day.

I turn back to my new best friend Trudy. "Did Emma Lou say she was running around with a new guy?" I ask as casually as possible. "I hope so. Cody is not my favorite."

"Ooooh, don't say that too loud around here." Trudy play-slaps my arm. "He and Deandre are thick as thieves." She leans a little toward me. "But I get it."

"Family is family, even if we don't pick them." I smile at her. "Purple really is your color. You should wear it every day."

"Well, aren't you as sweet as your sister." Trudy lets out a little sigh. "We really miss her. She would deliver free vegetables from her garden with the prescriptions. She wants to help people."

"She's amazing," I say, not adding she's an Oxy angel. "Do you know who she was delivering to the last day she worked?"

Trudy grimaces. "That's confidential medical information, sweetie."

I try for admonished and know I must keep pushing. "I wouldn't ask if it wasn't so important. Trudy, I'm going to tell you something even my mom doesn't know."

"Oh." She scoots her chair closer as I lean forward.

"Emma Lou . . . is pregnant."

Her hand flies over her mouth as if she's already keeping the secret. "Sweet Jesus," she whispers.

I feel both guilt and relief at sharing this with someone. "I'm thinking maybe she said something to someone about where she was going? I wouldn't bother anyone, of course. Just say I'm doing a random search. Wings would never be mentioned."

Trudy's gaze skitters back to where I assume Deandre's office is and then back to me. "I wish I could help . . ."

I stand there staring into her eyes, making it as awkward as possible. Trudy seems to be the type to hate silence. Finally, she breaks.

"Tell you what." She takes my hand. "You ask Deandre, and if she says yes, then you can take a peek. Between us, I think you're right. It might tell you something you need to know."

That would have to be good enough for now. "Thank you so much." I go in for a hug and enjoy her grandmotherly softness.

"Now, let's get you in there." She hops up and leads me down the hallway. "Deandre has a big presentation for the Miami business committee for her newest real estate development. Have you been to Elevated Estates yet?"

"Been where?" I ask as we zip past a closed door.

"Deandre and her husband, Tyler, built a development. The nicest houses outside of Grand Lake. But Toby Keith has a place there, so who can compete with that?"

I pause to glance inside an open office and see a large desk with several graduation certificates for Dr. Anthony M. Canter. "Does he still come in?" I ask.

"Best he can," she says, quickly rushing us past. Trudy pauses outside the last door, which is open a sliver. She waggles her thin eyebrows and puts a finger over her lips but motions me closer. We listen at the crack in the door.

"And so, Councilmen, I again come to you and the city of Miami with an opportunity. But this time, it's not only because of a demand for quality housing. It's also about the people of Picher seeing justice. To create real and lasting homes for those who have had so much taken away. Thank you."

Trudy begins to lightly clap, and I follow her inside the office. "Absolutely brilliant, Deandre. The city council would be idiots not to approve your plan."

"If only intelligence were a requirement to be elected," she says with a smile that falls as her gaze goes to me. "Hello, Syd. This is a surprise."

I grin in the way I always did when Deandre, a pretty, popular girl, looked my way. I immediately feel stupid that the reaction still lives inside me. "You look great," I stammer, trying to be cool and failing. "You have changed since high school . . . but all for the better."

She lets out a deep chuckle and looks at Trudy, adjusting her tight leather suit jacket. "I never get tired of hearing that. Have a seat. Let's catch up before I have to run." She hands a stack of papers to Trudy. "Can you get these filed by one p.m.?"

"Of course." She pauses before she leaves the room. "Oh, Jill RSVP'd to the party. Sorry!"

Deandre rolls her eyes but then focuses back on me. "I have four minutes before I have to haul these Louboutins over to the presentation." She taps her chin. "Now, remind me. You got married to a . . ."

"Mallory," I say. "We've been married three years. She's an optometrist."

"Fab," Deandre says. "You're with the BIA, right?"

"Archeologist."

She looks at me, surprised. "Like dinosaur bones?"

"More *Indiana Jones* than *Jurassic Park*."

"Oh, got it," she says, and then her face lights up. "Don't they have a new one out? A new *Indiana Jones*, I mean?"

"In a couple weeks. *Crystal Skull*, I think." I hold back a sigh because Mal and I had plans to go see it in the theater. Guess we'll have to wait for Netflix to mail us the DVD instead.

"Always gotta mess with a good thing for the almighty dollar." She shakes her head and slides her laptop into a red leather briefcase. "What can I help you with?"

"First, I want to thank you and your husband for organizing the search tonight." I mean that sincerely and hope it comes across that way. "I'd be happy to help. Plan routes or outline areas of town."

"Tyler is all over it," she says. "We'll knock on doors and cover as much ground as possible. I bet she's home safe and sound tonight."

I swallow thickly, wanting that to be true. I watch Deandre's face very carefully, and though Botox minimizes her expression, I can read eyes. Her fakeness is burned in my memory. How she'd lied about missing my phone calls or that she didn't have a sleepover with our friends. I don't see that falseness there now. "You're sure? I can help with mapping search zones, at least."

"Everything is handled. Pizza to eat, pop to drink, and even a preacher to bless our search. After your mom speaks, Tyler is going to say a few words about the new development. Approval meeting is today."

I am grateful that they're helping even though the reason all this happened may be because Emma Lou had a slipup at work. I don't want to make that accusation yet. "We really appreciate it."

"I always support Picher." She gestures to a shelf with framed newspaper clips and photos. Several have Deandre holding big checks. One is with the BIA and a new Tahoe next to a blond who looks like Sue Dove. "I really need to go, Syd. It was great to see you."

I realize my small hope that she'd reveal a clue or even a little insight was misplaced. Nothing worth knowing comes that easy. "The last day that Sister worked—"

"Yes?" Deandre says softly.

"Do you know who she was delivering to? Maybe there could be clues . . . or information . . ."

"Oh, Syd," she says sadly. "I wish I could help with that, but there's client confidentiality." That ask was too big. She doesn't owe me anything like that. Still, I can sense there's plenty she's not saying.

"I have a silly question." I throw her a playful smile.

"Ask away."

I clear my throat and make a game-time decision. "It's kind of embarrassing."

She pauses and suddenly looks as if she's listening for the first time in our conversation. "Go on. It'll stay between us."

Deep breath. "I hoped to get your opinion about what colors would look good on me." I don't have to fake my embarrassment, because I feel it, even as I lie. "I worry that I'm not as . . . I want Mallory to keep noticing me."

"Really?" She sounds as if she thought I'd be a hopeless fashion case forever. Fair enough. She looks me up and down. "That's my thing . . . Hmm . . ." She stares hard at me for a moment. "You know . . . I have these parties at my house, and I'm having one tomorrow. Might be fun for you to join. I have a few girls from the neighborhood coming."

The embarrassment switches to relief. "Sure, if I wouldn't crash the party."

She checks her flip phone, then slides it into her Coach purse. "Not one little bit. See you tonight, Syd."

I follow her as she gets a call. I pause at Trudy's desk and watch as Deandre leaves. The two women are still in the waiting room.

I have to step carefully, but I can't walk away empty-handed. "Hey, Trudy?" I motion her to come close as she hurries over with a stack of paperwork. "Deandre didn't want me to take a copy."

She shakes her head. "Oh, I'm sorry."

"She did say I could take a look, though." I shrug. "Maybe you could tell me what stood out to you? You do know everything about everyone, right?"

She swats away the compliment and then glances around. She pulls a sheet of paper out from under a folder. "See anyone familiar?"

Trudy watches as I scan the list. There are ten names with milligram dosages written in pencil scratches in the dosage column. I find who's receiving the largest quantity: *DAWESON, MANDA.*

Deandre's mother. I remember her at the casino handing a wad of money to the old man on the Rascal scooter. The pills are ten milligrams at a dollar a pill, which would be ten thousand dollars. "Wow," I whisper, "you weren't joking."

"I know. I'd look at his house first."

I stare at the list, realizing we're looking at two different names. "You would?"

"He might know your dad from heading up the buyout committee, but that don't mean he's not capable of something. Or knows something. Emma Lou was out there once a week."

The buyout committee? I run over the list until I recognize the name from the civic center meeting that was on the plaque right at the center of the table, sitting next to my dad. And he was visiting Sue this morning for those allotment maps. "Chairman Rhett Caine?" I say, surprised to see he's getting five hundred milligrams of Oxy a week.

"Just because he has a fancy house don't mean he can't get into a little trouble like everyone else."

I check the address. "Fifty-Seven Elevated Estates," I say.

"Mmm-hmm." Trudy slides the piece of paper away with her puckered lips to one side. "Deandre's neighbor with a big ol' mortgage."

18

~~~~~~

Mom isn't wearing her floral Deandre shirt as she stands in the back of the fire station pickup truck bed with a bullhorn. She faces a crowd of at least one hundred in her dingy khakis and a long-sleeved Picher Gorillas shirt.

As I scan the crowd, I recognize DNA. Everyone looks like someone I used to know, but I can't quite place a wiry build or crooked nose with a name. I stand at the front of the crowd and feel the stares like I'm an awkward teenager again, desperate to be seen and to disappear. The crowd is murmuring, and I can almost hear the old whispers:

She's the one who killed that Daweson.

Her sister went nuts after.

They say she had something to do with killing that girl and her parents.

"Memories are a mudslide, if you're not careful," says Ghost Luna at my side.

I focus on the bright pinkish-orange streaks in the sky as dusk begins. Soon the chat piles will glow purple as the sun sets behind them. I wonder if anyone still admires them after living with the price of such beauty.

"Thank you all for coming," Mom says into the bullhorn she borrowed from the fire chief. "It means the world to us. We've lost too many girls around here. With your help, we'll find Emma Lou tonight."

People are nodding and some "amens" are murmured. Mom is not being hyperbolic. Women and girls have gone missing. It's easy to say they ran away. Or fell into a cavern or abandoned mine. Some families accept that fate. Others keep looking. Never giving up, not until their dying breath. And some in the community help. Tonight, as I scan the familiar faces, I feel gratitude.

As many issues as I have about the way Native tribes were treated, especially the Quapaw, whose very land we're standing on, there are things to admire about Picher. The big companies took all the minerals, left poison, then abandoned the whole venture, giving the men working the mines black lung as severance. Then the yards, the homes built as the American Dream come true, began to literally cave in and disappear. But the evil continues long after the companies are gone. The poison takes your loved ones. Gives you diabetes or cancer or bad lungs, though you never smoked. Your kids are sick and developmentally delayed. You know more people on dialysis than have a steady paycheck. You'd have every right to tell the world to go to hell since it feels like that's where you've been damned to live.

That's not how people in Picher decided to go, though. As much as I never felt like I belonged, the town wasn't a bad place any more than your average tiny town in a flat state. People care about each other. I wouldn't chalk it up to "good people" like the narrative usually goes. Instead, it's the deep and real bond that develops after the world kicks your ass every which way from Sunday.

"You all saw my daughter Syd is here to help," Mom says, and that pulls my attention back. "Syd helped Tyler out organizing, and they have directions for each group of ten."

Mom holds up her master copy with every group, cell phones, and where they're assigned to search. When we got here early, it was clear Tyler didn't have a plan as much as lots of enthusiasm. But it hadn't taken me long to put one together.

"There are tips for how best to search," Mom continues. "My cell number is on the handout sheet if you have questions. Or find anything."

There's a question about logistics, and I take an extra copy over to a man in overalls and no shirt. I give him bug spray, too.

"When we're all back in exactly two hours," Mom says, "Deandre Monterey and Wings Addiction Recovery have provided pizza and pop. Tyler will say a few words about the new housing development that may be interesting to those taking the buyout. Please be safe out there. Pastor Ray will lead us in a prayer."

Mom gets down from the fire station pickup truck and hands the bullhorn over. She stands near me and places a trembling hand against my back. I lean my head down to touch the top of hers, as if I could somehow give us both strength. The prayer is longer than her speech, but when you get the megachurch preacher to come, you better expect him to settle in and stay awhile.

"Oh, Lord," he calls through the bullhorn. "When your sheep are lost, you know how to find them."

I open my eyes and glance at the bowed heads as the prayer continues. I watch as Ghost Luna wanders off, and completely irrationally, I'm a bit jealous of her freedom.

Finally, we are blessed, and I hurry to a group with their hands waving and a question on their faces. I answer a few more questions and hand out more bug spray as people start heading toward the neighborhoods to knock on doors. Others are going to walk the fields.

"I'm going out east." Dad runs his fingers through his floppy black-and-silver hair. "You want to come?"

"Is Mr. Caine going with you?" I ask, scanning around for him. One way or another, I'm going to find out if he saw Emma Lou before she disappeared.

"He's got back problems." Dad scratches at the side of his head and his braid bounces. "He donated some money to help with supplies."

I nod, seeing my choices for how to spend this time are now cut in half. "I'm going to search outside of town, but see you in a bit."

As I'm about to find my mom, two big trucks pull up blasting music, with some guys hanging out the back with yellow bandanas around their necks. I remember Sue saying that Kaleb and some of the guys, aka dipshits, would be volunteering. I'm glad to be leaving as the fire chief approaches them with the handouts we hadn't assigned yet.

As I head down the main street, it feels cruel to call this downtown Picher. The faded and broken signs, rotting wood, busted windows, and weary look of being abandoned. I find my mom at a check-in site and tell her I'm driving out to the edge of town. I hurry to my Jeep and take Connell Street, where there's a couple knocking on doors and holding flyers with Emma Lou's photo.

I feel bad for all the times I snidely called my hometown a shithole or wondered what my life would be like if I had been born somewhere else. Would a hundred people be out searching for my sister in some leafy suburb?

As I leave downtown, I see Mr. McClain, the drunk who got in my face at the civic center, hurrying into the pharmacy. He's alone, so likely not in the search party for Sister. I don't know why it surprises me, but it does. A reminder that there are dangerous layers here that can't be ignored.

I continue southeast past the town limit, through the sticks. A part of me knows I should be there knocking on doors alongside the volunteers, but to find Sister, there's somewhere else I must go.

Rolling down my window, I inhale the smell of sweetgrass. I notice a black truck behind me but ignore the suspicious feeling. Instead, I focus on how the drive is familiar to my pre-devil days. Passing the lone gun shop, I'm halfway through the fifteen-mile drive. The smell takes me back to church hayrides out to the Spook Light. Another little fun fact Mal could not believe.

It's a bright floating light that just goes through your car. On one dirt road in Oklahoma? Seriously?

I laughed and told her she hadn't even heard the best part. The Spook Light is in a town called Devil's Promenade.

You are lying to me.

But I wasn't. I even took her on that dirt road the night before our wedding reception, which we'd miss out on attending because Emma Lou OD'd. I teased her that if the Spook Light goes through your body, it'll steal your soul and take it right to the devil.

I leave the thick woods behind and approach Devil's Promenade Bridge over the Spring River. In the distance a white teepee signifies the Quapaw tribe's former powwow grounds. The truck is still behind me, so I pull over on the empty bridge. The truck speeds by and I catch little more than a shape through the tinted windows. Trying to find calm and focus for what's ahead, I close my eyes and listen to the fast-moving river. It's on this side of the Spring River that the Quapaw tribe were forced by soldiers to leave their land for a second time. What they were given was the land on the other side of the river and no way to cross.

It's easier to remember the spooky Native legends rather than Native pain.

I force myself to look at a small overhang. Almost like a cave, it's where I've seen glowing eyes. I know the shape of a bobcat stare in headlights. It wasn't that.

People say those eyes are from the devil, and you can see them when he's dancing. People say the devil started dancing as the Quapaw tribe marched into the fast-moving river toward death. That's why this bridge and this land are named Devil's Promenade. Because the devil watched and watches still.

The night of the devils, I know he danced.

I remember Deandre's fifteenth birthday party. We'd told scary stories of the Tsgilis and dancing devils around a campfire that Pete himself had made. His eyes had been on Luna. He'd even tried to talk to her about something . . . offered her a swig of his beer, but she'd refused. His twin, Skeet, lurked in the shadows, spitting tobacco in our direction.

Fire blazed red in Pete's gaze as he watched Luna. I grit the back of my molars, so angry at myself, even if I shouldn't be. I'd been scared of the devil from stories, when all the while the real devils were sitting right across from us. The next time I'd see those brothers would be a few weeks later at gunpoint.

But now it's my turn. Whatever devils remain, they will not keep my sister in their hell, and I am more than ready to go there to save her.

AGILVGI

There's a light in my eyes. "You're shiverin'. Use it."

A *whoosh*, and I flinch at something on my arm.

I scramble back, gasping, looking for a nasty snake.

The light is gone, and he leaves.

With all I have, my fingers creep like spider ghosts, whispering across this cold floor.

Scratchy wool and tattered edges.

A shawl.

I feel gratitude, and I hate myself for it.

At least you're not chained in this new place.

I've never been left here before.

I need to see if there's anything here to help me survive.

My fingers brush something hard. Turning my head, I can almost make out a shape in the dark. My God, it's a bottle.

Gently, gently, gently, not to spill a drop.

I stretch out with a belly full of water for the first time in days.

He does not want me to die.

He wants me to live in this new cold cage.

19

~~~~~~

"This is a mistake," says Ghost Luna from the passenger seat of the Jeep.

"Where else would Cody hide her?" I ask. "Not his trailer because Gracie is there. Not at the strip club or we'd have seen her. If Emma Lou is anywhere, she's out at that compound."

"You have no proof he's involved."

"Well, Manda's name was on Emma Lou's delivery list. If she's anywhere, it's there."

I cringe and feel stupid for explaining myself to air. I focus back on the two-lane highway. This is the right path, the only path. I will trespass onto the Daweson compound and find some evidence of Emma Lou, or even Emma Lou herself. My fingers grip the wheel of the rental, not only from anxiety, but also from something more dangerous: hope. This was the last location on her routes the day she went missing. Tonight, within hours, I could save Sister again.

When I consider last night, being facedown in a pickup bed,

a gun pointed at me, with a zip tie binding my wrists, it's bringing Rayna into the danger that was my biggest mistake. If I'm alone, only I will suffer the consequences. It'll be easier to control my emotions.

Ghost Luna pops a bubble. "Lone Ranger rides again?"

I turn too quick and fishtail on the dirt road where the Spook Light appears. Tapping the brakes, I get control and pull over, parking to the side as if I'm early to watch for the eerie light. Before too long, the road will have other cars pulling to the top of the second hill on this road. They will park and flash their headlights, one, two, three times, and then turn off the engine to wait.

The sun has disappeared behind the hill, casting a pinkish-purple hue on the fields. All around are wide ditches and cattle fences before the open flat land. I pull over, lock the rental, and start to walk down the dirt road.

It's only seconds until I see the Daweson compound, marked by the ten-foot fence with barbed wire on top.

At the edge of the property, I scan for cameras. I don't see any on the fence line, but I'd guess there's plenty I can't see. My eye catches a blurry shape near my Jeep. Ghost Luna is watching me but not following.

I take out the dipshit bandana from last night, washed with the rest of my clothes, and I tie it around my face as they did. The overgrown trees packed into the property drop darkness and shadows like a dusty curtain. There are strange rooflines, some sheds or trailers seeming only half there. I wonder if Emma Lou could be strung out in one of those buildings. If somehow Manda or Cody gave her some meth and she's tweaking somewhere.

For a whole week?

Feeling anxious, I search the sky. Only Venus is shining like an early evening star.

I've seen how drugs squeeze all the good out of a life. How even when someone manages to claw their way out of that sinkhole, it's a daily battle to stay free. Of course it's possible Emma Lou slipped. Anyone could. Even after the past few years of being sober. I hear dogs barking in the distance. I'd forgotten that from the party, all those big, vicious dogs in kennel cages. Trying to keep people out.

"Trying to keep people in?" says a soft whisper, but I do not turn around, even if my memories conjured her. "Keeping Sister like a secret."

I jump the ditch to put some distance between us and make it through weeds grown high on the west side of the compound. The effort doesn't keep my mind from considering whether Sister did know something.

FIND ME.

A secret the Dawesons wanted kept hidden. To find Emma Lou, I must retrace her steps to see where she was caught in their trap.

The property goes way back, as we'd say, though it's hard to tell much from the road. Earlier in the day, I'd mapped this land as best I could with a combination of the BIA software on my work laptop and Google Maps. It was like knowing the corner pieces of a puzzle. Helpful, but a long way from complete.

Walking along the fence, I count eighty-eight yards before the turn to the back of the property, where the fence is an old, rusted chain link.

Even though there are honeysuckle bushes and climbing weeds over the fence, I can see about fifteen feet into the property. This section of the compound is how I remembered it, with old pickups and rusted-out John Deere equipment. Most are riddled with bullet holes. Not a piece of glass in sight.

I throw a stick against the fence. There's a slight buzzing noise, which means it's electric. Most electric fences are made to give livestock a jolt and then reset, so I should have a few minutes before it can electrocute me. Now I tap the wires and feel nothing. Well, not nothing. My heart is about to rupture against my ribs. I peer deeper into the darkness, and there's the faded blue of a mobile home with the window AC unit whirring.

Cicadas rumble their warnings from the overgrown and ignored trees. Most have limbs ready to fall, if not the whole tree itself.

I head to a large elm tree that's grown into the fence. I squat down, and my fingers graze the tree bark that's being pressed into a diamond shape by the wire of the fence. I'm tempted to take out my pliers and snip it free, but what's done is done. The tree will never be whole again. It had to absorb what man has forced on it and decide whether it will grow or die.

I pull at where the bottom of the sharp metal fence is curling out of the ground. My wrists ache as I heave a couple more feet up. Lying down, I swing my head and shoulders under. Flat on my back, I scoot, inch by inch, onto the Daweson land.

As I'm bringing my legs onto this side of the fence, one of the sharp points slices my jeans and stabs the bottom of my thigh. I curse and find an angle, pulling it out with a grunt.

Butt in the dirt, I breathe heavily as I lean against the fence. A growing red circle stains my jeans. Blood isn't the best scent to be giving off when dogs are sniffing the air.

I rip the dipshit's bandana from my face and wrap it tight around my leg. Another day of the bandana stopping blood the Dawesons have drawn. I hate that my face is now exposed, but I'm not turning around. I head to the closest tree and crouch down to get my bearings. It's still evening, but within the trees this land brings night. I throw a stick, but no security lights flash on.

I take a few steps and my leg throbs, but I can walk. More old trucks with weeds and small trees growing through the rusted-out places.

I stay low and limp toward a blue trailer about fifty feet ahead. As I reach the back of it, the front door slams and I freeze. There's silence except for my breath in my ears, and then another slam. I edge around the corner to see it's the metal screen catching in the breeze. The air conditioner is rumbling, and I count sixty seconds, then find the courage to peek inside. Putting my boot on the hitch, I am high enough to peer through a window, but it's thick with dirt. I consider wiping it but don't want to give any indication I was here, even if everything inside me is screaming that Emma Lou could be trapped inside.

Returning to the back of the trailer, I see there's a bigger window. It appears a little less dirty, so I pull over a busted milk crate. On my tippy-toes, I peer inside and scan for Sister. But there's nothing inside except a few pots and pans, a long plastic tube, and boxes that look like they're from cold medicine littering the floor. I squint at a shape in the corner, and it's a milk jug and two-liter soda bottles.

That all but confirms what I'd feared. The Dawesons are still involved with meth. I am no expert, but when Rayna told me about the Mexican cartel moving in, I'd done research at the library in Miami after leaving Deandre's office. Things took a turn for local meth cookers after I left.

Oklahoma was the first state to pass a law to limit how much cold medicine, which has two meth ingredients, pseudoephedrine and ephedrine, you can buy in a month. I'd read local meth lab production was way, way down. Meth use, however, was not.

So the Mexican cartel is trying to move in. Different supply, same demand.

Stepping down from the crate, I'm relieved Emma Lou isn't in there high on a nasty mattress on the floor, but also cripplingly disappointed. As I'm considering which shithole trailer to check next, there's yelling. Two deep voices rise closer to the main barn in the middle of the property.

Checking my phone, I see I have forty-five minutes before the volunteers return to the firehouse. To be safe, I'd hoped to make it back to be seen. I could search these outbuildings, but I wouldn't have time for much more. I take a deep breath and whisper to my grandma Ama, "Where is Sister?"

I flush, feeling silly, and the voices near the barn get louder, as if taunting me, and my choice is made.

Staying low, I creep in the shadows of the trees. Ahead is a large oak tree that I remember being near where we'd built that campfire with the devils and heard of Tsgilis. There'd been boards nailed into the bark for a tree stand and we'd climbed into the branches.

As I get closer, I find the tree is smaller than in my memory and there's something tied around it. A rope or a chain, maybe. The hairs on the back of my neck stand up, but I don't stop long enough to consider why. Through a patch of bushes, I can see a huge slab of concrete leading to the main barn and house. I don't see any movement, so maybe they went inside.

I duckwalk over to the oak even as my leg throbs in the tight bandana, which is hopefully slowing the bleeding. A security light on the barn turns on and I freeze. I scan the pavement, which was too busted for basketball even back then, but don't see anything. My breathing doesn't slow down, but I move forward until I reach the tree. I creep around it until there's a metal clank under my foot. I jump back and blink at handcuffs in the dirt. They're connected to a long chain wrapped around the tree. I crouch down to look closer, whispering terrified nonsense. There's something written in the dirt.

As gently as I can I move the chains, like they're sleeping copperheads. There are five letters drawn into the mud: *GRACE*.

"No," I whisper, and my heartbeats feel vise tight. I pick up the cuffs, and there's dried blood along the edge. Dark spots in the dirt and what looks like a smear of blood on the tree.

Trying not to scream in the shadows of the Daweson compound, I feel a new terrible fear arrive: they stole Sister and chained her to a tree.

20

My shaking fingers hover above where my niece's name was scratched in the dirt by my sister. My whole body starts to tremble, mostly from rage. The Dawesons are trying to take her away again.

Trying to wear my archeologist hat, I peer at the depth and shape of the markings. Best guess, the earth was wet when Emma Lou wrote these letters. It rained four days ago, so maybe around then. I trace the air above the letters *GRACE* and must curl my fingers to keep from shoving them into the earth. To pull out the truth about Sister and where she's been taken. Or buried. Or lost to us all.

Wiping a few tears, I make myself stand up. The main house of the compound is about fifty feet ahead. I try to imagine any scenario where sneaking in would go well, and fail. I press my back against the tree. Breathing deeply, I work to return to this moment and press my fingers into the bark.

A minute and likely more pass before I'm able to step one foot in front of the other, and then again, to make it to the tree closest to the concrete.

I crawl over roots that have broken through the ground and created cracks at the edge of the pavement. I'm in the shadows, on the edges, but not invisible.

The big metal barn is now straight ahead. The security light creates a halo of brightness at the center, as if a UFO were shining down. My eyes adjust and I see there's more scattered trash and boxes.

The light reveals suitcases, some open, some closed. The front door slams open and a woman hurries outside. I catch a flash of a long gray braid as she stops in the shadows farther along the barn.

Her gaze narrows in my direction and then back toward the barn. "Hey!" she yells.

Before I can run, a skinny man stumbles onto the concrete from the shadows a few feet from where I'm hunched down. He's in sweatpants and no shirt and shuffles toward the light. "Lookie here, Manda."

"Don't got time for you, Doc," she yells, and stomps forward. They meet in the light, and I confirm it's Deandre's mom, Manda.

"Look at this sweet thing," he says, his bare back to me, but cradling something gently in his arms toward Manda.

"No," I whisper, and my fists grow tight. "Not a baby."

I consider intervening now or calling Sue. I squint to be sure I'm seeing what I think I see. But the shape in his arms is odd, large and almost more like a ball. I scoot to my right to get a better view.

In his wiry arms, he's cradling something . . . but it's not a baby. It's a milk jug with a long tube running out the top.

I almost laugh—that hysterical kind with no joy in it—but

bite down on my lip until I taste blood. There's liquid in the jug, and I realize he's carrying it not like a baby but like a bomb.

Doc is rail thin and he's hunched as if even carrying that jug is a struggle. People called him Doc because he was the resident meth chemist. He's a cousin, best guess, a couple of times removed.

"No one cares about that science shit." Manda points toward the shapes in the shadows where she'd been. "Can't you see I've got our future right here?"

"Now, give it a chance." Doc raises the jug. "That Mexico crystal is gonna kill me. My buddy in Tulsa swears by this shit."

"Like I'm taking the word of one tweaker to another." Manda laughs, a deep, raspy sound that's more cough than anything. "Shake and bake over in your trailer. I gotta count glass."

Doc mumbles and heads over to the front of the garage, plopping down on a plastic milk crate turned upside down.

Manda is cursing as she heads back to the shadows. I watch her shift one object, and there's the sound of a zipper. Those are suitcases. Reaching inside, she picks up a small bag, holds it up to the light. White reflects for a second and she drops it back inside.

Doc had mentioned the meth from Mexico, and it makes sense that the Mexican cartels would send their crystal in suitcases. Easy to transport and a little less conspicuous. She unzips one suitcase and dumps out what looks like old tighty-whitey underwear. She grunts and then marks it down on a notepad. She unzips another one and squats down. "Take this one inside, Zeke. Don't give me no more lip."

A young guy with a yellow bandana around his neck steps out from the darkness of the barn. Doc holds out the jug and gets the kid's interest.

"Doc, leave him alone and get your ass back to the trailer," Manda yells.

Doc rises off the crate as Zeke walks over to him. He starts explaining in a professorial voice how he made what Manda called a shake and bake. He uses words I've read about in reports about homegrown meth: lithium, camp fuel, and two packs of skittles, which means Sudafed.

Both of them are distracted, and I scoot behind another tree to get a better look at what Manda is doing with those suitcases. Proof of drugs could lead to a search warrant and turn this place upside down.

"You can't have no oxygen, or KABOOM," Doc says, and they laugh. "Shake and bake fry you like a chicken thigh."

As they're laughing again, Manda yells for Zeke to hurry, but he doesn't even look her way.

Another security light turns on, casting a circular beam where Manda is now standing. There are more suitcases, weatherworn and piled along the side of the barn. Slipping my flip phone out of my pocket, I check to see the time. I've got twenty minutes left before I should be on the road, if I'm going to make it back in time to be seen.

"Easy there, slick!" shouts Doc.

"I can do it better'n you." Zeke snatches the jug and swirls. "Your hands are too weak, you old peckerwood." He starts to shake the jug hard. "Feels like it's gettin' bigger, Doc."

"Give it back." Doc grabs for it, but Zeke is fast, laughing in his face.

"Take that shit over to his trailer," Manda calls. "I'm late on this count."

"Watch me twist this, you old fucker," Zeke says with the same punk-kid arrogance that emanated from the dipshits last night. "Shake and—"

The explosion is a single clap of painful detonation, like a bomb, and sprays fire into Zeke's face. His scream is bloodcurdling as his shirt bursts into flames and his body is lit up like a Roman candle.

Manda yells for help, but Doc is frozen. She hurries over to the suitcases, pulling them away from her burning nephew.

Zeke falls on the ground and writhes in the flames. Doc grabs a rag from his pocket and smacks and stomps, but the burning continues. Zeke starts to scream again, as if the pain has brought him back from unconsciousness.

"We need the hose, damn it!" Manda yells, now that all the suitcases are shoved off the concrete, into the dirt.

I blow out a breath, realizing I'm going to have to get caught to help this idiot on fire. I start to step into the light but stop as the front door clanks open.

The *thud–thud* of boots echoes on the concrete from the shadows. There is a man's shape, as familiar as a recurring nightmare that replaced every dream: older face, wide gait, slower steps, as he strides into the security light reflecting those ice-blue eyes.

The memories arrive like a mudslide and pile thick earth around me until I am suffocating. The shining white devil masks. The mothball smell of the closet Skeet crammed me into, where I found the shotgun that would drop him dead moments later. The smells of gunpowder and blood fill my nostrils and coat my tongue.

Thump-thump.

I drop to my knees and press my hands over my mouth to cover a scream. The devil never stopped dancing.

Pete Daweson is alive.

21

〰〰〰

I should have brought a gun. I didn't think I'd need it, but I didn't know the devil would be here.

I cannot catch my breath but manage to force my eyes open and see that Pete Daweson is moving fast. He grabs a garden hose and rushes over to Zeke, spraying him down. There could be more screams or total silence, but all I hear is my breath in my ears as I scoot back on the ground until I feel a tree at my back.

Pete Daweson is alive.

He is here.

The devil is back for my soul.

"He's back for your sister," whispers Ghost Luna, though I don't see her. "My life wasn't enough."

I lean the back of my head against the tree, digging my stubby nails into the bark to get control. With my eyes closed, my senses are overwhelmed by the stench of burning skin and screams from Zeke. I pull myself out of that hole where I try to keep the devil and remember the Dawesons are distracted. Manda is screaming at Doc. Zeke looks dead, unmoving as Pete sprays him with the garden hose.

This is about Emma Lou. Finding her here. Saving her from the devil again.

"Get the keys to the truck," Pete yells. "Gotta drop him somewhere far from here."

Manda rushes over with her hands on her cheeks. "The hospital! We gotta get him help."

Zeke lets out a long, horrifying wail before thrashing and then he collapses in silence.

"That'll bring the heat, you fucking idiot," Pete barks with that cruel voice. "Clear as could be, it's a meth burn." He snaps his fingers at Doc, who is frozen over Zeke. "Make sure there ain't nothing on him cops can trace back here."

Manda runs into the house, and Pete kicks Zeke over to hose down the other side. I gasp at his skin coming off with the spray.

Warrant. Evidence. Proof.

I manage on weak legs to hurry in the shadows to the closest suitcase. I'm on the edge of the security light, but if one of them looked, they'd see me.

I fumble with the zipper on the suitcase. I pull and pull again, finally getting one corner open. There are gallon ziplock bags inside. Unzipping the other side, I open the suitcase completely with quick glances at the chaos. No one notices me yet. As I inspect a bag, my first thought is of the rock candy on long sticks we'd buy at Gary's Pharmacy in downtown Picher. Emma Lou always liked the white ones, which tasted like pure sugar to me. Luna and I liked blue. Obviously, these are not bags of candy, but meth. I feel one bag, probably about a pound. I count ten bags and ten suitcases. That's one hundred pounds of meth.

I swallow thickly and open the top of the suitcase wider, then take out my phone. I scroll over to the small icon of a camera and press it. I flinch at a flash I wasn't expecting and reflexively snap my gaze toward Pete.

He's staring right at me. "Get the goddamn dogs." He sends a spray of water at Doc, who is slumped over Zeke's wet body. "Now. We got company."

Pete shoves Doc toward the back of the barn. "Hey, you! Get your trespassing ass over here." He throws down the hose and starts toward me.

I cannot move. His big body is so fast, and his blue eyes are full of hate and dominance that hold me like a moth on a pin.

Tires screech and an engine roars. A big truck backs out of the barn right in his path. Manda jumps out and screams to get Zeke in the back of the truck. Pete slams both palms on the side of the truck and growls.

"Hurry," Manda yells as she rushes to Zeke. "If that boy dies, and we gotta bury him at the boneyard, his momma will kill us in our sleep."

Terror has nailed my feet to the ground, but I can't stay that way and survive. I move slowly at first, but soon I'm sprinting toward the dirt driveway and open fields beyond this place.

The cut on my thigh sends a shooting pain up my leg, but it's like a blast of cold water, reminding me to go faster if I don't want even more.

Dogs are barking again, but the sound is hungrier and more aggressive, as if they know there's a meal waiting. The growls get closer even as I limp-run down the driveway toward Spook Light road.

I'm only halfway there when an engine roars behind me. I

turn while still trying to run, but the headlights are blinding and too close. A gear screeches in acceleration and the truck swerves for me. I hit the ground and roll, with dirt and grass and wet ground whirling around me.

The truck gets loud, until there's a smashing noise. I stop myself and jump up. The engine screeches, but the truck is stuck. I'm in the beam of a headlight, the other one smashed and dark after running into a tree.

Smoke spews from the crumpled hood, and Manda screams at Pete to get back on the road.

He revs the engine, only headlight on me, as if he's considering finishing what he started. The engine roars, but the truck rips backward. They hit the ditch so hard Zeke's legs and arms fly up from the truck bed along with the suitcases.

Pete slams on the brakes and leans out the window. "You call the cops, and I'll fucking kill her," he yells. "I've been waiting fifteen years to do it."

I start limp-running toward the truck. "Where is she?!" I scream. "Where's my sister?"

The truck speeds away, spewing dirt and dust in its wake. I cough but start running again, and I realize why: the dogs are coming. They growl, sounding so close they can taste me. I keep pumping my arms and legs and sprint toward some unknown miracle saving me.

About to be attacked by dogs, I pray to my grandma's god out on stolen Quapaw land.

Great Spirit, Great Spirit.

I can be more.

Please let me try.

But there are no prayers answered in this cursed place. I stumble and spin around, scanning for a solution. In the darkness, I can't see the dogs, but I sure can hear them.

Finally, I see an answer. There's an old deer stand in a big tree up ahead. I have no idea if there are even boards nailed into the bark that I can climb, but I'm not going to make it much farther before the dogs get me.

When I jump over the ditch, my boot lands deep in mud. I stumble as I yank my foot out, but it's my sock that emerges, and I don't have time to stop. I keep going, limping and running, as sticks and hard ground cut into my foot.

I throw myself around the tree. My fingers claw for nailed pieces of wood, bark, boards, anything I can climb. The growls get louder, closer. "Please, please, please."

I can hear the dogs leap over the ditch. They are seconds away now and even I can smell my blood leaking from my cut thigh down my leg.

I raise my hands higher and frantically search again. My fingers stretch and grasp until I smack a piece of wood nailed into the tree. It's too dark to see if there's another one above it. I don't have time to do anything but hurry. With my good leg, I jump onto the tree and pull myself up as I clench the small piece of wood. I lever myself up the tree inch by inch. The breeze pushes at my back as if saying to hurry, but it's too late, the dogs are here.

One of them snaps at my foot just as I pull my leg up. The bark is wet and vicious as he reaches the tip of my toe and sinks a sharp tooth. I shake him off, and he falls to the ground with the sock in his mouth. I scoot a few more inches on my good foot. With a grunt I use the other leg to press so I can get a better grip on the small piece of wood.

The dogs gnash their teeth as they jump, higher and higher.

They stretch as they leap, as if exploring how high they can climb, too.

My arms begin to shake from my weight, and my foot slips. My wrists are weak and scream from the unhealed cuts. I scoot up an inch, then a few more. The dog with my sock violently shakes it and leaps up the tree, nearly grabbing my ankle. Suddenly a gunshot rings out and dirt flies below me where the bullet hits the ground. The dogs yelp and bark. Another shot, and as it echoes, another one rings out. There's a whistle in the distance, back toward the compound. The dogs jump at me a few more times, then rush away into the dark field.

My breath is stuttering as my body trembles, about to collapse off the tree. I search the fields for one of the Dawesons coming to shoot me and feed me to the dogs. I imagine the glowing eyes over the promenade. The devil starts dancing because he almost has my soul.

"Let go, Syd."

The words sound a million miles away. My arms are shaking so hard, my focus only on staying right where I am.

"Please, you can come on down."

I blink several times, wondering if I'm hallucinating. But the dogs are running away. Is my prayer answered?

The relief causes my arms to finally give out. I slide down the bark and strong hands guide me onto the ground.

"Breathe slow."

I'm held by the shoulders. I'm shaking so hard I can barely see the shape of the man. I listen for vicious dogs or nearby gunshots or an engine roaring or the *thump-thump* of footsteps.

My breath keeps getting caught in my chest, rattling in my throat as the panic continues to control me. There's so much to say, so much to do, but my mind cannot talk my body out of this war of shock and survival.

"Emma Lou said you get the panics."

Sister?

"You're safe," he says. "Keep breathing."

I nod as if it's working, and I grapple to find the earth instead of all I fear. Finally, I can feel the air, and it's cool on my cheek.

I exhale one last shuddering breath and hate what I have to say. "Thank you, Cody."

He watches me for a few seconds, then releases me to pick his rifle up off the ground. I hobble to where I'd jumped earlier and lost my boot. I take out my phone and shine the light into the mud. It's still there and angled from where I leapt out. I slip my foot into it and see Cody is still standing where he held my shoulders. The dark silhouette of him and his gun slung over his back. I limp toward the dirt road and begin making my way through the tire tracks left by Pete and Manda. I hear Cody's soft steps behind me.

"Where are you going?"

The question ignites my anger. "Pete is alive. That devil is alive."

"I know," he says gruffly.

I stop, stunned at his lack of surprise, that he's not upset. "Is she in there?"

"Who?"

"Sister!" I scream. "She was handcuffed at their property. She wrote Gracie's name in the dirt. There was . . . blood . . . on the cuffs."

"Calm down, Syd. She's not there."

My mouth falls open. "Then where the hell is she, Cody?" I shove him in his silence. "What did you do with my sister?"

"I didn't do anything," Cody says. "Pete is back for a drug deal, okay? Forget you were ever here. He'll go back to Mexico soon."

"Back? He's alive. That fucking monster is alive, and you knew?"

For a moment I consider tackling Cody and taking his rifle. Then walking him to Sue or the sheriff or anyone who can lock him up again.

Or I could take the gun and raid that goddamn compound myself. The idea of dealing with it on my own feels right—not that this instinct worked so well over the past hour. I picture kicking in the door and demanding my sister. But who knows what I'm walking into? Likely, it's another gun or four pointed my way. I have to be smart if I'm going to make sure she's returned safe and the Dawesons go to jail.

"Where are they taking those drugs?" I ask.

Cody keeps his face still and merely takes a long, obstinate blink.

I swear at him, then pull my phone out of my pocket and dial Sue's cell phone.

"This is Superintendent Dove," she says quickly over people talking in the background.

I remember she had that banquet honoring her dad tonight. "It's Syd. Sorry to interrupt, but I'm at the Daweson compound and just had visual confirmation that Pete Daweson is alive and transporting a hundred pounds of meth—"

"We can't talk on the phone. Not about what you're trying to tell me."

"We need law enforcement here, now," I say.

"You trespassed," Sue says as if it matters. "If they'd have shot you dead on their property, they'd have been within their rights. People have died for much less."

"Emma Lou might be in there. Please," I beg. "Search the compound. Search wherever they're taking those drugs. I have to find her."

Cody steps toward me as if he's going to take the phone.

I inch back from him and say, "We don't have time to waste, Sue." No way they'd risk going to the hospital before off-loading the meth. "They're hiding the meth somewhere right now. Can you try to stop them? Can someone come search this place?"

She swears under her breath. "You're sure?"

"Pete is driving a Black Ford F-150 with his nephew, Zeke, in the back. A shake and bake burned his face off."

"I'll look into it," Sue murmurs. "You get home."

I hang up on her and start toward the road again.

"Where you going, Syd?" Cody yells behind me. "It better be to your parents' place."

I don't respond but start to jog.

"Hey! I saved your goddamn life tonight." He rushes up behind me and pulls my arm, yanking me back so we're face-to-face. "You can at least answer my question."

"That was you behind me in the truck on the way here," I yell, unable to control my rage. "You followed me and you knew I'd find Pete here and alive."

"I didn't know what you were doing but figured it was dangerous, and I was right."

"Did you hear Pete threaten to kill Emma Lou after he almost killed me? He has her, you selfish asshole. Maybe you knew that, too."

"That's not how this is—"

"That's exactly how it is." I shove away from his tight grip. "I'll tell you one thing for certain. Once Emma Lou is safe, I'll make sure this time you rot in prison. Along with everyone else in your godforsaken family."

22

I'm squinting over the steering wheel when everything goes dark, like the shutter of a camera closing. I slam on the brakes with a gasp of air and the road returns for a second, illuminated by my Jeep's headlights, before blurring back to black.

"Not now, not now," I beg.

"Stay focused," Ghost Luna says from the back seat. "You gotta get out of here."

I blink at her fuzzy image. A cloud of kicked-up dirt glows red in the taillights. My breath is coming too fast, but I can't stop here for long. I shake my head as if I'm one of those Magic 8 Balls we played with as girls. The message is clear: *You're failing Sister again.*

My cell buzzes, and it's my mom. I toss the phone over to the passenger seat, and every vibration seems to reinforce the message like a punch to the chest. I pound my hands on the steering wheel, and pain fires in my arms with a finale biting in my wrists. My bleeding thigh throbs as if to keep pace. Inside and out, everything hurts. Tears burn my eyes, and I blink a few times to focus on the road. I realize where I am.

Near Aunt Missy's and Rayna's houses.

My mind is clear enough to remember what Aunt Missy said: *Dipshits are always out at Netta.*

The mines that belong to the Dawesons. That's where they're taking the drugs.

I put the car in drive and flip a U-turn. It's only a mile until the chat piles rise from flat emptiness in a silvery shimmer.

Slowing down, I approach the barren and bulldozed landscape. The rusted-out and abandoned mining equipment looms like monsters in the moonlight. Beneath a single security light, the gates are wide-open, with a clanking chain wrapped like a snake around the bars. The dirt road into the Netta mine site appears dark, but I don't dare get any closer to confirm. I grip the wheel and try to find an answer.

Survive, my body says. *Do whatever it takes to survive.*

If I stop moving, I will die. If I think about Pete, and how he's alive, I will crumble. Instead, I hurry from the Jeep and slip the keys in my pocket. Staying in the shadows, I creep toward the gate, where there is a growing glow. Once I'm in a muddy ditch leading past the gate, I stay low and trespass on a Daweson property for the second time tonight.

There are two trucks with their brights on, and they are illuminating the back of a third truck that's loaded with the suitcases. Figures with yellow bandanas covering their faces cross the truck lights, creating giant shadows across the chat piles. One has the unmistakable shadow of a shotgun barrel.

I flinch at the sound of my cell phone vibrating in my truck. Or am I hearing things? They don't understand that I must do this on my own. They can't be put at risk.

Don't do your loner thing, as Mal says.

It might be true, but it doesn't matter. Pete has Sister. It was never that she was back on drugs. I assumed the worst and was so wrong.

I see a shadow shaped different than the others, the movements terrifying and familiar because they've haunted me for fifteen years. I reflexively scoot backward and knock against the gate, causing that big snake-chain to clang and echo. My hands are trembling as I press my palms into my eye sockets and think of the two skulls I've seen in the past two days. Then I picture Luna's skull buried along with her parents a hundred feet from where Emma Lou and I were able to live.

I cannot let Emma Lou be another discarded skull desecrated by men who should never have drawn a breath. Or who should at least be stopped from drawing any more.

Opening my eyes, I see Pete again. He's throwing a suitcase from the back of his truck. I won't let myself shrink away. This is good. I can tell Sue to get here. She'll have evidence for a warrant or maybe even an arrest.

But what else could be in this mine?

My wrists and legs scream in pain, but I crawl forward in the wet trench to see if there's any sign of Emma Lou. Another suitcase is unloaded, and the tailgate is slammed shut. A high-pitched howl fills the air but no one shows any reaction.

My hand flies over my mouth. The image of Zeke in flames returns. The way the ball of fire shot into his face. The awful scream and his trembling body being sprayed with a hose.

He's *still* in the back of the truck.

"We're good! We're good!" a dipshit yells, and slaps the hood of the truck. "We'll get'um in the mine!"

"Let's go," screams Manda from the passenger seat.

My truck is just off the road and as conspicuous as hell.

"Shit, shit, shit!" I whisper as I hobble back the way I came. I'm almost to the gate when I hear a familiar engine roar. The terrible sound from only an hour earlier locks my knees.

I turn my head, and there's a single headlight. I cannot move except to shield my eyes as the truck skids in the mud and accelerates right at me. From behind the steering wheel, Pete's eyes lock on mine. There's a fence at my back, but he doesn't care. He will smash into whatever it takes to finish what he started fifteen years ago. I cannot look away. Those pale blue eyes.

Is this what Luna saw moments before her death?

Manda flies across the truck and jerks the wheel hard. The truck returns to the road and shoots through the gate instead of slamming into where I stand. Pete's truck fishtails, and I hear her scream as he slams on the brakes.

"You fuckin' bitch!" he roars, and there's another scream and thump as she's slammed against the window.

"Please," she scream-sobs. "We have to get that boy to a hospital."

For a breath it is dead silent as Pete makes his choice: both of us die or both of us live.

The truck tires screech, and a giant cloud of dust is caught in the wind and washes over me. I cough as my eyes burn, but the point is that I am alive. I fall against the gate and the chain rattles.

There's lightning and a rumble of thunder that pull me back to my body. Like the old wives' tale about snapping turtles that never let go of your finger until there's a storm.

"Get her!" yells a male voice.

The shadowy shapes scatter and two engines roar. I limp-run with a frustrated scream and use all I've got left to throw myself into the Jeep. A giant cloud of dirt and exhaust rises from the center of the mines. I fumble with the keys, cursing myself for taking them with me. They drop to the floor and tires screech.

I find the keys on the floor mat and have to brace my right hand with my left to keep it steady. The key slips into the ignition. The engine is on as the first truck flies past the gate.

I downshift to reverse and hit the gas. The rear of the Jeep swings wildly to one side of the road and then the other. I turn around to peer out the back glass to see where the hell I'm going. Even though the road is long and straight, it's tough to keep the truck centered enough to accelerate in reverse, which I desperately need to do.

The dipshit truck gets closer as a second truck barrels out behind him.

I have no choice, so I press the gas harder and keep the wheel as straight as I can. The barbed-wire fence whirls past and the reverse lights allow me to see the turn coming up.

I must make a choice. But the road makes it for me.

The back of the Jeep swings left and fishtails all the way around to face forward and the dark road ahead. I shift into drive and press the gas to the floor, and the ability to steer going the right way makes driving feel effortless. The dipshit lights are behind me, but they're farther back.

My speed hits seventy, which will roll the Jeep if I turn, which I'll need to do to get onto the highway. I should have another mile, so I keep going fast.

The dipshit truck gets closer and the highway approaches. There are headlights coming, but I can't stop. Not all the way.

I slam on the brakes and gently turn the wheel, using all my strength to keep from rolling. My tires stay down as I slide onto the highway, just as a big truck blasts by.

Taking tiny gasping breaths to be sure I'm alive, I don't let myself think about anything other than going fast and getting away.

In the rearview mirror, I watch as the first dipshit launches onto the highway too fast. The tires screech as his truck rolls like a barrel all the way onto the opposite side of the road and into a ditch. An oncoming car stops, and their lights illuminate the wheels spinning in the air. I let out more gasps and start to pass the truck ahead. I pull into the other lane, suddenly blinded by the headlights of an oncoming car as the horn blasts. I whip back behind the truck.

In my rearview appears the second dipshit's truck pulling back onto the road.

They're coming after me.

23

Tires screech as the dipshit truck races behind me and doesn't slow down until it knocks against my fender. I scream as my head jerks forward, but I keep the wheel steady.

Taking a breath, I ease around an eighteen-wheeler and punch the gas. There are headlights oncoming again, but I manage to slip in front of the giant truck before the other car—horn blaring—whips past me. There are more cars coming to keep the dipshit stuck. I accelerate as fast as this Jeep will take me.

I pass another car before I see the dipshit has made it past the big truck. He's caught behind the car I just went around.

Here is where Picher ends, and the last chat pile disappears in my side-view mirror. Ahead is the turn where Highway 69 meets Highway 67. I slow down enough to skid around the corner and press the gas. There are no cars in the oncoming traffic lane, so I switch and use it like my own private road.

The dipshit truck makes the turn onto the highway just as I'm about to take a left exit toward Miami. I mutter a few curses and quickly brake to turn the wheel with screeching tires. The road is dark ahead except for lampposts along the fence line. There will likely be more traffic as I get closer to the casinos. Not that I know where I'm going.

I consider trying the Miami Hospital. I doubt Pete even slowed down before rolling Zeke out of the back. Plus, I know where the drugs are, though it's likely they'll move them soon. They may move Emma Lou. Maybe kill her.

A wave of panic hits me as I realize I've probably made things worse for Sister. My conspicuousness has put them on high alert. She's a liability if found. My phone buzzes in the seat, and I ignore it again.

I must save Sister. But I need help.

Taking the back way, I quickly turn onto NEO Farm Road leading into Miami. A few seconds later I recognize the dipshit truck. Losing someone in a town isn't easy. I speed by the Jurgensmeyer Mansion, over the Tar Creek Bridge. I take a hard left to cut through the NEO junior college campus, hoping they don't know about the speed bumps.

I hit the bumps just right, and I see their headlights smash up and down. Once I'm through the campus, it's a hard right onto Central toward downtown. The detour bought me a half block, maybe less, so I take another right and make it to Third Street, heading back toward downtown. I blast past the NEO Feed Store as the Nine Tribes Tower looms ahead.

My rental rattles over the train tracks and there are headlights nearing the intersection we're both speeding toward. The dipshits get closer in the rearview mirror, and if I want to get away, it's now or never.

Distant headlights illuminate the stoplight of the NEO Feed Store as I approach the blind corner on the truck route. The light turns from yellow to red, so I hit the gas. The truck's headlights burn in my peripheral vision, but it's slowed enough that I blast past. The dipshits have to slam on their brakes, and there's no crash, but they spin toward a ditch.

I'm able to fly down Main Street, which should give me almost a block of distance ahead of the dipshits. I zoom around a car that's turning and see the bright marquee lights signaling I've arrived at my destination. Even going almost forty, I read the glowing words: HONORING RONNY DOVE.

Did he know Pete Daweson was alive?

My vision blurs, but I shake off the panic and memories of the man the morning after the devils.

The dipshit's headlights are getting closer. I hit the brakes to make a turn down the alley behind the Coleman Theatre. The backstage door is where my dad would drop me off for *Annie* rehearsals, and it'll get me inside quicker than the long hallways leading through the front door.

I throw the Jeep in park as the dipshit's truck flies by and then the tires screech to a stop. I run as fast as I can on my throbbing leg, fearing the shotgun shadow appearing behind me. Bolting toward the big metal door, I pray to someone's god it's unlocked. My palms slam into cool metal, and I cry out in pain and fear. I heave the handle and there's no movement. I kick it with my good leg and pull again. The door slides open about a foot, and I slip inside just as footsteps start to pound behind me.

I push to close and lock the door, but the damn thing is stuck. There's no time.

My body tenses as a loud burst of applause echoes in the cavernous theater ahead. Standing offstage, I can see almost nothing is different from my memory. The velvet curtains hang alongside ropes and weights and backdrops on long rolls.

I dart toward a curtain and try to wrap myself in the folds. My breath is coming quick as the applause quiets. Heels pound up the stage stairs and across the wooden floor. I scoot closer to the edge of the curtain to see who is there.

A hand grabs my arm and yanks me out of my hiding spot. I cry out in the silent theater. The dipshit rips off his mask, and it's Kaleb, Sue's little brother.

"Shut up, okay?" he says, pulling me back toward the door.

My gaze darts toward the stage, where the spotlight is on Sue, staring at us from the lectern.

Kaleb freezes in her confused glare, and I jerk my arm away. "Let go of me."

"It's such an honor to be here," Sue says, returning her focus to the crowd. "My father, Ronny, loved Ottawa County. He served the people here his whole life, and the people of our many strong Native communities in particular, leading the BIA office for thirty-five years."

As applause starts, she glances back at us, and Kaleb grabs for me again. I shove him hard and his eyes bulge.

"I'm so happy my brother has joined us," Sue says. "Kaleb, why don't you come onstage while I tell a few stories about Dad."

He tenses up, but I shove him toward her and the spotlights onstage. He runs his hands through his hair and gives the lightly applauding crowd a nod.

"Dad told us that people have to make way for the next generation," she continues. "He felt that particularly because hard times had fallen on so many. Mines went bust. Goodrich closed. More people without jobs than with. But Dad kept fighting. For justice. For peace. For a place to raise kids that was safe. A place for those kids to raise their own someday. Not because they had to, but because they wanted to."

Sue beams a smile, and I can see how proud she is of her dad. He was their only parent, since their mom passed away right after Kaleb was born. Her dad worked all the time, and not only for the Bureau of Indian Affairs. It seemed as if in any decision made in Ottawa County, from the new pool to the Section 8 houses, Ronny Dove had a say. That meant Sue basically raised Kaleb and took care of her dad as much as he let her.

More applause, then Kaleb glances in my direction. I flip him off to let him know I'm not going anywhere.

"Dad loved to close cases. In fact, I was going through his files when I took over his office and confirmed what he always said: 'I've closed every single case.'"

The crowd chuckles. Even though there's no way it's true. There's a billboard asking for JUSTICE FOR JESSICA, who disappeared a couple of years before Luna was killed. Her permed hair and big smile in her Picher cheerleader letter jacket. I remember playing in the park while my parents walked the neighborhood looking for her.

"I saw Syd Walker is here as well. As you can imagine, the Myers case stayed with him his whole career. It stays with me through mine. There are too many people killed on Native land, particularly Native girls and women. We honor Ronny Dove by continuing this important work. For the next generation and the generation after."

The crowd applauds and the seats creak as people stand. Sue

waves and smiles while Kaleb shifts from one foot to the other. His forehead shines with sweat. I hope he's thinking about how he tried to make sure Rayna and I disappeared.

Sue strides off the stage toward me, and Kaleb follows with his head hung low.

"What the fuck is going on here?" she hisses at me, and then whips around to her brother. "Did you hurt her?"

"No!" he yells, and then flinches.

Another speaker takes the stage and Sue grabs both our arms and drags us deeper backstage.

She shoves a finger into his chest. "Start talking."

"She was trespassing. Again. I was going to turn her in, which is my legal right. But I had to catch her first."

Sue stares at her brother for a long moment. He does not look sorry or even slightly bothered by what he's done. It feels as if she's searching for a reason to believe him. Screw that.

"Your brother was hiding suitcases of meth," I say. "In the Netta mine area you'll find about one million dollars' worth."

"She's lying," Kaleb says. "We were running some security drills."

I grab the yellow bandana around his neck and twist it so tight he's coughing. I yank him close. "The man you are protecting, Pete Daweson, he murdered my best friend and her parents. I don't know how you became the kind of person who'd help him, but I know your father would be ashamed."

He coughs and gasps. "I don't . . . I'm doing my job."

I smile at his pain, finally feeling like I'm doing something good. I pull tighter so we're almost nose to nose. "If I find my sister and learn you knew where she was this whole time, or God forbid I find her . . . in a goddamn mineshaft, I will fucking end you."

I shove him to the ground and turn to Sue because I'm not done with this family yet.

"Did you know Pete was alive?"

Her eyes go wide. "Of course not."

I stare for a moment and realize I'm searching her as if she's still the friend I once had. Not this new person with a decade of life between us. "Did you know your brother is running meth for *him*?"

Sue shoots Kaleb a hard look. "Do you have evidence?"

"I have a photo." I grab my phone and shove the picture in her face. "This is one suitcase of ten. They have one hundred pounds of crystal meth. I saw your brother unloading those same suitcases at the Netta mines. Get a search warrant and you've got the bust of the year."

She narrows her eyes at the photo and then at me, as if she's not convinced.

I pull back my arms. "You should arrest your brother right now."

Kaleb is wheezing on the ground. "She needs to arrest *you*, psycho bitch."

"Enough." Sue closes her eyes and presses two fingers between her eyebrows. This is a new gesture to me, perhaps one she had to grow into to control her temper. "The situation is more complicated than that, Syd."

"I'll go to the Miami Police Station," I threaten. "They'll at least check it out."

"They don't have jurisdiction over Native land," Sue says. "Whatever they find will be inadmissible."

I understand the extra layers of difficulty with tribal law and police enforcement that must be navigated. BIA can only get involved in a crime on tribal land if either the victim or the possible criminal is Native. The BIA can patrol the land that's Native, but if it's leased to white men, which it usually is, then you have to tread carefully. "To get a warrant," Sue says, "we'd need a lot more evidence. *Admissible* evidence."

"It's Daweson land," I say. "Not Native."

"The land is leased," she says. "Members of the Quapaw tribe technically still own all the mine land. You think the Dawesons are going to take responsibility for the land once they sell off the chat, the only thing of monetary value still there? They use it and then walk away from all consequences, leaving the mess behind for the Quapaw tribal members who own the land. The same people who haven't seen a dime in generations."

"We're not talking chat. It's a missing person. It's my sister. It's the man who murdered three people."

"I do believe you think you saw him—"

Of course that's what she'd say. If Pete's alive, then someone lied about his DNA. Maybe the very man they're honoring tonight. "You read the files? Did they identify his body?"

"Science was different then," she says. "Let's not jump to conclusions."

"Whatever happened," I say, inching closer, "it's time for justice. To finally do the right thing and put Pete Daweson away."

She raises an eyebrow. "Are you implying the wrong thing was done?"

"I don't know," I say. "What matters now is finding my sister, Sue. She was at the Daweson compound. She wrote Gracie's name in the dirt and there was blood where they handcuffed her to a tree."

She swears under her breath and glances at Kaleb, as if he has a say. She seems frustrated but not surprised about Pete or her brother's involvement. Sue has conflict in her gaze. As if she wants to say something like *I'm on your side.* I don't try to make her feel better and only stare right back with my eyebrows raised. *Prove it.*

"Judge Allen is here," Sue says. "I'll talk to him about a warrant for the compound."

"The drugs are at the mine and maybe Emma Lou by now," I say. "Are you willing to overlook them to protect your brother?"

"Just like you want to protect your sister."

"Emma was taken by Pete Daweson. She doesn't willingly work for him. That's a big difference. Sister didn't do anything wrong."

Sue looks at me for a long minute. "I'll have the sheriff drive by Netta. I can get a warrant for the compound much easier than the mine, especially if we tie it to Zeke having meth burns. But it's still a potential Waco situation, so I'm asking a lot."

"I'll be the first one in," I say, meaning it. "If you let me."

"Looks like you've done more than enough. Now, you got enough blood left to drive yourself home? I've gotta get to the reception."

"Sure, if your brother doesn't try to ram me into an eighteen-wheeler."

She glares at Kaleb. "We need to talk."

"You can only protect him for so long," I say. "He'll pull you down, too. If he hasn't already."

"Watch it, Syd." Sue steps toward me. "I've been working these local cases eight years. My father, when it comes to the Dawesons, his whole career. You've been back two days."

"It's long enough." I turn toward the stage and the exit down the stairs into the main seating area.

I don't want to go into the alley. I need some fresh air, but somewhere within the crowd, so I don't get abducted by a dipshit. I need to decide if I'm as dumb as those yellow bandana idiots for taking Sue at her word.

24

I rush down the few steps leading from the curtained area off-stage to the main theater. I step onto the lush red carpet and freeze as I stare down at my muddy boots. I take one step onto the carefully woven Coleman family crest and thankfully don't track much. The lights come up as I begin to head up the far aisle. The giant chandelier hanging from the center molding illuminates rows and rows of people.

"Syd? What are you doing here?"

I'm almost to the exit into the lobby when I run right into Deandre. Backing up a few feet, I stand up straighter, wondering if she's got the same agenda as the dipshits. She was certainly trying to hide her mother's name on that list of deliveries.

She gives me a smile like I'm a feral animal. "Wow, you must have searched the ditches in Picher."

I'm not explaining myself. "I need to go."

"You heard?" Stepping toward me, she takes my hand. "Can you believe it?"

There are so many answers to what I could have heard. Her cousin Zeke nearly dead. Pete back for vengeance. Suitcases of meth at the mines her family controls. "Heard what?"

Her mouth makes an O, and there's a shimmer of excitement in her eyes before she tells me. "They found Emma Lou's car."

The room swirls, and I can hear the tinkling of the chandelier as it prepares to crash on top of us. Or at least that's how it feels.

Deandre watches me and shifts her grip from my hand to my shoulder. "Why don't you sit for a second."

I shake her off, though she's probably right. "Where did they find it?"

She holds up her hands. "The car is fine. Not like burned up or in a mineshaft, I mean. It was just covered with a tarp in a field."

I let out a breath, since that's good news. "Whose field?"

I don't let myself think of the meth trailers. I don't let myself fear it's some dealer in the outlaw lands. I will not put up that wall of anger and blame toward Emma Lou to protect myself, even for a few seconds of spared pain.

She leans close to my ear, glancing around before she whispers, "At Chairman Rhett Caine's farm."

"What?" I shake my head, trying to picture him from the buyout meeting. "His place by you?"

"No, he's got a family farm south of Picher."

I remember that we'd had several search teams out there. In fact, Tyler had insisted on covering outside the city limits, which I'd appreciated. And now I'm so grateful for that because we finally have something about Sister. Still, I'm having trouble understanding. "Would he . . . hurt her?"

She shrugs. "I don't know. He's being questioned right now by the sheriff."

"What reason . . ."

"Anyone can have a reason for anything," Deandre says sharply.

Anyone . . . I think of Emma Lou's delivery locations the day she went missing. That list had led me to Manda and then Pete. To the drugs. The thunder rumbles and the chandelier tinkles above us. But maybe I should have focused where Trudy said. On the chairman with the big mortgage.

"I'm surprised no one called you. Weren't you out there searching, too?" Deandre's eyes glitter with knowing, and I stare back hard, wondering how deep it goes. "You better get home before the storm hits, Syd."

"Yeah, I will." I'm strangely relieved to have someone give me a direction. To tell me what to do, because I feel as if every single choice I've made today has been a mistake.

I follow the crowd into the lobby. Lightning flashes through the glass doors ahead, and I have never wanted to be home more in my life. Hurrying past the snack counter, with Coleman mugs and hats, I glance at old photos from the heyday of the theater. It had been lovingly restored, so it felt like a step back in time to when Bing Crosby sang or the Three Stooges performed.

I take one last long look at the beauty the mines built. A token of appreciation with gold-leaf trim, silk damask panels, stained glass windows, and a carved mahogany staircase. A grand escape that's not so close that you can see the mines where the money was made, but close enough for those who benefited to enjoy it.

Stepping outside, I glance around for dipshit trucks, but how can I discern them from the dozens of others parked along Main Street?

The wind is frantic in that before-the-storm way and pulls at my matted ponytail. I glance at the Coleman's Spanish Mission–style architecture with a terra-cotta roof and gargoyles outside. In the crowd are a few familiar faces, but mostly this seems a Miami crowd. Ronny and Sue moved here from Picher right after the murders. It's hard to fault them. I left as soon as I could.

Why stay in a place where there are no answers, only whispers? *Why didn't you do more to stop them?*

Only one bullet. Only one bullet in the gun.

"Hey, cuz, you go to this fancy event looking like a mud flap on a truck?"

The question pulls me back and I see Rayna in the fluorescent lights of the Coleman. "I look like a mud flap?" I point toward a nearby truck. "One of those, with the naked-woman silhouette on them?"

"Sure, and usually truck nuts."

I frown at her. "What the hell are truck nuts?"

"You ain't seen any before?" She glances around and takes my arm toward a line of trucks parked along Main Street. "There!"

I narrow my eyes at the back of a Chevy Silverado, and on the hitch dangles a fake scrotum. "Wow. As if these trucks weren't Freudian enough."

We giggle and Rayna sticks out her tongue before running up to the back of the truck. She squats down in her tiny shorts and tickles them.

I really laugh, and some of the screaming pressure in my chest releases.

"Come feel this shit. They feel real." She laughs and makes a grossed-out face. "Why do they have to be so lifelike? I think I see veins!"

I cackle. "Shut up, you do not." A couple give us a dirty look as they cross to the other side of the street.

"Come feel these! Now's your chance to see what you're missing," Rayna calls, and the couple hurry to their car.

We laugh like the good ol' days as she makes inappropriate noises and fondles them.

Our laughter dies but the smiles linger. She heads over to me. "Better, cuz?"

I nod, wiping a few tears from my eyes. "Yeah, thanks."

"Then we better get to your house."

She puts her arm around my shoulders. As we walk, I inhale whiskey, cigarettes, and her too-sweet perfume. I hug her tight because she's always saved me, in her way.

"Easy there. Your parents are liable to take the homestead apart looking for extra keys to Emma Lou's car. They're really scared, Syd."

"About time they are." I lead us toward the dark alley, far from the bright lights of Ronny Dove's marquee.

AGILVGI

The damn bolt is rusted.

 My nail bleeds as I push it into the rough metal edge.

My whole arm shakes.

Not stopping, I cry out from pain and being pissed off the bolt won't budge.

Like the others.

With bars holding me.

My muscle seizes, and the cramp twists my arm into my chest.

Withdrawals again.

Dosed me with more of that heavy shit.

I'll have to save myself or I'll die alone.

That's a certainty.

More thunder.

Another crack of lightning.

I shiver on the cold floor and whisper a prayer to Gracie. *Don't give up on Momma.*

There were men here.

I heard their voices.

Could almost smell the whiskey on their breath.

I screamed and screamed, but nothing.

Over and over, I rub the small scar on the tip of my finger.

A memory, bright and warm, appears.

The sun is hot and reflecting off my dad's truck. I'm in the front yard making Syd a dandelion chain necklace. Dad's bare feet stick out from under the truck, which is up on cinder blocks more than wheels. Dad says something about the lug nuts being too tight. "Probably rusted from all that rain." He rolls out from under the truck. A lit cigarette hangs out of his mouth. That's only 'cause Mom is busy visiting someone and wouldn't see. "Sister!" He waves me over. "Need to show you something."

My fingers are stained yellow and green from the dandelion crown. I wrap it around my neck so I don't lose it in the clover.

I shade my eyes from the sun and lean against the truck. It's hot against my skin through my T-shirt. "What, Dad?"

"Come here and learn a thing or two."

He helps me onto the roller board and pushes me under the truck. There's a lot of old and rusty stuff, but it's still interesting to see how a truck is put together. Dad scoots next to me.

Chat dust swirls around us as he flicks the lighter and moves the flame. I shift away as it touches a rusted screw. "Why are you doin' that?"

"Life lesson, Sister." He pulls out pliers and twists. "Anything will move with enough heat."

25

Early thick drops of rain plop against the windshield like warning shots until the hard stuff settles in. This is one of those storms that roars in with energy gathered from the flatlands of Kansas and is gone just as fast. Lightning flashes, and it rains harder. I slow the rental down and switch on my brights.

Rayna pulls a bottle of Fireball whiskey from her big purse. She offers, but I shake it off. The plastic lid cracks, and she takes a long swig. The wipers work hard as they squeak, squeak, squeak.

Our faces are lit by an oncoming car, and I switch my lights back to regular. My heart speeds up as I have a flash of being on this road just a couple of hours ago and almost meeting head-lights head-on. I don't know how to say that out loud, even to Rayna. Words like "Pete is alive." Or "I saw where they chained Emma Lou to a tree." Instead, I'd rather cup these painful flames and shield others from the burn.

"How'd you find me?" I ask, finally giving in to distraction over the protection of silence.

"The Great Spirit led me to you," she says, and takes a swig when I don't respond. "I needed cigs. I saw you outside the Coleman."

"Were you at a bar?"

"Pope shit in the woods?"

"No?"

"Huh," she says. "I always assumed."

"Is the comedy routine over?" I ask.

"Bo Don took me out for a drink and slots at the Stables, but we got in a fight. I was walking it off. Your mom called, so I had my eye out."

Lightning flashes as we pass the first chat pile on the road into Picher. "I hate to think of her freezing out there," I say quietly.

"If she's shivering, she's alive. That's what matters."

There's a question I need to ask, but it admits how far away I've been. "What was Emma Lou like before she went missing?"

Rayna gives me a sad smile. "She was talking to Luna. Not all the time. She kept her job and seemed pretty normal with Gracie when I saw them. She told me Luna asked for help beyond the veil. That it had grown thin."

"Emma Lou always believed she'd help Luna's spirit to the other side."

"It was scary." Rayna takes a long drink. "Sister said she was meant to take Luna's place in hell."

"Luna is not in hell," I say, thinking of how much hell is on earth. Emma Lou should have been satisfied being right here working for devils.

I consider telling Rayna more about what happened, but the silence is too alluring. For a moment, I can breathe and only focus on the road as I pull into the long dirt driveway to the house.

"Where's that damn buffalo?" Rayna rolls down the window

and cold rain hits both our faces. "Charlie!" she screams into the night. "Hey, big boy? Your auntie wants to ride ya."

I laugh and she does, too, as I press the switch on my side to roll up her window. "You don't know how to act in a car with real leather." She snorts and leans her head back. She's cresting and that's good. She'll be asleep before long.

I park by my dad's old truck. We sit in silence, and if Rayna wasn't here, I'd cry.

Lightning flashes, and the thunder is only a few seconds behind. The heart of the storm moves over us. The clouds are thick and roll across the sky like a sheet tumbling in the wind. I do not miss this about spring in Oklahoma.

"Anything with a tail?" Rayna asks about the telltale sign.

I crane my neck to see the sky better out the front window. After a few more lightning flashes, I don't spot anything unusual for a cold spring storm. "Let's get inside."

We hurry through the rain and run up to the covered front porch, which leaks in several spots. Rayna stumbles over to a rocking chair and collapses into it with an exhilarated *whoop.*

A loud rumble of thunder rattles the windows. On the porch, the deep wet cold is settling into my bones. I wonder if Emma Lou is in the dark. If she's also cold and wet, but alive, alive, please, alive.

"Good grief, there you are." Mom stomps out onto the porch. "What's the point of having a cell phone if you don't answer it?"

"Sorry," I say. "Rayna found me."

"At the bottom of a glass?" she asks.

I turn to see Rayna rocking the chair like she's trying to make it flip over. "Careful!" I say, and rush over to her.

Mom leaves as I try to keep Rayna's legs on the ground. "Chaaaaarlie!" she yells.

The screen door slams behind us and Mom is back with our family blanket. "Put this around you, girl. Wet as a dog and wearing less than a collar."

We tuck the blanket around Rayna, who curls into it. I run my finger with the scar where the red and yellow stripes meet. Sister and I were wrapped in this blanket as babies.

"Where's my Fireball?" Rayna whines.

"I'll find it," I lie as lightning crackles, hitting the ground with a *boom* in the distance.

Rayna stares out at the storm. She's always loved them. As girls, we'd stay on the porch until we fell asleep and Dad brought us inside.

Mom watches her as the lightning flashes and a quick crack of thunder shakes the ground. "You want something to eat?" she asks.

Rayna shakes her head and snuggles into the blanket more. "I'm fine, can't you tell?"

Mom sighs and nods for me to follow her into the house. All the lights are on, and the drawers and cupboards are wide-open, the insides out. "You tore the house apart looking for Emma Lou's car keys?"

"Looking for anything," Dad says at the kitchen counter, where he's sipping a cup of coffee. "It doesn't make sense that Rhett Caine would do something to . . . You bleeding, Syd?"

"Maybe," I say. "I'll take a shower in a minute. Did you talk to Caine? What did he say?"

Mom slams a drawer behind me. "He said he didn't know anything about the car. Then he called his fancy Tulsa lawyer."

For the first time, I see my mother's distress. The red eyes and dark circles under them. Perhaps it was searching for her daughter's remains that finally made the possibility true. My father has looked wrecked since I first saw him. Now he and Mom have joined me in this place of panic for Sister and I am . . . relieved. As if I can trust them with some of my fear and truth.

"I found something out," I say to them. "At Wings."

Mom freezes. "How's that?"

"I was able to look at the delivery list for Emma Lou on the day she disappeared."

"I've been looking for it," Mom says quietly, glancing at Dad. "What did it say?"

"Caine was on her list the day she disappeared. So was Manda Daweson."

"If the sheriff would listen—" Mom shakes her head with her lips pressed together.

"We could try again," Dad says to her.

Mom holds up her hand. "I can't stand those idiots' judgment again. Asking about drugs and prostitution. About my missing baby. Sister had problems, but—"

I didn't know my parents had gone to the sheriff. "With evidence, though . . . they have to do something now?"

Dad lets out a long sigh. "I don't know. Caine draws a lot of water."

We are silent for a moment, and the awful possibilities are as loud as the rain on the roof. Would Caine just take her? Do awful things, then kill her?

"It don't make sense," Mom murmurs. "If the police would let us talk to Caine . . . Maybe she left her car with him."

"You're making excuses for him?" I snap. "This is why men like him think they can do whatever they want."

"Easy there," Dad says. "We know him, is all. It's hard to imagine he'd hurt Sister. I go fishing with the man."

There's no arguing with that, so I focus back on their ransacking. "Are you looking for her keys?"

"Anything," Dad says. "I'm sure they got her car open by now. Still, we had a second set of keys. I think . . . maybe Cody has them."

"Tell the sheriff," I say. "Send him to Cody's house."

"He's Gracie's dad." Mom slams a drawer. "The only parent she has right now."

"Where was he that day?" I inhale deeply, knowing we're all frustrated, but it has to be said. "Where was he that night?"

Dad glances at Mom, who's digging through another drawer. "I saw Sister at lunch. She made two sandwiches and left."

"Who was she eating with?" I ask, already knowing the answer.

"She said Cody was at the Body Shop to let the keg guys in."

"Was he the last one to see her alive?" I demand. "Why have you kept it from the sheriff?"

"We haven't," Mom says. "We went to them first thing. They searched his place. They questioned him. He accounted for himself all day. His mom, the keg delivery guy, and someone at the bank when he dropped off a deposit."

I shake my head, nowhere near convinced. "He had all day. Maybe even night—"

"He had dinner with us at that very table," Mom says quickly. "You think he could hurt Emma Lou and then eat spaghetti facing her family? Cutting up his daughter's food after he'd killed her mother? What kind of monster—"

"You know there are monsters like that," I say. "I killed one, remember."

"He ain't like his uncles." Mom puts her hands on her hips. "Now, where were you tonight?"

I stare at her hard, wondering if I should tell the truth. If sharing even that small fact would make a difference. "Pete isn't dead," I say quietly. "I saw him tonight. At the Daweson compound."

"What on earth were you doing there in the first place?"

That was not the question I expected. "Did Cody call you? Do you already know?"

Mom closes her eyes for a moment. "He wanted to tell us that you were okay."

"He's working with Pete. He's trying to get into the meth-from-Mexico business."

"He wouldn't," Mom says with a deep weariness. "People talk about the cartel like they're a boogey monster."

"I saw suitcases of meth." I step toward her. "Pete's alive, Mom. Cody knew his uncle was alive. Probably this whole damn time. The man who almost killed us. He hid that from our family. We can't trust him on anything. Just like always."

Dad holds up his hands. "Take a breath, Syd. We should ask before we accuse him. Besides—"

"Move on, Noah." Mom shakes her head at him.

"Besides what?" I say, angry they're keeping secrets, which makes me a hypocrite, and that makes me angrier.

Dad glances at Mom, who shakes her head but continues. "I don't know what it means, but when they found the car . . . we went over there. To verify it."

"Okay, so?" I'm breathing too fast, but I can't slow down, can't stop. "What?"

"Cody said she never came by his place for lunch," Dad says. "And it's a small thing, but . . . tonight we saw the car and . . . the two sandwiches were still in ziplocks on the passenger seat."

"So what?" I laugh, the terrible one that says I'm close to

breaking. "So he killed her before lunch! Why are you defending him?"

"Because he's been here," Mom says as she slams a drawer and whirls to face me fully. "We know him. We believe him. He's a good dad and he was good to Emma Lou since he got out. He was here, Syd. He was here."

My mouth falls open. "And I wasn't?"

"No, you weren't," Mom says simply, with disappointment in her gaze. "You're off half-cocked like you know more than us. Like you're more terrified."

"You need to stay away from the Dawesons," Dad says a little too gently. As if I'm a child who's found a loaded gun, and he needs me to hand it over. "Ain't nothing on that compound but more pain for our family."

"I will look for Sister anywhere I damn well please," I say. "I'm just getting started."

"You listen to your father and stay away," Mom says, her eyes filling with angry tears. "Or God help me, I'm gonna lose both my girls after all."

26

After a sleepless night, I get up before dawn to put my anxiousness and fear to use and finish the dig assessment on the Myers land. It'll be a while before Sue hears from the lab, but I want to be sure I'm not missing anything still waiting to be found.

I quietly shut the screen door and inhale cool air from a light spring mist hovering over the yard and fields in the dark distance. I don't look toward the graveyard because I'm afraid to see Ghost Luna. Worried she'll be joined by another dead woman, our Sister.

Headlights suddenly appear down the road. They are coming fast at first, but slow as they approach our fence line. At the entrance to our place, the big truck stops. The engine revs and I take a step backward, closer to the door.

Thump-thump.

The engine releases one more roar in place and the truck peels out, kicking a thick cloud of dirt into the air behind its chaotic pace away from our property. It's a warning or a threat, I'm sure of that.

I think of my boss Jo's request: *This is about more than the skull and the badge. You need to figure out what they're hiding.*

Damn right I will.

I slide my tools over my shoulder and balance my sorter against my hip as I walk east. My boots crunch on the road as the stars are fading to morning overhead.

I wonder how Mal is doing, what she's thinking, or if she's thinking of me at all. Perhaps me being gone is a blessing like the new life growing within her.

"Pity party?"

I ignore the question and keep striding toward the Myers land. The place where I'd once dreamed as a girl. The place where all my nightmares came true.

And they didn't stop. Another skull, another woman, found on this land where I stand again, at the terrifying center.

There's enough light to easily sort my tools. I find where I left off and begin to dig. The familiarity kicks in and my mind is focused on what I was trained to do. Dig, sift, document, and move on.

At some point the sun is shining bright on my face and I slip on sunglasses. I realize I didn't even bring water, but the pleasure of getting lost in work is more important than anything else at this moment.

My hands are trembling as I shake the last of the dirt through the sieve. Wiping the sweat from my face, I inhale deeply as if waking from a trance. I stretch my back and my muscles are already sore.

There's a woman in the distance, and for a moment I think it's Emma Lou. But the Lolita heart-shaped sunglasses are a quick giveaway that it's Rayna striding toward me with my niece on one hip and a picnic basket on the other.

"Brought some brunch. Looks like the prairie dogs been digging out here," she says toward the dozen piles of dirt around me. "You need a hat, cuz. Don't think a farmer's tan will suit."

"I'll put some sunscreen on in a minute," I say, not in the mood to be mothered. My niece is watching me with a tiny smile, as if she has a secret. "Gracie, did you bring me something?"

"Peanut butter and honey sammich," she says softly. "I share my rainbow Goldfish."

I slide off my dirty gloves and reach for a towel and Purell in my backpack. "You are the sweetest," I say, meaning it.

"Hey, I helped!" Rayna bounces Gracie as if she's going to drop her.

"Bare-wee help, Way-nah." She giggles. "I need my dolls."

"It's a good thing you're cute." Rayna gently places Gracie on the ground and digs various naked Barbies out of the basket. "Don't go too far," she calls to Gracie as she twirls away in a Disney princess nightgown, arms full of dolls.

I'm guessing Rayna is still wearing her short shorts, but she's drowning in a Sonic T-shirt so big it looks like a dress. "Is that my dad's shirt?"

"Gracie girl wanted us to both wear dresses, and I'm scared of Aunt June, so I asked your dad for help." She watches Gracie until she finds a spot not too far from us. "She and her momma play dress-up a lot."

We watch Gracie arrange the dolls, and then she runs back

over to us. "I need their treat!" she shouts as she digs into the basket.

Rayna crouches next to her until she finds a chocolate Hostess cupcake.

She snatches it from Rayna. "Birthday party time!"

We stand there in silence as we watch Gracie try to feed her dolls the cupcake before taking her own big bite. The frosting smears and she picks the doll up and licks her face clean. Rayna and I laugh, and it's so pure and simple, I have to blink tears from my eyes.

Grabbing the blanket, I stride over to a tree and spread it in the shadows of a half-dead maple. Rayna drops beside me and starts to unpack the picnic basket.

"Gracie seems to like you," I say as Rayna hands me a sandwich.

"I watch her now and then. Guess there's worse things than having a kid. Hey, you'll know that soon enough."

I take a bite instead of letting myself dwell on the fact that Mal hasn't responded to my texts today. The sweetness of the sandwich hurts my teeth, but it's an ache wrapped in nostalgia. The creamy peanut butter folded into fresh honey, all on white bread, of course. I must have eaten peanut butter and honey sandwiches a hundred times on this very land. Emma Lou likes them with extra honey, and Luna, more peanut butter.

Last night slams into my thoughts. The face older, but still sharp from hate, which weathers the skin like sand. The truck this morning.

Thump-thump.

I shake my head, refusing to fall back to the night that happened here. Not when he's here now. "Pete Daweson is alive."

Rayna sucks in a breath and starts to cough. "Jesus, warn me next time." She clears her throat and takes a sip of Sprite. "You're sure? You seen him?"

"Last night. Out at the Daweson compound. I was sneaking around looking for Emma Lou while everyone was busy with the search in town. He almost ran me over. Twice."

"Shit, girl." Rayna leans back, steadying herself on one arm. "I'm sorry. That's messed up."

I drop my sandwich onto a napkin, the sweetness making me feel queasy. "You think after all this time . . . that sick fuck would come back just to get at us?"

She blows out a breath and stares up at the dead section of the tree. "Until we find Sister, you are the only witness left. Get rid of you, then run for president."

I snicker. "Shake and bake in every pot kind of thing?"

Rayna releases a belly laugh that makes me laugh, too. Soon we're quiet.

"I wonder why . . . they thought he'd burned up, too."

"What did they say?" she asks softly. "When they told you he was dead?"

I realize Rayna has never asked me about that night. Not ever. She's always given me space. Tried to tease me into remembering who I was before. "DNA evidence," I say, repeating what the sheriff told my parents. Or maybe it was Sue's dad. "They had evidence of all five bodies that burned in the fire."

"God, that's so sad. An angel like that forced to burn with those devils."

"Just one devil," I say. "Pete got out somehow. It's always the ones who don't deserve to live that do."

Rayna frowns at me. "You survived, Syd. You saved Sister."

I don't want to go down this familiar road. A path of survivor guilt and regrets that have stolen more than weeks of sleep. "Pete's alive. Sister's missing. A skull is found out here. The land is telling us something."

"Don't you sound like Grandma Ama," Rayna says with a smirk. "What else happened at the Daweson place? Bad as it ever got with me, I refused to go out there. Even for a fix."

"I'm sure everything is about drugs." I let out a long, shaky exhale. "I saw a meth shipment. Ten suitcases with ten pounds in each."

"Holy shit." Rayna turns to face me. "Are you sure? It goes for about ten thousand a pound." She lifts her heart sunglasses. "That's one million dollars' worth of meth. That's definitely cartel level."

My mind continues to search for logic amid all my anger and fear. "Emma Lou must have been mixed up in it, or maybe knew and shouldn't have. That's why Pete or those dipshits took her."

"You really think Sister is stolen?" Rayna's voice is calm, as if she's searching for answers, like me.

I stare down at my trembling hands but force myself to speak. "She wrote Gracie's name in the dirt. Right next to a pair of handcuffs. There was . . . blood. They had her chained to a tree."

"Oh, Sister," Rayna whispers as her face twists in pain. "We should burn that place to the ground."

"The thought has crossed my mind." I pull my cell phone out of my pocket. Sue hasn't responded to any of my texts. My anxiety about how I approached her last night mixes with anger that Pete was alive this whole goddamn time. "Sue might get a warrant for the compound."

"I can't imagine what shit they'll find out there."

"The meth isn't there anymore. You know Zeke Daweson? He blew his face off with a shake-and-bake thing, and they took him and the drugs out."

"That's depressing." Rayna leans back. "Zeke was kinda hot."

"He's still alive. Mom got a text the church is having a prayer service for him there tomorrow. I guess Zeke's mom is a member."

"She's going to be on the warpath," Rayna says. "Zeke is her only child and walks on water."

"Huh." I wonder if having her son blown up might make her view her family a little differently. "Maybe I'll go see her."

"Good luck with that."

We sit in silence for a moment aside from a light breeze, and the cicadas' song comes and goes in pulses.

"Waaaaay-naaaaah!" Gracie calls from an old tire she's playing on. "Can I have another cupcake?"

"I guess." She grabs one and delivers the plastic package. "What?" She drops back onto the blanket. "I ate sugar all the time and look how great I turned out."

I frown at the joke because I hear the edge to it. "You are great, Rayna."

She swats at me. "Go piss up a rope."

Gracie stuffs the cupcake in her mouth and jumps on the tire to get the dolls to fall.

"I need a smoke. Let's head over a little so it doesn't blow her way."

I follow Rayna as she lights up. After a deep inhale she leads me closer to the yellow tape and dig site.

"You said you were in town because they found a skull?"

"Yeah." I glance at Gracie, who is still on the tire.

Rayna's pointy boot connects with my leg right in the spot where the fence stabbed it.

"Ouch. What the hell was that for?"

"You can't do this alone, Syd."

I start to argue but I don't know why. "It's what I'm used to doing."

"That work out pretty well for you last night? Twice?"

I swallow thickly. "Not really."

"Then try something new." She stands up straighter. "Hey, Syd! Whatcha up to?"

I roll my eyes but know I must answer. Rayna sees me in a way that reaches all the way back to the crib. She knows I have our grandma's brown eyes. She knows I was too stubborn to tell anyone when I broke my arm and it ended up infected. She knows that being scared and mad go together with me. She knows I try to hide it all.

I bring over my backpack and hand her the folder. "Someone left a skull right over there." I point toward the tree. "My old BIA internship badge was between its teeth."

"Whoa." Rayna flips open the folder and curses as she sees the photo of the skull. She glances through the report. "Yeah, I heard that cadaver dog is good at finding bodies. Happens a lot here with all the sink-ins and mineshafts."

"But why leave the skull?" I say. "Why leave it for me? In our old tree."

Rayna continues to stare at the top photo. "What about that tree?"

"We'd hide messages to each other there. I guess it's possible Emma Lou—"

"No you didn't." Rayna holds up the photo where the caution tape gently blows in the warm breeze. "That tree used to have the swing, right? You girls hid messages in the other one."

I point west toward the tree in between our properties. "I know. We used both trees—"

"Um, no. I'm five years older than you and I used to have to watch your asses all the damn time. For no money, by the way. I remember you hiding messages in the trees. But not that one, usually. It was that one."

My gaze follows where she's pointing. To a tree with high grass around it. Memories arrive in flashes of leaving notes there, especially Emma Lou. In fact, I think we each had a tree we used more and that one was hers. The one with the skull was mine. The one on the fence line, where we'd gaze all the way to Kansas, that was Luna's.

How could I forget? Why didn't I let anyone else help me remember?

I grab my gloves and jog over. There's a similar V, but it's shorter. Running my hands over the bark, I feel familiar knots and creases. I get closer and see scrapes from a pocketknife or rocks. Near the V is a giant heart with the word "Agilvgi." The low broken branch that allowed us to climb up far enough to reach inside. I was wrong.

Rayna walks up behind me. "Whoever left that skull probably left the receipt and ring for you to find. But there still might be something in there."

I inhale sharply. "Something from Sister."

Taking my flashlight, I peer into the rotted tree. I can see all the way to the bottom, and there's nothing but leaves. "Empty."

"Feel around. You girls would have half your bodies inside there. You had weird secret spots."

I smile, remembering Emma Lou loved leaving things in the rotted branches that you could only access from inside the tree. I reach deeper and my fingers feel until I come to one of those small, rotted spots. There's something inside. I pull out the object and bring it into the sun.

It's a smooth, flat rock. The kind we'd paint and draw on as girls. But there are no little hearts or sticks on this one. Just three numbers.

"Five, eighteen, eighty," Rayna reads. "Missing some numbers for Powerball."

I turn the rock over and there's a familiar message on the other side of the stone: *FIND ME.*

27

I leave Rayna and Gracie playing outside and head back toward home. As I cross the field, I call Sue, but she doesn't answer. "It's Syd, and I've been out at the Myers land. I found something. Call me back as soon as you can."

I text the same thing, but there's no response.

I'm relieved she didn't answer, because I'd have more evidence but no answers. Emma Lou was always playful, even after the devils. She loved Easter egg hunts. Would hide my car keys with little notes and clues.

I walk into the driveway and see my dad yanking weeds in the Three Sisters Garden. He scowls at where he's digging, as if angry the weeds chose to sprout there. Or maybe it's the fact that Sister isn't around to see how her plants are growing. Then there's the terrible question of if she'll be back for the harvest at all.

Dad glances up at me but doesn't stop his work, so I don't either. I consider the messages. I don't think Emma Lou is playing a game. But she might be trying to get me to play so I can understand. So I can help.

FIND ME.

Crossing the lawn, I stride toward the family graveyard. I haven't been out here in years, and there's a welcome familiarity as I open the squeaking gate and start down the gravel pathway.

"You should go to my grave."

I stumble at Ghost Luna's words at my back. A chill spreads down my neck, and I rub my arms. Though she's not real, there's a cruelty I can't shake to seeing her own grave.

I head toward the three graves, but there's only two under the trees' shade. I jog over to the maple tree, which is so much taller than I remember, but I know this is the spot.

Luna's parents' gravestones are there, but hers has fallen over. I crouch down and see a muddy boot print across the gray granite. Not fallen, knocked over. Someone has vandalized Luna's grave.

I still have my gloves in my back pocket, and I take them out. I gently lift the stone so it's returned to upright. But it's more than being broken. Someone spray-painted over where her name, the day she was born, and the day she died were carved.

"Tsgili," I murmur at the crude devil image defacing Luna's grave. My hands begin to shake as I glare out at the dirt road where the dipshits had revved their truck engines at our property line.

This time they'd crossed onto our land. To this sacred space to desecrate Luna's grave. The place where she could finally be at peace after such a terrible death.

I press my hands together to secure my gloves, and I kneel at her broken grave. My finger lightly traces the letters of her name and then the day she was born: five, eighteen, eighty.

Something is familiar, and I touch the three numbers again. The numbers Emma Lou left for me. It's Luna's birthday. I take a long inhale and try to stay focused. The numbers feel like a code or . . . a combination.

My gaze shoots toward the house, where there is a lock inside. FIND ME.

I jog toward the porch and take the steps two at a time. It's quiet inside, and I don't stop until I'm standing at the hallway closet.

There's not much to the lock. A simple hasp with what looks like a bike lock and four numbers. I quickly add Luna's birthday and there's a click. I inhale sharply, not sure what I hope is on the other side of that door.

It's possible Sister has gotten mixed up in illegal drugs again and that will explain why she might be in trouble with someone like Pete or the dipshits. Maybe it's chaos in there. Papers and clothes and pills not delivered. Perhaps she was overwhelmed by work and motherhood. Maybe she was too embarrassed to admit how tough life had become.

I let the lock dangle and slowly open the door.

Pulling the light string, I blink as the small space is illuminated. I'm face-to-face with a laminated piece of paper taped onto the shelf so it's hanging right in my line of sight.

"Frito-chili-pie Fridays?" I read on the simple weekly menu from my aunt Mercy's community center. I laugh, a little too loudly, and it makes an eerie echo in the house. *What are you trying to tell me, Emma Lou?*

As girls, we'd often have free lunch there with our grandma and aunt. The menu is dated last week.

I get a paper bag out of a kitchen drawer and, with my gloves on, gently place the menu inside. The evidence—if that's even the right word—is stacking up, and I have absolutely no idea what any of it means.

Except I need to finally go see my aunt Mercy.

I grab a bottle of water from the refrigerator and head back outside. Dad is still absorbed by pulling weeds. Maybe I get my focus from him. My need to pour everything into the work in front of me as if my life depended on it.

"Dad? You need help?" I call after I put the paper bag in the Jeep.

He shakes his head and doesn't break from what he's doing.

"You see Luna's grave?" I ask.

"Yeah, I saw it."

He keeps going, and I recognize something in the pace of his movements. The way the frustration and fear cause him to rip the weeds from the ground. With a big sigh, he suddenly stops, red-faced, probably thirsty, and I doubt he has any idea what time it is. Just like me.

He leans back and wipes the sweat from his face, smearing dirt across his cheek. I hold out the water bottle, and he takes a long drink before speaking.

"The police let Rhett go."

I curse under my breath. "Why?"

"His statement is that he had no idea her car was out there. They searched his house this morning and didn't find anything. Sheriff says he tried to get Oklahoma State Police involved, but they still think Sister just ran off."

I shake my head, feeling the Myers land at my back and the tree that held a skull. "Like all the other Native girls around here. Saying they left is a lot easier than accountability."

Dad presses his lips together as if what I've said disappoints him. "Sister is tough. She's smart. She's lucky. Don't you give up."

"I'm trying to be realistic," I say, and then stop myself. Another fight won't help anything.

"You're doing your loner thing," Ghost Luna says from behind me. "Mal warned you. Rayna. How many times does it take?"

I squint as if I'm getting a headache, and I'd take one over hearing Ghost Luna's opinion. Still, I listen. "Dad, can you talk to Rhett? Maybe go by his place. See how he acts. If he really thinks Emma Lou just left the car behind. I'm not saying he did anything to her. But if you ask, maybe he'll tell you something that can help us."

"I doubt he'll say much."

"But you're friends. You guys fish together. Actually, why don't you try that? Go fishing."

"Take the man who had my missing daughter's car on his property fishing?"

"If we're not giving up, then we're trying to find her."

He takes another long drink. I know he's fighting his nature. To weed and tinker and worry instead of facing what's really going on. That's one way to survive, but it comes with a high price. In this case, it could mean the life of Emma Lou.

"Okay, Syd," Dad says simply, and some tension releases in my chest at having help. "I'll go over there with some grub worms."

"Thanks, Dad." I start to leave but decide to keep going. "The lock to Emma Lou's closet was Luna's birthday. Inside is a menu from Native Senior Center."

"Aunt Mercy will be glad to see you," Dad says as if what I've shared is the most normal thing in the world.

"Why would Sister want me to go there?"

"She spends a lot of time with Aunt Mercy lately. Be good to check in."

My list of to-dos is growing. "I'm also stopping by to see Zeke's mom at the hospital. Maybe she knows something."

"She's been going to church the past couple years. She sure loves her boy. Has us pray for him every week." Dad sounds sympathetic at having a child on the edge of death.

I keep my comment about forgiving a Daweson to myself since they clearly don't have a problem with that when it comes to Cody.

"Your mom organized a prayer chain for him after his mom, Lisa, called the preacher about what happened. Been getting 'prayers up,' as June calls it, all morning. Tell her hi."

"I will."

"Grab Lisa a candy bar. She's got a sweet tooth."

We're quiet for a moment. "Love you, Dad."

"Gvgeyui, Sister." He clears his throat. "Good luck with Aunt Mercy. She's been stewing that you ain't visited yet."

"Then she'll have to stop stewing that I'm working for 'the man' at BIA, as she puts it every single time I see her."

"We can hold more than one truth in us, kiddo." He grins at me. "We contain multitudes, maybe most of all your aunt Mercy."

I head toward Miami, past the mushroom farm and the casino signs flashing in the sun. I pull into the parking lot of the Tribal Senior Center. It's after lunch, so there aren't many cars.

My phone buzzes, and I see it's Ellis's number from the Narragansett tribal office.

"Hey, everything okay?" I ask as I park. "I'm about to go into our Native senior center."

He laughs. "What's on the menu?"

"I have no idea," I say. "Fry bread, maybe."

"Sounds good. Hey, I've got a lead on the Narragansett woman. My sister remembered a young woman going missing right after she got married twenty years ago. I'm going to talk to the family later. See if the Swatch or dress are familiar."

"That's great," I say, a pang of relief that he's moving forward and jealous that my own case is stalled. "I'll check in soon. Seeing the remains of two women in one week . . . I'm angry." I blink at my words, not expecting them. "Sorry, I'm just rambling."

"No you're not," Ellis says. "Focus on justice, not the unjust. Keep digging, Syd."

"Thanks."

I quickly head inside the senior center, where I'm hit with a welcome blast of cold air. There's a smell I'd forgotten, some mix of cafeteria Frito chili pie and leather, like the old-time gift shop off Highway 69.

There are long tables set up with a few older folks eating dessert. The kitchen area is mostly quiet, and several games of dominos are being played by old men in faded denim shirts. A group of ladies are in a corner chatting and knitting. Another woman sorts beads by color while the other threads them onto a thin piece of leather. There are several peyote-stitched key chains next to them.

I think of my own on my key ring that Emma Lou sent me for Christmas. The cylinder shape with blue and red beads stitched in a V pattern. Sister probably made it here. That stops me for a moment, lingering where the women are beading. The one sorting beads looks up.

"Who you looking for, sweetie?"

I swallow back my first answer, Emma Lou. "My aunt, Mercy Walker."

The other lady nods solemnly. "She'd normally be right here, but she's been staying in the library since . . . her little niece disappeared. Are you Emma Lou's sister?"

I nod and clear my throat. "She made me one of those key chains."

The woman laughs. "She must have made fifty that year. I imagine everyone got one for Christmas."

"They're really beautiful," I say. "I'll go check on my aunt."

"We miss her," the other woman says, and runs her hands through the purple beads. "Oh, Luann, let's give her Gracie's bracelet."

"It's in my tin." She pulls out a cookie tin that's full of scraps and beads. "Here you go. We finished it for her."

The little bracelet is all different shades of purple and trimmed with silver beads that match larger silver beads on the wrist tie. "She'll love it. Thank you."

The ladies give me small smiles and Luann points down the hall. I slip the bracelet into my bag and head in that direction. I pass a glass cabinet displaying corn-husk dolls decorated with black yarn hair. A familiarity returns the farther I go down the long hallway. There's a door propped open with an old dictionary, and I suddenly remember the circular-shaped room has bookshelves for walls.

I loved this round room as a girl. The tribes held summer programs here where we played Indian marbles and made little dolls out of panty hose. One year I learned to write my name in Cherokee. It's where the three of us learned the word for sister, "agilvgi," and we whispered it like an incantation.

I remember Aunt Mercy being impressed when she heard us using the term. She pushed me to learn more. "You do not have to speak Cherokee tomorrow, but know that it is there for you," she'd said to me, in the passenger seat, as she pulled her brown

Buick out of the parking lot. "The most famous and beloved Cherokee, Sequoyah, is the creator of our alphabet. He gave us a way to share our heritage and communicate our ideas."

I hear the words as my gaze lands on Aunt Mercy, alone at a large round table in the center of the round room. She could be my grandmother, and even though there's a three-year difference, people always thought they were twins. I'd never connected how that's like Emma Lou and me.

Just as with us, there were many differences. My grandma dyed and permed her hair to the very end. Aunt Mercy's dark hair turned wild when the silver strands began to grow. She'd say she was born to be a crone and greeted old age with "wide wiggly arms and saggy boobs."

She is hunched over a book in a ribbon dress with red and orange stripes sewn over a yellow fabric.

"You're like the sun in that dress," I say quietly to reflect the stillness of the library.

"Sunset, maybe. Siyo." After she greets me in Cherokee, she snaps the book shut. She extends her hands, covered in turquoise rings and other colorful stones. Aunt Mercy is not a hugger, but I like that she takes my hands into hers.

"Siyo." I smile down at her. "Good to see you."

She inhales deeply as if drawing my spirit into hers. "You smell like dirt."

"I've been digging," I say with a smile. "I tried to clean it off. Sorry."

"Don't apologize, it's a sacred smell. Dâyuni'sï brought mud to the oceans to create the Earth," she says of the water beetle in the Cherokee creation story before switching gears. "Heard from your dad."

"It's ridiculous the police let Rhett Caine go already."

She shakes her head, and her beaded earrings tap. "It's a shame, but it's no surprise."

"Dad is going to talk to him," I say, glad I spoke to my father honestly. Testing out my weight on the ice of asking others for help. I sit down in the chair next to her, keeping our hands together but resting on the wooden table.

"We're beyond engaging with people who don't care." Her forehead creases exactly as I remember. I've been studying the lines deepening on my skin, and I keep thinking of Aunt Mercy. How she wears her wrinkles like a warrior wears their scars. "This epidemic of girls going missing has a choke hold on Native people everywhere. No one is listening, so we gotta solve it ourselves."

Aunt Mercy has always been a bit tradish in her style. The ribbon shirts and moccasins. But her ideas about modern Native life are radical, if prescient. She's marched on the Oklahoma City capitol many times. For water rights. For land back. For environmental justice. For missing and murdered women.

"Did Emma Lou visit here a lot?" I glance around, easily imagining Sister picking out books for Gracie or a gardening book. I don't want to jump into the menu immediately. I'd like to understand, and that takes listening.

"She'd bring Gracie for us to watch while she's in here on her projects." Aunt Mercy sighs and stares down at the book. "She's researching our family history."

I drop our hands, trying to push away the jealousy and, of course, guilt. I temper the feeling by telling myself I'm glad Emma Lou has been here. To learn and carry on the past. "She find anything interesting?"

"I'm sure she did." She doesn't move, as if I don't have a right to know.

"She *will* be back."

Aunt Mercy closes her eyes and takes my hands again. Her thumb rubs up and back over the ridge of my knuckle. "Something is coming. Truth, maybe, and something else. Like a dark cloud."

Thud-thud.

"Pete Daweson is alive," I confess softly, back to business. "I saw him last night. He has Emma Lou."

She spits out some curses under her breath. "BIA is worse than the sheriff. I told that damn BIA man, Ronny Dove, he needed to do more. Giving him a parade when there are still girls missing under his watch. Shameful. Don't know how you work for them."

A familiar refrain, and I don't take the bait. "Do you have what Sister was working on? I'd like to see it."

"She'll be back to finish it," Aunt Mercy snaps.

"I know. I won't let Sister be another missing person. I'm not leaving until Emma Lou is home," I say. "Not until Pete is dead or in jail. I think there's something here that Emma Lou wants me to see. Something that could help find her."

Aunt Mercy frowns at me as if she doesn't trust me to share what she knows.

Before I can press her, my phone buzzes and there's a text from Sue:

Just left Lisa and Zeke at the hospital. Not looking good. She will only talk to you. She knew you were there last night.

28

Everything is eerily calm, like a storm is coming. Any minute, the still warm air will be subsumed by a too-fast wind as only spring in a flat state like Oklahoma can produce.

I pull into the Miami Hospital parking lot with the hope that Zeke's mom, Lisa, will give me something useful about Pete, Emma Lou, or both.

The hospital is yellow brick, and I glance at the window display at the gift shop as I enter. The small store is a reprieve from sickness or dying. I remember the tea towels, books, and magazines with perfect people I had enough sense to know I'd never grow into. I wonder if they still have miniature horse carousel statues. It'd be nice to get one for Mal to remind her of the wooden one in North Providence she went to as a girl. A place she mentioned wanting to take her own child one day.

I should call her, or text at least. But I don't.

Inside, I smell sickness, a scent even the regular cleanings

can't cover. It takes me back to long days waiting for my grandmother and, soon after, my grandfather to pass.

I pay for a magazine and Snickers, then head toward the hospital elevator and press the ICU floor. My nerves feel as if they're
stretching my skin in that way of needing something but having
almost no power to get it.

I exit into a long hallway. Passing the quiet nurses' station, I
arrive at the waiting room at the end of the hallway. There's a
man in a crinkled shirt in the corner, and opposite him is a
woman who looks like a Daweson. The ratted hair dyed with
stripes of rusted blond. Her barrel-shaped body shifts as I approach. Her red-rimmed but icy blue eyes narrow on me.

"Are you Lisa Daweson?" I ask gently. "I'm Noah and June's
daughter Syd. They send their prayers."

She looks down at the ground as if I've come to collect a bill.
"Thanks."

"I brought you this magazine," I say.

A pencil-thin eyebrow arches. "Looks like trash."

I drop it into the chair next to her anyway. "And a Snickers."

"My ass not fat enough for you?"

The man snores awake for a moment and then eases back to
sleep. "I'll eat it," I say, and fake like I'm going to open the wrapper.

She snatches it out of my hand and opens it. "It's better than
nothin'."

"How's Zeke?"

"The same." Every line on her face deepens, and then her hardness fades. "Cooked like a marshmallow at the end of a stick." Her
chin pulls tight. "You hear I wanted to talk to you?"

"I did."

"Well. What happened?" Lisa snaps her gaze in my direction.
"He doing something stupid?"

"Doc had a shake and bake," I say. "It's meth in a plastic—"

"I know what it is."

"Zeke was trying to shake it on his own and . . . *boom*."

Lisa swears under her breath and swipes a tear. "Them being dumbasses don't make you love 'em any less. Best and worst thing that can ever happen is being a momma."

Her comment feels like not so much a warning as an inevitability. Our children will disappoint us, perhaps deeply. "I'm sorry," I say, meaning about Zeke, but also about how it feels damn unfair to give a part of yourself away like that.

"You don't have kids?" she says, and chews through the last bite of the Snickers.

"Not yet."

"Come on in and meet mine, then."

I follow her to Zeke's room, and my unease only grows at the sight of him covered in bandages. A machine breathes for him. I almost want to ask her if it's worth having your heart outside your body. If she would tally up more good marks than bad. If it would even matter, because once you have that child, you are changed. No mark can tip that scale.

She stands over his bed but nods at a vase with daisies dyed bright pink and purple. "Church sent those. Ugly as sin."

"What's more perfect than a daisy?" I agree.

"Exactly. People ruin everything." She starts to touch her son's arm but pulls back. "Who was there when it happened?"

"Pete," I say, and watch. She does not look surprised, but I continue. "Manda, too. Pete wanted to drop him down a hole. Manda said you'd burn them in their beds."

"I still might." Lisa's mouth draws into a tight line before she dabs her licked finger in the Snickers wrapper and returns it for the last crumbs. Her stare at me is a challenge as she throws the wrapper on the ground. "What I'm paying, they can pick it up."

I know what she's doing. Trying to be the bitch instead of the upset mother. I get that posturing. Better to be the villain than the victim. I do have sympathy for her. But not enough to change what I'm here to do.

"Zeke could bring some heat to the compound," I say. "Anyone can see it's meth burns. Pete might come after him."

"He ain't even awake to say anything."

"Is that worth the risk?" I ask carefully. "With the big deal Pete has going on?"

She frowns at me. "What's your angle here, girl?"

The Dawesons aren't smart, per se, but a suspicious nature can take you pretty far. "You know my sister is missing. Pete has her. It's too much of a coincidence that he's back and she's gone."

"Look, I wanted to hear the real story from you. But if you think I'm saying shit against any of my kin? I know you don't think much of family—"

"What does that mean?"

"You're asking me to go against my own blood. I hear you ain't been back for years. So what do you know about blood anyway? Don't seem like family matters much to you at all."

I step closer to the bed, where she stands sentry. I can't let myself get mad. This moment is too important. I need her help more than I need to defend myself. "If I find Emma Lou and they arrest Pete, your son will be safe. That's not something your family can promise you either." She shakes her head, but I can see she's listening. "Do you know where he might take Emma Lou?"

"Man like that don't go to prison." Lisa gently lays a hand on the edge of the bed.

"I'll do everything I can to make sure he does."

She rolls her eyes as if that means nothing, but I keep holding her gaze. I don't know what it means either. I'm learning how far I'll go minute by minute.

Her gaze goes back to her son. Her face contorts, not from sadness but from a white-hot rage that's like looking in a mirror. "I got a son to pray over. Maybe you should try the same for your own sister."

29

I barely have time to change and turn right back around to be at Deandre's house by six o'clock. I call Mal as I'm walking out the door.

"There you are," she says. "Things busy?"

"Crazy. I'm heading to a . . . party, I guess, at Deandre's place."

"Really?" Mal laughs. "I pictured you digging until midnight."

"Well, it's another kind of digging, I guess. I just can't figure out what is going on around here."

"Anything new on Emma Lou?"

I tell her about the note and the lock combination. My worry about drugs and Pete and frustration at how much I don't know.

"I'm sorry, babe."

"Thanks. Can I call you later? I need to go."

"Oh, sure. I just need to talk to you about something, okay?"

I don't like the sound of that, so I say I love you and goodbye, feeling weak and not sure how to be strong.

———

As I hit the Miami city limits, the sun is setting, and I follow my printed-out MapQuest directions to a newly paved road east of town. I remember this being a big field, but instead there's a brick sign that says, ELEVATED ESTATES.

"Perfect for Miami," I murmur with my old chat-rat chip on my shoulder. Before I enter the long block of new-build houses, I see farther down the road there are construction vehicles. I think of the development that Deandre and Tyler are building for people taking the Picher buyout. Chat rats and Miami snobs unite.

Continuing into Elevated Estates, I note the houses are large and boxy in that nice-for-the-Midwest way. As if the muted creams and browns on the exteriors are meant to match the Kirkland's oversized wood bedroom sets or whitewashed coffee tables. These are the artifacts of the new build in a flat state.

At the end of the road is a cul-de-sac with what appears to be the largest house right at the center. The style is country chic with cream-colored brick and brown siding and wood-beam pillars. Like most of the other houses, this one has small bushes and young trees that aren't properly staked in the yard.

Parked in the driveway are two red Lexus SUVs, a Mercedes, and a Land Rover.

I wonder if they're all Elevated Estates neighbors who drove the fifty feet to show them off. Another red Lexus pulls up and zips around my Jeep, quickly parking in the last spot in front of the house.

A door slams as the woman in the Lexus gets out of her car. Her sunglasses are on even though it's twilight, and she pauses to stare at my rental with a hand on her hip. I get that jittery teenage feeling that I don't belong and she knows it. I'm annoyed at myself that I'm still susceptible to those insecurities. Annoyed at how much I worried about what to wear.

Running my sweaty palms along my dark jeans, I pull at the shoulders of my mom's black button-up. Clothes were an issue for me. We wore hand-me-downs. Mom stitched them and pressed them and did her best to make them new. But they weren't, and honestly, no one thought we could afford new anyway.

The clothes arrived in big black trash bags and never felt like me. As if the bodies who wore them sucked up all the identity from the Laura Ashley floral pattern or tie-dye sweatshirt. I dug out the dark shirts, the flannels, though I didn't know why. I wanted to be invisible. To not seem to be trying because that was a signal that I cared. Even though I desperately did.

All this sits like an anvil in my stomach as I get out in front of Deandre's big-for-Miami house. I've never even seen a new house built in Picher.

I remind myself I'm an adult with a good job and a great wife and live in a beautiful place far from here. I wave at the woman still staring at me.

"Hey, there." I hold up the bottle of white wine I picked up from the liquor store on the way. "Ready for a drink?"

She reaches into her car and pulls out a bottle of Veuve Clicquot like it's a one-up, and she's not wrong. I head toward the front door, approaching three bright red rocking chairs with a pillow in each saying HOME, then SWEET and HOME. There are red, white, and blue hanging baskets with American flags in them and a matching door wreath with the last name MON- TEREY on a sign in the middle.

"You must be the special guest," she says. "I'm Bree Stratton." She offers a wave from beneath a Burberry-style plaid wrap that Mal's sister would love.

"I'm Syd," I say. "Dea . . . Deandre and I went to school to-gether."

"*Oh*, you're from *Picher*?" She smiles wide, a little red lipstick on her front tooth that I don't mention. "Chat rats forever, right?"

"That's what they say." I knock on the door, thankful it's opened quickly.

Tyler grins with his perfect white teeth in a way that says he knows he's handsome. "Hey, ladies."

I hold up the wine. "Thanks for having me, Tyler. I really ap-preciate your help last night."

"We call him Ty-baby." Bree wiggles around me to grip a muscular shoulder and plants a kiss on his cheek.

"All right, now." He waggles a finger. "I'm going to have to wash my face for the third time tonight."

"Well then, I better do the other side, Ty-baby." She leans in and kisses his other cheek.

He grins at me, both cheeks bright from the lipstick, and I hold up the wine like a shield. "Here you go."

"Thank you, Syd," Tyler says with a startling sincerity as he takes it. "I think we'll find Emma Lou soon. I'm glad you're tak-ing some time to have a little fun tonight with the . . . you know what they call them?"

I shake my head, glad I don't.

"Don't say it, Tyler!" Bree swats at his chest.

"The Miami MILFs." He laughs and steps aside so we can enter.

I fake laugh. "Good thing I'm not a mom." *Yet*, I correct my-self. I don't know why I jumped to that place.

"This needs to be opened and poured," Bree says as she hands her bottle to him. "I'll take Syd to the girls."

We cross the dark hardwood floors through the entryway and

past the large kitchen. There's a limestone backsplash and brown-and-cream granite countertops that could seat a dozen. A metal pail with fake sunflowers sits among bottles of wine and an untouched cheese platter. We head through a large family room with leather furniture and matching throws and pillows.

The music is blasting as Bree swings open the slider to the patio. "I Kissed a Girl" blasts over the speaker.

There are two women in tiny bright-colored dresses dancing around the fire pit. Deandre is refilling her rhinestone glass, which says BLING QUEEN. She's shaking her hips in leather pants and a yellow tube top.

"Oh my God!" one of the women says. "Bree is here! Don't you love this song?!"

They all answer by belting out the chorus and shouting about cherry ChapStick.

Deandre grins at me as if she's in on the fact that I do kiss girls, or one girl now, and do, in fact, like it. It's annoying, but I have to play nice, so I shrug as if she caught me.

"Perfect timing," Deandre calls, wiggling her bright nails at us. "Girlies, this is an old friend of mine, Syd Walker."

One keeps her grin, but the mousier one nearest me goes wide-eyed. Of course they'd have talked about my sister's disappearance. She's one of Deandre's employees. After a few more glasses of wine, maybe the mousey one spills about what she's heard. I'm even curious about how Deandre explains her family's involvement with drugs. Maybe she pretends she's one hundred percent all Monterey now, zero Daweson.

"Thanks for having me," I say after the song mercifully ends and these adult women quit shaking their asses. "I'm underdressed."

They all laugh at once, and I get that sickening all-the-seats-are-taken feeling.

"That's the point," Bree says beside me. "We come in our grubby whatevers and then buy something new from Deandre's collection."

The two ladies in the short dresses spin around like models and strike poses.

"You don't have to buy a thing," Deandre says to me. "It's a certain look for certain people."

I shrug. "I'm open to whatever."

"Makeover!" shouts the mousey one. "I'm Jill Warner. Soon to be Foster."

I smile and realize it's probably her family who own the tractor dealership right before you get on the highway. "Congratulations."

"I'm Adriene Bellsmith," says the one in the hot-pink dress. That name is familiar, too. Pretty sure her family owns the concrete plant next town over.

"Tyler will be out with the good stuff I brought," says Bree. "He's heading to the country club?"

"Poker night," Deandre says to me. "We drop the kids off at his parents' and have fun."

"Nice." I inhale, the social anxiety spiking. I question why I did this. Like Deandre is going to spill her guts? Confess everything her family has done. Where they put Emma Lou. Why she never told anyone her uncle Pete was alive. "I'd love to see the clothes," I lie.

It's so much worse than I imagined. They want me to try on everything. Deandre explains she only has three sizes of each piece, so everything is exclusive.

"Sometimes she skips the large," Adriene says with a cackle.

I proclaim my size medium and am forced to try on, literally, every top, every dress, and even leather pants like Deandre is wearing. I actually kinda like those.

I've gone shopping with Mal and some girlfriends, but nothing like this spectacle. There's a competitive element to who picks out what, and the hierarchy among them becomes clear, with Deandre at the very top.

I try to get through this excruciating hour by observing them like an archeologist. As if I've discovered the lost tribe of Forever 21.

I observe how they one-up one another, especially Jill. They establish hierarchies through their likes (*good* champagne) and have ceremonies to raise their drinks to their hot asses and to the nickname "MILFs of Miami." They also raise their glasses to well-hung husbands.

It's about as cringey as any scenario I've experienced, but my catty observations keep me calm enough to endure. I am not comfortable for one second of the makeover, but at the same time the attention is weirdly nice. What I imagine it'd be like if all the cool kids invited me to hang out after the football game.

The drinks flow and occasionally spill. I'm told, "You're *actually* pretty!" several times.

Jill pulls something from a pile of clothes in the corner. "I love this tube top from last season. It's cuter on. There's a heart cutout. Is this your last one? It's a medium, Syd!"

She jabs her fingers through the open cutout. I've seen that sparkle tube top before. Sue had it on two nights ago when she saved us from the dipshits. She's been invited here, too.

"We have the large somewhere," Deandre says in a friendly but measured voice. "Try it on if you want."

I can't ask point-blank if Sue regularly comes to these parties. But I saw the photo with Sue in Deandre's office. They were not friends in high school. Sue's dad would never have allowed it.

Always seemed as if he hated the Dawesons as much as my family did.

Interesting that a friendship bloomed, likely since Sue's dad died.

"I'll go with the turquoise. The one that actually has sleeves." I also don't hate it, though it's more than I've ever paid for a shirt, or even pants, for that matter.

We pick at a cheese-and-veggie tray and then head back out to the fire. Jill trips on the way there and skins her knee. She seems too drunk to care, but it's going to hurt tomorrow.

Bree and Adriene are dirty dancing. Jill tries to join in but mostly gets hip blocked. Deandre watches and takes pictures with a small camera.

"I'm going to blackmail you bitches!" she says as the light keeps flashing.

Bree shakes her ass as they laugh and slosh booze onto the patio.

I guess this is what Deandre wanted when she got out of Picher and away from the illegal drug business. I can sympathize, since I'd wanted the same thing. I mean, not this, but I grew up restless for something else, somewhere else. I took out every student loan. Worked two jobs until I graduated and left the state for good with Mal. New house, new friends, new wife, new life.

I think of Sue again. How my leaving and dropping contact must have felt like a betrayal.

"I'm tired of dancing for you all. Let's go shake it at a bar." Bree grabs Deandre's arm and pulls her inside. "I want to borrow your black dress that makes my ass look like I got a Brazilian butt lift."

"It looks like that because she got one," Adriene murmurs to me with a wink before she follows them and shuts the slider in Jill's face.

Jill's thin shoulders slump, and she pulls her dress up for the hundredth time. I bet they made her take the large even though she's the smallest. Of course she did it so she could match the other two.

"You girls are a lot of fun." I lean against the back of a wicker chair as she stumbles away from the door, toward the outside furniture. "How often do you get together?"

"Every few weeks." Her tone is snooty, as if she can pretend to be queen bee when the real queens are gone. "So many ladies want to come. It's the talk of the town."

I nod, hiding my smile at her slurry little speech. "Who else usually comes?"

She stammers for a moment. "I'm busy a lot so I don't come to all the parties." She gulps whatever is in her glass. "Deandre knows I'm busy. I have a big wedding to plan."

"Sure," I say, terrified she'll start talking about that instead.

"But Deandre invites other Miami Country Club friends. Neighbors who bought into the Estates like us."

"Any chat rats?" I say with a grin.

Jill lets out a big laugh that's high and repetitive like a jackhammer. She swirls her drink. "If you say it, that means I can say it, right?"

That's definitely not what it means. "Does she invite anyone from the good ol' days?"

"Ugh, that blond one that kinda looks like a Playmate."

"Sue Dove?" I say too quickly, not wanting to be right. Wishing she was still the vintage-loving bookworm I used to know, not some Country Club Barbie.

"Yeah, that's her. She's totally boring if you ask me."

"How long have you been friends with Deandre?" I head over to the bar and grab a bottle of white. "Refill?"

"A little more." She trips in her high heels but recovers.

I pour her a splash, and then we toast. I pretend to sip, as I've done all night. "Tell me about Deandre and you."

"Well," she begins as if this were an Oprah exclusive. "We were friends early, before even these girls. I was her first country club friend. When Tyler started bringing her around, they were bitches to Deandre. But I was nice."

That makes sense. "Was she already working for Dr. Canter?"

Jill shakes her head. "She was in physician assistant school. She said she wanted to work in Tulsa. Thought she and Tyler could move to the Utica Square area. All the girls rolled their eyes, but I believed her. She's the type that if she wants something, she gets it done."

"People started to like her?"

"It took a while. After the wedding, at least. I mean, he did marry a chat rat." She giggles. "Sorry, you said it earlier."

"I did," I say. "Plus, her family. She's a Daweson."

Jill grimaces and slurps in a breath through her small, square teeth. "We don't *ever* talk about those people. This ex-friend Becky, she asked once, I mean, one question . . . once, and she's been on the O-U-T-S ever since."

"Wow," I say, not surprised. "After Deandre's honeymoon, she started Wings?"

"They got back from Florida, and it was like . . . *boom!*" She sloshes the wine in her glass. "Deandre never talked about Tulsa again. It was all the clinic this and the clinic that. We will help people blah blah and we won't have insurance companies calling the shots. You should see the lines around the block for these places in Florida blah blah blah. She got on her high horse like she was the Nurse Nightingale lady, you know?"

I nod along with her as I process what Jill is drunkenly telling me. Deandre saw a pill mill on her honeymoon and was so inspired, she started one where she lives. Talk about shitting where you eat and making a mint off it.

"When did the . . . Elevated Estates happen?" I glance inside and see no one dancing back our way in a tube top. "Around then?"

She squishes her nose as if thinking hurts. "A year later? It was a huge deal."

"I saw they're building more?"

"Yeah, that's kind of annoying because it's for chat . . . sorry. It's for Picher people. But they say it's good for our property values." She shrugs with a smirk but then hiccups. "They run Miami now. And she's my, like, *best* friend."

"Can I grab you a water?" I consider taking the wineglass out of her hand.

"I'm good, I'm good." She hiccups again. "Did I tell you those girls were mean at the country club? Everyone was mean except me. I'm her first friend. That makes me her best one."

I'm saved from the same rambling stories when Bree dances back onto the porch. She's wearing a tight dress, and her long blond hair is pulled into a messy bun. "Deandre let me borrow her new Louboutins. Hot bottom." She turns to show us the red sole of the shoe. "Hottest bottom." She slaps her ass and cackles.

Jill gets up and starts fawning over her about the dress and shoes. Bree doesn't even look at her. "You going with to get your dance on at Buffalo Run, Syd? You know Deandre will want to hit the blackjack tables."

"Not sure that's my scene," I say. "I can drop you off there."

"Yes, please, sweet pea." Bree puckers her lips at Jill. "Are you going? You seem too drunk."

She gasps, which makes her hiccup. "I am not."

"At least wear something that fits. Don't want that fiancé dumping you again."

Jill's eyes go wide as Bree drags her inside and yells at Adriene for help. Deandre watches them go before heading toward me. She closes the deck slider behind her with a serpentine smile.

"We're alone at last," she says, not looking as drunk as the others.

"Thanks for inviting me," I say, kinda meaning it despite myself.

"That shirt does look nice on you." She crosses her arms. "Not that you're here for the clothes."

I'm not surprised by the accusation, though I'm not ready to reveal the whole truth either. "I was curious about my sister's new boss."

She glances through the window as if making sure we're alone. "Let's sit down for a minute." She waves me over to the largest couch. The fire lights up her sharp nose and blue eyes. My heart speeds up a little being this close. A stupid reaction I ignore. "This is probably our only chance to talk, Syd. I hope this can stay between us."

"Sure," I say. "Unless you're about to share the location of my sister."

"Oh my God." Deandre swats at the comment. "I'd have told in a heartbeat. I know Emma Lou had a tough life. Both of you went through something awful. If I knew anything about her, I swear, I'd have taken care of it myself."

"Sure," I say, wishing it were true, but doubting it just the same and not keeping that from my voice. I don't like her buddy-buddy flirt routine.

"There's something I want to explain to you. Why I asked Emma Lou to work for me. Well, Cody suggested it first. But that's not the real reason." She sets her drink down and scoots closer. "I don't have words for what happened because of my uncles. My momma is completely nuts. Nearly every last Daweson isn't worth slowing your car down for."

I hate that I'm relieved at her admission. "What does that have to do with Emma Lou working for you?"

"I owed her. I owe your whole family. I pushed her to take the job. Even your mom wasn't sure, but it's good money and they deserve it." She puts a warm hand lightly on my knee. "If your sister had a relapse because of me . . . There were signs, but . . ."

"Signs? What do you mean?"

She sighs and squeezes my knee. "Some pills had gone missing. I haven't told anyone. Maybe it wasn't her. Miscounts happen."

I scoot away from her hand, but the warmth from her fingers lingers like a phantom limb. I don't want to go back to thinking all of this is because of drugs. That Pete is some kind of coincidence. That she's strung out like I first feared. But I know it's possible.

I'll kill her.

Pete had screamed that at me after he'd barely missed running me over. "I saw your uncle."

"My uncle?" Her thick lashes blink as she licks her bottom lip. "Which one?"

I don't answer and instead watch her. She was raised by liars, so I don't know what I'm hoping she'll reveal. "At the casino.

Forget it," I say, not wanting to admit anything more and feeling stupid for thinking she would.

"I don't know if you ever wondered why . . . they would kill like that. A girl. A friend. They knew Luna. She was at my party just a few weeks before." She shakes her head sharply. "Their dad, my grandpa, has been sick and bedridden for a long time. But there are stories. And his dad, my great-grandpa, was kicked out of a big mining deal. He was mean and bitter and passed that on. Grandpa beat my uncles. Beat my mom. Still tries when they let him out."

"I don't care why they did it."

"I just want you to know that it's not . . . pure evil. Or whatever bullshit people say about us. Pete and Skeet's dad used to lock his kids up in a box behind the house for hours. When they were bad. When they weren't."

My throat tightens. "Why are you telling me this?"

"Because I wonder. Don't you? If what it takes to survive in this place makes us this way? We can run from it. Hide from what kept us alive. How far away can we really get before it comes calling?"

"Evil is a choice. Hurting other people . . . killing them. That's a choice."

Her eyebrows rise and she doesn't have to say it. That it's a choice I made. To kill her uncle that night to save Emma Lou.

She shifts closer again and leans only a few inches from me. "Look, before those crazy bitches come back, I need to ask you a question."

I hold my breath. "Okay?"

"How did you do it?"

"Do . . . what?"

"Break away from your family." She turns her gaze toward the fire. "Leave everything. Let your mom and dad know there's no next generation to handle the family farm?"

I shake my head at what she's saying. "You're equating your family's drug dealing with my family farm?"

She releases a flirty grin. "It's just business."

"I help out when I can," I say honestly as I try to decide her angle with this question. The problem is she looks sincere, so I will be, too. "But mostly I learn to live with being a disappointment."

Her mouth falls open and there's a sadness in her gaze as tears sparkle in the porch lights. "Did they ever . . . get mad that you were such a disappointment? Threaten you?"

I take in her question and realize what she's asking. This girl from Devil's Promenade can try to hide who she is from the Miami MILFs, but this chat rat can see the truth. "Threaten you with what? Kidnapping an employee who knows too much?"

Her gaze snaps over to mine and now the fire dances in her pale blue eyes. "Careful, Syd. I'm the only Daweson on your side."

30

While the MILFs of Miami are pouring roadies, or to-go cups of wine, I head toward a dark hallway to call my dad. I see a couple of missed calls from Mal but decide to deal with it in the morning.

"Dad? Find out anything?" I ask when he answers our land-line at home.

"Rhett seems pretty skittish. He didn't want to fish or even see me. Shut the door in my face."

"Wow," I say, surprised. "He was mad?"

"Scared," Dad says. "As scared as I've seen any man. He finally let me in and drank about a fifth of whiskey. But he started talking."

When whoops and hollers begin echoing, I duck into a dark room. I click on the light and am greeted by a sleek white desk with a black marble top. "What did he say?"

"He swore he had nothing to do with Emma Lou disappear-ing. He said they are friends, so maybe she thought she could leave the car there."

"Bullshit."

"He'll be at the Saturday morning prayer service for Zeke tomorrow, if you want to try him," Dad says. "He let me look around. Nothing seemed out of place. It doesn't make any sense."

My eye catches a big wedding photo on the bookshelf that takes up the whole wall behind the desk. There are many more photos than books. In the center is a nice shiny vase and a sculpture of a tree without leaves that looks out of place.

"How was the hospital?" he asks. "Lisa doing okay?"

"Zeke doesn't look good. She knows something about Emma Lou, but she won't budge."

"Try her at the prayer service with a little of the Lord greasing the skids."

I see Sue's smiling face in a photo. "I'm leaving Deandre's soon." I step back onto something. "Shit."

"What's wrong?"

"Nothing." I bend down to find a long paper rolled tight and tossed on the floor. I wedge the phone between my ear and shoulder and slide the plans open. "I found their plans for the Picher development. They've got twenty lots to build on with potential for more."

"Not sure that's going to happen. The business committee didn't approve her plans. They're going to revisit it later."

"Is Rhett on that committee?" I ask.

"Sure. He's the chairman."

I stare at the plans, millions of dollars in real estate, even if the houses are small. "He voted no?"

"Yeah," Dad says, sounding surprised. "Good guess."

It's not a guess. "But now that he's under suspicion for Emma Lou, does that take him out of commission for a while?"

"Probably. It should, anyway."

I pull my hand off the plans and they roll back with a snap. "Talk to you soon, Dad."

I only have a few minutes, and I quickly check the photos, seeing Sue is in several of them. Smiling by a big check for BIA research with Deandre. Cutting the ribbon at the Wings clinic's new look and name.

I pull on the top drawer and it's paper-clip stuff. The middle drawer has a few folders, but they're folders with numbers I don't have time to understand. But there's a feeling, an energy, that says, *There is something here.*

Help me find her. **FIND ME.**

I go through the rest of the drawers and strike out. I stop my mad dash and really look around. There are no traces of Deandre being a Daweson. She's totally reinvented herself.

The tree vase stands out, though. It almost reminds me of the message tree at Luna's place. I take a step forward. Dea played with us, too. Not all the time, but she certainly climbed the trees and knew about the messages.

"Syd?" I hear her call. "You in the bathroom?"

I jam my hand into the vase and suck in a breath at the feel of beads. My hand begins to shake as I pull out the long cylindrical shape.

I hold the beaded peyote key chain tight in my hand. It's identical to mine, with AGILVGI beaded into the side. Deandre has Emma Lou's car keys. Deandre was the one who planted the car at Rhett Caine's house. As punishment for the vote?

Once a Daweson, always a Daweson. There's a buzz on the desk where Deandre's phone is charging. She's gotten a text.

It's from Sue. And I have to go.

I grip Sister's key chain tight in my hand and hurry to throw open the door. Deandre is standing there with her roadie in a relaxed pose, but her gaze is on fire. "What are you doing in there?"

"I got lost." I elbow past her and the gaggle of drunk women. "See you at the compound."

She frowns at me as if I've started speaking in tongues. "What?"

I don't answer and instead head toward the door. I can't trust Sue. I can't trust anyone at the BIA. This is why I go alone. Because other people can only get you so far.

I leave the front door wide-open because I expect Deandre will be right behind me once she reads the text Sue sent her.

COMPOUND RAID HAPPENING NOW.

31

~~~~

I drive so fast that the Jeep is shaking like the engine is about to drop onto the dirt road. I know going to the Daweson compound is a mistake, but the fact that Sue was alerting Deandre tells me this raid can't be trusted.

I turn too fast, and the back tires skid. Dirt blows up like a plume of brownish-red smoke in my taillights. I wrestle back control in time to miss the telephone pole I was careening toward and tell myself to calm down—then press the gas.

There's a police car ahead with red and blue lights spinning and blocking the Dawesons' driveway. I can barely breathe at the thought that Emma Lou is there. I picture a blanket around her shoulders as she's treated by an EMT. Pete and Manda in handcuffs.

This is hope. It's dangerous, as I told Emma Lou time and time again. Hope is for those who have room for more pain.

Stopping next to the officer, who is out of his car now, I wave as he heads over with a flashlight.

"Howdy." I smile, though I'm screaming inside, and blink in the bright light. I get a flash of memory from the dipshits with their own lights but push it aside. "Sue Dove said I might need to identify someone. Can you let me through? Or should I call her?"

He stares at me a moment and then another. His patchy hair is thinning, though his face is round and youthful. He doesn't look menacing. More like he's processing who I am.

"They ain't found your sister," he says as if that will be the end of our conversation. "Place is clean as a whistle."

"They know that already?" I tightly grip the wheel but keep my tone polite. "Sue said I needed to see something. If she's changed her mind, I'll come right back out."

"I'm not supposed to let anyone through."

"But it's not a crime scene, right?" I give him a half smile, as if it's a joke between us. "It's clean as a whistle. I should double-check with Sue."

The blue and red lights whirl across our faces as he scratches the back of his neck. "Ten minutes." Indifference replaces concern as he flops back into the seat of his cruiser.

After giving him a friendly nod, I slowly creep along the driveway. My heart begins to fire as I strain to see anything at all. The flash of dirty-blond curls, most likely without shoes.

I realize Ghost Luna hasn't been around as much since Pete came back. I miss her, in a weird way I don't want to analyze.

Keeping my gaze forward, I ignore the tree where I was nearly eaten by dogs. Then a violent bark, and I tap the brakes. Is it real?

The angry barking continues, but in the distance. It's not only the terrible memory. I tighten my grip on the steering wheel and keep my mind in the present. Otherwise, I'll have to pull over before everything goes dark.

I ease past the dead grass, which is bent from tire tracks where

Pete tried to run me over. Death is everywhere and coming for me.

Not yet, Devil. Not yet.

Crossing the cattle guard, which rattles the whole Jeep, I park in the ditch. A vehicle may need to get in or out of the driveway. I slam the door and realize I'm not scared anymore—I'm real pissed off.

While everything isn't Sue's fault, my anger is narrowing in on her, and I'm not trying to stop it.

My phone rings from inside the truck and I grab it to see it's Mal's mom calling. My heart seizes in a panic just as I hear a man yelling behind me. "Hello, is everything okay?" I ask her quickly.

"Oh, Syd, I'm glad I reached you. Mal has been calling."

"I'm so sorry, I was at a . . . this thing earlier. Is she okay?" There is more yelling nearby, but I ignore it. "Is she okay?"

"She's in the emergency room. She was spotting and—" Her voice cuts off with emotion. "I don't know anything more. The doctors don't know what's going on. Do you think—"

The punch to the side of my head comes from the right, spinning my whole body in a semicircle. I double over and manage to keep hold of the phone.

"Hello, Syd? Hello? Are you there?"

I gasp at the pain but am shoved down onto the ground before I can say anything. I drop the phone and protect my head as the kicks start into my ribs. "Trespassing bitch!" a man yells as a foot connects.

"You think you can come in here."

"We'll show you what happens to bitches who mess with us."

I curl tighter into a ball and the pain is everywhere. I don't scream but pull myself tighter to protect against the boots.

Suddenly, I'm up on my feet and being dragged through the

mud. I pull against their arms, but it's useless as I try to stand and keep up with their big steps. I catch a flash of a yellow bandana and confirm I'm in deep dipshit again.

"Look who we found," one of them yells as he drags me into a security light. "The trespassing bitch who started all this."

I'm thrown onto the concrete and I drop like a rock, huddling again as I wait for more pain.

"Hold her up so I can get another good one in."

I'm jerked up onto my knees. I protect my face with my arms just as another kick connects.

"That's enough, boys," says a voice, and I open my eyes to see Sue with her hand on her gun. "I got it from here."

I blink at the men holding me, and the yellow bandanas blur before they let go.

"What the . . . what the hell?" I stammer, my vision darkening as my breath speeds up. I have to talk to Mal. I have to find Emma Lou.

"You okay, Syd? Hey, Syd?"

The hands holding me up disappear. I am floating and falling and connecting with the ground. Everything inside me says, *I am going to die.*

I am going to die alone.

Just like all the other girls and all the other skulls.

You failed them again.

You promised you could help.

You promised you'd be here.

Now all the Sisters will reunite under the earth.

32

SATURDAY, MAY 10, 2008

I wake up in total darkness. There is the drip of a faucet. The floor is cold against my cheek. I'm curled in a ball as if to protect myself from more swift kicks.

The wind howls. Do I know these sounds? Do I know this place?

Surrender.

Isn't that what my grandma said when I told her about my panic attacks? She said to feel the pain and not fight against such a strong current.

Let the river carry you until you are strong enough to swim against it.

My breath shaky, I wrestle for control. Inhale, exhale. One command, then another. Inhale, exhale. Deep belly breathing is what Mal calls it. Inhale, exhale.

Surrender.

I let the pain and frustration fill my chest. I acknowledge

what's happening even as I gasp for breath and am sure I'm about to drown.

I suck in at more pain flooding my body, pulling me into a depth that feels impossible to escape.

The same familiar panic: *I'm about to die.*

Still, I hold these emotions close, as if choosing to stay below the surface in the darkest parts of the water.

Tears begin, and I can feel my body and mind acknowledging my pain. I don't let myself look away. The strobe light of awful thoughts flashes, but I realize it's a lie. My mind wants me to hide. To stop. To survive.

I cry harder, never understanding such an experience was possible. All along, it's been to survive no matter the cost. Survive no matter the walls I must build. Survive no matter the love I no longer give or accept. Survive by hiding. Survive by dismissing. Survive by living in fear. At the cost of everything, *survive*.

I can see the panic clearly now, for the first time, and it is not Pete. He is a water moccasin that skitters across the surface of my consciousness. A symptom of the truth I could not acknowledge. Surviving is not enough.

I must live, even if the cost is more pain. Even if the cost is failing those I love again and again. Love is trying. Living is trying. *Show up*, Mal said. Show up and live.

Inhale, exhale. The panic begins to drain with each breath. *Inhale, exhale.*

I find myself and steady myself. The panic is a lie. I am not dying. Surrender and survive.

I return to myself.

And everything hurts.

I cannot open my eyes from all the pain. My heart races, but I focus. I'm on a hard surface. Cold ground. I reach out my hand and feel a cool metal bar. I am trapped.

"Emma Lou?" I call out, but it's a scratch rather than a true sound.

I hear the soft pad of feet as a bright light turns on. I flinch and then open my eyes to see I'm in a jail cell.

"She's in here, Mrs. Walker," says a woman's voice down the hallway. "She passed out. Doctor said she's fine."

There are footsteps, not just Sue's, whose voice I recognize. But shuffling, slow steps. I pull myself up with a sharp stab of pain in my side. I feel it's been taped, probably by that doctor.

My eyes adjust as Sue stands in her BIA uniform in front of my barred door.

"I called your aunt Mercy, Syd. She offered to put up the bail."

"Don't think because I'm old I don't know when civil rights have been violated." Aunt Mercy gets in Sue's face. "I've got all the time in the world to make your life miserable."

"Okay, Mrs. Walker, just slow down. You can be mad at me, but Syd trespassed on private land. Twice. That's not a joke around here. Manda Daweson agreed to not press charges, but the DA might step in to prove a point. He's sick of people crawling all over private land."

I glare at her as I try to stand up, but the pain spikes my side. "I need a phone. Mal is in the ER."

Aunt Mercy pulls an old-looking flip phone out of her big purse. "I get charged per minute, so talk fast."

I take the phone and they both watch me as I dial Mal's number, but there's no answer. I try her mom's house and it's the same. I shake my head and try to shift gears. "Did you find anything at the Dawesons'?"

"Nothing." Sue has a placating look. "That judge is furious I pressured him to sign off on a warrant that went nowhere and already has lawyers breathing down our necks."

"You want sympathy for your fake raid?" I manage to stand so I can really say what's on my mind. "My sister was at that godforsaken house. She wrote her daughter's name in the dirt. It was next to handcuffs with blood on them." I'm yelling and can't stop myself. "You wouldn't see that because you waited twenty-four goddamn hours to execute the warrant."

"That right?" Aunt Mercy says to Sue.

"No," she says, sounding a little chastised. "I got it done as fast as I could. I can't use your photo of the meth as evidence. The Dawesons have this sleazy lawyer who'd love it if we issued a warrant based on evidence illegally obtained."

"What about Doc? Will he tell the truth?"

"No, Syd." She smirks as if I'm a child and asking about unicorns. "He's an old meth head who can barely remember his real name. The same lawyer had his hand up his ass like a puppet."

"And Pete?" I whisper.

"Everyone says he's dead. Manda has no idea what you're talking about." She stares at me hard. "The house was clean. Real clean."

"You made time to text Deandre to warn her." I lean against the cold bars and look up.

There's real pity in her gaze. Like she's standing in the eye of a tornado while the rest of us circle to our deaths. "I know you're hurting. You and Emma Lou have a special bond. Stronger than most because of what you went through."

"You are in on this with them," I say.

Aunt Mercy's eyebrows rise at my accusation, as if warning me to step lightly. But I'm so far past the point of stepping. I want to destroy. To do whatever it takes to get Sister back.

Anger flashes in Sue's eyes. "You insisted there was evidence. This was the best I could do."

I laugh at her weak-ass claim. "You gave the Dawesons time to clean up. To move the drugs to the chat piles, where you refuse to go."

"There's more at stake than your sister. I swear to God, Syd, I'm doing my best."

"Your best?" I shake my head and my lips press together. I should stop talking. "You're hanging out with Dea a lot, right? The family at the heart of this investigation. Your *best* is being *besties* with Dea?"

"She goes by Deandre." Sue puts her hand on her gun. "You're being ridiculous."

"You wear her slutty clothes. Go to parties at her house."

She shrugs. "Free country."

"Your brand-new Tahoe? That might keep you looking the other way?"

"It's a truck, Syd. I'm not selling my integrity for four cylinders and satellite radio."

My anger has overtaken my pain. I press my face between the bars. "But there's a price?"

She sucks in a sharp breath but doesn't move an inch. "Careful."

I shoot her a long, angry look. "I may have left, but you changed."

She curses under her breath and pulls out the keys. Unlocking the door quickly, she swings it open so she's on the other side and the door is a barrier between us as I exit. "I got missing girls all over my corner of the state. Cases that go back twenty years. Cases my dad never closed or barely opened in the first place."

"I thought your dad closed every case."

"These didn't count since the police said they just ran off."

My anger mirrors Sue's. "Easier to ignore."

"Much, but listen, I care about Emma Lou. I care about them all."

Aunt Mercy loops her arm around mine. "Then help us."

"That's what I thought I was doing." Sue inhales deeply. "I won't charge you the bail, Mrs. Walker, if you keep her away from me."

33

The morning sun reflects off a senior center van parked outside the county jail. I keep holding Aunt Mercy's arm as we shuffle outside. "Did you take that to get here?" I ask.

"Herman was excited to come to the jail." She raises a hand to the older man behind the wheel. "I told him not to wait."

"Is my Jeep here?"

"Cop parked your getup this way." She hands me a bag with my car key and phone. There's one bar of battery left, and I dial Mal's mom.

"Hi, Syd," she says with a coolness in her voice.

"I'm so sorry about last night. And to call so early. I'm just so sorry. Is Mal okay?"

"She's fine. She was discharged late last night. The baby is good, but Mal needs to rest. The doctor thinks maybe stress. She has to take it easy."

"Oh, sure," I say. "I didn't mean to—"

"I know you didn't, Syd. But you did."

"You did this to her," Ghost Luna says. "She's better without you."

I swallow thickly and blink back tears. "Can I speak to Mal? Please, just to say hi. She wanted to tell me something."

"I know. Mal is going to move in with us for a little while. She was thinking about it, but now . . . after last night. It's really for the best."

"No, I'll be back home soon. I can come right away."

"Mal wouldn't want you to leave your family right now. She needs hers, too. Please, I'm asking you to respect that."

Mal is my family is what I want to say, but she's right. "I'm here . . . if she . . ."

"Sure, Syd. She knows."

"Thanks," I whisper.

"Oh, Syd. It's Mother's Day tomorrow. Tell June we wish her a good one. We hope Emma Lou comes home soon."

"Happy Mother's Day to you, too."

She hangs up and I curse, swiping at a tear. "I really screwed up," I murmur to Aunt Mercy.

"Means you're trying," she says. "Now, let's get your rig, and you can drop me off. I don't like how Herman grins all the time." She swats toward the van as she takes my arm again. "Shoo, Herman. Shoo!"

I laugh a little harder than I should, but I'm desperate for some of this pain to subside.

Surrender.

I start the car and realize I have to stop holding back if I want Aunt Mercy to trust me enough to tell me whatever Emma Lou was working on.

"Sister left me two clues on the Myers land. The first one was one of those coin rings that were popular when we were kids. The second was to come find you at the senior center."

"I remember those rings," she says. "Lots of girls wore them. What year was it dated?"

"Oh, um, 1991."

Aunt Mercy shifts in the leather seat. "You better start driving."

I drop my phone in the bag. "Why?"

"I just got you out of jail. You can listen to me for a minute."

I give her a nod and get her buckled. I put the bag between us on the console. "Which way?"

"Out by them trailers where all the Picher people moved," she says, pointing west.

I do as I'm told and start to drive. We're still quiet as we pass the road that leads to the hospital. That leads to Wings. That leads all the way back to Picher.

"I don't get you all to myself this much, usually," she mumbles in passive-aggressive Okie Auntie. "We walked this land for thousands of years before *they* ever stepped foot here. *They* remove us from our medicines, our land, our plants. *They* destroy our art. *They* silence our songs." She pauses to take my hand. "It's not a secret that I don't like you working for the BIA. All they've taken from us and are still taking. I see you are fighting within that place just as many of us are fighting outside of it. We need both. We need everyone. Justice requires many paths and many hands."

"It doesn't always feel like I'm doing enough," I confess. "I try to remember a time when I wasn't letting someone down."

"Listen here." Aunt Mercy leans over to smack my leg. "You fight for our land. You fight for our culture. You can't move forward if you're looking back. Don't be sorry. Fight instead."

I feel such a relief I nearly smile that she sees my work as fighting, too. Something I've always admired in her. I take the turn on the far side of Miami, crossing the Spring River Bridge. We pass fields with horses and blooming yellow wildflowers before taking a gentle curve leading to the gas station on the corner.

"Stop, stop." Aunt Mercy taps her hand on the dash. "Right here!"

Confused and glad there's no traffic, I swing us into the unmowed ditch. Grasses scrape the sides of the Jeep as we bump off road. I blink at the pasture ahead, where a brown horse is eating a round bale of hay. "What?" I ask.

She points toward the dash and my gaze goes over the Jeep and up to a billboard that reads JUSTICE FOR JESSICA.

Jessica's photo takes up almost the whole billboard, along with a phone number for tips. Her letter jacket catches my eye again, and then her big early-nineties hair with her shy smile. Her hands are folded over each other and—

"Her ring," I whisper.

"One of them panda types," Aunt Mercy says. "Rayna wanted one for Christmas one year. I went to Goforth Jewelry to see about it. Costs two hundred dollars for a little coin ring."

My body tingles as if there's something I should know. As if there's some answer somewhere, but I can't reach it. "What year did she go missing?"

"She went missing in 'ninety-one. What seventeen-year-old girl just runs away? Don't make no sense. Lazy police work, you ask me. One of my protests, I made a sign to remember her. It's 1991, her senior year, I'm sure of it."

Thud–thud.

I suck in a breath. "Someone wants me to find Jessica?"

"Not someone, Sister," says Ghost Luna's voice from the back.

"You know that ain't Myers land. Not really. BIA leased it to the Dawesons generations ago. After some mining deal went bad. Like an I'm-sorry gift that wasn't theirs to give." Aunt Mercy shakes her head.

We're close, but there's something missing. Simple facts I can't get from Aunt Mercy or anyone on this side of the law.

"What time does the prayer service start?" I ask.

Aunt Mercy looks at the clock on the dash. "Lord will wait for sinners like us," she says. "But a lead foot wouldn't hurt nothing either."

34

The big white church spire rises ahead. There are drops of rain as gray clouds swirl. I pull into the tiny parking lot, which is full of cars. I blow out a long breath and glance over to Aunt Mercy.

"I hate church," I say. "Maybe this is a bad idea."

"Follow your instinct," she says. "Surrender."

My gaze snaps to her as if she'd read my mind earlier. Her demeanor is placid. And she's right. "I will," I say.

"Look, about Emma Lou's research." She reaches into her bag. "I brought it for you. It ain't really about genealogy."

"Really? Oh."

She drops a folder into my lap. "She's researching land rights. Native land. Cherokee and Quapaw."

"What?" I flip it open to find dozens of maps printed out. I frown, realizing most of them are in Miami. Sister circled an area and scribbled "EE."

"You know what that is?" asks Aunt Mercy. "And that." She stabs her finger at the plot of land next to it.

I see the road and realize it's where I was last night. "Elevated Estates?"

"Bingo," Aunt Mercy says, her grin nearly malicious. "That Daweson girl and her hotshot husband are building on Quapaw land. See the name there? That's Becker land. The property that belonged to someone they once called the richest woman in the world."

"Wait, that's Rayna and Aunt Missy's other side. Are you saying that they own Elevated Estates?"

"Based on this map, they own that whole side of town." She giggles like a girl. "Them Dawesons can fold that in four corners and stick it where the sun don't shine."

I flip through more maps and pages. "I can't believe people just build on Native land. Like they have the right. Like no one is going to stop them."

"No one does," Aunt Mercy says. "Well, maybe your sister tried."

I close my eyes at the implication. "When did she start this research?"

"Let's see." Aunt Mercy stares at the church. "Rayna got out. Then Cody. Probably after she and Cody started running around again. He even came with her a few times. Over eighteen months, at least."

"Is that around the time she got her job with Deandre?"

Aunt Mercy purses her lips to the side. "Yeah, sounds right."

Emma Lou could have told Deandre what she found. That this new development and future projects weren't theirs at all. Her get-out-of-Picher card belonged to someone else.

Deandre had Emma Lou's car key. Maybe it wasn't Pete after all. Just a terrible coincidence.

"Not that it matters," Aunt Mercy says. "Newspaper said they voted down that development project. Lost by one vote."

"But they could vote again. And Rhett Caine won't be there." I stare at the maps. There's another one that's in Picher. "Where's this?" I show it to her. "I recognize that road, but—"

"Rhett Caine's farm west of town," she says, as if she knew I'd get there. "Looks like he's on Quapaw land, too."

"He's head of the buyout committee," I say. "What would this research mean for him?"

"Might mean he's got nothing to sell." Aunt Mercy shakes her head, and the strands of her beaded earrings make a soft ticking noise. "Just like that Daweson girl. Can't imagine either of them would like that much." She points toward a big Cadillac.

"Course, you can ask him. That's his car."

I get out and walk around to help Aunt Mercy onto the pavement, which is more chat than anything. We head toward the white door that is propped open. The paint is peeling, and the handicap ramp is closed because the boards are falling in. This whole town feels like it's on its last gasp. Holding tight until someone finally says, *No more.*

As we step into the entryway, I'm relieved we're very late. People are taking Communion. I see the reason for my visit, Lisa Daweson, slumped in a pew. My parents are behind her with Gracie. I lead Aunt Mercy near them and pass Lisa, who silently sobs into her hands. I decide to start with Rhett.

The altar call hymn begins and the congregation stands. Aunt Mercy takes a spot by my parents and nods my attention toward Rhett Caine in the back.

As everyone rises, I slip over and tap him on the shoulder. His eyes go wide, but he stands. We take the side door into the small stone courtyard, which hasn't been able to grow a flower in decades. I think of my father's words, that Rhett Caine looked scared. There are purple circles under his exhausted eyes. His trembling hands match his whole jittery body. He's nothing like the confident man who stood in front of the whole town just three days ago.

"Look, I didn't hurt your sister. I would never—"

"Your farm is on Quapaw land," I say softly, as if he's about to spook and run away. "So is Elevated Estates and that Picher development."

He stares down and runs his fingers through his gray hair. "I don't think . . . that can't all be true."

"Emma Lou must have shown you her research." I watch as his gaze darts around. "The question is, what would you do?"

He crosses his arms. "Nothing."

"At first, I feared the worst. Kill her to keep it quiet."

"I'd never hurt her. Never."

I hold up a hand. "Oh, I know. That's why you voted against the deal with Deandre. That's why Deandre planted Emma Lou's car on your land."

His face contorts as if he can no longer hide the pain. "You think . . . Deandre took Emma Lou? Because of the land?"

I inhale deeply. "It wouldn't be the worst thing that's been done for land before. Especially not around here." I think of Deandre telling me about her great-grandfather. How he had his stake in a mining company taken away. His one shot at big money stolen. Did Deandre think that was happening to her?

"Who else knew?" I ask. "Who else wanted to stop Emma Lou?"

He shakes his head. "I told her I'd do my best. I told her I'd do the right thing . . . I mean, not say it's Quapaw land—"

"It is."

"Well . . . it's complicated. The government treaties and BIA management and all that."

I can't hold back my disgust. "That sounds like a bunch of horseshit."

He rubs his palm over his face. "Your sister gave me the same look and basically said the same thing. The Dawesons are coming after me. It won't stop with that car. It won't stop until . . ."

I swallow thickly. "Say it."

"Until they blame me for her death." He puts his trembling fingers to his forehead. "Oh God, this is all my fault."

"She ain't dead," a voice says from behind me. Lisa strides over in a Deandre-style dress, all purple and tight. Her eyes are red rimmed as if she's been crying for hours. "I saw Cody. Told him he better tell me the truth. He said Pete took your sister."

The wind kicks up and for a moment all I can see are the gray clouds turning dark. "Took her? Where?"

She shakes her head. "I don't know. But you better make damn sure that bastard goes to prison." She bursts into tears. "My baby passed this morning." Her whole body shakes. "This goddamn family killed another one and they ain't stopping until we're all in Pete's boneyard."

35

The few drops of rain begin as I sprint from my Jeep to Cody's trailer door. The clouds are elongated and warn of a fast-moving spring storm. I realize it might flash flood, and Sister could be in a floodplain as easily as not. Or belowground. Hand-cuffed and unable to move.

We could be so close and then she'd drown.

"I know you're in there!" I bang on the door. "Open up right now and tell me the truth." I am running on anger, and even though every muscle is screaming, I kick at the door. "Open up!" Another boot to the lock and I make a dent in the aluminum door. "I'll kick it in if I have to—"

The door flies open, and my anger is frozen at the sight of Cody. He's been crying. He's pale and trembling. "I can't do this," he whispers, and drops to the first step. "I can't . . . Go find her. Find them all."

I lean over to grip his shaking shoulders. "Cody, I will help her. Where did he put her?"

"Emma Lou found . . ." He drops his head into his hands. "The day she was gone. She was bringing me lunch, but I was at the old Myers place . . . I was digging up . . ." His body tenses. "That goddamn boneyard."

"What boneyard? What does that mean?" I can hear Lisa, who just referenced it. And Manda, that night with Pete, she screamed, *If that boy dies, and we gotta bury him at the boneyard, his momma will kill us in our sleep.*

"Jessica," I whisper. "That's her skull? *You* put it in the tree. With my badge? You were the one who brought me back here?"

"I needed help. Emma Lou always says how smart you are. I thought getting someone outside this fucking place could help us." Cody starts to shake harder.

"But how did you know it was her—oh God. The ring."

Tears stream down his red face. "I recognized it from the billboard on the way to my mom's place. I thought maybe you could do some lab stuff to figure out it was her. That she was buried with the others."

"But what about Sister? Tell me what happened."

He puffs a few breaths. "Emma Lou saw my car and came onto the Myers land where I was digging . . . There were five skeletons at least. Different parts. Different bones. Different girls."

"Oh my God, Cody."

"I know, but I had to do it. Pete said if I didn't move them out of there, then he'd put Emma Lou right alongside them. I know that's what he wants to do anyway. He don't like knowing there are witnesses that could put him on death row. He wants you all dead."

Pete had more than proven that with me in the past few days.

"You were digging up the bones. Emma Lou caught you? Keep going."

He stares up at me with wild eyes. "She lost it. Pete came by and saw her freaking out. Said I had to kill her or he would. I couldn't let him do that."

I drop to my knees into the dirt. "Oh God, Cody, you didn't." I press my fingers against my mouth. "Not Emma Lou."

He cries hard. "I know, I know. But I was stuck."

I launch myself at him, all the anger and rage. "How could you kill her? My God, she's the mother of your child."

He grabs my arms to steady us both. "Jesus, Syd. I didn't kill her. I hid her. She's alive! I swear to God. I just lied to Pete about it. I'm not some fucking psychopath like him."

"What?" I gasp. "Emma Lou is alive? Where?"

His gaze darts up at the clouds coming in even faster. The wind pulls at our hair. "Somebody saw Emma Lou and told Pete. He knows I was hiding her. He's going to really kill her. He'll kill us all. Please, you have to keep Gracie safe, Syd."

"We are not giving up." I hold his shoulders tight. "Where is Sister? We have to get there before Pete."

He falls forward. "You can't stop him."

"Where?" I shake him like a rag doll.

He falls against the door. "She's been hiding out at my mom's old place. There's this cellar she goes to when the dipshits come round. They kept hunting dogs in there . . . like a cage. But there's nowhere else to hide her."

I keep my voice calm and steady. "Where, Cody? Tell me."

"The trailers the Picher people moved into west of Miami. But it won't work, Syd. You're too late. He'll have her by now. That raid last night scared the shit out of him. I fucked all this up. It's all my fault."

As silent tears fall down his flushed cheeks, I drop back onto my hands as if he's struck me.

I see Cody now. Just as alone as me. Trying to survive doing as much of the right thing as we can stomach.

We tried to keep everyone safe but ended up doing the opposite. Because we couldn't ask for help. Because we were too ashamed to admit our role. Our fault. Our mistakes. We'd bury all that poison deep down rather than open the wound so we can heal.

I stand up and his defeated gaze meets mine.

Surrender.

"Come on," I say, holding out my hand. "We'll get to Sister first."

AGILVGI

I roll onto my side and sit up, blinking in the darkness.

The rocks I've gathered from the floor are waiting for me.

The fibers I pulled out are gathered on top of the rusted bolt.

My fingers find the largest rock.

I press my weight onto the tip of the rock against the bar.

The metallic scrape echoes in the cave.

A spark lands directly on the nest of threads from my shawl.

A glowing amber circle appears, like the devil is winking at me from the dark.

I gently blow, keeping it stoked for a few seconds more.

I grab the blanket, the shawl, the small miracle the devil gave me.

The metal screw is hot through the blanket, but I like the burning feeling coming from somewhere other than my infection.

A scrape and squeak, then the screw moves.

I twist harder.

It cuts into my thumb but moves again.

This is a pain that feels good, like a loose tooth, nearly out, but pinching.

My cries turn to joyful sobs.

The screw twists free from the rock floor.

Anything will move with enough heat.

Three more.

I'm coming, Gracie.

36

As I drive us past the JUSTICE FOR JESSICA sign, Cody starts to murmur. "How could he kill all them girls? The families never knowing. The lives never lived."

"Let's focus on saving this one." I squeeze his shoulder. "The one we love. The one who needs our help right now." I think about calling someone, but I can't be told to stop. If we don't keep moving, this chance to save Sister will disappear with her for good.

He lets out a shuddering exhale. "Turn up here on the left. It's the third trailer. My mom's old place. Before she got sick."

"Oh shit," I whisper as I see three black trucks in front of the trailer he's pointing toward. There are at least a dozen dipshits lingering outside with those stupid yellow handkerchiefs over their faces. I keep driving and then take the left along the other road bordering the trailer park. "Okay, so do they have her?"

Cody stares out the back window. "I don't think . . . No, they're not by that basement. It's far back, near the trash cans."

I pull over a quarter mile up the road, and we get out. The rain comes faster, and the wind rips at my clothes. The clouds are rolling over one another, and something about all this storm's energy makes me feel fearless, or maybe it's hopeless. Either way, I'm not stopping until we have Sister.

Crossing a field, we stay low to the ground but hurry.

"This way." Cody's face is stern and serious. His eyes are still red, but he's focused for the first time since I almost kicked down his door. "We'll go in the back way."

I keep my hands on the few tools I was able to grab from my Jeep. Cody said she may be hiding in the dog cages. Or even locked in there, if Pete or the dipshits found her.

The thought of having to unscrew bars to save my sister doubles my pace. Cody keeps up as if he has the same thought.

I can see the small dugout cellar ahead. A dipshit is walking and smoking close to where we're headed. We lie on our stomachs in the sharp grasses. The wind continues in steady bursts, and the grasses hiding us sting like switches across my face. Finally, the dipshit turns back the way he came. We raise ourselves enough to look around and, both nodding at the other, run.

Thunder rumbles in the distance. The storm is coming fast from Kansas, picking up speed and energy along the flatlands.

We creep behind the industrial-sized dumpsters, which smell like diapers and rotten food. A flash of lightning hits the ground not too far from us. The dipshits seem to notice, and they scatter to start knocking on trailer doors.

"You think she's down there?" I nod toward the cellar.

"It's where she's been hiding out when they come looking."

"Can you be lookout? Stomp on the door so I can get us out if they get close."

He nods quickly, his gaze clear. "Thank you, Syd. I don't know why I thought I could handle this on my own. I'm sorry."

Squeezing his shoulder, I understand on a cellular level what he's feeling and to some degree, what he's done and not done. "I'll go get our girl."

I open the door and a strip of cloudy daylight illuminates several stairs. "Emma Lou?" I call, and my voice echoes. This is a big place. "Are you here?"

The wind gets quieter when I shut the door. I shine my small flashlight down as I descend to the last stair. My arms chill from the cooler temperature and everything smells damp.

"Hurry," Ghost Luna whispers. "She needs us."

"Emma Lou?" My voice is a loud echo into what could be a pitch-black mineshaft. "I'm here, Sister."

From deep within, someone yells back.

My heart races, leaping into my throat as I hurry down the loose rocks. The cavernous space is like a microphone for the wind, a howling tunnel. I shine my flashlight all over the walls, searching for a cage.

"You're almost there." Ghost Luna hovers ahead. "Find her."

I yell for Sister again, darting the flashlight all around, but only see rock and packed earth. "Emma Lou?" I call into the darkness.

"Help!"

That small voice stops me for a moment. Emma Lou is here. "SISTER!" I yell.

"Help," she calls weakly.

"I'm coming," I scream as I stumble forward in the dark. I can hear the air blowing and then there's another sound, not natural. Something new, something familiar and signaling a waking nightmare.

The long, steady sound carries all the way down here. The middle-range note holds, and being raised in Oklahoma, I know it'll blast for three minutes before dropping off at the end. The unmistakable sound of a tornado siren.

Somewhere ahead I hear a cage rattle, as if someone is trying to get my attention.

I rush ahead until I feel something: not a wall, but bars. She is in a cage. "I'm here," I say gently, not wanting to scare her. "Are you okay?"

"Yes," she whispers, and her warm hands wrap around my fingers. "She said you'd find me."

Tiny hands grip mine. I realize the voice isn't just soft but childlike. Find her. I did, but it's not Sister I found.

There is real terror in Ghost Luna's voice, something I feel. "You found a child locked in a cage."

AGILVGI

A voice breaks through the fog of my dream. The fog needed to survive being his prisoner.

I'm here! I'm here!

Sister!

Sister!

I shoot straight up as pain rockets from my fingers through my whole arm. For a moment I'm trapped back in the trailer before it burned. But no, not there—I'm here in this dark place. In this cage.

My finger with the tiny scar throbs. If it wasn't so torn up from turning the screws, I'd touch it. That scar has been my touchstone since that summer night the three of us cut the tips of our fingers to become blood sisters.

Sister!

Wait, I did hear something. What woke me?

The air changes, getting thicker, and the wind whistles far, far away.

As I close my eyes, I can hear something, words or my name?

The scar on my finger throbs like there's a storm coming, but of course I can hear it, too. I rub my thumb in soft circles around the old cut and listen.

Are you here?

That's not possible.

Crawling over to the bars, I lean against where I took out the first screw. "Help me," I yell into the darkness, my voice weak and scratchy. "I'm here!"

I realize this is what hope promised me. Someone would come. I wouldn't die here and leave Gracie all alone.

"Help!" I scream again. There's someone climbing, then falling. A woman. She's cursing and scrambling.

The footsteps are coming for me. I hold my arms out, through the bars, ready to live or die, to be decided at last. My heart rattles with hope and terror. Please let me finally be free.

A light shines in my eyes, and I squint. There's heavy breathing. A siren begins far away, familiar as an old nightmare. A tornado is coming for us.

The flashlight moves, and my eyes adjust after only a few seconds. "Emma Lou?" I say, not expecting her. Not after all this time.

"Luna," she whispers to me and begins to cry. "I came as soon as I knew you were alive. When I finally figured out how to find you. Oh, Sister, I'm here."

Sister. I smile at the old nickname from those days as girls I play on a loop in my mind. How Syd and Emma Lou called me Sister, too. Blood sisters, they'd said, as real as any kin. I shake off the feeling of betrayal from being left behind.

Emma Lou's sobs are quiet, but still they echo. "We've been looking and looking."

I want to believe her. I hold her hand tight.

"We have to hurry." Emma Lou's eyes go wide. "The devil is here, Sister. He wants to take us both to hell."

37

〰〰〰

Hello," says a soft voice.

There's movement, and I blink at what looks like a small hand reaching from between the bars. I feel the fingers and I flinch, realizing the hand is too small to be Emma Lou's. It's a child's hand. A child in a cage.

I breathe, in and out, not sure if I'm dead or hallucinating.

"Hello?" I say softly as I crouch down. My eyes adjust after a few seconds of just our mingling breath in the cool damp air. She's tiny, around my niece's age. "I'm Syd. Can I help you get out of there?"

She clicks on a small flashlight and aims it at my face. "¿Habla español?"

"No." I flinch in the light and try to pull college Spanish 101 from my rattled brain. "Um, me llamo Syd."

"You're Sister?" she says in English.

I wonder if she's repeating what I yelled for Emma Lou. "You can call me Sister. What's your name?"

"I'm Gracie. Is my dad back yet? He said it wouldn't take long."

"You're *Gracie*?" I blink rapidly at the strange coincidence. This kid is not my niece and yet there is something familiar about her. And her dad is . . . a Daweson? "How can I get you out of here?" I start to feel around the bars. Searching along the ground, I find a screw and take out my pocket wrench.

"That one, too." She points her flashlight toward the ceiling, where there's another screw that looks smoother and used, unlike the rust around it. "Then it lifts."

I do as I'm told, and it takes me a minute, but the screw loosens. I pull it up and there's a mechanism that swings open the two bars closest to the wall. This is an old dog kennel, just as Cody had said. And this poor little girl was trapped in here.

"Come on." I hold out my hand. "It's not safe—"

"I am safe here." Her little flashlight shines around the cave to show me the small sleeping bag, few toys, and food in the corner. There's even a little plastic potty.

"Of course you are safe. What a nice room," I say quickly, smiling the best I can. "There's a big storm. Do you hear that siren? This is an old shelter and it's not safe. That means we need to get out of here, so we don't get trapped."

She moves to the corner where the toys are in a circle. A stuffed buffalo is tucked under her arm. "But Dad's coming back."

I glance around, and I hope I get to meet her father so I can give him a piece of my mind about leaving a child down here. "Let's see if he's up the stairs, okay?"

She steps outside the cage closer to me, as if curious. "Blood sister?"

"What?" I ask, wondering where she heard that phrase, but she only smiles. "May I have your flashlight to lead us out?"

She hands it over so I can combine it with mine. I gently take her hand and move much quicker, heading back the way I came. When the ground is uneven or there's something in the way, I'm sure to shine the light where she's stepping.

As we near the door, I accidentally shine the flashlight on her face, a worried frown that's so familiar, I say the name before I realize why. "Luna?" I whisper, though that's crazy.

She looks like Luna as a girl, with dark hair and dark eyes.

"That's my momma's name," she says proudly. "Daddy says she's in trouble again." She waggles her finger. "Mommy is bad."

I can't move—is it shock? Relief? Hope I never imagined being answered nearly knocks me down. I stare at Ghost Luna, who's smiling as if she knew this moment was possible all along. "Did you say your momma . . . is named Luna?"

Ghost Luna's voice returns and she pleads, "Luna is alive. Find her. Find me."

"She's in big trouble but she's okay. Daddy said she's in a cage like me. Emma left me to find her."

"Who?" I drop to my knees in front of this child. "Who left?"

"Emma Lou. She's a sister, too. She said I look just like my momma. And she went to go find her."

I keep my breath measured and my voice calm. "Where did Emma Lou go? Where did your dad put your mom?"

She frowns as she thinks. "Daddy puts her in the dark when she's bad."

I swallow thickly. Jesus, what this kid has lived and seen. "Where is the dark?"

"Down with all the treasure." She itches her nose. "Those sirens are loud. Should we go hide?"

"Yes," I say. "Can I carry you?"

She smiles at me. "Sure, Sister."

I get us outside to find Cody jumping around as if that'll get me to move faster. The gusts of air are so strong that I press Gracie to my chest, afraid she'll be sucked off to Oz.

When Cody sees us, he doesn't look surprised that I've got a child with me. "Come on!"

Running back across the field, we dodge leaves and branches the best we can. At the Jeep, Cody takes Gracie from me and puts her in the back cab seat. He gets in the other seat and buckles her in across from him.

Just as I slam the door, a branch smacks my window and the corner shatters but doesn't break. I throw the Jeep into drive.

I can't stop looking in the rearview mirror at this little girl. Luna's little girl. Is it possible? Ghost Luna hovers over the child from the back like a guardian angel. I try to slow my breathing as I keep the truck steady. Could Luna be alive? And this is her daughter?

How the hell did this happen?

"They lied," Ghost Luna says, and runs a hand over Gracie's feathery hair.

"Who lied?" I ask, realizing I said it out loud. "I mean, how do you know this Gracie, too?" I say to Cody from my mirror as I press the gas. "Is she . . . who she looks like?"

"I didn't know until earlier this year," he says. "She started coming with . . . Pete . . . from Mexico. I let her play with my Gracie but didn't tell anyone. I only just found out that . . . Luna was a part of it."

"I'm her imaginary friend," Gracie says with a grin. "Isn't that a silly name to call me?"

When my niece mentioned her imaginary friend, I never dreamed it could be real. Only that she was creative like her mom. "We'll get you right back to her," I say, watching the clouds and feeling some relief that we're getting ahead of the storm now that I'm back on the highway.

I put on my brights as cars are speeding down the road, both away from the storm and toward it. My heart begins to thrum, trying to process this Gracie's words. The idea that her mother could be . . . that she is.

FIND ME.

A car comes screeching by me with a loud honk as if twenty-five over the speed limit isn't fast enough. "So how did you keep Emma Lou from Pete?"

"She hid in the cage when he dropped off Gracie."

"Emma Lou had to break out of a cage?" I ask, horrified at what my sister has gone through.

"No!" Cody says from the back. "That was just for a little while. She stayed in my mom's house. Like a guest. Both she and Gracie. But when the dipshits started sniffing around the trailer park, I had to move them both this morning."

Gracie is humming softly, as if everything is totally normal. I know kids are resilient, but it's terrifying she was in a cage under the earth and appears completely unbothered. What on earth has she seen in her few short years?

I focus back on Sister. Both of them. "Where would Emma Lou go to find Luna?"

He's trembling. Fear has made him hard and allowed him to survive. I can't fault him for that, but I can try to help him do better.

"I'm scared of Pete, too. But we can stop him."

He looks at Gracie. "I want my daughter to be safe. No girl is safe with that kind of evil in the world."

"Then where is she? Where are they?"

"He'll be there, don't you understand? He'll never let her go. He'll kill us all."

"No he won't, Cody. Please, where?"

He closes his eyes as if about to pray. "Pete put Luna in the West Netta mine. Emma Lou must have talked to Gracie and figured it out."

"My God, they put her in a mine?" The long, dangerous tunnels snaking under this whole county. Hundreds of miles of tunnels, many of them flooded with toxic water. So many people through the years have made the stupid choice to go exploring and died. "It could kill her to find Luna."

Cody stares down at his lap. "That won't stop Emma Lou."

"It won't stop me either." I press the gas as we fall silent, driving for the first time without a ghost in my ear, chasing one instead.

AGILVGI

I don't know what I expected Emma Lou Walker to look like after fifteen years, but a filthy fairy wasn't it. She's in this long, dirty dress. Her curly hair is everywhere. Her eyes are wide and unfocused. She can't stop talking about the devil.

Still, I feel steadier with another person here. I am returning to myself, whatever that has become. No longer withdrawn to my place of survival. Focused on nothing but living another minute, hour, day.

"I've been hiding from the devil." Emma Lou's voice is a whisper and eerie with the siren blasting. "I saw your little girl."

"Is she okay?" I say harshly, not used to talking to an adult who isn't evil itself. "Is my baby girl okay?"

"She's just fine." Emma Lou places her hand on my arm. "Come to find out, Cody's been letting her play with my Gracie. I never met her until today. But my Gracie would go on and on about her 'imaginary friend,' and I guess she wasn't so imaginary."

"Your . . . you have a daughter, too. You have a Gracie? And they've played together? I had no idea. She said she played with cousins . . . I never thought . . ." I grin, and my eyes sting with tears I didn't know were left. "Grace was always our favorite name as girls."

"We promised we'd all have our own three Gracies together. And they'd be sisters, too."

We reach for each other at the same time, pulling as close as we can through the bars. "Everyone said you were dead." Emma Lou squeezes tighter. "I knew you were waiting for me."

"My finger was throbbing all day," I whisper about the scar on the tip of my finger that we all have from when we became blood sisters. "I didn't dare hope it meant anything."

We both cry. The tears are a relief when I'm in the arms of someone who actually knows me. The real me, who I was before my life was stolen. Before I was sacrificed. I let go of her first, and as I pull back, the fear returns. The siren seems louder. The devil is close.

"There's another screw to loosen." I crawl on the ground to show her where I stopped.

"I brought a screwdriver. Your Gracie said you were in a cage. We're getting you out." Emma Lou holds out the item like an offering, along with the flashlight still creating shadows on the walls.

"That's real good." I grab my blanket and pull it tight around my shoulders to ward off shock that sets my body trembling. "Can you try to loosen it? My fingers are barely working."

Emma Lou is on her knees, and I shine the flashlight on the spot. She twists hard and her hand slips. She adjusts the screwdriver and tries again.

My ears pop as the air changes. We don't have much time.

"Got it!" Emma Lou holds up the screw. "I was meant to save you."

"You were. Now, you pull and I push."

We shove together and something at the top of the cage creaks. I notice two of the bars are thinner. "Wait, this might move now." I feel along the edge, and two bars are connected. I pull up, and now that the screws are gone, the bars lift and the cage door swings open.

I am trembling as I step outside. The devil has threatened so many times to put me in the ground, one way or another. Only this time, deep under the earth, he made good on it.

"I want you to meet my Gracie," Emma Lou says. "Come on."

She sounds like she's in a dream, but I take her hand. She leads me from this nightmare toward the sirens and howling wind.

My heart hurts with something like joy, but that won't do us any good. My ears need to pop so bad I can almost feel blood coming out of my eardrums.

We're careful through the tunnel. Suitcases are stacked on the side, no doubt full of drugs. There's another bag there, too. "Wait, Emma Lou. I need to see something."

The devil threatened to throw me in this cave. But the other threat, when we'd come back recently, was to throw me in the boneyard. I believed every word. He'd bragged about the girls before me. What he'd done to them before he killed them. Before he buried them out on his land that used to be my family land.

The boneyard is what started my living nightmare. My dad saw Pete digging one of those shallow graves. He uncovered the remains, the skeletons, the terrible secret. He and my mom had gone to Ronny Dove that very night and been turned away. But it was too late. Pete and Skeet busted into our trailer in devil masks and silenced us all.

My hands are suddenly steady, which I've developed over the years when panic sets in. Emma Lou follows me to the bag.

"Don't, Luna."

I stare up at her and realize she already knows what's inside. "We can't leave them." I open the bag and there is a white skull right on top. There are more bones underneath.

Emma Lou starts to cry. "Oh, those girls. The devil killed so many."

"How did you know?"

"I caught Cody digging them up." Her face goes tight as she tries to speak. "Families looking for years, just like I looked for you. I didn't care what anyone said. I knew you were alive. I knew I could get you from the devil."

I close the sack. "We have to get them from him and let their families know. Lay them to rest, finally."

Emma Lou takes the heavier end, and with what little strength remains, I help her to relieve some of the weight. She was always strong. The one who'd open the pop bottles or pickle jar. Who reached the top of the tree first and stretched out her hands so Syd and I could follow her.

I slip and feel Emma Lou's hand support me as she steadies the bag. We readjust and continue up a steep, muddy incline. A few more falls but we follow the dull beam of daylight. Finally, we stumble to the mouth of the cave, and the siren's blare hits like a wave. I blink at a thick cloud swirling in the distance. The wind rips at my blanket as we gently place the bones on the ground. My heart races that I'm nearly free.

Emma Lou points across the field of chat and machinery to the big black truck the devil's had the past few years. Bile rises and burns, but I swallow it down.

She grabs my arm to point from the devil's truck to the sky. A tail comes down from a wall cloud, and it does not go back up. The tornado is on the ground and heading in our direction.

The sirens are screaming. Branches and debris swirl with the clouds of chat. I trip over rotting wooden beams that keep the cave accessible. I scan around for the devil. If he sees me, he's going to kill me. My freedom means his imprisonment.

The devil only puts people in cages. He's not going in one.

Emma Lou grabs my arm tight. "Are you ready?" she shouts.

The tornado is maybe three miles from us. The wind is devastating. My eyes are on fire from chat and dust swirling. I don't see the devil anywhere. "Let's go!"

As we heft the bag up, I stop Emma Lou and point toward a red Jeep in the distance. "Who is that?" I scream.

The vehicle barrels toward us and stops halfway. The driver's-side door swings open, and I step completely outside the mouth of the cave.

"Sister!" Emma Lou screams. "Syd is here!"

There is my old friend, my best friend, my blood sister. Fifteen years later, the three of us are joined in the place that tore us apart.

Syd is running across the chat pile, trying to dodge the debris, but it's getting worse. There's nothing but chat piles and open fields. The wooden support beams keeping the mouth of the mineshaft open ache and moan as if making sure we know that it's ready to swallow us whole.

Emma Lou grabs my shoulders and pulls me to her chest. "He's here!" she shrieks. "The devil is here."

———————

The devil runs toward Syd, and for a moment it's in terrible slow motion. "I have to stop him," I yell to Emma Lou, pointing in his direction.

We fall back against the mineshaft entrance wall. "He can't get you." Emma Lou shakes her head as if possessed. "No, no, he can't. Not again."

"It has to be me," I call. "I'm the only one he wants. I'm the only one he can't let go." I have expected to die more years than I haven't. The devil is hobbling, but he's still unnaturally fast as he runs at Syd. She falls.

"No, Sister." Emma Lou's eyes are wide. Her curly hair is on its ends from the wind. She places a kiss on my forehead as if saying goodbye. Her brown eyes are wide, tears shimmering in them, but something else. Relief?

She rips the blanket off my shoulders and throws it around her so it's covering her head. Then she runs toward the devil in her disguise.

38

~~~~~

As we approach the West Netta mine, I see a black truck with the front light smashed in.

"Pete is here." I turn to Cody. "Where would he put Luna?"

Cody points ahead toward the opening of the mineshaft. The dark hole must be one of a handful that still exist and haven't collapsed on themselves.

"That's where the drugs are," he says with his gaze down. "There is a cage in the back of the cave. I bet she's there."

"Stay in here with her," I say. "With your gun, okay. Pete comes close, you do what needs to be done."

He nods and I can see the shame and I feel it myself.

I get out of the Jeep and slam the door shut. Panic and anger, always the screaming twins, are strapped to my back as I blink at the tornado, enormous on the horizon, swallowing more of the sky the closer it comes.

"Surrender," I murmur, half curse, half prayer.

They say a tornado is as loud as a freight train, but like any kid growing up near train tracks, I know that sound too well to say it's true. Just as a tiger is more than a roar, a tornado howl is beyond a train—as if all the power and destruction of gravity and nature unifies to tear us apart.

A mile away, less even, and we don't have much time to get away.

My breath is sputtering when my face is hit by something sharp, a stick, and I reflexively whip around to make eye contact with a hard blue gaze.

Thump-thump.

Pete is narrow-eyed fury. I'm more scared of him than of the tornado, and he's still far away enough that I think I can make it to the mine before he does. Only one way to find out. Run.

I start to sprint, trying to ignore the pain from last night and the past few days. Pete is barreling after me, and I run as fast as I can, but in this wind, it feels like I'm pumping my legs underwater. To cross the field and reach the cave opening, I dodge huge limbs and swat at debris slamming into my body. I turn to find Pete.

He is closer than before. He is faster than he should be. I won't make it.

I am running backward, and something connects with my injured leg. I fall onto the ground, and it feels like slow motion. I am living a horror movie as Pete charges toward me in the wind.

I scoot and brace myself, closing my eyes for a moment, and when I open them, he's not there.

He turned away from me. He's chasing someone. Someone else is out here.

She's in a dress with a blanket around her head and shoulders that the wind whips like a sail in a storm. The woman runs toward him and then back, as if taunting him. And it's working. She runs in the opposite direction, and he chases.

The shape of the woman is familiar. Even at a distance and being pulled in the wind. As he gets closer, she runs in the opposite direction, as if luring him away. The wind tears at the blanket and there's a flash of curly dirty-blond hair I've known all my life.

It's Emma Lou. She's alive—and she's taunting Pete in the path of the tornado.

There's another woman who falls out of the mouth of the cave. Not a woman. Luna. My God, Luna *is* alive.

Closer to me, almost exactly between us, Ghost Luna appears. Her dark eyes are full of tears. I watch one fall and feel it on my own face. As I brush it away, she does the same thing, as if we're mirroring each other.

I look back out toward the real Luna, and my trembling hand wipes more tears as I blink to see her more clearly. She's changed, of course, but I'd know her face and sharp gaze anywhere.

Ghost Luna appears in the swirl of debris. The wind pulls at the edges of her and she begins to disappear like ripples in water. I reach for her, not sure what I want, but I know she's leaving me.

She holds out her hand, lifting her pointer finger, where if she was flesh and blood, there would be a scar. For a moment the scars we share touch.

"You found her," she whispers in my head. And then Ghost Luna is gone.

A flash runs past me, and it's Gracie, who's escaped my Jeep and is sprinting with her hands out toward her mother.

"Stop!" I scream, and jump to my feet, limp-running after her. "Gracie, wait!"

A chunk of tree hits me in the back of the head. I stumble,

pretty sure I feel blood, but keep moving forward. Gracie is fast and reaches Luna, who has crossed part of the field to scoop her up. It's only a few seconds before I'm right there and Luna motions for me to hurry to the mouth of the mine.

We duck inside and it's dark and the wind is only slightly quieter. "Is she okay?" I ask Luna, and put my hand on Gracie's head to look for any blood.

"I think so," Luna says, with her big eyes wide, peering over her daughter's body wrapped tightly in her arms. She puts her mouth right to my ear and yells, "I need your help!"

She leads me back to the edge of the cave, and there's something there, a big bag.

"You have to carry this back somewhere safe," she says, as if she might not be with me. "Promise."

"Sure," I call into the howling wind, and check to be sure Emma Lou is still a good distance from Pete. She almost seems to be toying with him, as if she's having fun, and God help her, maybe she is.

Luna is strangely still, as if she's making sure I mean it that I'll bring the bag. I lift it to see how heavy it is—very—and open the top. Something white flashes. Something familiar . . . Oh my God.

I turn toward Luna, who is looking solemnly in my direction. She holds her daughter tight against her. These are bones. Luna's eyes close in pain, and that's when I know they are the women and girls from Pete's boneyard. Where he buried the bodies of the girls he killed. They could weigh a thousand pounds, and I'd die using the last of my strength to put them to rest. Throwing the bag over my shoulder, I step into the storm.

Luna runs ahead, across the field with Gracie, toward my Jeep, and I follow as fast as I can with the sack. There's a loud pop and I freeze, realizing it's the sound of a gun. Cody is near Pete and fired in the air. Emma Lou is about fifty feet behind them.

Luna has the door open and is putting Gracie inside. I run to the back and open it, dropping the bag as gently as I can before coming back around to find Luna.

I look up to see Pete within striking distance of Emma Lou. I scream, but it's lost in the wind. Pete picks up a thick piece of splintered wood and throws it at my sister. It strikes her on the side of her head, and she drops to the ground.

"No!" I scream, and run toward them.

Cody charges with his pistol aimed at Pete, who he sees coming. He smashes his big body into Cody, tumbling them both to the ground. Another loud pop and only Pete stands up. He's got Cody's gun.

The chat and dirt swirl around us. Pete approaches Emma Lou with the weapon pointed at her body on the ground. He rips the blanket away, and his face is shocked, then angry, as if he expected to see someone else. He shakes his head and then hefts Emma Lou's limp body over his shoulder.

I search for a weapon, anything to attack him and get him away from her.

Within me stirs a truth: *I'll die protecting those I love.*

Pete aims the gun in my direction as he hurries toward his truck. He throws her body in the back, and I call in anger as he gets inside.

I run toward him and the truck as he pulls away. A horn blast at my back, and it's Luna behind the wheel. Pete's truck is through the gates, and I cry in frustration again before turning back to Luna.

She's jumped out and is over Cody's body. I see her shriek the word "Help," but the actual sound is lost in the roar. This tornado is about to swallow us whole.

I run to help her with Cody. He's slumped over and holding his shoulder. He manages to walk on his own, with us supporting him on either side. We get him loaded in the back seat with Gracie.

Once we're inside, Luna crawls into the back with a wad of tissues out of a box on the floor. She presses them against the bleeding place in Cody's shoulder. "This might hurt."

He makes a sound as if confirming it does. I turn on the Jeep, suddenly feeling all that dark sky as if it's falling onto us. Trees are stripped bare. A huge branch thumps the side of the Jeep, but Luna doesn't even flinch.

The funnel spins toward us, sucking all life as it subsumes the horizon.

A scream is lodged deep in my chest. But it's not the tornado spiraling me into total panic—it's that the worst has happened: the devil has Sister again. "I have to go after him," I say simply. "I will save her again."

"We will." Luna turns from Gracie toward me. "Go to the Daweson compound. Devil's Promenade is where it ends."

39

I start to breathe with some control once the tornado is in the rearview mirror. My mind gauges where the twister could be headed after striking the mines. I am terrified for my parents and Aunt Mercy, for Rayna and Aunt Missy. For a hundred other faces I've known all my life who may not make it past today.

I don't think the tornado has gone that far northwest yet. It hasn't even reached Picher.

"Shit," Luna whispers, staring in the mirror.

My first thought is Pete and the dipshits. But she's looking far out east, where the highway crosses between Oklahoma and Kansas. Another tornado tail emerges. It's on the ground, too, and within seconds both tornados merge into one.

I face forward and tears burn to be released. Cody has his eyes open and is holding the tissues now against his shoulder. Luna keeps touching Gracie, giving her child comfort and likely taking some herself.

"You're okay, baby girl," Luna murmurs over and over.

Quiet minutes pass, and I peer at Luna in the mirror and quickly look back at the road. I know we are not girls anymore, though the child she was is in there. Perhaps the same is true for me. Luna's face is longer, thinner. Hair a rich brown.

Every question is too stupid to ask. *Are you okay? Do you hate me? Have you been living in hell? What happens now?*

Luna keeps checking her wrist and wincing. I open the glove box and grab a couple of Sonic napkins, since the tissues were all used on Cody's shoulder. She takes them and hisses as she touches the angry red slashes.

"That's infected," I say softly, and then I realize the truth.

Luna wrote *her* daughter's name in the mud at the compound. Those cuffs were around her wrists, where she pulled and pulled until she bled.

I tighten my grip on the wheel and focus on my anger, not the panic.

Surrender.

The turn to my parents' house is coming up. The tornado is far enough east that we should be fine. "We can take your Gracie to my parents' place."

Luna frowns at me and I realize we moved after she was . . . taken.

"At my grandma Ama's place," I explain. "My parents moved out there."

"He needs help," she says, glancing back. "Is it Cody? Emma Lou's old boyfriend?"

I nod, relieved she didn't know for sure. Because maybe that means Cody hadn't known she was alive all this time. Maybe he'll just have to live with the pain of his ignorance like the rest of us.

"It should just be you and me." She glances my way and there's that hardness I remember. "We'll leave them with your parents."

"You don't have to go," I say, meaning it. All that she's gone through. I can spare her this at the very least.

"Syd." She smirks at me. "I'm going. He's mine."

"Okay," I say quietly, the relief overwhelming that I won't have to do this alone.

"Gracie girl, remember I called Syd and Emma Lou my sisters?" Luna holds up her index finger. Scraped and bruised, the scar is there on the tip of her finger. "We are blood sisters. That's a bond that lasts a whole lifetime. You can trust her to keep you safe."

I swallow thickly at her words because hearing them is powerful, but hearing them from Luna means everything. "I will always try to keep you safe," I say.

Luna kisses her hand and taps it against Gracie's cheek. "Te quiero, hija mía. To the moon and back."

My parents are on the front porch as we pull up. Mom is holding my niece, Gracie, and I hate that we're not reuniting her with Emma Lou. Not yet.

I go around a giant maple tree that's fallen across the driveway and park on the other side, closer to Emma Lou's Three Sisters Garden. I stare at it for a moment, marveling that it looks untouched despite the fence being ripped down not twenty feet away.

Mom runs over and flings open my door. "Thank you, Jesus." She hugs me tight and looks expectantly across the seat. "Emma Lou, are you . . ."

Luna shifts away from where she's checking on Gracie and toward my mom. "Hey, June," she says. "We'll get your daughter back."

Mom's mouth falls open in a gasp. She blinks several times, and her gaze shoots out toward the graveyard where the woman behind me has a headstone. Where we buried what we thought were her remains. "Oh, child." Mom reaches over to take Luna's hand. She stiffens but doesn't pull away. "I'm so . . . sorry."

Luna nods once, not like an acceptance, but an acknowledgment that June is sorry. Maybe even that we're all sorry, but what difference does that make?

"This is my Gracie." She leans back and unbuckles Gracie, pulling her onto her lap. "Sweetie, this is Miss June. She took care of me when I was your age."

Mom grins at the little girl. "Did you know your momma and my daughters thought Grace was the most beautiful name in the whole world?"

The little girl hides in Luna's arms for a moment, then looks back at my mom. "That's my name."

"Every doll in my house had your name once," Mom says, and her chin quivers. "Do you want me to show you some dolls? My Gracie is inside if you want to meet her."

"I don't need to meet her. I'm her imaginary friend."

Mom's eyes grow wide and watery as Gracie slides out of Luna's arms. There's something unnerving about a child who is that brave. Who is able to quickly bounce back from being in a cage, being separated from her mother, from a bleeding man and a tornado.

Mom takes her little hand and they pass my dad as he hobbles over to the Jeep. I get out to meet him before helping Cody. He watches Mom walk by with the little girl. "Rolled my ankle getting some cows into the barn," he explains. "Who's that little girl? She looks like—"

The passenger-side door opens, and Dad's eyes go wide. He whispers something in Cherokee and strides toward Luna. He holds open his arms and Luna gives him a hug.

She loved my parents, and I'd never really understood how

much they meant to her, especially my dad. I can see Luna holding back emotion, and she pulls away from him, wiping her eyes.

It's quiet now that the tornado has passed. The sun, setting soon, even peeks out from behind light gray clouds moving fast. The calm after the storm feels almost as scary as the storm itself. Too good to be true. A bit of beauty among the wreckage.

I head toward the back and open Cody's door. He looks okay, if a little pale.

"It went through my shoulder," he murmurs to me. "I can go with you. I gotta get Emma Lou back. The baby." His voice breaks on the whisper. "Pete can't . . . he can't take them." He presses his eyes shut, and he looks so exhausted, so gaunt, I almost hug him.

"Stay here with your daughter. Take care of yourself. We'll get Emma Lou, I swear to you. You will have your family back."

He presses his lips together before looking up at me. "Our family."

I nod as if that's what I meant, but it isn't. I'd never considered us kin, not even close. But what could be more powerful than being connected by the love of my sister and my beautiful niece? I am humbled by his words. Ashamed of my own. How I treated him when I know, if I was in his circumstances, I would have crumbled long ago.

"Listen, Cody," I begin, feeling the weight of what I'm about to do. The possibility that I won't come back. "You need to tell Sue about the bones. I'm leaving them here with you and no matter what happens, their families must know. They deserve to bring home their girls. That's why you tried to get my attention with the skull and badge."

"You're the only one I knew who'd done it," Cody murmurs.

"I hoped . . . that you could get Emma Lou away from him again."

"I will do everything I can, but you need to see this through. You need to be sure these remains are taken to their homes. To rest in peace with their families at last."

He wipes a few tears with his good hand. "I will."

I help Cody out of the Jeep, and he shudders as he begins to walk. I go around to take his other arm and help him. He hisses with each step but keeps going.

"Is Aunt Mercy okay?" I ask Dad, who hobbles behind us.

"She's just fine. Now that the storm is gone, she's lying down."

"She bailed me out of jail this morning." I stumble when Cody pauses. "Yeah, you heard me."

"Well, well, Miss Too Good for Oklahoma," he says with a pained half grin. "I coulda given you some pointers."

I let myself relax for only a moment, then the fear is back. "Do you think the tornado hit the town?"

"Yeah, I do," Dad says. "I'm going to go check as soon as we get you settled." He motions toward the field. "Don't know if Charlie made it. He's a tough buffalo, but he's wild."

"Dad, we're not staying," I say as I guide Cody up the porch steps. "We need guns. Pete has Emma Lou."

Dad stares up at the sky, whispering again, and I know what he's reaching for, finally. To find courage to face the truth. To step forward, even when it's difficult. To reach out our arms, like the branches of a tree, for help. For love. And extend our own arms out to others. That's what's kept us here, right or wrong, on this land generation after generation.

Dad limps onto the porch. "He has her because of land, not drugs."

I blink at him, shocked that he knows, then hurt that he kept it from me. "Did Emma Lou tell you what she was doing?"

"That's why Sister took the job with Deandre," Dad says quietly. "To befriend her. To learn more about the land deals. Sister wanted some justice against . . ." He trails off and looks toward Luna. "Against the Dawesons. For what happened. Or didn't happen. Even Cody tried to help. We should have told you."

"Why didn't you?" I take a long breath. *Surrender.*

I think of Ghost Luna's warning about my family. *They're hiding something from you.*

She was right, but not in the way I feared. They were hiding their lives from me because I'd walked away and stopped showing up for them. "Actually, it's okay, Dad. I haven't been there for you and the family like I should. Like I will be in the future, I promise."

He blinks at me as if I've really shocked him. Kind of shocked us both, actually. "I love you, kid." He limps over to give me a big hug. "Hey, let me drive you and Luna."

"We got it," Luna says quickly as she comes up behind me.

"I can't have you do this alone."

"I'm not alone," I say. "And neither is Emma Lou."

Dad shakes his head. "But if I could—"

"This is for Syd and me to finish, Mr. Walker." Luna pauses on the bottom step in her dirty white dress, gaze as brilliant and hard as a diamond from a mine. "Now, how many guns can you spare?"

40

After we have all the available guns and ammunition, I grab some clothes and sneakers for Luna to change into. She's in as much of a hurry as I am, so she stands behind the truck and strips down. My hand comes over my mouth at all the scars covering her body. A web of terror woven into her skin.

I can't hide from this truth. Not when there's been so little truth for her. Her entire existence hidden by lies.

"Luna," I say finally, finding her gaze as she dresses in my jeans and a black T-shirt. "I'm sorry."

She blows out a frustrated breath. "You don't want to know, okay? Let's drop it."

"Are you sure?"

"What do you want to hear?" Luna says as we both get into the Jeep.

"Whatever you'll tell me."

Luna is quiet for a moment, picking at nothing on the passenger-side window. "I was his prisoner. The first five years, I barely saw the sun. I lived, if you can call it that, in a closet at the first shithole he had in Mexico. Or that fucking cellar on the compound when he started coming back to Oklahoma again with drugs."

I cannot wrap my mind around her words. First weeks. Then months. Then years. "You were trapped? A prisoner. In a cage? How did he bring you back to Oklahoma?"

"'The box' is what I was in when we traveled. My second home for the first few years." She says it almost like a joke, and that makes me wish she'd scream it instead. "He kept me in it on the long drive from Mexico to Oklahoma. Or it'd be into the box when I was mouthy. Or even when I wasn't. He'd lock me in that small coffin he built for me in the back of his truck like a toolbox. The first years were in the box. In the end, it was the safest place I could be. When I wasn't in the box . . ."

She lets the words hang between us. I bite back my selfish guilt. My panic wants me to say, *We thought you were dead. We didn't know.* I won't let myself do it. Luna deserves more. She deserves everything good we can ever give her.

"I don't know how you . . . survived," I say, wanting to take her hand but afraid it's too much. That I don't have the right. "You are a survivor."

Luna closes her eyes and tilts her head to the side as if in pain. "Not yet."

"Yes, you are." I take her hand. "You have survived."

She opens her eyes and then lifts her face to the sky, as if sending a prayer that my words are true. I hold up my finger, the one with the small scar that matches Luna's if hers weren't under clean bandages. Emma Lou's if she were safe with us again.

Luna faces me and touches her bandaged finger to mine.

All this pain, it all goes back to one man, one family, one simple truth: it ends now.

We cross the Devil's Promenade Bridge, and I can't imagine a prettier sunset, which is just like Mother Nature. To remind us beauty is possible after destruction.

"Maybe we'll see the Spook Light," Luna says. "I thought about the church hayrides so much. All the fun we had. All the good times. All the love. That's what saved me. That goodness of our days as girls, as sisters, kept me alive. And then Gracie was my angel. She really saved me."

I squeeze my lips together, eyes on the road but full of tears. "Your Gracie is incredible. She gets it from her momma."

"She gets it from who her mom had to become," Luna says. "Like those scars all over my body. I wouldn't heal them even if I could. They are more me than my skin or hair or name. They have formed me. The scar tissue healed, but those discolored lines mean I am changed. That I will never be whole, but something else. Something stronger."

My anger is overwhelming, and we are silent until I pull over about a mile from the compound. I turn off the car and face Luna. "We save Sister first. Then we do whatever you want. I'll back you up."

"I won't need you." She grins at me, but there's no joy. "He's mine to kill."

I get out of the Jeep and call Jo's office line, where she won't be, so I can leave a long message. Then I head around to pop open the back door and slide the guns forward. I inspect them as Luna walks up behind me and takes a rifle. Her dark eyes narrow at the scope as the wind pulls at her hair.

I'm struck by how much my memories didn't do her justice. By what a pale shade Ghost Luna is compared to the woman. I feel shame and a lot of anger. Did I ever see her?

"Syd, why are you looking at me like that?"

"Sorry," I say, and fumble with a box of shells.

She sighs deeply. "Look, Syd. You tried to be brave. Promised to protect us. But we were girls. It was not a promise anyone can make. A promise no one can keep, not really."

"Yet, when you love someone, it feels like the very least you can do."

She doesn't respond, and we focus on the handgun and two rifles. Once we're armed, we crawl low to the ground through the grasses toward the compound.

She starts to hum the tune to "Cherub Rock," the song that was playing before the devils burst into her parents' place.

"Is that a joke?" I say, horrified to hear it.

"It's not the song's fault," she says. "'Who wants hoooooney? Let me out. Let me out.' Try it."

"No." I lightly smack her shoulder. "I forgot you have a triggering personality, Luna."

She laughs and adjusts the rifle so it is tight across her back. The adrenaline is already pumping as we approach the devil's lair with loaded guns.

"You think the side entrance?" I ask, and try to ignore how my elbows burn from crawling.

"Emma Lou is bait," Luna says. "It always comes down to me. The possession he wanted most. Remember him at Dea D's party? He watched us as girls, you know."

My stomach drops. "What?"

"There were deer stands out on my family land. He'd watch us. He got obsessed with me. And angry that my dad was selling weed. But it's that my dad found out about the boneyard. That's really why he killed us. Killed them. I'm sorry you were there."

"Don't be sorry; he's what's evil."

Luna sits up on her elbow. "You do not have to go. I need one shot, and I can do that on my own."

"You're not alone anymore," I say softly. "Not ever again."

We keep moving together.

Leading us to the place where I entered a couple of days ago, I throw the stick again to knock out the electric fence. We listen before going under. There's the evening silence and an unenthusiastic breeze rattling the trees as the sun disappears.

I get out a map and a small flashlight to point out different markers: Doc's trailer, the concrete where Zeke shake and baked his skin, the larger buildings of the house, the big concrete slab. "Let's stay against the fence and head northeast until we're at the entrance."

"You're sure?" she asks me one more time, because this feels like an end. "You don't have to go."

I squeeze her arm. She needs to know I'm not only here for Emma Lou. "The devil dies tonight."

41

〰️

I want to scream Emma Lou's name, but of course I stay silent. We crawl under the fence and stay low as we creep along the route. There are quite a few fallen limbs from the tornado, but we manage to crouch-crawl. There are a few dipshits lurking with their guns drawn. Pete has them on high alert. We are all ready for whatever comes next.

Checking the rifle and taking off the safety, I press my back to the wall of the barn at the center of the compound. I sidestep as slowly as I can and make it to a window.

Luna lingers behind me, looking so calm it scares me. "You see his truck?"

I glance in through a broken window to confirm, but I already knew it'd be there. Luna is right: Emma Lou is bait. He wants us in his territory to finish what he started fifteen years ago.

"Through that door." Luna points toward the north side of the house, if you can call it that. It's strangely long, additions tacked on, one section with plastic siding, another with plywood. The carelessness is terrifying.

We run. As fast as we can with loaded rifles on our backs toward that long house with the plastic over Sheetrock flapping near a metal door. I turn the knob and there's a deep voice from across the yard. Pete is outside. He's found us.

"Go get Sister," Luna says. She grabs the door and kicks it at the same time. When it swings open, she shoves me inside. "Hurry!"

The door slams in my face and I stand in total darkness. I grab my rifle and point it at the blackness of the room. I feel my way along a wall and there's another door. I try to open it like Luna did, but it doesn't budge.

I know enough to not shoot the lock off. That's in movies and the bullet would ricochet right into me.

I shine my flashlight around to confirm I'm alone in this room. Then I steady the beam as I hold the rifle and fire at the top hinge. I quickly reload and hit the bottom one. The top of the door sags, and I kick it open enough to get through.

There are voices yelling as I squeeze in the two feet or so I'm able to access where the hinges came apart. I'm guessing dipshits are heading my way to investigate the shots. I have to hurry.

Inside another small dark room, I feel along the wall, and there's nothing there. The room looks empty, but then my light shines on a thin, dirty mattress. A bucket in the corner. My light trails along the walls where there's a letter written in blood. A giant *G*. I step forward and see *RACIE* written next to it. This must have been where Pete would keep Luna. One of a dozen dark and terrible places of torture.

There are no windows. No light. A room that served as a cage.

I see a sliver of light and head toward a door partly open to a dark hallway. I start to hurry, sensing Sister is close.

Surrender.

I do not think about the dipshits, but I do lock the door behind me to hopefully trap them in if they follow me. I do not talk myself out of helping, or hide somewhere. I do not use anger, and I do not listen to my fear. I search with my heart and pray to the spirit of my grandmother that she guides me to my sister.

FIND ME.

There's a noise from the room I just left. Male voices, and someone shoots at the door.

They're coming.

I stumble down the dark hallway. My shaky flashlight helps me avoid broken boards and disgusting buckets through this terrifying maze. My breath pounds in my ears.

I come to a door, but it's locked, so I keep going. There are locked doors all along, and finally I find another hallway. It feels as if I'm going west, which is in the direction of the front of the house.

I hear the dipshits shooting. One of them screams, likely getting a ricocheting bullet.

I run until there's another turn, and this portion of the hallway floor isn't plywood anymore, but old carpet. I rush forward and it feels like a real house, a house I know. But instead of a dining room, I find an old card table in the middle of the room filled with scales and drug-packaging materials.

Next is the living room and three worn couches. The TV that's on creates an eerie white light as a soft static sound plays like a warning. The room smells like death, the rot of skin and untended wounds. I startle at someone on the couch. I exhale when I see it's a little old man, sitting in the dark, staring at the wall.

I don't want him screaming, so I back up toward what looks like a kitchen. He turns and hisses at me with a gummy, putrid mouth. My flashlight goes to his face, and it's covered in red veins and his blue eyes appear cloudy, as if covered in cataracts. "Help me," he bleats. "Who are you? Help me!"

"Where is Emma Lou? The girl Pete just brought here?"

And alive, please, Spirit, let Sister be alive.

"What would I know about that?"

"Luna is here, and she's free," I say, and the man's eyes go wide in recognition. "Luna is armed and angry. She's putting a bullet through Pete and anyone else who gets in our way. You want her coming for you?"

The man's face contorts. "He deserves everything he gets, not killing that little bitch. If he'd just buried that one like the rest, we'd be fine."

"Then I'll send her your way." I start toward the other hallway.

"Wait, no! Listen, I don't want to pay for what my son did. I got some use, too, but ain't that my right?"

"Pete is your son?" I say, putting this dynamic together. Thinking of what Deandre told me of his cruelty to his children. As if that explains how a monster like Pete could be created.

"The fuck do you care?"

"Oh, I care a lot," I say. "I'm Syd Walker. I killed your son Skeet."

The man screams and lunges at me, but I'm much quicker. He falls to the ground with a *thump*, and I realize both his legs are stumps. "Come here, you little bitch!"

I obey as he struggles to get up. He uses his arms to pull himself across the room. "I'll kill you!"

I take the butt of my rifle and smash it against his face. "Do I kill another Daweson today?" I point the barrel at him.

"Just do it," he spits out.

I consider it, but there's more I need from him.

My mind goes back to the skull in Narragansett, her neck snapped and rotting under the earth.

I press my boot to his throat, and he kicks and swings his arms, but he's weak. He sputters and coughs as I press. "I'm not going to kill you," I say. "I don't trust there's enough suffering in death." He takes silent gasps, but there's no air. I smile. "Where is the girl?"

"Fuck you," he hisses when I lift my boot, so I slam it back down. He cries out, and it's possible I broke his windpipe. "Kill me, you goddamn bitch, kill me."

"After you tell me where he has my sister." I press down harder, and he pisses himself. "Where is she?"

He starts to point toward the hallway I haven't been down. "Third door," he gasps. "Locks on it."

I squat down to create more pressure. "Where are the keys, Mr. Daweson?"

The hate in his blue eyes is so familiar. Something I saw only seconds before Skeet hit the ground.

One bullet.

One bullet.

There was only one bullet.

I shake off the panic and focus back on this old fucker. "Where are the keys?" I scream, and press until I can feel his throat collapsing.

"Kitch . . . en . . . table."

I pull off my boot, and he spits blood as he struggles to breathe. He grabs my leg and pulls me to him. "Kill me, you bitch. Kill me!"

I shake him off with a startled scream and sprint to the kitchen.

There's nothing on the table except a vase. I run over to it, realizing it's identical to the one Deandre has. Again I reach my hand into the trunk and feel the keys.

He's managed to pull himself across the room. I stand over him as he grabs for me. *Kill me*, he mouths, and shakes so hard it may be a seizure.

"Naw," I say. "I'll leave you for Luna."

Running to the hallway, I jam a key into a lock and then bang on the door.

"Sister, are you there? It's me!" I bang again and try another key. It clicks. "I'm here to get you out of here. Gracie wants to see you so bad."

I throw open the door and see Emma Lou. But she's not alone.

"Hi, Syd," says a familiar voice from beneath a yellow bandana. He stands up, pistol on Sister's bruised head.

"Kaleb, you don't have to do this." I aim my rifle at him. "Please, Sue wouldn't want—"

"She knows," he says, keeping his aim on Emma Lou. "She knows everything.

Two other armed dipshits run up behind me, yelling and laughing as if it's a reunion. They have their guns on me, too. "I got this one," Kaleb says after one of them grabs my gun. He pulls me by my ponytail. "Let's hurry. Pete won't want us to miss any fun."

42

Kaleb shoves me outside, and I stumble forward to brace myself on the edge of the barn. Emma Lou is thrown next to me, and I grab her arm to loop it into mine.

"I'm so sorry, Sister," I whisper.

"We're together." She squeezes us even tighter. "All three of us. At last."

"Oh damn!" Kaleb yells toward the field ahead. Luna is standing about twenty yards away with her handgun pointed right at Pete, who has his own weapon drawn. "Move."

We're shoved forward until we're close enough to hear Pete screaming.

"You belong to me," he yells as he aims right at her. "Since I first saw you as a girl. I knew you were mine. Only I say when you live and die."

Luna responds by dropping to her knees and firing at him.

"Stop!" Kaleb shouts from behind us as Pete falls to the ground.

He runs up to Pete and helps him sit up. He's holding his leg where a red stain spreads.

Kaleb moves us closer to Luna. Luna shifts her weapon toward him. "Put your hands up!"

"Please," I beg. "You don't have to do this."

Pete gets up, and he's laughing hysterically, even as he's limping forward. "Luna, you put that weapon down, girl. Or I'll finish what I started right now. No playing possum this time. All three of you girls will christen my new boneyard."

Luna keeps her gun on the dipshits, then back to Pete. "Stay back."

"I'd be doing you a favor if I put two in this boy-looking bitch," Pete says as he aims his gun toward me. "She killed my brother. She left you to die. I know you didn't forget, Luna."

I frown at her in confusion. "What's he talking about?"

"Can I tell her?" He grins as he pulls back the hammer. "Or you want to do the honors? Maybe I just kill her. She'd never have to know. That's what sisters are for, right? Keeping those deep, dark secrets?"

Luna keeps her gun on Pete but shifts to look my way. "There was another bullet in the gun. You killed Skeet. But there was another bullet."

"No, there was only one bullet. Only one bullet," I murmur like a prayer I've said a thousand times before.

The dipshits start to mock me, repeating the phrase in a high voice. "Only one bullet. Only one bullet."

"There were two, Syd. You dropped the gun and ran. I watched Pete put it into my mother's head."

I collapse onto my knees under this terrible truth. "No, no, no." I'm shaking violently, clawing at memories. "No, that can't be right."

"It is," says a familiar voice, and Sue steps around the side of the barn. "Hey, brother," she says to Kaleb, with his gun still pointing in Luna's direction. "Don't let her out of your sight."

For a moment I feel stupid relief. As if Sue is there to help us. Then I realize what she's said. How no one seems alarmed that she's walking into the middle of this scene. Kaleb had said earlier that "she knows," and hadn't I been suspicious all along?

"About time you got here," Pete says to her. "Gonna get real messy."

"This isn't a social call. You got the drugs or what?" Sue says to Pete.

"They're in the house." He licks at his lips. "I can show you after we finish here."

Sue's calm breaks for a moment, but she brings it back. "Sure. Let's get rid of these girls and get the deal done. Let's put them in front of the barn. Better light."

Luna shifts to aim at Sue. "We're not going anywhere."

Sue smiles as if proud. "It's five to one as far as weapons go. Those odds you want?"

Luna watches Pete as he limps closer, and then the two dip-shits plus Kaleb also have their guns on Luna. She throws her weapon down with a curse and puts her hands up.

We are marched to the slab of cracked concrete under the se-curity light. "On your knees," Sue says. "Keep facing the barn."

Before I turn, I search Sue's face for the person I used to know, but she doesn't even have the courage to make eye contact.

I join the other two, my sisters, and we kneel together, heads bowed, like at the pastor's altar call. Like the last time we were together, huddled on ratty carpet in a trailer about to burn.

We are back together, by new devils and old.

Emma Lou wraps an arm around me, but I can't stop shaking. "I'm so sorry, Luna. I don't know what happened that night. I think . . . I think I got scared. I couldn't do it. I couldn't kill Pete, too. So much blood."

"I bet Ronny convinced you there was only one bullet," Luna says loud, so Sue can hear. "He wanted to just brush everything under the rug. To pretend I was dead along with my parents. He even burned the trailer himself. So they'd never know Pete and I survived."

Sue's jaw sticks out, and I can see she's not made her peace with her father's misdeeds. I hope she never gets a moment of solace after all she's done.

"Ronny Dove told me that if I ever came back, he'd arrest my whole family," Pete says with disgust, blood dripping down his leg onto the concrete. "Well, I did what I was told. Took my prize to Mexico and made some money. Now that he's dead, I'm back for what's mine. I'm even going to make his kids rich."

"All right," Kaleb yells as if he's embarrassed. "Let's get this done." He points at the other two dipshits. "Get in front of each of them. I'll take out Luna, if that's all right with you, Pete."

"Hell no, boy." He spits on the ground and grabs himself. "She's mine."

"Use my gun," Kaleb says. "Military-issue."

Pete smirks as he takes the nine-millimeter Beretta. With the two dipshits, he approaches. Sue and Kaleb keep their weapons on the three of us. As if it takes five guns to stop three unarmed women. It's never been fair. I close my eyes and realize there's more I need to say.

"Sisters, I love you."

They murmur their love. We lock arms, tangled limbs

familiar, just like the moments before the devils came through the door.

I close my eyes. I think of Mal. Of our child she's carrying. A child I'll never meet. How could I let what happened with the devils ruin my whole life? *Please let Mal forgive me.*

"Ready?!" shouts Sue. "Aim!"

The shots echo, and I fall to the ground holding the bodies of my sisters.

43

I open my eyes and there is no pain. I take a deep inhale and realize I am alive. But am I the only one? Where did those bullets go?

Turning to my sisters, I see Emma Lou first. She is frozen in the exact same position but with eyes closed. There's a trail of blood along her scalp and I blink in shock before realizing that it was there before. She wasn't hit. But Luna is on the ground.

"What the fuck?" screams Pete, and there's the sound of *click-click-click* as he tries to fire his gun. "There's no goddamn bullets!" He throws it down and pulls the other one out of his waistband.

The other two dipshits writhe in the dust, their legs bleeding as they moan in pain.

My hands fall to my sides as I realize that shots were fired not at us, but at the two dipshits.

Sue comes up behind the dipshit closest to me and kicks his gun away. "Hold steady on Pete," she says to Kaleb.

He keeps his aim straight and yanks the yellow bandana off his face. "Here," he says to me, but he doesn't move from Pete in his sights. "For your sister."

I turn to Emma Lou and dab at the blood. My finger throbs, the small scar suddenly hot, as if remembering the blood we shed that day. "Is Luna okay?" I whisper, not seeing any blood.

"No one move," Pete yells.

"You're not doing shit," Sue says coolly, her weapon still drawn on Pete like her brother's. "The FBI is expecting you."

"You fucking bitch," Pete roars, his blue eyes bulging. "Think you can double-cross me? Over my dead body."

Sue steps toward him. "Say the word."

Pete laughs and moves toward her. "Takes a lot to kill a man, little girl. You made of that kinda shit? Ready to carry it with you the rest of your life?"

Sue glances at me as if she remembers I did carry that guilt. That it haunts me still even though I wouldn't change my choice.

Only one bullet.

I don't regret killing Skeet. I wish my courage hadn't ended there, but it did. For the first time in my life, I don't hate myself for that fact.

"Step back," Kaleb warns Pete.

"Luna," I whisper as I scoot closer, "are you okay?"

She doesn't move from where she's lying facedown on the ground.

Pete takes another step toward Sue. "You think you got the grapes to do what your daddy couldn't?"

"We do," Kaleb says. "You'll rot in prison, where you've always belonged."

Pete begins to laugh, and it's clear he's not going there. His gaze becomes wild, and his aim follows, as if he's deciding who gets a bullet first.

Suddenly, Luna moves. She puts both palms on the ground and rises slowly.

"Want it to be you?" Pete says, still bouncing back and forth where his gun is aimed.

"It's always been me." She steps over a dipshit and picks up the gun beside him. She aims it at Pete and grins, her gaze feral and knowing, as if even with guns to our heads, this moment was inevitable. "And now it's you."

"Whoa! Whoa! Stop her!" Pete yells, and aims at Luna. "Take me into custody. Jesus Christ, she'll kill me."

Pete is there, gun drawn, fear in his eyes. Something I've never seen, not in any terrifying moments we've shared. Perhaps this is the first time the terror hasn't been from his hands.

"St-stop, Luna. Right there," Pete stammers, taking a step backward. "I'll shoot you, you crazy—"

He stumbles on piece of cracked sidewalk where a tree root broke through.

Luna doesn't hesitate.

She empties six bullets into him.

She strides over to his body, where his pale eyes are open. His mouth is twisted, as if he never expected justice to come calling at last.

His blood runs toward her on the concrete. She drops her gun and heads over to the other dipshit, who's crying on the ground. She takes his weapon and goes back to Pete. She unloads another six.

No one says a word.

There are no police lights in the distance. No one else to witness. This devil will dance no more.

"Wipe those," Sue says to Kaleb, nodding toward the guns Luna has thrown near Pete's body. "Kaleb and I did it, as far as the FBI is concerned. Everyone clear?"

No one responds, but of course we understand. This is justice, which we'll uphold at any cost.

"Let's get out of here." Sue helps me up, and then we both take Emma Lou's arms.

As we limp toward the driveway, then toward the road, the injured dipshits scream for help. We slow to look back toward them, near where they punched me in the face while I was trying to talk to my wife.

"They'll figure something out," I say. "Or they won't."

We pass where Pete tried to run me over. The tree where the dogs attacked me and the branches I climbed to save my life.

We're still silent as we spill out onto the dark dirt road where our vehicles are parked. To leave Devil's Promenade and never, ever come back again.

As we approach Sue's SUV, a car comes from behind, shining a bright headlight on us. We turn, but the white light is floating and grows brighter and brighter as if calling for our attention.

The Spook Light floats above us on the road, then crashes to the ground and disappears, as if leading the last devil to hell, as if finally, we are free.

44

~~~~~

ONE MONTH LATER

One of my last tasks before returning to Rhode Island is to trim the persimmon tree branches down to the live wood. The trees can be survivors if you keep the rot away.

I toss the branch onto the big pile and smile down from the ladder at Emma Lou. "We have enough to make a ceremonial fire, if you think Aunt Mercy would help us build it."

Sister is sitting in the sun with Mom's Cherokee blanket on her lap. There's a bandage on the side of her head, but otherwise she looks like herself.

"She might." Emma Lou runs her hands along the red floral pattern. "Be nice to teach the girls about fire. Maybe remember those we've lost. Sooner rather than later."

I climb down the ladder and sit on the ground next to her. "You have a whole lifetime to teach Gracie."

Emma Lou doesn't respond but takes my hand in hers as if she's still trying to get used to the idea that she survived. That we all did.

We stare out toward the cemetery. Where Luna's grave remains.

We haven't told anyone but our small group she's alive. Even Sue has been able to keep the FBI at bay for now. Not until Luna is ready to live again on this side of the veil.

"You feeling okay?" I ask, and watch Emma Lou's hand relax on her belly. She nods quickly, once, and I leave it there. She hasn't told Mom and Dad yet, though she's just starting to show. A secret she keeps, as if what's growing inside her is healing her, too. Soon she'll be ready, but not yet.

"The mom monster is coming!" yells Luna from the front porch as both Gracies burst out the front door. She chases after them across the yard. They scream as they run to us and crawl under Emma Lou's blanket.

Emma Lou is very focused as she gets them tucked into both sides. I notice the girls are wearing purple beaded bracelets from the senior center where they visit Aunt Mercy. "No little girls here, Mom Monster."

Luna raises her arms and growls. "Are you sure, Sister?" She sniffs the air. "I smell tiny dirty feet."

The Gracies giggle and wiggle. Luna picks up the edges of the blanket and then throws it off them. Little-girl squeals fill the persimmon grove, and we laugh as the two Gracies run back toward the house.

"Save us!" they yell as Mom emerges from the house. "The mom monster!"

"Hide on the porch," Mom calls as they storm up the stairs toward her. "Behind the rocking chair. Under Paw-paw's feet."

My dad starts to laugh as the Gracies try to use him for cover. Mom heads toward us, and I give her a little wave. No more anger. No more hiding. No more excuses.

We are all worthy of love, just as we are all worthy of forgiveness, including ourselves.

"Sue called again," Mom says. "Sounds like the committee is moving forward to give Rayna and Missy the property."

I whistle at the news. "I always wanted a rich family."

"I'm sure your aunt Missy will burn through it in a month." Mom tries to suppress a little smile. "Rayna says they're moving into Deandre's house."

Mom stares at the three of us sitting together on the ground listening to her news. She quickly wipes a tear and turns to head back.

"It's okay, Mom." I hop up and run to her. There have been too many tears shed alone. I put my arm around her shoulders. "Come sit with us in the sun."

She doesn't resist as I walk her back to our circle.

A warm wind brushes our faces and pulls on our hair, no longer the same color. Very little is the same as when we were girls. We are together again, and that's what matters.

Luna leans over and plucks a yellow dandelion. She splits the green stem in half as she reaches for another one. "Let's teach the girls how to make dandelion necklaces."

"Will you make me a crown?" Emma Lou asks.

"I remember, Sister." Luna smiles at her. "That was always your favorite."

Once the crown is done, Luna gently places it on Emma Lou's head. She shifts back on her arms and nods toward our family's pecan grove in the distance. "We'll have to make pies."

I smile at a memory of making pies with my mom from those very trees as girls. Staring at them now, I know pecan trees seemingly stand alone, but they are connected in their groves like a family. They don't need much to stay alive, surviving droughts for years at a time. Pecan trees endure and even adapt, with a grove producing nothing for years, even decades.

But if you want the trees to do more than stay alive, to bloom and grow and produce pecans as they're meant to do, they need care. Sometimes, lots of it. Dad told me that his pecan trees had a different problem every year. He understood that problems only meant they needed help. If one solution didn't work, they'd survive, and he could try another until at last they bloomed. *Never give up*, he'd said.

My stomach is like a butterfly in a jar. Seeing Luna again, something I'd never imagined in any real way, shocks me each time my gaze catches hers. I try not to study her, like a rare species of tree among rocks, not supposed to survive and yet, it grows.

How would I study such a tree? Pick at a piece of bark to see how healthy it is underneath. Study the roots and how they're growing through the ground. Remove a leaf, hold it up to the sun so it's green and glowing.

"What are you thinking about, Agilvgi?" Luna asks quietly, using the Cherokee word that's a whisper from summers long ago.

I smile at her, though her gaze is still far off. "Trees that grow despite where they're planted."

That gets her to glance in my direction with a hard, knowing stare. She understood survival before the devils, and that's what kept her alive. She grew through the rocks, and for the first time in a long time she's no longer alone. Agilvgi broke free of the earth and stands in the community of our grove.

EPILOGUE

I'm nervous when Mal parks her Acura in front of our home. Today is the first time she's been back since we both left. I know I'm different. Stronger and more certain I can protect those I love. I don't know how to get her to see it or believe it.

Not that Mal's moving back in. Not yet. I check myself in the big mirror, smoothing my hair and adjusting that turquoise shirt from Deandre.

Doubt ol' Dea cares for inmate orange.

Heading outside, I take our porch steps two at a time. Mal shuts the door and gives me a little wave. I wonder if I look different. If the death of the devils and the resurrection of Luna have healed something broken within me. If helping to identify the women from Pete's boneyard has restored a part of my soul that wanted justice but never believed it was possible.

Mal is in a flowy red dress that she bought right after we were married. She seems calm. Her chest looks bigger. She has even more glow than usual.

She let me come to a doctor's appointment last week but said no to lunch after. Small steps. Actions, not words.

Surrender.

As she approaches me, I let out breath. "Hi there."

"You look nice." Mal gives me a quick squeeze. "Are you okay?"

I nod. "Are you?"

She puts her hand on her stomach. "We are. I feel good." Mal smiles wide. "Still mostly lemonade and crackers."

"Del's?" I ask about the Rhode Island icy lemonade she loves.

"Every day." Mal laughs. "Sometimes twice a day."

My heart hurts at what I've missed. In four months, our whole lives have changed. A life we could still share together if she'd let me.

"We'll talk later," she says, as if reading my mind. "I'm ready to work." She holds up her drawing supplies.

"Thank you for coming." I hear hope in my voice, but I'm not afraid to share it.

"This is good." Mal points toward the backyard, and we start down the gentle slope that leads to the pond.

She slows our walk toward the deck stairs. Staring out at the trees, her gaze lingers on the calm pond and green leaves only starting to turn yellow. The frogs and crickets are already talking in their soothing, pulsing song.

"I love it here." Mal turns to me. "I miss our home."

Looking into her beautiful dark eyes, I can see the *I miss you.*

There's the sound of fast feet on the deck. We both look up to see Gracie's black hair shining as she peers over the wooden deck rail. She doesn't say anything, which is pretty normal lately, but she does look curious.

"Who is it?" Luna calls. "The Big Bad Wolf?"

Gracie rolls her eyes.

"Hi there," Mal says, slowly approaching where Gracie stares down at us from the deck above. "If you like to color, I brought art supplies. Pastels were my favorite when I was your age."

Gracie glances back at her mom. "Can I?"

A chair scrapes and Luna joins Gracie over the deck. "Sure thing, baby girl." Her gaze goes between Mal and me. "Nice to meet you."

"Same here," Mal says.

There's a relief I didn't anticipate that my wife is able to meet my blood sister who haunted me, even though she was alive.

Mal squeezes my hand as if she senses how overwhelming this moment is for me. I close my eyes for a second, breathing deep and absorbing her warmth, palm to palm.

Surrender.

The emotion passes soon enough, and we head up the stairs.

"You've been reading." Mal grins and raises an eyebrow at the books scattered everywhere.

Luna has been making up for lost time with Gracie, especially reading together. They didn't have many books in Mexico. I've bought out three Savers discount stores of all their picture books and a few short chapter books.

"She also loves to draw." Luna puts her hand on her daughter's shoulder. "Gracie girl is better than me already."

Gracie rolls her eyes again. "I *have* to draw."

She doesn't like going to the child therapist, but it's gotten easier the past few visits. She's stubborn, like her mom, but that's good. That can save your life.

"I drew this picture yesterday." Mal pulls her portfolio out of her bag and gently opens the leather cover. "There's a horse down the road. He lives in a big field with apple trees. How nice it would be to eat apples all day in such a pretty place."

She hands the sheet of paper to Gracie, who studies it carefully.

Gracie asks softly, "Can you show me?"

"Sure." Mal leads her to the picnic table and slides a blank piece of paper over. She opens the kit of pastels. "Find a brown you like and start with the eyes."

Gracie glances at Luna, who nods for her to continue. She gently lifts the darkest brown and draws two circles.

Mal focuses on Gracie, and they talk quietly.

I watch the tension release in Luna as it often does, starting in her jaw and easing down her body. Like she's suddenly floating on water instead of drowning in it.

Luna and I made a pact when we arrived in Rhode Island. We'd both go to therapy, and we wouldn't ask questions of the other. That way when we do feel the need to share, it's from a place of trust, not guilt. We never discussed how long she and Gracie would stay, because we were healing, and that lived outside of time and expectations.

After Gracie is comfortable with Mal staying with her, we say goodbye and get in my truck. As I drive, Luna scrolls through my iPod and finds the nineties mix she likes. She always skips a few songs to start with the Smashing Pumpkins' "Cherub Rock," and the joy I felt while listening to it as a girl is returning.

"Thanks for coming with me," I say as we turn toward the Narragansett land where I first got the call about the skull on the Myers property. That feels as if it could have been fifteen years ago, too.

Emma Lou continues to do better, day by day. My parents are there for her and so is Cody. My niece is resilient, as I'm learning we all can be with enough love.

"Sue called again." Luna leans her head out the window and

the breeze blows her hair across her face. "Case is coming to-gether. She really wants my testimony but won't force it."

I was wrong about Sue, though she was wrong, too. She knew about Luna. She found out after her father died when she was going through the boxes that were in the flooded office. She'd found the real autopsy reports, which never included Luna or Pete. There was a secret memo outlining the deal her dad struck with Pete to get him out of Ottawa County. How he'd made this deal with the devil, making Luna a sacrifice for all the other girls who'd be safe with Pete Daweson gone forever.

Sue had convinced her brother, fresh out of the military, to join the dipshits undercover. To finish what her father never could. An undercover operation she ran in coordination with the FBI. That had been why Sue didn't want the BIA's help in the first place.

Luna says she can live with what happened because she knows it saved a lot of other women, at least those in Oklahoma. That's not to say she's not angry or betrayed, but it helps to have a bright touchstone of hope when things go dark. At least, that's been my experience, and I hope it's true for her.

Deandre was prosecuted for taking Emma Lou's car from the Wings parking lot, where Cody put it, and then planting it at Rhett Caine's house. She was also charged with falsifying documents to show she owned the land. There are other charges pending, related to her mother's prescription and selling Oxy. Manda's tied to the meth they found at Netta, so word is she's willing to deal, even against her own daughter.

My mom has been keeping us updated, relishing every drop of justice.

"You're going to have to testify," I say to Luna for the tenth time.

Her eyes are closed against the wind. "I'm not ready."

"You can't stay dead forever."

She shoots me a look, but I can tell she knows I'm right. Sue isn't going to push because Luna being alive will bring a difficult conversation about Ronny Dove. Something that may also get her into trouble, since she tried to keep it quiet. The truth is, professionally, neither Sue nor I are out of the woods yet. But if that's the price of justice, we will pay it.

Luna's cell phone buzzes, and she shows me the text from Rayna. "She got that tiger-print couch." Luna presses a button, and a picture pops up with my cousin sitting naked on the couch with a pillow over her bits. We cackle and it feels really good.

Luna and Rayna struck up a quick friendship back in Picher, my cousin proving again she knows how to help heal the broken.

"I can't believe she bought that boob bar," I say, grinning at Rayna's entrepreneurial spirit. She took over the Body Shop for next to nothing since it was seized as Deandre's property. Now only women work there. They are treated well and paid even better. Plus, the drugs are gone. She's painting the bar bright pink next week.

"She's going to let us know how opening night goes," Luna says as she puts her phone away. "Did you call your boss?"

I shake my head no because I'm not sure how to answer Jo. She wants to assign me to another region where a girl went missing a few months ago. But I'm going there as an archeologist, not an investigator.

"It's the perfect cover," says Luna, who thinks Jo is going to be some kind of Charlie, with me as one of her angels. "Lots of bad men out there. Lots of women and girls who need help before they're forgotten."

I've always wanted to see Montana and of course help another family find justice. But I'm an archeologist, not a detective. "I'm not sure I'm ready."

Luna lets it go. She fiddles with the iPod and plays Tori Amos's "Silent All These Years." She hums along with the opening piano notes and then sings along with the chorus as I drive.

We arrive at the open gate to the Narragansett land where I found the skull. The dirt road is bumpier as we head deeper into the woods. I park next to Ellis's truck. There are several other cars along the road.

"I'm glad all her family made it back for this," Luna says softly.

She'd been interested in the case. I've spent most of my time since we returned tracking down family to honor the woman who was murdered and thrown away.

I grip the wheel and take a deep breath.

The family was relieved to finally know what happened, especially her only sister. The ex-husband lied and said she'd run off with someone. The sister had held out hope it was true. As she cried into her hands in her small living room, I knew the shame she felt. The anger at never asking more questions. Of letting someone go too easily when they needed to be found.

"Why don't you carry the blanket." I hand Luna the soft woven fabric, in vivid reds and yellows.

My mother heard my story about the skull and how the case was coming together when I left to come back to Rhode Island. She wanted this woman—Melody Hollows—to be covered and protected as she finally passes from our world to the next.

The family appreciated the gift and asked if we wanted to join them for the ceremony. They invited Luna after getting to know her and pieces of her story. A great honor we do not take lightly.

An elder from the Hollows family called Luna a wounded warrior. She is someone who fought, earning her scars. A warrior who has endured and risen again. The battle wounds signal strength, not defeat.

Perhaps the same is true of the polluted land in Picher. The same is true of the stolen homelands of the Cherokee and Quapaw. Of the land and profits taken by the government. As with justice and as with the earth, there can always be a balance returned. There is healing in the very pursuit.

Luna runs her finger along the flower pattern, and I know it's the one with the scar we share. She finds my gaze, and I hope she feels what I cannot say. Now that the devils are dead, we will do more than survive.

We are still here. We will live.

AUTHOR'S NOTE

There's a lot of truth in this fiction. Over the three years I worked on this novel, I did my best to research, interview, and see for myself this place where I grew up, but from a writer's perspective. I feel an obligation to readers to capture real issues, past and present, particularly within my own experience as a member of the Cherokee Nation of Oklahoma.

The story and people are from my imagination (though I did use my Cherokee family name, Walker). But the events, the places, and the history were written to be as close to the truth as I could find—from the May 10, 2008, tornado to the EPA Superfund site housing buyout program (and resulting lawsuits) to, yes, Mexico meth coming to Northeast Oklahoma right around the time of this story. For events of the past, the Trail of Tears, the taking of land and profits by the BIA and the government, and more removal from land, I assure you what I included is but a fraction of the atrocities and injustices.

The crime at the heart of this book is tragically inspired by the real case of two missing girls that happened after my senior year in high school—a case I've watched with hope for some resolution, though I'm sad to say as of writing this, the family still searches. There's a powerful book on this case by Jax Miller, *Hell in the Heartland* (edited by my editor, coincidentally), that I highly recommend.

I am hopeful folks in Northeast Oklahoma will read *Blood Sisters*, and so I must ask if you know anything about the murders of Lauria Bible and Ashley Freeman, or any missing persons—particularly indigenous women and Two Spirit, who are disproportionately affected by violence—please consider reaching out with information.

While this book is set in 2008, and at that time the Missing and Murdered Indigenous Women, Girls, and Two-Spirit People movement didn't have this name we use now, the statistics have always been staggering, including the fact that nearly eighty-five percent of American Indian and Alaska Native women have experienced violence in their lifetime (www.indian-affairs.org /violenceagainstnatives.html).

I'd encourage you to seek out information in your own states and communities to support journalists and organizations doing the important work of elevating this MMIWG2S issue.

Finally, *Blood Sisters* is written within my narrow window of experience as a white-presenting Cherokee woman from Northeast Oklahoma living in Rhode Island. I'm still learning, growing, and connecting, but I am so honored to share what I have with you.

Finally, we are lucky to be readers in a time with so many incredible Native authors, though we need many, many more. If you reach out over Facebook or Instagram (@VanessaLillie) or my website, I'd be happy to send you a list of some of my favorites.

ACKNOWLEDGMENTS

Wado

Osiyo, my friends. This story began with my family and the Cherokee pride and heritage I am blessed to have been given. To Mike and Carla and all the ancestors surrounding us, wado. To Zach, August, and Violet, the dog who nearly ate the copyedited version, I love you. Thank you to the Stolz family, Lillies, Knights, and everyone in between for their decades of support.

Thank you especially to my brother, Nathan Lillie, who was always happy to talk ideas, read pages, and connect me to people within the Bureau of Indian Affairs, where he worked with pride and dedication for sixteen years. Love to Dez, Knight, and Walker, too.

Thank you to my agent, Jamie Carr, who saw the potential in this book (and me) and guided me with kindness, joy, and grace every step of the way. Shout-out to her amazing colleagues at the Book Group.

As far as dreams coming true, being on the Berkley team of authors with Jen Monroe as my editor has been nothing short of magical. The way she's championed *Blood Sisters* has been remarkable, and I'm so grateful to Jeanne-Marie Hudson, Claire Zion, Craig Burke, Loren Jaggers, Candice Coote, Jessica Plummer, Daché Rogers, and everyone on the marketing and sales teams.

Thank you to my TV/film agent, Michelle Weiner, at CAA and to my foreign rights agent, Jenny Meyer.

A special thank-you to Rebecca Jim (Cherokee) for reading an early draft, for her guidance and insights about the land, laws, and history. I don't know how we got so lucky to have you in Northeast Oklahoma, but I am grateful all the same.

Thank you to Chelsea T. Hicks (Osage) for her editorial and cultural guidance, for the classes she's taught, and for the kindness she's shown to me on this journey. Also, don't miss her incredible debut story collection, *A Calm and Normal Heart*.

Thank you to reader Rory Crittenden (Cherokee) and editor Gretchen Stelter. Wado to the Native American Writers Seminar, teachers and fellow fellows. Your humor and creativity inspire me. I hope to work together again in a writers' room someday.

Thank you to so many bookstores for their ongoing support, especially Chapters in Miami, Oklahoma, and to the late Lee Dell Mustain. Thank you to Lisa Valentino of Ink Fish Books in Warren, Rhode Island, for being my first and best bookstore-owner friend.

To my friends who have read drafts and chapters and answered really odd questions at all hours, thank you. To my writer and author friends in the text trenches with me day in and day out, I love you. I literally couldn't do this without you.

Kutaputush to Lorén Spears and the incredible Tomaquag Museum for their guidance and resources about the Narragansett tribe, on whose land this story opens and closes and where most of it was written.

Thank you to the amazing #bookstagram fam and social media communities where I'm able to connect, laugh, and celebrate all things books. Thank you to Dennis Michel (@scaredstraight-reads) and Abby Endler (@crimebythebook) for your incredible early support of this book. Shout-out to What Cheer Writers Club, ITW, MWA, and, especially, Sisters in Crime.

Finally, thank you to the people and land of Northeast Oklahoma, particularly Miami, where I'm from, and Picher, whose history, pain, and beauty have impacted me all my life. From the orange rivers I grew up beside to the environmental justice it inspires to this day, I'm honored to share a little of what you have given me.